LOLA...

Beautiful, lively, completely without sentiment or scruples, she begins her career seducing a middle-aged man into seducing her. At nineteen she becomes the favorite in a fancy brothel . . . at twenty she's the mistress of a man who dies mysteriously . . . at twenty-three she's a top-ranking movie star.

LOLA...

the most exciting young girl who ever tempted men with her intrigues and amoral passions.

LOLA...

one of the most unforgettable heroines in contemporary fiction.

Other SIGNET Books You'll Enjoy

THE WORLD OF SUZIE WONG *by Richard M*~~~~ between an
The daring bestseller about a love~~~~ meets in a Hong
artist and the enchanting girl~~~~ Kong brothel. (#D1552—50¢)

TWO WOMEN *by Alberto Moravia*
The shattering story of a mother and daughter who
are driven by the hardships of war into thievery and
prostitution. (#D1657—50¢)

CAT ON A HOT TIN ROOF *by Tennessee Williams*
A drama of the seething passions that beset a Southern
family in a shattering moment of revelation.
(#S1590—35¢)

GIGI AND JULIE DE CARNEILHAN *by Colette*
A delightful novel of a willful young girl who plays
the game of love more shrewdly than her worldly
aunt and grandmother. (#S1525—35¢)

LOLA

A DARK MIRROR

by *Dario Fernández-Flórez*

TRANSLATED FROM THE SPANISH BY
BARBARA PROBST SOLOMON

A SIGNET BOOK
Published by THE NEW AMERICAN LIBRARY

FIRST PRINTING, JULY, 1959

This book was published in Spain by
Editorial Plenitud under the title
Lola, Espejo Oscuro.

SIGNET BOOKS are published by
The New American Library of World Literature, Inc.
501 Madison Avenue, New York 22, New York

PRINTED IN THE UNITED STATES OF AMERICA

Author's Prologue

In the personal epilogue at the end of the novel I inform the reader just how the manuscript of this autobiographical story came into my possession. But I advise you not to use the epilogue as a prologue out of contrariness. And now, despite your impatience to get on with the story, I must first set some things straight.

First of all, I reject all responsibility for any similarity between the real people who live between these pages and those more or less fictitious beings who inhabit Madrid, where most of this story takes place. Names, events, and places have been altered in order to avoid unpleasant coincidences. If by any chance some similarity still exists, it would be in respect to people and things that have no relation with those who have nourished these pages.

I also wish to add that the opinions and attitudes expressed by the characters—few indeed as they are strong and independent types who are above all concerned with the business of *living* life—have no connection with my own feelings, which in this case are irrelevant.

Concerning the amoral life of the protagonist, I have little to say. It is the same milieu and life, modified only by a different century, that has been recorded in our greatest literature. It is the world of the *pícaro*, the trickster, the shrewd thief, the conniver, and the sinner. It is as well the life of the stoic, the rude and the quarrelsome, recorded with all its hardness, truth and toughness. I should warn those who have been misled by the questionable profession of the heroine, and who are hankering after a boudoir novel, that if they are not interested in looking beyond the sensational, they should close the novel without further ado. I don't know whether or not I have succeeded, but with great effort, I have tried to show something more profound.

There are sin and ugliness in what you are going to read because there are sin and ugliness in a world which lacks pity. But the wicked, the sinners, are also creatures of the Lord, and realizing that, St. Augustine wrote the following compassionate words:

God sees those who will be good and he creates them. He sees those who will be wicked and he creates them. . . . He forgives mercifully and punishes justly; or he judges mercifully and forgives justly. Nothing feared by the malice of another; nothing needed by the justice of another; nothing gained with the works of the good, but the good gain with the works of the wicked.

> . . . I strip her naked, and set her as in the day that she was born, and make her as a wilderness, and set her like a dry land, and slay her with thirst. . . . I will hedge up thy way with thorns, and make a wall, that she shall not find her paths.
>
> HOSEA, 2:3, 6

> Now we see through a glass, darkly; but then face to face. . . .
>
> SAINT PAUL, I CORINTHIANS, 13:12

Part 1

❧❧❧❧❧❧❧❧❧❧❧❧❧❧❧❧❧

One

I have never been a great literary fan, and if I hadn't known Juan I never would have dedicated myself one afternoon to buying some decent paper and one of those fancy American fountain pens which, after an annoying initial effort, really work quite well and lend tone.

I have always guessed that my life was not the life of just anyone. Since I was a child, and even before I was born, according to what I believe, I was destined for great things. People were going to take notice of me, many would even like to kill themselves over me, in order to satisfy my desires. Pachín, the mayor of Zamarrón, who because of his age and position really must know a lot, said that everything which has happened to me has been due to my prettiness and nothing more. But Juan insists that I am a marvelous headstrong creature. He is capable of spending hours amusing me with this sort of pleasant nonsense. I am grateful to him for this. Most men, once they've gotten what they wanted, start thinking about their other obligations.

I am, after all, someone unique. I've always known this and am delighted to be different from the rest of the world. But until I met Juan I didn't realize that my special qualities could bring me immortality; that alive or dead, I could cause envy and admiration in people—something very important to me. Though despite what Juan says, I believe that the mayor was right when he said that after one's skin becomes wrinkled and the flesh crumples, and one's bones rot under six feet of earth no one gives a damn about you. I think Juan has a crazy streak in him like I have and the other night I had occasion to prove it. I told him that I wanted to die with him and I seized the steering wheel while the car was going at full speed and aimed the car directly toward a thick wall at the end of a sharp and ugly drop at the bottom of the street. He laughed wildly and made no attempt to put his foot on the brake until we finally turned over at

7

the corner. The crash could have been the end of us. I wasn't in my right senses, being terribly tight, and I couldn't say now whether I meant it as one more joke or whether I would have really liked to take him with me smack into the next world.

Actually, it never occurred to me before that one could leave something which lives on after one's death. Something which, according to Juan, would make immortal the image of a fascinating woman—a woman worthy of becoming known beyond the circle of her friends. Until now I've been content with being known among this vast group, who are after all the cream of Spain today. But that is no longer enough now that Juan has filled me with these strange new ideas. I am going to die while still very young and still very beautiful, and I want people for all time to know how I really was. I don't want to teach or make an example of myself. I only want people to realize that a girl like me existed. I want them to feel badly because they can never find another one like me.

Here I don't intend to lie to anyone. This is going to be difficult. Not only because my well-being has always depended on my ability to lie, but because after one has repeated a story two or three times, one ends up by believing it. I want to be truthful (favoring myself just a little) and I want no romanticizing or sentimental babblings, which I detest.

I confess I don't know where to begin. Juan, who really knows how to go about it, says that the less he mixes in it the better. Juan says I should just start writing. The male reader will obviously be interested. Women will be too—provided they haven't forgotten their basic nature. He says that the real reader opens a book with the anticipation of a lover, that the first page is like the first kiss. Everyone surely remembers how that is!

Anyway, I make no pretense at being a woman of letters —though in some ways I know more of life than they do. Best not to dillydally, but begin talking to the reader as though we were in some tavern eating breast of fowl *suprême,* and washing it down with a good ordinary red wine, wine that I drink only in the company of old friends with whom I can talk freely. With fancier people one must pretend at being very finicky and carefully study the wine list and insist on something very rare and potent which costs a small fortune.

Two

I am a very beautiful young girl. Very beautiful and very expensive. Even though everyone is aware of this, I repeat it so that no one will be misled. In these matters men are such big innocents that one always has to remind them of the miracle good luck has brought their way. By this technique I manage to hide my single defect—spindly legs. Why, they even rave over the shape of my calves!

I don't know of any other girl who can compare with me. They realize it and my superiority burns them up. They'd enjoy showing me up, but can't.

I don't intend to go into descriptions of myself, saying that my eyes are like this, my mouth like that, or that I have a marvelous figure and a slow, swaying walk that's really breathtaking. I will only say that I glow with the kind of magic which captivates men—and it isn't, as many believe, a magic that passes quickly, but rather one that lasts a long time, even though, in the end, it too passes away. It is a mixture of flesh and spirit, though leaning a little toward the first when it is a case of business. Between sweet murmurings, tender looks and convenient languishing on one hand, and sudden bursts of fierce jealousy, odd caprices and passionate gestures on the other, I hold my victims in my spider's web until their wallets are empty. Then I toss them into the rubbish heap.

I detest men. I'd like to see them all ruin themselves for me.

The other day Juan asked me the reason for my hatred. I told him the truth. I've been hurt a great deal. He laughed —his strange laugh which completely unsettles me, as I can never win with him—and he said that wasn't a good reason. There must be something else behind it. Well, I might as well confess it. When I see them suffering on my account a cozy, pleasant feeling warms me. I guess I'm incapable of really loving a man.

Perico says I should hide this attitude which at times becomes very disagreeable. I am convinced that he is mistaken. Knowing that I hate them gives men pleasure. It excites them more. They have to maintain a tenseness and vigilance which make it easier for me to trap them with my embraces.

This is not to say that I am not *simpática*. To the contrary, everyone agrees that once the economic question is out of the way (in which I am most demanding), there isn't another girl as amusing and lively as me. I'm sure this is true, because I try my best to adapt myself to each man, changing myself like a chameleon, according to who I have at hand.

9

I can be the clinging vine, the understanding companion, the drunken devil-may-care, very *flamanca*, the desperate type, the fascinating personality—even vicious, sensual—though that role bothers me the most. I let each man see me as he wants me to be. They all end up with their own notion of my basic nature, each man believing that I've revealed myself only to him.

As for Juan, no point in saying more now. I have already mentioned him several times. He knows me better than anyone. Unfortunately, nothing escapes him. I can never fool him. Still, I have a hunch he'd give anything to be able to be fooled just a little—enough to believe in the sincerity of my love-making.

This is why, when I begin my work, he becomes angry. He has forbidden me the use of sighs and gentle gestures. Sometimes he hardly lets me open my mouth. He says he'd prefer having me embalmed and silent, encased in a mammoth crystal bottle stretched out alongside of him. He likes looking at me. Actually, he's the only man I haven't been able to conquer. He spends what *he* wants, not what I want him to.

But as for the others—that's another kettle of fish entirely! When I pit my twenty-five years against their strength how quickly they weaken. All I need do is bashfully lower my head and look dewy-eyed, carried away by their speeches, to get them in their weak spot. Then how quickly they unburden to me their miserable illusions, their foolish hopes. When I let my hair fall loose against my bare shoulders at just the right moment, my face glowing with passion—what agitation and desire I manage to awaken in them! How quickly they lose their pose of being men on the hunt, of being brilliant and powerful. Underneath their show of dominance, what giant cowards they are, corrupted by the fear and the dirtiness of their lives! All the false dignity of these magnificent superior beings melts in the face of my splendor, and they are left horny and . . . oh, no, I mustn't use ugly words here. Juan says I must put it all down just as it comes to mind. But I'm an educated girl—the good nuns of Almería taught me everything necessary in order to become a young lady.

Also, I've noticed that in books people never talk the way they do in real life. Instead they are always expressing noble and tender thoughts. That's why I'm not putting anything bad in here, even though I curse and use bad language when I get angry.

Three

It's all right for old people to dedicate themselves shamelessly to spinning out their memories because that helps them forget about death. But I, in the full bloom of my twenty-five years, can look back at my childhood without any romantic reveries.

I do wish to mention, though, that my life started under a cloud of great mystery. When I think about it I still shiver in awe. Twenty-five years ago, on the twenty-third of March, 1921, I was left during the middle of the night in front of the orphanage of Almería. Someone knocked loudly and impatiently on the door, then disappeared. It all happened exactly as it does in one of those sad novels which one reads when one wishes to be distracted from one's own troubles with the troubles of others. There they always begin with a baby left on a doorstep.

I was a tiny thing, rosy-faced and beautiful. The Mother Superior (whom I have always loved and respected as though she were my true mother) took me in, and I began to grow, as all small things do.

The orphanage was part of a larger building which was mostly used as a hospital. It was near the harbor, opposite the town park. I remember very well how the large patio was warmed by the soft sun in the winter, and baked by the brutal heat in the summer. There were four giant palm trees, which swayed like gypsy women, the trunks whitened by the dust from the constant dryness of the arid land. Masses of daisies and all kinds of plants brightened the pretty blue, white, and rust tiled patio. In the spring when the tamarisk shrubs burst into bloom I always felt happy.

Life was very simple then, I went my way always daydreaming, much more so than now, when I am adorned like a queen with fifteen models from the best couturière, twenty pairs of shoes, three fur coats, and a silver fox stole that is the envy of all my companions in the trade.

Thursdays and Sundays all the girls in the orphanage were taken out for a walk—our chance to have a breath of freedom. The rest of the week we were prisoners behind the high walls. We walked in a line, two by two, some quiet, some troublesome, some chattering away about a million things. We looked nice in our blue uniforms, brightened with white ties, and people stared at us with curiosity and sadness. Other young girls who still had both their mothers and fathers opened their eyes wide with anticipation and fright whenever they passed us by. Impudently, when the nuns weren't looking, we stuck out our tongues at the silly idiots.

I must say that at that time I came to the conclusion that to have parents, though very convenient, must weaken the personality and make one stupider. For my part I didn't miss all those silly endearments which other girls who had parents were used to. With the sisters at the orphanage I had plenty, sometimes even too much. My way one grows up with a truer sense of life, a kind of experience which, as a pilot friend of mine puts it, takes much practice and many flight hours to obtain.

This is why, I confess, it always infuriated me to see that look of commiseration which spread over people's faces when they saw us walking down the garden paths or along the harbor. As though being an orphan meant that our lives were condemned to eternal sorrow! Since that time I've been convinced that there are many fools in the world and I decided that when I grew up it might be amusing to trap some.

We got up at seven in the morning every single day. At eight we went to early mass in the chapel, then we breakfasted on coffee and bread—the bread either soaked into the coffee or eaten separately, as one chose. Afterwards we busied ourselves with our work, which depended on one's age and cleverness. We embroidered, sewed, washed, swept and scrubbed during the entire day and were in bed by nine at night. The older girls helped the sisters care for the sick in the hospital while the younger ones amused the children. I always preferred to go to the sick. My hands were gentle, my voice soft, and I had great patience, which is what they needed.

We were given a simple meal of potatoes, beans or cod—always welcome, and to this day I like my food. On Sundays and holidays we had meat. The Mother Superior solemnly blessed the meal before eating, finishing with a *padre nuestro*. Indeed, the meal needed blessing—the cod was so tough it nearly broke my teeth.

We never missed teatime, which was similar to breakfast, and for dinner we always had noodle soup, fish, salad, and eggs with more air in them than yolk. And, of course, rosaries, novenas and sermons in abundance.

Certainly I earned my keep at the orphanage, because by the time I was ten years old I sewed and embroidered for the people outside, never getting a cent of it for myself. But I haven't forgotten my gratitude to the place—though today no one would dare slap me or grumble at me, and I only wish that certain people who did their share of grumbling and slapping in those days could know that before it's my time to go out of this world feet first. But anyway, one must give each his credit as I know from a certain Señor Caesar and from God. In the orphanage I was treated well and when I left, at thirteen, it was by the front door and not by climbing out of a window and down a ladder like one young enamored idiot that I knew.

I myself never took up with boys. I got on famously with the wet nurses who came to the hospital to give milk to the newborns, but it was never because of any trouble I had gotten into with men. I was dying to learn more of the outer world and they were my best source of knowledge.

As I have said, I left the hospital when I was thirteen. I was already extremely pretty, tall and slender as a reed. The face God had granted me was charming and delicate. I had two very long thick braids which held tight my reddish brown hair. Even though I wasn't yet fully developed, I realized that as I walked down the street I was followed by men's stares. But as I wanted nothing from them, I paid little attention.

I was adopted by some caretakers who lived on the Calle Real. Really, I don't know how all this comes back to me as I have a terrible memory. Things escape me, and any concrete effort to remember the past bores me. But Juan says that one is formed in childhood; it is then that all our traits are created which later give us so much trouble, so if you really want to understand people you must know how it was from the beginning. I think that's nonsense, but as one is never bored talking about oneself, I shall continue with my story of the caretakers, whom I always considered my parents.

Before I left, the Mother Superior locked herself in her office with the caretakers for over an hour, an unusually long interview which excited the imagination of my companions. They were aware of the shadow and mystery concerning my birth. Bastard I may be—but well born. There were rumors of titles of nobility and the tragic death of a young gentleman. What was definitely true was that when I left I had with me, in addition to two thousand *duros,* some beautiful clothing and a valuable jeweled medal with the sainted image of the Macarena. The medal was large and heavy, of real gold; and the date of my birth and the initials M.V. were inscribed in rubies. That's why they called me María de los Dolores and gave me the last name of Vélez.

This jewel, as well as the two thousand *duros,* had been on me when I came to the orphanage and had been kept for me by the Mother Superior. The other young girls constantly daydreamed about the medal. Several insisted that they had seen it when the Mother Superior had been in a

13

good mood. Others let it grow in their imagination until it became as radiant and enormous as a sun on fire. On the day of my First Communion I had been allowed to hold it in my hand for a short while. The sisters remarked that I conducted myself very discreetly upon seeing it for the first time. Unimpressed, I looked at it with a calm curiosity —actually it didn't seem so big to me. Still, I have never, never forgotten the feeling of its weight, the fresh heat of the gold as I squeezed it in my palm. . . . Oh, if only men paid one that way, instead of in miserable dribs and drabs, how much more they'd receive in return!

The Mother Superior told me that my adopted parents had been informed of the details concerning my origin and birth, and at the proper time they would tell me everything. She asked me to pray for the souls of my true parents regardless of whether they were still suffering in this valley of tears, or whether they had been taken away already by the infinite pity of our Lord. I must always continue to be as good as I had been up until then, and I should realize that the path of righteousness is better than the road to sin, a tempting and false mirror held up by the corrupt and cruel Devil. I must always honor God and honor my adopted parents as though they were my own. If at any time God should permit me the joy of discovering my true parents I must not forget that pity and charity are the virtues esteemed by our Lord.

Afterwards the Mother became sad, for she had always had a soft spot for me. She kissed me and said that I was very pretty, and would no doubt have the misfortune of turning into a beautiful woman. Misfortune because the only beauty which brings happiness is the beauty of the soul. For this reason I must always pray to our Lord Jesus Christ, so that I wouldn't lose my own soul and be abandoned entirely to the beauty of the flesh.

Though I didn't understand too well what she was talking about, her words had a pleasant sonorous ring, as though she were speaking to herself. The Mother had been a great lady and beauty. She was still good to look at as she went about her business, her habit always sparkling clean, never losing patience when one of the sick spit up on the sheets.

There were kisses and hugs, but I shed few tears; I was impatient to get out and acquaint myself with this world of evil that roared and blustered beyond the walls of the orphanage.

Four

My father, as I have always referred to him, was a Cordovese, forty-five years old. He had been in the Civil Guard and from his experiences had developed a wary eye, a tight mouth, a quick hand, and a generous kick. I never cared for him because he was quick to give me what-for and he was a coarse sort, always unshaven, tough, and of few but foul words. My mother was younger. She still had a good figure which she was proud of, though she insisted it had never been of any benefit to her. Loquacious and gossipy, she always spoke more than she should have. She would get drunk on her own words and rarely stopped to think first. She didn't get on with my father and they fought constantly. Even though she was the female, she was the stronger one, which proved she came of tougher stock. Still, she loved her man and as far as I know never fooled around with anyone else, though more than one had admired her. I loved her very much because she was good and never laid a hand on me.

I spent several months with them. I either sewed, embroidered, worked in the house, or else ran wild in the streets. Then, one day, my parents had a really terrific battle, and the family went to pieces. My mother, who was the careless sort, burned our supper of beans. My father, miserable at not being able to satisfy his hunger, started to curse. He went into a fury, screaming insults at my mother, who retaliated by taking a pan and hitting him over the head with it. By then he was purple with rage, and he went after her with a knife. I got into the act too, and with all the strength of my thirteen years I grabbed a rock which we used as a kitchen weight and threw it at one of his feet. My aim was so good that it ripped one of his tendons and left him with a limp for the rest of his life.

Roaring and spitting saliva like a wild bull, he threw the two of us out of the house, creating a scandal that was the amusement of the entire neighborhood. We hastily took refuge in my mother's sister's house, who wasn't particularly delighted with her unexpected guests.

I quickly realized that the visit was going to finish badly. My mother was a stubborn woman who never knew how to give in in time, and who always magnified situations, never capable of listening to reason. This created an atmosphere of constant warfare between the two women.

I was innocent about life. But I'd already begun to realize that one has to judge people shrewdly—one's reason has nothing to do with one's love. My father, for example, was

15

a rough, glum sort, as I have said. He didn't seem to care for anyone except maybe the baby, yet he could spend hours caring for our little garden, he would die for the flowers, even the ordinary daisies.

I didn't love him but I've always had an extraordinary fondness for my mother, who at fifty is still a strong and independent woman incapable of being touched or softened by anything.

As our stay with my aunt was obviously going to end in disaster, I abandoned my adopted family to join some gypsies I'd become friendly with in search of the world. A world where what I longed for belonged to the Devil, rather than to God.

Five

Juan assures me, whenever the occasion arises, that I am a very intelligent woman. Too intelligent for a woman, and especially for one in my profession. As far as I am concerned, the one thing I am sure of is my beauty. I am proud of my looks, but on the other hand have never pretended to be particularly wise.

But maybe he's not completely wrong—in the lives of all famous people there are all sorts of weird things. Their lives are disturbed by strange doubts, and sometimes where others miss the mark, they have a sixth sense about what is right. I don't know if I've always guessed right in my short but busy life, but I think I did well in joining the gypsies. I spent with them the best months of my entire life. Indeed, I often dream about those dusty roads of Andalucía and of the extraordinary adventures that each new day brought me. A few days ago while driving with Juan, the one person I feel at ease with, I was overwhelmed with a sudden desire to relive those days a little.

It had been raining continually, the earth smelled damp and the sides of the road were filled with puddles. As I came from a dry and dusty region, this humid, gray weather drives me out of my mind. I told Juan I wanted to get out of the car and walk a few miles alone and barefoot and feel once more the pleasant sensation of the ground beneath my feet.

He looked at me surprised. Then, as he has great sensitivity about these things, he gazed at me sadly and helped me remove my silk stockings. I didn't feel like being with anyone so he promised to drive on and wait for me two miles ahead. He warned me that I was fooling myself—it is impossible to recapture the past.

I wasn't fooling myself, not at all. Still, I felt a bit slowed down, almost old, and my chest bothered me for a week— I suppose from going barefoot in the dampness. It's true —one can't recapture the past.

The gypsies were a couple getting along in years. The man was tall, old, very erect, and had a large frightening mustache which drooped like a Chinaman's. He was a real artist and he knew how to play the flute, the guitar, and the accordion. He had two trained monkeys who danced to music, and recently had lost a bear, a great misfortune because he loved the animal very much and because he earned a lot of money with it. His gypsy nickname was Cuchiyiyas—the "Knife"—of Andalucía. He drank a lot and spent all his money on wine. But he never hit me, and he called me "the little one" with tender affection in his voice.

The woman was a little younger, very quick and sure of herself. She knew more than he did. She was terrific at stealing—no one could ever catch her in the act.

Even though these two fought, it was in a different way than my adopted parents. There are ways and ways of fighting. The way of the gypsies was sympathetic and loving. She was the sort who always sees the joke in everything and he was solemn and serious, even when talking to his bear—which according to him had been a phenomenal animal.

We left Almería at dawn on a March morning, walking along the road to Málaga. Punta del Río was shining like gold, and the tip of Cape de Gata could just be seen through the veil of mist on the gulf.

I had been able to leave the house without any trouble and I had joined the gypsies at the outskirts of the town. There behind a grove of trees I'd changed my clothing and put on a long and graceful skirt and a blouse with a kerchief around my neck that my new mother, La Bermeja, gave me. We made a package of my old clothes, planning to sell them at the first occasion. I had just turned fourteen and was completely carefree and lighthearted, delighted to be traveling along the coastal roads.

Between the gypsies and myself there was little familiarity, the way of really noble people. I joined them, and they took me along. Nothing more.

We had neither a cart nor a horse, we walked as long as our feet held out. Mine, more pampered, killed me the first few days but as I hadn't yet realized how pretty and precious they were to me, I was perfectly content to mistreat them. It took us a week with an occasional generous lift to get to Motril. Meanwhile we lived off the land.

We didn't stay there long. People were suspicious of us, which made it difficult to rob them, even though I made my debut there. My fingers lighted on the wallet of a young fool who was standing mouth agape watching the monkeys' tricks. We didn't really mind cutting our stay short as we were in a hurry to get to Málaga, a city of great possibilities, according to my new parents.

Still, it wasn't a total loss. In the outskirts, in Pedregalejo, we filched two linen sheets which we sold later in El Perchel. We spent three nights in the Inn of the Sun, until the itching fingers of La Bermeja made it imperative for us to go on to La Pelusa, the most marvelous place I had ever seen. There everything for sale was wonderful and it was sold freely and openly, with no pretense. I was delighted.

During the day we took the monkeys over to the park where we carefully avoided the guards. The old gypsy, his face very solemn, made the monkeys dance to the sound of his flute, guitar, or accordion, depending on the size of the crowd, while I passed the plate and my mother dextrously exercised her hands.

La Bermeja also managed to get part-time work cleaning people's houses for the weekend. Once she got the hang of where everything was, she certainly did do a good job—and her employer's cheerful weekend ended in Monday blues.

Those were good times, but I liked even better the days spent on the road where one's feelings had more to do with nature and less with people. In the happy weeks spent in Málaga I flowered into a young woman, opening up like a bud in springtime.

As everything must end sometime, those days ended too. We left the city, taking the road to Algeciras. We took with us some money, a bundle of fine clothes and the bad wishes of all the good people of the town.

Six

Until we came to Marbella everything went well. Our feet were more rested than usual because we had met up with some happy-go-lucky independent muleteers. They were kind to us, though La Bermeja assured me that their generosity had another name which she didn't care to explain to me for fear of opening my eyes too much. But my eyes were open wide enough and I knew how to act aloof enough to dampen their ardor. God knows, they certainly didn't give a damn about what might happen to me.

Then in Marbella one of the muleteers, miserable at my

rebuffs, tried to obtain from me that which a man of honor never attempts to take from a woman by force. Hearing my screams, the old gypsy came to my defense and gave the fellow a good thrust in the arm with his blade. This incited the whole band, who threatened to become ugly. Instead of continuing with them along the coastal road to Estepona and San Roque, we cut over to San Pedro de Alcántara toward Ronda, a city renowned for its magnificent fairs and bullfights, according to Cuchiyiyas.

I don't expect to live long, but even if I do get to be old and senile I don't imagine that I will ever forget the tough trip through the Sierra Bermeja and the mountains before Ronda. Our loot from Málaga, instead of getting smaller, had grown since Marbella, thanks to the trusting nature of the muleteers. This made traveling even harder. The gypsies carried the bundle between them, and I helped as best I could but I wasn't very strong. In San Pedro de Alcántara we began to climb up cliffs and over gorges and it took great will power not to throw our loot away in some forgotten ditch of that accursed road.

Finally we made a sensible arrangement which relieved our fatigue. We divided the bundle into three smaller packages—two large and one very small. The little one was for La Bermeja, who was suffering from a puncture in her lung and who had begun to spit up blood. The old gypsy and I took the other two. I would stay behind, waiting on the road with my bundle while they went on ahead for maybe a couple of miles. Cuchiyiyas then would leave La Bermeja and return to help me. In this back-and-forth fashion we climbed the first sierra.

I became fond of the old gypsy at that time, and when, some time later, the police took him away, I confess my eyes filled with tears. It was one of the few times in my life I honestly wept. But I suppose the old man had it coming. He was one of those types always getting involved right in the middle of a situation. He never learned to stay to one side, hold back, and let others fight the battles as most men do. He taught me many things about life, and among them how to drink wine like a señorita. "Look . . . little one . . . don't gulp it down in one swallow. Slowly, gently . . . put the flask to your lips and sip a little at a time, pretty one." He was a real man, of the stamp that doesn't exist any more today. And if he had been younger . . .

We reached the first sierra which, as I have said, was called Bermeja—"Crimson." My gypsy mother was very proud that because her skin was always somewhat coppery, she had been nicknamed the same. It occurred to me that she was a lot like those mountains—very hard to get at. Only her man could do anything with her. I remember going on to think that she was going to die soon, and that it would please her to be buried in those mountains if possible. All these thoughts came to me, I suppose, because I myself had some of the peculiarities of that strange woman.

After reaching the top we stopped awhile to rest and look about. We were fiercely proud of our success, of being able to dominate the earth below from our exalted heights. We had finally made it. This feeling of conquest never comes when one is riding in a car, no matter how many miles one travels, or how powerfully the motor roars.

I looked down, enthralled. In front, below us, the earth stretched out like an open hand while behind us, it tightened into a closed fist. Ahead the land rolled gently, flattening out, leading to the glittering blond sand of the beach and the smooth blue water of the sea. But when I turned around I saw the earth crumple and fold into rough ridges that grew higher and higher until the crowded mountains seemed to touch the sky.

Looking out to sea, life seemed easy, simple and good. I could almost feel the gentle water breezes caressing my face. In contrast, the sierras seemed frightening and menacing. The peaks, huddled close to one another, looked like weird faces peeking out curiously, half-hidden behind windows. A cold wind blew through the mountains and now the world seemed harsh, complicated and threatening. Later I learned to love the sierras, but at first I was scared. I was a child of the coast and the gentle murmuring roll of the waves had lulled me for fourteen years. I hadn't known that the earth could rise up that way.

We had already passed Benahavis, and we were climbing up to Igualeja when my parents decided to spend the night in an abandoned shepherd's hut, which was a real find, as it started to freeze as soon as the sun went down. In spite of its being only the end of September, the chill went through our bones. This harsh cold was a new discovery for me.

After making a supper from a healthy hunk of bread with oil and pork, and washing it down with a long drink of dry red wine from the wine bag, we lit a fire and the three of us huddled together under one blanket, drawing warmth from each other's bodies, and in this way I slept in the mountains for the first time in my life.

We arrived at Igualeja the following morning. We entered the village, and as soon as they spotted us, the neighborly villagers threatened us with sticks and their dogs. We hid in a pine grove, so frightened that we stayed there during the entire day. Finally, at the end of the afternoon, we found a swineherd who was willing to lead us back to the road.

The earth glowed with color. As I have said, it was the end of September, just before the fair of San Francisco which is celebrated in Ronda on the second of October. It was the end of the day and the warm autumn lights were everywhere. The mountains rose so high, so filled with ravines and deep gorges, that when I looked down from above I became nervous. Down at the bottom, the valleys were hidden behind soft greenish-purple shadows.

Though I've seen many beautiful views in my life—I've always been fond of nature—there have been few like that. The colors were beautiful, and there was a kind of menacing calm that was terrifying yet strangely irresistible, pulling me toward the risks that could be imagined there, lurking among the shadows, the rocks, the trees, and the rushing torrents that roared away unseen.

We were about to go on toward the road when the swineherd pointed to a fire which had been blazing away for three days in a pine grove called La Palmitera and was traveling toward El Cuscús, in the direction of a ranch called La Honda. The boy was a swineherd there, he knew the region, and he told us that the best thing for us to do now was to accompany him to his cabin and spend the night. This was no place for Christian people to be traveling alone at night, and even though we were poor, it could cost us plenty.

The old gypsy laughed at the boy's fears but the swineherd insisted. He looked at me tenderly and said that I could be kidnaped. Cuchiyiyas understood and he finally agreed to go on to La Honda.

It was a large ranch. To reach it we had to climb over a steep and rocky hill and pass over the Lairín Daidín—a place so difficult that even mules were scared out of their wits and balked. That we ever managed to get out of there alive was a miracle. Poor Bermeja spit blood constantly, so much that the boy helped carry her, which made it easier for her to breathe. As for our bundles, there was a moment when I noticed that Cuchiyiyas was contemplating abandoning them behind a pine tree, but he was a stubborn man. He took them on with him even though it was like carrying a ton of bricks.

We reached the Lairín Daidín by twilight and we stopped to spend the night at the bottom of a valley. A river ran through the valley—the swineherd called it Guadaira—which appealed to my imagination. The boy told me that he had hunted martens there, the soft animal whose skin is later used to flatter the faces of rich ladies. He said he was going to give me one for being so beautiful. Well, I didn't get to

21

see either animal or skin, but I learned something new and I dreamed of covering my neck with a magnificent scarf like that in some distant future time. Today, when I casually let my silver fox fall from my shoulders, I sometimes feel nostalgia for a certain small skin of an unknown marten, hunted in Guadaira and offered to me by an enamored swineherd.

We eventually reached his cabin. He did the honors as best he could. He gave us thick, well-seasoned garlic soup, fresh bread, and a hunk of sausage so good I was transported with bliss. After the hot meal, when our stomachs were full of soup and our feet well warmed by the fire, the boy suggested that we continue with him the next morning to the ranch to watch the weighing of the pigs. He was anxious to postpone our departure, wanting to spend as much time with me as possible.

Cuchiyiyas thought awhile—he wasn't a man of flighty decisions. After soberly appraising the situation he decided to go with the swineherd. He hoped that in the commotion of the moment something would fall into our fingers. Something fat and greasy.

We rested up from the tiring trip and by dawn we were ready to leave for the main house of the ranch which was more than five kilometers away.

It was a difficult hike. Not one step was easy that cold clear dawn. While we followed the brook which flowed past the house we saw clusters of cork trees, pines, chestnuts, almond trees and oaks. The ranch itself was huge, more than seventy-five hundred acres. It extended from the hill of Abanto, which was very high and cold and covered with pine-saps, down to San Pedro de Alcántara which was by the beach. Surrounding the ranch were the villages of Istán, San Pedro, Igualeja and Benahavis. According to the swineherd, who was from the region, everything could be found on that one ranch—from the cold pinesaps of the Sierra de las Nieves to the warm orange groves down below, from the common Spanish goat to the beavers and martens. In order to get to the ranch, he added with fierce pride, it was necessary to sweat plenty, as no road went through there and even the animals were afraid of the Lairín Daidín.

The ranch was called La Honda—"the hidden"—as it was buried deep in the sierra, next to the river bed of Guadaira, a fantastic place. The owners never bothered to come down from Madrid where they were busy with parties and society life, so it was poorly run. The earth is good to people who care for it and work it well, and if one doesn't take care of it, it's better not to have it. We all agreed on that.

Before reaching the main house, huge, dilapidated, and surrounded by an orange grove and almond trees, we could

22

hear the grunting of the pigs corraled in the yard with the men who weighed them. Nearly all of the five hundred animals came from a man in Jerez who was a tenant. Several were from farmers from the nearby villages. They all seemed small and young and they grunted sorrowfully. We spotted a dozen suckling pigs and fell in love with them immediately, dreaming of the meal they'd make.

During the weighing there was a terrible commotion of squealing animals, men shouting, and a cloud of dry dust rose that made my eyes water and my nose itch. I became frightened and pressed myself against the hinges of a gate so that no pig would bite me, or any boy get fresh. I soon noticed that the pigs always pulled in the wrong direction, tugging against the cord fastened to their tails, though it would have been much easier for them to submit quietly. But after all, it's not fair to expect animals, especially stupid ones, to be smarter than people who do just the same. It's my own little custom to appear to be contrary, to give a pull in a direction opposite to where I intend going, and by doing that, I manage to get my way without anyone being aware of the truth, and to flatter men's egos as well.

Cuchiyiyas weighed many pigs and did it well. He took nothing for his special use as the occasion didn't present itself and he was a man who knew how to bide his time patiently. But La Bermeja, with her itching fingers, filched a wallet with three *duros* in it from one of the boys and stuck it for safekeeping in between her skinny breasts.

Later, after the racket of the weighing was done with, we quieted our hunger with a good breakfast. While the swineherds were leading away the pigs, the boy missed his money and raised holy hell. The old gypsy sized up the situation, realized we were in a spot and might get quite a beating. After calming them down, he led all of us out into the yard where we started to search for the missing wallet. Sure enough, it was there, half-hidden in a dusty corner.

We were hurt by their lack of trust in us and we decided that it was time to leave the ranch. We had ahead of us the difficult trip up the Lairín Daidín, which was murderous and took nearly three days.

Seven

When we finally got back onto the road and could count the distance to Ronda from where we were—Puerto de la Llanailla—we sighed in relief. We didn't even mind the local people, who seemed tough and belligerent. According to an impressionable swineherd, who knew by heart the history and miracles of the Pasos Largos, a bandit named Flores Arocha had wandered through the mountains with a tremendous machine gun. Though he was a swineherd who saw bandits on every side, it's true that later during the war . . . or maybe a little before . . . I never get these things straight . . . the Civil Guards did kill Flores Arocha in La Honda, which was a very safe and natural place for bandits.

We arrived in Ronda safe and sound on the last day of September, 1935. We came with the intention of improving our fortunes at the fair of San Francisco where there were the most fantastic herds of pigs that I've ever seen.

We had had to cross mountains, gorges and streams, as the country near Ronda is rough and mountainous on all sides. When we arrived we decided to rest a day in what they called El Barrio—"the quarter"—which was the best place for us as it was thickly populated and very free. We sold some of the sheets we had carried with us and we were able to stay in the Posada de la Herradura with people of quality. I tasted there a rare fruit, neither pear nor apple, which bothered me. I like things to be clear. Men men, women women and pears pears.

After eating, as we were making a holiday of it, Cuchiyiyas took us around to see the town. He was very fond of it. I'm not sure whether it was because of the good bullfights or because of some ancestor from Ronda whom he had never mentioned to us. He never spoke of his personal life, not even to La Bermeja. She didn't even know where he had been born.

First we went to La Ciudad—"the city"—which is the old part with narrow streets, a mixture of Castilian and Moorish design typical of Andalucía. He made us stop in front of the church of Santa María la Mayor, the Palacio de los Antienza and the Palacio de Salvatierra and the House of Mondragón. He let a sheet go very cheaply to the lady there, so that we could see the inside patio. Personally, I didn't think it rated all the fuss.

Later we went to El Campillo. We went down in the mine that leads to the Casa del Rey Moro, the House of the Moorish King, which had me really scared—the steps going down seemed never to end and I imagined that I was going to end up in the entrails of the earth where they say everything is on fire. We also saw the mills and we crossed the Guadalevín by the old bridge. After wandering about this way for a while we came to Mercadillo, the new city, where most of the business goes on. Naturally we gave this our careful attention.

Ronda is built high on a steep rock, unlike anything I'd

ever seen. Cuchiyiyas led us up along the lookout which hangs over the brink of the Tajo, a deep gorge cutting the city in half.

At my feet the earth crumbled away sharply, I stood there suspended in air, looking down on the eagles flying about below. Down below, way down, I could see the mills, the vegetable gardens, the farmhouses, the olive trees, and grape vineyards lushly spreading over the lowlands. My eyes traveled far beyond the valley until finally I saw the peaks of a huge reddish mountain looming over the town of Grazalema.

It all seemed fantastic, most of all the Tajo itself. I liked best the quiet world I found there. Even though there were the usual noises of nature, a silence dominated the Tajo, a silence which calmed my soul. Time passed, but I was unaware, lost in a dream of happiness.

I know that there are many things I am ignorant of. But sometimes it suddenly comes to me that I understand everything without thinking. At that moment, numbed by the peaceful silence of the Tajo, I had a sense of things . . . an intuition which has unfortunately proven to be inconsistent and fleeting, like all worth-while things in life.

La Bermeja also was very moved. She felt death near. She said that the earth below pulled at her stomach and this was a sign that it was hungry for her long-suffering body. The old gypsy, tired of her foolishness, took us away. We went to the Plaza de Toros which Cuchiyiyas said was very old. I admired the pretty filagree of bulls over the gate; it's one of the best bull rings in Spain.

Later we bought some ice cream in the Alameda—just like real ladies. To top off the day we had dinner in the Posada de la Sangre. In the Posada de la Herradura three spoons and a knife were already missing, so we didn't go back. I don't know what it is with our fingers—everything sticks to them.

After dinner we moved over to the Barrio where we stayed in the hut of a gypsy, an old woman who had known Cuchiyiyas during his boyhood. During the day she took care of our one remaining monkey. The other one had caught cold and died during a bad night in the sierras.

The family, which was five on leaving Almería (I count the monkeys as they were more intelligent and loving than most human beings), was getting smaller. The good times were coming to an end. Maybe because I was only fourteen I remember that period as the happiest, most carefree time of my life. Not just because I was young, but because I had a splendid indifference to the necessities of life which I later lost. Now I yearn for material things, and when my wishes are fulfilled I become bored, sad.

I always felt that my gypsy parents were noble people even though they were thieves both from necessity and habit. The three of us lived close to nature, which makes decent people happy. The crowded life of the cities, buried under air clouded by cigarette smoke and choked by the same monotonous conversations, never can end in anything good.

Now there are many nights when I dream I hear water running. A water crystalline and fresh that I can never see. I am grateful to Juan because a few days ago he took me to a river that rippled and murmured happily. It was a pleasant time, nothing more. An interlude between the eternal Casablanca, Pasapoga or El Abra, the Casa Carmen, La Rosa, Montserrat, the apartments of Ricardo, of Perico, and the bedrooms of the good hotels. An interlude between the terrible embraces of men, their faces desperate with anxiety, while I try to pierce their indifferent hearts with words of love, to see if there is even a single drop of blood flowing through their veins.

Just the way time seems to go by swiftly sometimes and drag on interminably other times, so it is with the way I remember things. I go on at great length over this, and skip rapidly over that, depending on what seems important. I've written about these weeks with great detail and care though I hardly bothered to tell about the months we spent following the road along the coast from Almería to Málaga.

We left the Barrio the day of the fair of San Francisco, fed up with that motley collection of pigs and humans, disgusted by our failure to get hold of one of the animals. Even a little suckling pig would have done. Cuchiyiyas then tried to filch a bolt of cloth during a small business venture in Mercadillo and the affair turned out badly. We escaped for the moment, but the Civil Guards followed us and came for Cuchiyiyas during the night. When we heard their voices, Le Bermeja and I managed to hide behind an elm tree which kept the two of us from being caught. The soldiers handcuffed the old gypsy and took him away. He couldn't even say good-by. We saw him go, calm and sure as always, not stooping to a false gesture, and with the dignity of one who knows, when the time comes, how to lose.

A few days later, thin as a scarecrow and spitting up blood continually, La Bermeja died. Before she went we talked and she spoke to me with all the sorrow and honesty of the dying, who finally admit to the things we know all along are true. I suppose death robs people of their false vanity as well as of their life.

"My child . . ." she said, already slightly delirious, "I don't like having to leave life without my man by my side.

26

But I am not surprised that things are working out badly for me, as he isn't mine. He belongs to another woman. . . . He left her for me. . . . I'm not happy at having you here. . . . You are very young and death is very ugly. The two don't go well together. You must promise me that when the time comes you'll leave. You must go out to the street. . . . I'll manage things presently with old Carmela. Do you understand?"

"Yes, Mother."

"You'll leave?"

"As you like." I promised her that I'd go in order to please her but I had no intention of leaving her side. Death has never frightened me. I'd seen many bodies grow cold in the hospital at Almería.

"While you are still here, I must tell you something that has bothered me since I've known you, child."

"What is it?"

"I don't see you going in the right direction in life. One can rob and even kill without deserting one's proper path and without losing hope of finding fresh water at the end of the desert—but you, I am frightened for you. You seem to be going nowhere; for you life seems to be merely a large circle which has you turning round and round . . . never arriving—" She started to choke and was forced to stop. After I arranged her head more comfortably against the pillows so that she could breathe better she continued her ramblings.

"When I was a young girl I also was very beautiful and all the men of Loja were after me. But I always went my own way, which was to fall deeply in love with only one man. Whether he was good or bad made no difference, I gave him all my love. I felt as though a fire flamed inside me, and I wanted to give of my whole being. Now you . . ." She stopped, sighing slightly. "You will be beautiful, little one. You are already—and you know it. But when you are fully developed and know what it is to feel like a woman, then the men will not let you alone."

"Oh, that doesn't interest me!"

"That's what I'm afraid of, girl. That men won't interest you—that they won't interest you at all," she said mysteriously. "I'm afraid that you won't give of yourself to anyone and that your heart will dry up little by little from disuse until one day it will crumble like a speck of old dust. Poor baby!"

"Don't feel sorry for me. I'll manage."

"A dry well doesn't give forth water, my girl, and poor you indeed if once in your life you don't lose your head for a man and fall so in love that you are ready to do anything."

"No, Mother, no—I'm not going to lose my head."

27

"Quiet! Don't talk such wickedness."

In this fashion La Bermeja raved on, talking foolishness, until the last sighs and rattles marked her end. She was, as I've said before, a strange deep woman who left me unknown riches, even though I never agreed with her.

Eight

I was left alone. Now neither the old friend of Cuchiyiyas in the Barrio hut nor the monkey was company. The monkey wasn't feeling well. He had a suffocating sharp cough that bothered me by sounding pitifully like the cough of a newborn baby. The old lady, deaf as a post, was very disagreeable. She had the nasty temper and anger which come from not being able to hear. So, what with one thing and another, I decided to leave and follow the first road that I came to, which turned out to be the one which went to Jerez de la Frontera and Cádiz.

When I told all this to Juan one night, while we were talking in the dark about my past life, I saw that my decision impressed him enormously. He didn't say anything right away, but later he confessed to me that he didn't think that there were many women in this world as courageous and adventurous as me.

Oh, I think he exaggerates—it really takes more courage to stay still in one place than to get up and leave, abandoning everything. Anyway, whenever I've gritted my teeth, blocked a fountain of tears, and gathered my forces, it has been to find something new, and I've had to make the journey whether it leads me to good or to evil.

But Juan is a strange person and I like him to keep his illusions about me. He is a man experienced in the ways of life, he tosses aside your lies and laughs at them without becoming angry because he himself has been through everything already. Still he hasn't become cynical. He is always searching, always curious—as alive with emotion as a child, and always able to discover something new in people.

This is terrific in a man almost forty. I have never known anyone with as much enthusiasm as he. He goes about life like a hunter and in one word, one gesture or look, with his intuition and imagination he discovers the truth. Nothing escapes him in spite of his habit of appearing to be introspective and unaware. Sometimes he's so uncanny I get gooseflesh.

Actually, I rarely bother to lie to him any more; the few times I do it is mostly not to get out of practice or to amuse myself watching him struggle to ferret out the truth.

Courageous or no, I left Ronda one fine morning happy as a lark with only a hunk of bread and a slice of salt pork to fill my stomach. I was still only fourteen and I had to fend for myself to see that I arrived at Cádiz as intact as when I left Ronda. True, I arrived a bit more handled and I had some bad moments along the waterfront, but I was tough enough to wiggle out of those situations.

In Cádiz I joined up with an old woman who worked as a maid and who helped get me a job as a nursemaid with a family who lived in the Calle de Columela, between the harbor and the Plaza del Mercado. They lived on the second floor which showed that they weren't very well off. In Cádiz everyone who possibly can prefers to keep his furniture and boredom on the main floor.

The man of the house—el Señor, as he liked people to call him, but which I never bothered with—was a boor. He was prying, vulgar and quarrelsome. While he worked in La Almadraba I helped his wife straighten up the house. Later I'd go out with the children to the Plaza de Mina while she did the day's shopping—she'd never let a penny out of her hand for fear that she'd be cheated.

Cádiz was to my taste. I liked being next to the sea, even though it wasn't the same sea I had grown up with, and when the wind made the waves rise and roar like wild beasts, my own mood was even stormier.

Actually, my life there was very dull. I became stupefied with a kind of numbness. I think this has to do with adolescence, the rapid development of the body mixed with a boredom toward daily existence. But as it was already the middle of winter I decided to stick it out until spring, which comes much sooner in Andalucía than in this damned Madrid.

Every day I took the children—two of them, and devils—to the Plaza de Mina which was paved with large chunks of slate. There were benches so we could stop and rest, and lamp posts which dogs continually peed on to the amusement of the children.

Up higher, in the center, was a garden with a lawn and paths. The best thing, though, was the four statues. "The four statues of the Fart," natives of the town nicknamed them.

The first statue has a finger of his hand pointing in a way as though saying: "Who has farted here?"

"Well, it wasn't me," the second statue assures, with his hand on his chest.

29

"But it didn't spring up from the earth," the third one remarks, pointing to the ground.

"Then let him speak up, whoever did it," says the fourth, looking angry with his arms sternly crossed.

There was a kiosk for a band which played on Sundays after Mass—a very odd bunch of musicians—and next to it was the Fine Arts Academy. The Academy caused quite a stir among the old nurses and women as it was rumored that inside were naked women. The women used to hurry past it, holding the children tightly and not even letting them glance at the building.

Though I strolled by many times and stretched my neck hopefully, I never saw anything. I would have liked to have gone inside on the pretext of looking for a job. It sounded easy enough—posing naked so that they could make idiotic paintings.

I consoled myself by going to another part of the Plaza. There I used to look at the pictures in Raimundo's Photography Shop. In his tinted portraits of young sweethearts and children dressed for First Communion one could see the future stupidity and vanity of grownups.

The square was filled with all sorts of vendors. An old woman used to stroll about shouting in a rough nasal voice which turned my stomach, "Cinnamon stick candy, filberts, nuts . . ." while young boys came around with anchovies and crayfish from the Island. When the children saw them coming, they cleared the way and started to sing:

> *I don't eat clams*
> *because they stink*
> *the boy that sells them*
> *pissed in the basket.**

* I have noticed that in books of importance they stick these little things in in order to make something clearer. I am putting in this one so that you can see I am doing things right, and in order to explain that instead of saying that "They pissed," children of the better families said "They made peepee." The children I took care of said "pissed." (*Lola*)

Other days we went over to the Parque Genovés, or to the Alameda—in the cities of Andalucía there is always an *alameda*, or park, where you can see the sea every time you turn a corner.

On Sundays and holidays my employers let me go out. I went with some other girls, also nursemaids, to the Plaza de San Antonio where one of the girls had a boy friend who had a car. He often gave us rides, and on one occasion took us to a very gay christening. The people climbed on top of the cars and full of high spirits drove through the Calle del Sacramento to the La Viña district, reaching out for palm leaves and throwing pennies to the godfather.

Living this way, I managed to stick it out through April, 1936—I had promised myself not to leave Cádiz until the end of my fifteenth April. According to what I was told, I was something to see, blooming more prettily than the most beautiful flower.

I continued to go my way, not wishing to be bothered by boy friends, and not getting close to any one man. The girls I knew didn't like me because their boy friends couldn't keep their eyes off me, and ignored them completely. In those days I went out with more than one sailor and there was dancing, petting, and kisses, all endured without any passion on my part, until the boy went his way the better for a few parting slaps of mine. I've never paid attention to men's looks, always minding my own business—except on one mistaken occasion which I will explain later on.

In May I finally left Cádiz for good. I wanted to see Sevilla. I went alone and as in the past on foot. Before leaving I helped myself to a few trifles from the house where I had worked in order to make the trip pleasanter. The truth is that I wasn't afraid of anything.

Nine

I left the house during the night. The sea was acting up, and a strong wind was blowing from the direction of the prison.

I walked through the streets, past the whitewashed houses with their Moorish towers and their cisterns, content to leave this "little cup of silver" which is more filth than anything else. I was tired of it all. Of the plazas, the walks, the port, the cathedral, and most of all of the Puerta de Tierra—a kind of castle which has a tower which can make idiots of the stupid. In a window high up there is a little man who makes signs with a flag to the trolleys that pass by the port so that they don't collide on the single line. I had had it, even up to the coffee, *el cafelito,* which is probably the best thing about Cádiz. I can still hear in my ears a song that an old nurse in her broken and lisping voice used to sing.

Cádiz has gone crazy with trolleys
See the good business the company has done
There are Gaditanas, there are Gaditanas
Who dream of the trolley and its bell.
And others who haven't even got a dime for coffee
Can spend their lives in San José. . . .

I went along my way, happy to be going. As I walked, I kept close to the sides of the houses so that no one would notice me, as people here are highly sexed and one thing quickly leads to another. I was glad to leave the city as the capitals don't please me at all. Even now, in Madrid, where I have such a reputation that men call me "La Estraperlo" —the Black-Market Queen—because I am so expensive that there are men who will give a thousand *pesetas* just to have a look at me, there are times when I am capable of committing some absolute insanity and hurting my own interests just to be able to leave the city and go on a short trip somewhere.

There is nothing like being alone and free in the country, surrounded by all the beauty of nature.

Living in the city poisons and destroys one—I myself wouldn't have done many things if I hadn't felt so lost, so removed from nature. Men aren't so angry or evil when they can use their strength working the land instead of jitter-bugging. But here in Madrid the whole point of going away for a weekend revolves around some elegant new clothes; a hunting party in the sierras smells more from poker and whisky than from rabbit.

In this inane life everything is prison, war, and bloodshed. Juan tells me that it has always been that way, and will always continue to be so, but even though I'm not as well read as he is, I don't believe it has to be like that.

Well, we'll see what the future brings! Now, why can't they take all the criminals—there are only a few real ones—and instead of locking them up in those miserable jails, put them all together on some deserted island? They could bring them food and also the women they love. That would be much better, and the poor devils couldn't harm anyone there.

Whenever I tell people of these marvelous ideas of mine, the idiots laugh at me. They ask me if that happened, what work would the police have? But it's really very simple. They could watch the criminals and see that they couldn't leave the island—at the same time taking care not to interfere in their private affairs. Men are blockheads who stubbornly go their own blind way and because of their vanity don't wish to hear you when you say something more sensible than they. But that's the way of the world, and it's in their hands. Indeed, I am sure that they even arrange it so that many things don't work out right—when it suits their own private interests. I know that from hearing them talk about business and about politics, which is a plague that consumes all those who take it seriously.

Getting back to my farewell to Cádiz—it ended up poorly for me. In the Puerto Real I joined up with an old man—a fish cleaner—and his woman. He wandered about, getting work wherever he could. But the very first night I heard him whispering and plotting, and when he thought I was asleep, and tried to take a silver tray from me, I threw a stool in his face.

His hefty companion helped him out and I couldn't escape from the rats who denounced me to the police. I was in jail for six days, six days which I don't like to recall. I was livid with rage at being shut up like one more sardine in the can. One man I bit on the wrist—oh, I carried on like a wild beast until the whole pack of them started to take an interest in me, and together they managed to calm me down.

Finally the police commissioner saw me and also took an interest. I don't remember too much about it, as so many men have passed through my life. Still, he wasn't a bad sort and when he learned the little I chose to tell him about my past life, he very quickly sent me back to Almería to my adopted parents. After all, I was only fifteen and I hadn't stolen anything of value in the home I had worked in at Cádiz. Only a golden crucifix which belonged to the owner and which had been specially blessed, three good trays which they had had since their wedding, a watch and some medals of gold on a chain which belonged to the children.

They could replace all the things. Not me. I was only a poor little orphan without any fortune except my sweet face which already was beginning to be worth more than all the rest combined.

Ten

Soon I was back again in Almería, cheerfully welcomed home by my mother and not at all inconvenienced by my father. He had recently left the house feet first on a one-way trip which ends in the cemetery. The man died of suffocation and a paralysis which comes from drinking too well of the local wine, which had poisoned his system.

I went freely about the city, doing whatever came my way. Sometimes I sold tobacco, sometimes stove kerosene. On other occasions I ran errands for people or held out my hand for charity. But I was very devoted to my mother, and when I turned sixteen I got a real job in the Casa Marcelino—a fabric store in the Calle Real—where I earned three *pesetas* helping out the clerk.

I liked working among fabrics. I liked the smell and feel of the material. The store was dark and musty and the air was filled with the delicious smell of wool.

Whenever I helped Bonifacio, the clerk, unwind a length of cretonne or of striped cotton duck and spread it along the counter, polished by the friction of so many dirty hands, or when I measured out some dark velveteen or gay percale, I felt good. To me each of the fabrics had their own special song which I could hear inside my head. It could either warm or chill me, depending on the nature—sometimes sweet, sometimes bitter.

This may sound strange—but is there a woman who feels the same way when she touches a beautiful blue wool from Béjar, hard and sturdy, as when she feels a light percale—gay and tolerant of all her caprices? Surely the excitement created by the sight of a lively cretonne is not the same emotion as the calm inspired by the majestic whiteness of first-class *Thread of Gold* for sheets?

Oh, those sheets! They seemed incapable of inspiring any but the most noble thoughts and pleasures and yet they were always the downfall of so many honorable women. They awaken in us such a desire to own them, such a hunger for conjugal life, that we can't resist carrying them away to hoard in the bottom of a closet or pack in some bundle.

To tell the truth, I took a few things from the store myself. First there was a length of cloth that I hid upstairs. Later I took two more lengths and finally an entire bolt. Then they kicked me out. They didn't have any real proof, but plenty of justifiable suspicions. But that whiteness—that smooth texture had so carried me away that I had to satisfy my desires.

Once more I was out in the street and suffering from an empty stomach. The Civil War had started already and men were killing each other with astonishing swiftness. Though they had no idea why they were doing it, they were becoming more and more inflamed. Instead of prices lowering—with so many deaths there were fewer mouths to feed—it was the reverse. As the deaths increased, what was left for the living decreased. There was nothing to eat and the prices soared. In order to quiet my stomach a little I decided once more to get a job as a nursemaid.

My mother, who was very shrewd, found me a position with possibilities. The head of the house worked in a sugar factory called La Esperanza—"the hope." Now, it was a business that was better than its name. It offered something more concrete than hope for the future—plenty of sugar right in the present. Pounds of it were taken from the factory each week. Because of the war, sugar was a lucky charm which found the key to many hearts.

The man of the house was about forty, good-looking and well built. Or so he seemed to me, and that's saying something, as I've said somewhere before I don't bother much with men's looks. Indeed, I dislike the pretty kind who try to get ahead on their appearance.

The man was married to the daughter of the owner of the factory, and there was nothing sugary about him—more likely vinegar. Whatever he had hoped to get by his marriage still was beyond his grasp. He had to work hard for his salary as his father-in-law was the sort who had sweated for his fortune and wasn't inclined to let it out of his hands without getting something in return.

This made for much arguing and shouting in the house. I had my hands full with the three children, and I say hands full as I had to be constantly slapping them on their backsides and face in order to control them.

But how we ate! And during that sweet war eating was a major problem. I sized up the situation very quickly and I realized that if the war were to last, soon we wouldn't have anything left to put in our mouths. The country was in complete turmoil. Even the fishermen had left the sea and were out for a soft spot on some committee. . . .

La Esperanza was controlled by the workers, but my boss had cleverly put one of his friends in charge of distributing the sugar so we had all we wanted. I even managed to get some for my mother, who waited for me to come with her mouth watering from hunger, she was so badly off.

I realize that the job saved our skins. Though in the process I lost that which one only loses once. I took the boss his lunch every day at the factory, which was in the outskirts of the town, and afterwards I returned home. But one particular day it was raining hard and I stayed at La Esperanza and waited for him to bring me home on his bicycle. On the way, the man persisted so that I finally gave him the only thing I had to give him in the shelter of a grove of trees near the side of the road. I mention this as with the passing of

35

years I've become convinced that it is capricious chance which guides our destinies. We ourselves have little control over the future. If it hadn't rained that morning just when I should have returned to Almería my whole life might have been different.

I had just turned seventeen. I was beautiful but still didn't possess that "radiant magic" which fires the air around me, according to Juan. Between the boss and me there had never been any forewarning of what was to happen. But he insisted, he insisted so much that . . . I saw myself without sugar, despised by my mother, cursed by my step-sisters, and, what was worse, maybe thrown into prison, as the man had power. For those reasons I gave in. The entire business bothered me quite a bit—though, to tell the truth, the man himself didn't displease me.

Eleven

This combination lasted four months. He was a looker who knew how to lead women about, but I also knew a thing or two and what started out for him as a quick dalliance with a nursemaid ended up by becoming an affair of passion.

Very soon the house was in an uproar as neither of us had bothered to keep up appearances. Then, to avoid trouble with his wife, he placed me in a pension, Casa Paca. He gave me everything I needed, and each week the sugar arrived in greater and greater bulk.

In the midst of all this I remained an innocent child, still filled with illusions about the world. Young and free as I was, I felt some sadness and pain at finding myself so defenseless and alone. But I had strength, I wasn't afraid of anything and I managed to go cheerfully about life. Even when I became pregnant, and had to get rid of the baby, I was able to keep up my good spirits.

But finally I started to tire of the man. He was losing his brusqueness and hardness and was becoming sweet and tender, like putty in my hands. I was bored with his constant drooling over me. I decided to take him for all I could, fortify myself with a load of new clothes, and try my luck in Cartagena.

Encarna gave me the idea for the trip. An old businessman in Murcia kept her here in this city, as he was terrified of his dragon of a wife and wanted to hide Encarna from her. The two of us had become friends, as we both stayed in the pension almost continually. We didn't intend to upset our gentlemen friends and give them cause for jealousy. After all, they were the source of our income.

Encarna was from Alora, two years my senior, blond-haired, green-eyed, a little plump and very good-looking. She generally was taken for an English beauty until she opened her mouth. That was fatal. Coming from Alora she had a strong accent.

We discussed our affairs daily and finally we decided to leave our friends and try Cartagena. First we fleeced them. They were hooked, but good, so it wasn't hard at all.

According to Encarna who had a boy friend there, Cartagena had tremendous possibilities. We could make lots of dough and still be our own bosses. The idea of spending our entire lives in the Casa Paca with nothing better to do than occasionally cheat on our men was driving us slowly mad.

We took care of our economic situation by playing a clever game of giving and withholding to our own advantage. We lit out for Cartagena and were immediately hired as taxi dancers in the Shanghay, a very busy ballroom. Busy but not productive. I've since learned that men who like to dance a lot don't do much of anything else. Then, I was still a silly fool who didn't understand much about life. For example, I never told anyone the truth, even when it was easier. And I lied poorly.

Cartagena was in a mess due to the war and we had much less to eat than in Almería. What with this, and our work at the dancehall which was quite strenuous, I became sick. I was still growing at an astonishing rate considering that I was already seventeen. During the night my chest was racked with an awful, painful cough. Encarna got worried and took me to a doctor who was a friend of hers, insisting that the kind of doctor who looks after girls in our profession doesn't know anything about chests. He gave me some very painful injections and warned me to take good care of myself. He said that the very thing which made me appear to be so beautiful was the same thing which caused a physical weakness. If I didn't watch out I wouldn't be long for this world.

For one whole day I took his advice to heart, but by the following morning I forgot it all. The injections made me feel better and I started up my old mad life again.

We lived in a rather fancy pension on the Calle de los Balcones Azules. The two of us got on well together and always divided our take. I even gave her half of the cash I got when I called up my man in Almería and asked him for money so that I could return to him.

I was discovering how easy it was to take advantage of men. They have a remarkable facility for believing what they

37

want to believe. My friend in Almería repeatedly fell for the same stories about my needing money for my return trip—a trip which never came to pass. I became convinced that he was a fool. Later I realized that this kind of stupidity could exist in men who were quite shrewd in other matters.

For a while Encarna and I managed quite well. We were free to do as we pleased and that was the most important. It would have taken an awful lot of money to have made me resign myself to losing that freedom.

One of my lovers wanted to marry me. He was an American seaman, the captain of the *Kansas,* a freighter which seemed incredibly enormous to me. He sailed as far as the Crimea and when he returned he always brought me a present, being a good spender.

He wasn't old, but not very young either. He was ready to marry me if I would come with him to a city called 'Frisco. Despite Encarna's urging, I decided to stay on in Cartagena. I wasn't very sure about what kind of wedding he had in mind, and I prefer trotting along through my own country rather than attempting a place where I'd have to speak such a strange and difficult language that would only get in the way of my art.

Encarna disagreed with me. She insisted that the language of love is universal. I don't say that this isn't so, but I'm convinced my extraordinary ability to win men is due to something more than my looks. (Even though they are unique.) What counts is the whole person—the way one moves, one's expression, and above all the way one speaks, which is what clinches the deal. If my tongue were taken away, I'd be like a wild beast with his claws cut off.

So I took the captain for what I could, meanwhile keeping my eyes open for whatever else came down the pike.

Life became a bit complicated for us as Encarna had a bad time giving birth to a baby. She had come from Almería four months pregnant and being terribly sentimental, hadn't wanted to get rid of the baby. The presumed father was the Cartagenian who had encouraged us originally to make the trip. She had to quit the Shanghay during the last months and lived on what he gave her. He was an army captain—we called him "Finger" as he didn't know how to read or write and had to sign his name by making a cross with his finger.

Even though he was a rough sort, he wasn't bad at heart and he gave Encarna whatever he could—but finally he was called to the front at Baza and there he let his finger rest forever.

His death coincided with the birth of the baby, and Encarna was completely unstrung by it all, being the mother of the biggest crybaby that I'd ever heard.

Actually, I had considered leaving Encarna. She wasn't much use and her baby kept me from getting any sleep during the day. But as she had always been a good friend and had looked after me, I decided to wait a month and see if things improved. Meanwhile, we had to make do with the *pesetas* the dead captain had left her. Also, I must confess that I'm not very practical about life. I'm one of those girls who are so much like the Civil Guard—they don't like to work alone and prefer going in pairs.

In the long run I was glad I had put up with our streak of bad luck. Encarna soon bloomed again. She left the baby in the care of some ragpickers who promised they would take good care of her providing that she didn't forget to send them seventy *duros* monthly. This is the way these sentimental affairs always end—in the hands of the ragpickers.

We weren't doing too well in Cartagena, and it seemed certain that the city was going to be bombed. We had already had an unpleasant taste of *that*, so we decided to scram before things got ugly.

A friend who worked in a traveling theatrical company, the Alady, got us jobs in the show. Encarna, being plumply beautiful and also a little older than I, soon became one of the chief attractions.

We did "The Girl from Valencia." I came out dressed as a gypsy and stood with a candle beneath a painted bridge while the whole company sang:

> *"Milkshake vendor from Valencia*
> *though you're pretty as a minx*
> *I really don't like your drinks*
> *I'd prefer first . . .*
> *to die of thirst . . ."*

Encarna earned thirty *pesetas* daily and I fifteen. Still, we went halves the entire trip through the provinces of Murcia and Alicante.

I was tone deaf which ruined the act. Being knock-kneed didn't help either and I wasn't much of a success in the tableaux. In Elche they threw rotten oranges at me. Encarna, though, was terrific and stirred the entire audience with her scene.

But once the farce was over and the theater lights dimmed, in real life I had the successes and she the failures. I've always had a gift for getting men, particularly the old ones, and did quite well. Encarna had to resign herself to going with the young ones, who are always more troublesome.

In my business affairs I've always been sober and sensible. A man in Alicante wanted to marry me but I took my time deciding. He was a captain in the Carabineros, ate well and paid well. He saw me perform at a function we gave in a hospital entertaining the wounded, and he fell in love.

He had been shot in one eye and was almost blind, but he saw me well enough with the other one, which was his bad luck. He was crazy about me and even made his mother visit me to try and obtain my consent.

For various reasons I didn't accept. First, because I didn't want to tie myself down to any one man, not even to a captain, and secondly because for me a marriage that isn't sanctified by the church is no marriage, but a brothel. As at that time they were killing priests and the churches had been converted into prisons, I decided that I'd end up with all the annoyances of marriages and none of the conveniences or stability.

I sent him away, but he was very high-strung due to his eye, and became hysterical, threatening to kill himself. He was in such a state that his mother came to see me again and threw herself on her knees begging me to reconsider. But I stuck to my word and I left Alicante with the rest of the company.

In Murcia the Alady disbanded, and we went with Melgarejo, who had formed a good company of operetta. We had to sing the songs and I had an idiotic bit of my own to do which irritated me because of its stupidity. Still, I took advantage of the part to show as much of myself as possible—more than the rest of the girls—and the audiences in the towns and villages went wild at seeing me. Then, no one threw anything at me, instead they all wanted to sleep with me.

We performed in Onteniente, Alcoy, Almansa, Albacete, and other places which I no longer can remember. It was a busy, lively life, full of the unexpected. We were always on the go in a train or bus, we never had time to be bored and we never spent two nights in the same bed. But in Villena, a crowded rich town, I became very sick. I had caught a chill, and the intense September heat only made it worse.

Encarna, seeing me lose my strength and becoming whiter than a sheet, became frightened. I started to hemorrhage and lost a great deal of blood. As I couldn't even move, she left Melgarejo and stayed behind to take care of me.

We spent one month in Villena in the Casa Nenét. Encarna saw to it that the old man Nenét footed our bill. She even got me to see the town's best doctor, Don Bernardo, as

40

I think he was called. He told me that my anemia and general frailty should be of real concern to me. If I didn't take care of myself the result would be fatal.

During the following month I led a life of ease. I did nothing but sleep and eat at the expense of Nenét and of a shoe manufacturer admirer I had acquired. On account of my interesting illness I was able to get some money from him in exchange for nothing from me.

With so much rest, spending the whole day in bed reading either the newspapers or some boudoir novel my shoe manufacturer had sent me, I became much stronger and got bored with such a dull life. We left Villena and went on to Albacete. The city was filled with strangers profiteering from the war.

In those days I was always a little nervous—I was still considered to be a minor. Times were such that generally those things didn't matter much and even very young girls were able to get away with a lot. Still there was always the risk of getting involved with a rat who took the government laws seriously and who would make trouble. I always tried to go about my business without calling too much attention to myself—with my delicate face and coltish body I looked even younger than I was. I never forgot that there was always someone around ready to complicate my life if I showed my disdain or refused to grant some whim. I tried to be very careful in the difficult and complicated maneuvers of women who live by the vice of men.

But in Albacete I lost all my caution and became involved with a soldier from the Brigade—a Pole who lived in the Hotel Stalin. He was uglier than a monkey's ass, more disgusting than a Pekingese. He was also a rat—but a rat who was a general, so I decided that it was healthier for me to live with him than end up one fine morning stretched out in the muddy dirty outskirts of Albacete.

This was a low period for me, and I swore daily at my bad luck. Even though I've never been too particular about myself, and am only interested in the money, I loathed him. His friends from the Brigade annoyed me as they spent the whole day cursing the Spanish—those on their side as well as the enemy.

Encarna had better luck. A colonel yanked her from the claws of the International Brigade and gave her a life that was fit for a queen. Eventually I also benefited.

Meanwhile, my situation became worse each day. The general drank more and more, while his friends had a ball with me. Finally, one night I couldn't take it any longer and I escaped to Encarna's house and decided not to return to the

41

Hotel Stalin, even if they killed me. Encarna's colonel promised me that if I spent a few pleasant days with him, he'd get me out of there.

The following week, carefully disguised, I drove away with him. He left me in Chinchilla where I lived a few days on Encarna's money. Soon she joined me. The boys from the Stalin as well as her colonel had made a dash for Barcelona. The war, now in the last stages, was going badly for them.

I hoped the worse for them—even now I sometimes wake up in a sweat dreaming of the terrible days I spent in Albacete. Though Chinchilla was one of the weirdest and scariest places I've ever seen, compared to Albacete it was a paradise. Encarna's weakness was that she was always in love, and in Chinchilla she became melancholy, spending hours crying about her colonel. She was so infatuated with him that the little fool climbed on top of the hill near the jail and stayed there watching the road to Albacete. She was convinced that her lover was going to come back and fetch her at any moment and if things went badly he would take her to another country.

I was amazed at her. I knew that the men had gone for good in search of I don't know which frontier, but Encarna wouldn't listen to reason. She spent nearly ten days on top of the miserable, desolate hill, not even budged by snow or the most ungodly storms I'd ever seen in the month of February.

I've always been cold-blooded and I need a great deal of warmth. One night when I was telling some of this to Juan, I started to shiver and I had to put the soles of my feet against the small of his back to warm up. He was very amused at my fear, but I spent an awful night. I don't like to talk of my life and with him make the one small exception. It isn't because I'm in love, as there is no one who can do that to me, nor is it that he deserves my confidence—as he is more or less like all men. But he understands me. I know I've already mentioned him a lot—so perhaps it's time I told how and when I met him.

Twelve

We met each other over a year ago. I remember exactly when. At that time a litre of oil was selling for twenty-five *pesetas* and I had just convinced Luis Rico—rich by name perhaps, but stingy in actions—to take me in his car to Talavera where I could buy fifty litres very cheap at ten *pesetas* a litre. Cheap for me, but costing him an arm and a leg. He smashed up the car on a curve because he was fooling around with me, and we had to be towed all the way back to Madrid. His wife raised holy hell as she had guessed who was with him, and that was the end of him for a while.

I was alone and decided to go to Casablanca, since it struck me as the best night club in Madrid at the time. According to the advertisements, Tomás Ríos and his band provided the entertainment, but I think I was a bigger drawing card.

Whenever I came I had a free table there—and still do—the very best in the place. It was high up on a small platform, and in the distance and dim light I looked very mysterious and distinguished.

First I used to grab a bite either in a tavern with some friends or alone in my pension in the Calle de la Reina. Then a coffee in La Elipa or in El Abra—I never frequented El Cóctel, let that be clear. I don't like rubbing shoulders with that kind of trash. After that, I would go to Casablanca. I'd sit down at my table with great dignity, and soon all eyes would be staring my way, and the men would ignore their dates.

Being alone that particular night, I had eaten first in my pension—I am particular about food, when I pay for the best I don't tolerate cat for rabbit.

I was also out of sorts because another lover, Perico, had had the nerve to go off suddenly to Bilbao, leaving me behind like an old shoe. Of course, he had his reasons—I had caught him in the Pasapoga with another woman, and had given him a present of a knife wound on his face. Still, I was in the right and I didn't think he'd bear a grudge. But after spending two months in my apartment—the apartment that Espichao gave me before entering the monastery—without a by-your-leave, Perico skipped out for good.

That night I looked marvelous. I had on a black lace dress, very low-cut and tight. My dark hair, lit with natural reddish glints, rippled about my shoulders like a stream of fiery water.

I had a drink of Marie Brizard and smoked cigarette after cigarette, not paying attention to any of the looks I was getting. That's my style. I'm only after big game. This aloofness is a system I've perfected after many years of research.

First I let myself be seen. I act proud and mysterious, and notice no one. This way they get a good chance to study my beauty. Then they become hungry for me, though they realize I'm not in a hurry. If one of them, more forward than the rest, asks if he can dance with me, I reply, "With

43

pleasure, but a little later please. Just now I feel a trifle tired." I say this in an appropriately languid voice. They are so jealous that they imagine that I've just come from the arms of another, and am exhausted, so they slip away. The idiots! *Vamos, hombre!* . . . the man hasn't been born who is capable of tiring me, because I am . . . but let's not go into that.

That particular night, as I've mentioned, I was perfection itself. No one dared to approach me, and they kept their wallets firmly in their pockets. As everyone knows, I'm an expensive girl.

Having just gone through a rather low period, I abandoned my pose of indifference just a little and permitted myself a light smile at a few of the imbeciles. Then I noticed that a man was watching me from the distance. He seemed somewhere between thirty and forty, was tall, dark, rather thin, and very well dressed. My policy is to stay away from the thin ones, even though I refuse them with great politeness. There are difficult elements in them that can lead to complications. Now the fat ones—jovial and solid—are definitely more productive companions.

Still, this one intrigued me. I suppose he could be considered good-looking, and I won't argue the point, though those things don't matter to me. What interested me was the way he kept looking at me almost with a certain hardness. He went from table to table, ignoring his friends, disdaining company, all the while staring at me as though he were in a trance. I'm not an idiot, and I came to the conclusion that I must remind him of someone who had died —his look was of someone not in his right mind.

His admiration flattered me even though I was used to that sort of thing. But as I stay away from the types who complicate life, who don't know how to get quickly to the point and call a spade a spade, I was cool and didn't give him one look in return. True, I managed to see that my beauty was displayed to its best advantage. I turned his way so that he could see the rosy glow of my bare shoulders and the loveliness of my face.

Later on, some friends came by my table and I spent the rest of the night dancing and chatting while he continued to stare at me from the distance, completely spellbound. At first I thought that maybe he belonged to someone and didn't want me to know that he was accompanied. But the crazy fool, seeing that I was occupied and dancing, went up to other girls, had a drink and a dance with each, and then let them leave. During the whole time that he was with them he never took his eyes off me.

I was in a strange mood that night, and his behavior piqued my curiosity. I decided to send away my admirers, risking everything to see if he would make up his mind once and for all. When the dancing was over and the lights had been dimmed several times for the benefit of the jerkwater customers, people finally started to leave, gathering near the exit. While I was collecting my things, he came over to my table. I was with another girl then—she'd joined me so we could go together. We both lived in the same general direction, and were afraid of the dangers that could befall a woman walking alone.

"Good evening," he greeted me.

"Good evening," I replied, raising my eyes in surprise. I stood up. He was extremely tall.

"No, please. Don't trouble yourself."

"But I'm leaving anyway."

"Wait a minute."

"All right. . . . I don't believe we've met?"

"That's why I came by, so that we could get acquainted."

"Well, now we've met."

"Yes, and up close you're even more fabulous."

"I'm extremely pretty, aren't I?"

"Uh-huh."

"Thank you. Now as you were saying—"

"Listen, let's get out of here."

"Fine, but—"

"*Anda, chica* . . . don't complain."

"Delighted to come with you. But first I must have five hundred *pesetas* immediately. I have rent to pay tomorrow. I want to give the money to my sister here."

"Ah—she's your sister?"

"Yes. I can't go with you if you don't give me the money."

"Maybe we can discuss it alone?"

We left my friend for a moment, who was a sister of mine under the skin, so to speak, and we sat down in a dark corner under a fake palm tree. For at least several years a stuffed monkey has been sitting on one of the branches and has been in the process of eating the same coconut.

"You're very expensive."

"I can afford to be. Take a good look."

"I have been looking during the entire evening."

"Well then—you've never seen anyone better."

"But five hundred *pesetas* is an awful lot, good-looking."

"Not for you, I'm sure."

"You're mistaken. No doubt you're worth much more. Why, I'd give it to you, and without even discussing it," he

45

went on enthusiastically, "but I don't have five hundred *pesetas* tonight."

"I'll let you go for four hundred."

"I can't."

"Three hundred?"

"No."

"Now, that old man standing around over there is waiting to see whether we'll come to an agreement, because he's offered me four hundred. But I can permit myself the pleasure of choosing, and you're really quite a good-looking man," I told him, even though I hadn't yet studied his face.

"How complimentary . . ."

"I'm going to do something crazy. Give me two hundred and we'll call it a deal."

"Thanks. You're very kind. Now, let's get out of here."

"First you have to give me the money."

"What?"

"Yes, right now. I prefer it that way."

"Do I look like I'm going to cheat you?"

"It's not possible to trust anyone, see? The bigger the guy, the larger the car, the more champagne flowing, the more of everything . . . the bigger the risk you run of being stuck."

"Until now, I've never had to swindle any woman . . ." he muttered angrily.

"*Hombre,* don't get sore. I really like you very much—"

"But pay first."

"One has to live."

"Here, take it."

"Thank you—you're a tough nut to crack."

"And you're really something."

"There's no one like me—see?"

"This is the first time this has happened to me. You are making yourself scandalously commercial."

"Nonsense. Now, excuse me for a minute. I have to give a message to my sister."

"All right, but watch out. Because now you belong to me."

"I'm a very serious girl, word of honor."

I gave back my girl friend the one hundred *pesetas* she had lent me and also handed her a message for the old man. I suggested an appointment for the following day—he was the kind who would wait. Then I joined my friend. He was singing—and I think with some malice—the *huanango,*

> *How pretty is your bell,*
> *Tell me who gave it to you*
> *No one gave it to me*

46

> *I spent my money for it*
> *Those who want a bell*
> *Let them buy it, same as me.*

"It's certainly taken you long enough, good-looking."

"Your impatience delights me."

"Really?"

"Yes. My boy friend left a few days ago and I feel like being with a good man."

"Oh, cut the crap!"

"As you like. Are you coming, my love?"

"*Caray!* Am I your love?"

"Yes, cutie pie."

"This 'cutie pie' we can do without, eh?"

"Why?"

"I don't like it."

"Whatever you say, my love."

"I can do without your phony coyness, thank you."

"What did you say, cutie pie?"

"Come again?"

"Excuse me, my love."

"That's a little better."

"My love, my love," I kept repeating, smiling at him.

"Your little Lolita is going to love you very much."

"Who's my little Lolita?"

"Me, my love, me."

We left the Casablanca together.

He told me that he was called Juan.

He was a big talker, cool and aloof.

Like the rest he fell in love with me.

But when he left I noticed that he was a little annoyed. He had started to sing again:

> *As it was only made of tinsel*
> *I broke it very soon*
> *I had a bell . . .*
> *With my money, I bought it.*

Thirteen

Getting back to that God-awful Chinchilla, I don't know whether it was the cold or her disillusion that made Encarna change her mind—usually when she decided to be obstinate, she was more stubborn than a mule. I took advantage of her brief moment of sanity and convinced her to return with me to Cartagena. We didn't know where else to go.

47

We took jobs again as taxi dancers—this time in the Bolero. We took in what we could, which wasn't much. The mood of the people was poor. The war was nearing an end and everyone was worried.

Encarna got herself involved in a new predicament which made it impossible for us to stay in Cartagena. She had a new lover and was seen around town frequently with him, until finally his wife raised hell, which is the way these things always end. Encarna hadn't been content to meet him in our pension in the Calle de Cuatro Santos, but had to be seen everywhere with him. Naturally this provoked the other one, who after all was his legitimate wife.

This was one of Encarna's big defects. I admit she was an exceptional beauty, and certainly no one could have been more good-hearted. But she was also one of those women who, when they get involved with a married man, instead of knowing their place, let their pride and vanity get in the way. They end up trying to separate husband and wife, which is ridiculous. Most men return to the bosom of their families like little lost lambs once the novelty of an affair has worn off and you've shown them your claws. If they don't go back it's even worse, because then it's impossible to get rid of them and you have to put up with their nonsense.

This always leads to unpleasantness and is only worth while when the man is rich and there is some security in his attachment, but I don't think that can ever be guaranteed. Now me—I always do just the opposite. I place on a pedestal the wives of my lovers. This makes them proud as peacocks, and suits my own interests much better.

We went from Cartagena to Alicante. It was nearby and we knew some people there. I asked after my captain who had lost an eye and found out that the last time he had tried to take his life he had managed to pass on to a better one.

It was the beginning of March; everywhere people talked about the war ending. Our hunger was more acute than ever. Even when the money flowed in freely you couldn't buy anything with it. Everyone knew that when peace was declared, money would become worthless, and those who had provisions hoarded the things for themselves. I felt very bitter that my hard-earned money couldn't even buy me a good mouthful of food or a decent dress or a pretty piece of jewelry. It was a mess, and many wished for the end once and for all.

But at the same time there was panic in Alicante. Those who had been involved in committing some outrage began to spread rumors about the Nationals in order to confuse and frighten people.

So much so—and I assure you that I know very well what

I am talking about—that I, too, began to worry, and I don't scare easily. Even though God knows I always minded my own business and never mixed into anything as dirty as politics. I could never understand why men become so passionate about this, unless they see money in it. We planned to go to Elda, a quieter place where we also had friends, but I became sick again. We were broke, and everything was sky high, so I had to go into the local clinic.

I was terribly ill. Finally my lungs had to be deflated in order to get rid of the pus. At times I think I must have been delirious. A young, sympathetic doctor saved my life. He cared for me and gave me calcium and vitamin injections in order to put me on my feet. In the process, he fell completely in love with me.

I don't remember very well what he was like—in my memory men's faces melt like wax into one common image. I think he was very good-looking, even though he was sickeningly sentimental.

I know I shouldn't say these things about a man who saved my life. Still I gave him everything he wanted—so that makes us even. I never actually went to bed with him, and that's the greatest gift that you can make a man who is as crazy in love as he was, and has his kind of notion of honor.

When my fever went down and I became better, he often visited me. I guessed what he wanted, and what he desired me to be and I tried to gratify him. I made up a lovely story which set his gentle heart on fire.

I told him that because of a series of events, which I won't go into here, I was left alone—abandoned in the Red Zone without any other company excepting an older sister, Encarna, who earned her living performing at the Olympia. My parents were Sevillians and caught in the other zone. The rest of the family had all been killed in Valencia. It was a pretty story, I don't deny it. Still, during the war there were many cases like that which actually happened.

We planned everything carefully. To appear respectable we married off Encarna to a young boy from the navy whom she had taken up with in Alicante. The doctor fell for it hook, line and sinker.

We were like lovers in a farce. He was a big innocent and sweated hard in order to give me all the things that I needed, which were plenty. I played my role perfectly, and Encarna's navy boy said I was a better actress than Garbo.

I was prettier than ever. My frailty and paleness made my beauty even more delicate. According to the doctor, I was like something out of a dream, fantastic and unreal. I had long shiny and wavy hair and I arranged it against the

49

pillow so that the coppery tints flattered my face. Somehow, I always managed to leave the top of my nightgown slightly unbuttoned. Later, when I was able to sit up, I caught my hair in two very becoming braids.

I sighed a great deal and each of my sighs echoed terribly in his heart. I barely spoke, but was very mysterious and had fainting fits which worried him. I appeared to be so affected by his attentions that he went to all lengths to please me.

Amidst so much care and so many presents, I soon became better. I became his girl friend and we started going out together just as the war ended.

Encarna then committed the last folly that I know of, though I imagine that it was followed by many more. She left Alicante for Orán with her navy friend, who was apparently quite a sailor and had some accounts to settle with the Nationals. I haven't heard from her since.

I felt very badly about this foolishness of hers and I also missed her companionship. Especially as at that time, I was busy making new clothes, and she knew how to cut and sew to perfection. At least before she left she had had time to make me three new dresses and some lingerie, all at the doctor's expense.

Even though I was better, I still wasn't completely cured. My boy friend took me out of the public hospital, which had become a madhouse in all the final disorder of the war, and put me in a private sanatorium. He was already taking care of all my expenses, although he never gave me anything excepting pocket change.

His intentions were to take me to the altar, and he introduced me to his mother. He was very respectful of me, and also introduced me to his married sister, who had just returned from Córdoba with her husband, who was a captain.

They were decent, good people, but my situation was becoming increasingly difficult. They were going to find out sooner or later that my story was humbug. My friend didn't deserve such a disappointment. Also, he wasn't my type and I had already emptied his wallet of everything worth while. Even though he loved me madly, and didn't budge from his notion of marrying me, I wasn't prepared to conform to his ideas and become the charming little wife of a middle-class doctor from the provinces.

I thought about it seriously and came to a quick decision. Without one word, without one single explanation, as that always makes matters only worse, I left for Sevilla. I had only my railroad ticket and five *duros* when I boarded the train. But I went extremely well-dressed.

Fourteen

I thought that it was going to be a pleasant trip, but it was worse than a wagonload of animals. The train was filled with troops on leave, and the soldiers, in the first flush of victory, figured that no holds were barred. I saw that I had better take up with officers.

In this manner, after a lot of stopping and starting, I was able to get to Granada with my five *duros*. There a captain gave me a safe-conduct so that I could continue to Sevilla. Before the trip was over, my money ran out. I pictured myself lost and stuck in all that commotion of those awful trains and I became terribly frightened.

In Antequera the engine broke down and I spent one day without eating as I didn't dare approach any of the men openly. I realized that I wasn't in Albacete and I didn't forget that in the eyes of the law I was still a minor. Finally one of the boys from the inn found me a bed to sleep in and a breakfast to chew on. Then, the next day, the train started out for Sevilla once again.

Before arriving, near Marchena, I began to worry about entering the other zone alone and without any money. I had spent the entire war on the other side—perhaps they'd throw me into jail here, if I didn't watch out. I had been silly to leave my young doctor so soon. I saw that these were different times and I couldn't wander about as in the past. I was a woman, and quite a woman—my appearance always attracted attention so I couldn't pass unnoticed.

For the first time in my life I felt alone and weak and I cried. Later on, near Utrera, I became suddenly dizzy. I still wasn't very strong and the jamming in the train was suffocating me.

My hands and face got cold, I turned as white as a sheet and fainted. That's how I met Dieguito who was traveling in the same car, on his way to Sevilla.

He was a Malaguenan, about thirty, short and fat, but not bad to look at and friendly enough. When he talked, he fortunately didn't pronounce the horrible *z* of Málaga, but the softer *s* of Sevilla.

When I came to, he offered his services. As soon as I found out that he owned a clothing factory I accepted. It was one of the few times in my life that I joined a man with pleasure, and in the station in Sevilla, when I leaned against his arm, he seemed to me to be a wonderful guy. I didn't even mind having to look down at him as he was much shorter than I, even though I'm well proportioned and only average height.

Dieguito set me up immediately in an apartment in the Calle Palacio Malaver, near the Europa. He spent more than five thousand *duros* for the bedroom which had nickel-plated fixtures and fancy lighting. I had a traditional Sevillian dining room and in the living room had shelves filled with costumed dolls which I started to collect at that time, and have added to ever since. Now I have an entire roomful.

I lived with him nearly a year; with age I had learned that it's true that a bird in the hand is worth two in the bush, and Diego was a nice substantial bird.

In Sevilla I became chummy with a girl who had worked in the Martín theater in Madrid. Her name was Tina and she was kept by a guy called Manolo. He was a pal of Diego's. They were both in the clothing business. Manolo's store sold lace, ready-made dresses, and costume jewelry.

The four of us often went out together in Manolo's car and while the men worked during the day, Tina and I bicycled around the outskirts of Sevilla, or amused ourselves at a local inn, la Conejera.

During the winter I became ill again. This time it was worse than ever. One night while Dieguito and I were in a movie I started to hemorrhage. Blood ran from my nose, mouth and other parts which I needn't mention among refined people.

Dieguito sent me to all sorts of consultants. He was ready to go to any lengths, not sparing doctors or medicines, to see me cured. I must have been very seriously ill, as they had to put clamps on and tie my veins and arteries in order to stop the rapid flow of blood. I was put in bed and in a very uncomfortable position, with my legs high up and face lower down.

I thought I was dying and no longer cared, since I didn't even have the strength to be frightened. But finally with X-ray treatments, transfusions and camphor, those eminent Sevillians saved my life.

Afterwards, when I was able to leave my bed, Dieguito sent me to the sanatorium of Aracena, a beautiful spot, cheerful yet quiet, where I was able to regain my strength during the spring.

I fished in the river, walked with the shepherds, and ran through the countryside with hardly any clothing on, delighted to be in contact with nature again. I benefited by this regime, and the terrible intestinal pains which I had developed in my last illness went away.

I got better but—oh, I won't hide it! They had given me morphine to take the pain away and when I returned to Dieguito in Sevilla I couldn't break the habit. Since then people started to call me the "drug doll." At first Dieguito was angry, but finally he let me continue. What difference does it make to live a little more or a little less? When you lead my kind of life the important thing is to live quickly.

Fifteen

Just before summer I quarreled with Dieguito. We were in Las Siete Puertas one night, and I acted stupidly.

"Don't keep looking at her," I warned him.

"At who?"

"The dancer. You are making an idiot of yourself."

"Oh, she's not my type."

"So, stop eyeing her."

"She intrigues me."

"I'm the prettiest girl in Sevilla and I won't stand for your insults."

"I'm not insulting you, girl, I just happen to like the way she dances."

"I said—don't look at her."

"Baby, take it easy. You're in a stew over nothing."

"Then stop looking at her."

"I'm only watching her dancing."

"This is going to cost you plenty."

"The morphine is making you a little—"

"A little what?"

"A little hard to take, sweetie."

I gave him a slap. It rang out like a shot against his full sallow cheeks. Then I left.

The next day his friend Manolo came to my apartment to test the lay of the land.

"*Anda*, don't be silly, girl."

"I don't have to put up with these things in a man, Manuel."

"He's very angry."

"So let him stay angry."

"He says that you have a lousy temper."

"There are plenty of people who like me the way I am. Look at me, Manolo. Don't you think that I'm the best-looking girl in Sevilla?"

"I've always thought so, Lola."

"But you've never showed it."

"Don't provoke me, *chica*, you've always appealed to me a lot."

"More than Tina?"

"—much more."

53

We went out on the town. We drank all afternoon and over dinner Manolo told me that Dieguito was already seeing a lot of another woman.

Later, we spent the night together in a pension owned by Trini in the Calle de la Línea.

The following afternoon, when I was alone again in my apartment, I became frightened of what Diego might do. Even though he had always been good and gentle toward me, one could never be sure with men. I called Pepín, my manicurist. He could give me good advice—he was fond of me and a fairy.

We talked it over and he suggested that I wait a few days and see what was going to happen. He said that I shouldn't go out with Manolo—Dieguito would never forgive me, and Tina wouldn't either. It would only end in double trouble.

I waited around for a few days, but Diego didn't show up. Maybe he knew about Manolo, maybe he was taken with the novelty of someone new.

I decided to sell the apartment and Pepín introduced me to a woman who made this her business. After much backing and filling, she finally put seven thousand *pesetas* in my hands. I packed my things, said good-by to the maid, called the janitor, and gave him the key to give to Diego, in case he came back.

Afterwards Pepín and I went out to celebrate the sale. We had dinner in the Casa La Viuda, and we both got slightly high. We took a large basket of fruit and started to hand it to everyone in the street, causing a sensation. I was dressed very elegantly. I wore a pale blue turban which flattered my face, and all the men devoured me with their eyes.

It was the time of the fair in Sevilla, and people thronged in the streets everywhere. Pepín ran into some of his clients, a married couple, and the four of us went to the Caseta 77. My arrival caused quite a hubbub.

I drank a lot and became annoyed at the advances of the husband. He didn't stop looking at me and behind his wife's back touched me at every opportunity. I told him that he needn't be so proud of her as I knew that she was a little tramp who worked in Las Siete Puertas. Also, she had been getting very chummy with the fairy. She heard, became furious, and started to fling a few insults of her own.

A fuss started, and everyone in the Caseta was very amused at our expense. It was time for Pepín and me to blow, and we headed for El Barranco. We were followed by a trail of men who didn't let me out of their sight during the entire evening. In El Barranco we drank a lot of red wine along with hot fried fish.

My manicurist friend immediately started to go into operation. Like nearly all fairies, he was a shrewd operator. He approached the men who were following me, and introduced me. We drank together and, dealing with each one separately, made arrangements with them all. They were rich and important and willingly forked over a lot of dough with the idea that at the end of our little party I was going to be theirs.

We made a good haul and enjoyed ourselves doing it. Later, Pepín informed each of my admirers that I was being kept by a very jealous and influential man. It was urgent, therefore, that I proceed with caution. With a great deal of mystery and drama I left El Barranco and entered one of the men's cars—he was already anxiously waiting at the wheel. I then slipped out the other door and repeated the same trick in another car, until finally there was the inevitable scuffle between them as they became aware of the fraud. Pepín and I had to jump over a ditch and run like mad to get away from them.

We made nearly a thousand *pesetas* on the deal, which I carefully stashed away in my stocking. Pepín said that if he ran into any of the men, he would take care of it saying that it was all the fault of my taking morphine. Everyone knew that I did, and they'd believe him if he said that I'd do anything when I needed to have it.

I spent two days with my manicurist in the Casa Juanito, a pension in the Plaza del Pan. For my own vanity I tried to change him, to see if he could be aroused, but he begged me not to bother him.

Afterwards he very disgustingly asked me to help him out in a difficult little love matter he was involved in; it ended when two policemen came to the pension and took him away.

Frightened by the police, I got out in a hurry and I came to Madrid with a safe-conduct and five thousand *pesetas*, all I had left. I was always a big spender and never knew how to hang on to my money.

Sixteen

I stayed in the Hotel Inglés a few days, having heard Tina in Sevilla refer to it as a very distinguished place. But there was no way of getting a nickel out of their frozen-faced customers.

I went over my resources and saw that I had better do something quickly. My money was rapidly slipping away, especially since I wanted to buy everything I saw. I got some beautiful dresses, some fancy lingerie and a Cyma watch with a bracelet of solid gold.

When I remember those days I could both laugh and cry at how naïve I was. I felt so proud of being in Madrid that instead of feeling overwhelmed, I was positive that I could conquer it all. I imagined myself becoming the reigning queen of the capital.

Besides dressing myself more splendidly than ever, and even acquiring some jewelry, I dedicated myself to studying the inhabitants, who didn't please me very much. I've always found them somewhat cool and aloof.

I strolled through Madrid, my arms burned by the hot June sun. Wandering through the bustling streets I frequented the bars, dancehalls, theaters, and movies, as well as other places especially fitting to my way of life. I needed to know about everything.

Many of the nights I rushed through the streets nervously. I'd already had a taste of the dangers risked by the solitary night wanderer.

Madrid at night is nothing like what I had seen in Andalucía and Levante. There are magnificently dressed couples, groups of men idly standing around, lying in wait for whatever comes down the pike—if it's cheap enough—prostitutes, suspicious and quick, blustering a false coquetry that has no one fooled, and finally, that solitary stroller who goes for a slow turn after eating dinner in his modest pension. This is a type that a woman would be well advised never to have confidence in—not on your life.

Everyone swarms like ants to the center of the city, picking their way through the labyrinth of excavations, holes, trenches, of mountains of earth and of pieces of pavement left in the wake of the war. Suddenly, unexpectedly, I'd come across a pipe with foamy water gushing out, or a loose cable I was scared of stepping on. I didn't want to be electrocuted and left a dead duck.

I went crazy with the awful sound of the drills blasting the pavement, burrowing in like birds looking for worms in the mud, and was blinded by the livid glare of the acetylene torches burning up the rails.

Very quickly I realized that though most Madrilenians find their city unbearably hot during the summer, they take a perverse pride in talking about the weather. They are proud of everything about their city. They make bitter criticisms and comic jokes about their City Hall, the way parents fondly tell what devils their children are.

Suddenly I realized that I only had a little money left,

so I went to a modest pension in the Calle de la Montera, the Casa Balbina, which only cost me twenty *pesetas*. At that time my hair was platinum. I combed it with a part on the side and made two braids. This gave me a delicate, somewhat foreign air. I was beautiful. A little thin, but well filled out on top. Sometimes I wore a large hat which had cost me a fortune and was very elegant, even though I was always a little startled at seeing myself in it.

In Casa Balbina I met Juanjo, a pimp in the perfume business. He sold perfumes, lipsticks, rouge, powder and other things to prostitutes. Mainly he was always going about receiving and delivering messages and negotiating business. He was a fairy, but didn't turn down a good girl when it was for free. He was about fifty and very experienced.

When he noticed that I was by myself he asked the owner of the pension about me. After making sure that I was really alone, he asked my permission to sit at my table and we ate our skimpy meal together.

I accepted. I knew where this was leading. It occurred to me that a certain Juanjo might be just what I needed.

From him I got a free bottle of *Scandal* and advice which was worth a hell of a lot more.

He said that I should be careful about my hat. Maybe it was expensive and elegant but it certainly frightened away the flies I was trying to catch. Also he said that it would be better if I dropped my air of being offended royalty and acted with greater naturalness. He added, though, that I should keep my mysterious and slightly out-of-this-world manner. In Madrid they had seen few girls of this genre and it made me appear more original and interesting, even though underneath I was like all the rest. I shouldn't speak much, but smile a lot. The smile accentuated my cheekbones and made my eyes look even larger. He wondered about my eyes. He had never seen such brilliance and asked if I used some secret drug in order to make them shine so.

I assured him that wasn't the case, only a little mascara. We formed a partnership and went forth in search of big game, he playing the role of my escort.

We went to the bar of the Palace, to the Abra, to La Elipa, the Capitol, to Suevia, Gaviria and to Fuyma. When we were acting like real big shots we went to dance at La Galera and the Tokio.

Everywhere we went I showed myself off to my advantage, and soon all eyes were following me. We chose carefully, generally the older and more serious types. Either Juanjo made the contact first or had me go, depending on the case.

What a blessing for women are those corners a bit hidden from all the hustle and bustle, where there is always an amiable florist, an old woman begging, or a bellboy who follows you to see what is going on!

Whether it was Juanjo in the bar or me in the dressing room, the friendship was soon established. Then with our companions we'd begin to make the rounds. We'd ride all over Madrid—from El Tropezon all the way to El Meson. And the sweet looks would come, and the murmurings, the smiles, the slow sexy fox trots—always with Juanjo nearby.

I liked working this way, at my own pleasure and ease, well protected by Juanjo's dignity. He created a good impression and he didn't take anything from me, though he ate and drank for twenty. My entire night's work passed directly intact into my purse, so I suspect that he found some shrewd way of emptying my lovers' wallets by wangling a loan.

This pleasant way of life lasted the entire summer and helped me out of my financial hole, though I didn't save anything. Whatever wasn't strictly necessary for my day-to-day expenditures, I threw away on whims and luxuries. I bought a beautiful cocktail ring which was very stylish at the time and also a link bracelet of fourteen-carat gold. Then Juanjo ruined it all. Those damned fairies always have the same weakness—they get a whim and they risk everything to obtain it. Juanjo's was a languid, sneaky Italian. Poor Juanjo couldn't pay all that the guy demanded in order not to squeal on him, and I, naturally, refused to get him out of trouble. He begged me on his knees, saying that he was very ill and jail would be the death of him. But I wasn't going to spend even one cent to see that there was one fairy more or less in this world and I broke with him. I had already decided to change my mode of operation and enter as a pupil in a first-class house.

Seventeen

I realize that up until this point there has been nothing particularly original about my life—I'm just one more among the millions of floating young girls that one finds in these difficult and unsettled years. But as I comb my long hair, slightly coppery when I don't bleach it and always silky and shiny in spite of the dyes, I myself am astonished at my own incredible beauty. Standing in front of the mirror I fall in love with my own gestures and expressions. Juan says that any motion of mine, no matter how idiotic, results in being a natural work of art.

I'm not forgetting that we all consider ourselves wonderful and perfect, and I've seen cases of vanity that could astound you. However, in my case I'm clearly aware that it isn't presumption or stupid self-deceit that makes me feel this way. The mirror that the men reflect never lies—and their pocketbooks even less. I've been able to open up and win the most stubborn hearts, even those embittered by life's harshness, and to loosen the tightest of wallets.

Even though I don't consider what men say of the slightest importance, I will put down here what I've heard. I'm not referring to what they say in the heat of passion—at that point their words are worthless and even the most ordinary woman inspires them. But with me it's not like that. The emotion I awaken is different. When they're with me, their false pride fades. Lulled by the sleepy atmosphere, the soft moonlight, they are transported by a sudden re-awakening of all their ancient musty hopes. A gentle, delicious bitterness comes over them, a consoling drug which soothes pain.

I don't know how to explain the unreal aspect of my appearance. Those not gifted verbally merely say that I am very strange . . . that I have a special quality they can't define. Those who are cleverer, and have more of a tongue, talk on and on and the words fall like music on my ears, pleasing me no end, soothing my vanity like a shower of pearls.

Though they each express it in their own way and according to their ability, down deep they all feel the same. I've known for a long time that I could treat men badly. Indeed, I *must* treat them badly. They are drawn to me. They adhere to me with a fatal ease. They are vicious and sensual, but with the vices and laziness of the soul that always end in bitter defeat. Actually, I don't conceal myself very much behind the mask of my good looks and frequently I lash back at them. Many times I've triumphantly showed my power, and have caused many faces to redden with the rage of humiliation from well-founded jealousy or the pain of being completely scorned. Yet even then I've seen their expressions soften and mellow when they gaze at the delicate beauty of my face, without my having uttered a single word of love, or apology, or sympathy. Then, just to be contrary, when they are feeling the effect of my magic more keenly than ever, I like to ask them for money, or give them a swift kick to remind them that I'm nothing more than an ordinary female, and a whore at that.

This hurts them. I know it hurts them terribly. Like something monstrous, deformed and infamous—an ugly trick of nature. Then I become quiet. I show them my face and my special magic leads them on once again.

This is why I've always had contempt for those poor females who only can triumph in the heat of passion and desire.

My empire is an empire of frustrated hopes which take wing, of purity crucified by the harshness of life, of emotions which open first with suspicious timidity, and finally end with impotent desperation. Until, hidden behind the faithful protection of my looks, I make my haul. Then I close all the doors with an abrupt, cruel slam. Never, God as my witness, did I feel pity for any of my victims.

I'd like to pass rapidly over this period. Not that I'm ashamed of anything, after all I was the highest paid girl in the entire house, but because of the two dull wasted years spent there. One day I suddenly realized that if I kept on using myself up living that way, soon I would lose both my high spirits and my youth. My pleasantly mounting pile of cash wasn't really doing much for me and if I continued at that rate someone else was going to profit from my savings.

I had entered the house more from fear than from a desire to earn money. I had been nineteen years old and I didn't want to become an ordinary streetwalker. Unfortunately, most of the *pesetas* that one worked and sweated for stayed right in the palms of the pimps and the madam. Half went directly to the owner and a certain per cent of what was left went for maintenance and service. We also had to hand out presents and bribes so that we could meet men of importance. My life there wasn't easy, but I learned a lot, I can't deny that.

When I left, in the spring of 1942, I was twenty-one. I took with me a false identification from one of the girls down the hall; in it my age was recorded as being twenty-four. On my own this useful bit of paper would have been impossible to get. You only had to look at my naïve childish appearance to know that I was very young.

I lived those years of apprenticeship like one frozen into a state of suspended numbness. I wasn't sad or happy, I wasn't sweet or mean, pleasing or unpleasing. I worked and I worked and I worked. With each new bill of a thousand *pesetas* that I greedily pocketed, or each new bracelet which jingled on my arm, I became more and more submerged in a lethargy where all spelled gold. Indeed, my crazy Juan said that my heart itself must have turned into yellow metal.

Being the most sought-after of the girls in the house, the proprietress introduced me to her best clients with a great deal of drama and mystery. Many of the men enjoyed corrupting young girls. These she assured that I came from a very distinguished family. She told them that I was a minor and had entered the house on my own in order to save my father from prison. He was supposed to be a very important man who had gotten himself involved in some embezzling scandal. Now really . . . as if they ever put high-class swindlers in jail! But men will believe anything, especially when beautiful women are involved. Then one can pass off the most incredible frauds as the truth.

During my time there I got a good education in envy, malice, and vice. In order to make my life more tolerable, I spent most of my money on morphine and cocaine, even though the cocaine made me feel worse. I got the shakes from it and it discolored my hands.

Then, one day, a man beat me. I didn't want to sleep with him and he struck me. I threw a bottle at his head. He covered my mouth, preventing me from screaming, then he gagged me and tied me to a chair. He beat me the entire night without anyone realizing my situation.

He was a dirty and ugly man who had been through several wars and always carried lots of money on him. I never liked going with him. It disgusted me to have to put up with him, but he insisted and he paid. He paid well. Everyone had to for me.

During the entire night he kept hitting me on my face and body. He'd drop off to sleep for a while, then with renewed determination he'd begin again. Finally at around ten in the morning, he left, after a very unpleasant parting. He told the maids that they shouldn't waken me as I was sleeping like a little angel. Damn his soul! What had happened was that I had almost lost consciousness, I'd been so beaten.

Afterwards I wanted to get back at him and I looked for the rat all over Madrid, but never ran into him again. If I ever do, I swear by all that's holy that I'll make him pay.

When I took my valises and left, the smells of spring filled the street. The house was located in the center of Madrid—everything was near at hand, convenient to it. From the walled-up, dirty, run-down façade of the building one could never guess at the fantastic splendor inside. There were elevators, thick wool carpets, fancy mirrors of all kinds and elaborate and fragrant woods. Above all, there were the bathrooms—black, red, green, blue, and yellow. These were the pride of the establishment.

From inside my taxi I looked back at the place and swore to myself, never again! Then, carefully clearing my throat, I spat on the sidewalk in front of the door. A just farewell. True, I was almost rich, but the price I had paid was high.

Part II

❧❧❧❧❧❧❧❧❧❧❧❧ ❧❧❧❧❧❧

One

At one point I became unwilling to continue writing my story. The spirit and necessary patience had left me. Also I was pressed for time. I was busy trying to empty the pockets of an Austrian black marketeer who was crazy about me until his money ran out. Juan provoked me though, saying that I was afraid to go ahead because I didn't dare mention certain things. He was completely mistaken and I'm going to prove it. Thank God I've had nothing to be ashamed of and have always been ready to try anything and everything.

Until now it's been practically a diversion for me to write about my early innocent naïvete, my simplicity and happy youth. Those were the years when for practically nothing anyone could take advantage of me. But now that I am giving my impressions of what my life became from the time I left the Casa Amparo until the fall of 1947, when I started to write this, it's going to be harder to do, and more disagreeable. There are some things which belong to oneself, which one doesn't like to share with anyone.

For one thing, I don't like putting into words my fondness for the poor and the sick. The day that Juan found out about this I was a little drunk and couldn't keep my mouth shut because of something irritating he had said.

"You are the most complete prostitute that I've ever known," he said, although he put it in another way that I'm not mentioning here out of dignity.

"What things you say!"

"You are a prostitute one hundred per cent through and through," he continued unpleasantly, but looking at me with admiration all the same. Prostitute or not, he's still taken with me.

"Oh, leave me alone!"

"All prostitutes have a weak moment when they least expect it. But not you," he continued obstinately.

"What do you know?"

"You've never been in love, you've never weakened."

"That's true."

"You've never for one moment felt compassion for a man who's fallen at your feet. At your prostitute's feet."

"No, never."

"You've never felt the need of giving of yourself, of bringing something of yours into life," he insisted.

"You seem to know everything, Juan."

"Because it's so."

"Maybe you're mistaken."

"No."

"Well, you're dead wrong," I shot out, unable to contain myself as I'd been drinking champagne, the good dry kind that always excites me.

"Don't drink any more and shut up."

"I don't like your talk. You always think you're so smart."

"I am."

I looked at him for a moment. He was lying back on the couch, drinking slowly and contemplating me with his eyes of a hunter. It was already dawn. We had spent part of the night together and before he took me home we had gone to Riscal to have a bite to eat.

I felt strange that night, and while I calmly listened to everything, inwardly I was crying with rage. Was he trying to provoke me into speaking? With that man one could never feel sure of anything. I have an idea that it isn't I whom he loves and admires but my shadow. A dark shadow which isn't really me even though it always follows close by. I should have kept quiet, but I couldn't. Suddenly I was ready to ruin everything just to show up this know-it-all.

"Idiot! What do you know about my poor? Tell me? What do you know about my sick, you—you bastard!" I exploded, furious.

"Of what?" he asked, his eyes suddenly shining. "No, Lola. I don't know anything about that," he admitted very seriously.

"*Anda*. Pay and let's scram," I cut in, getting up as well as I could.

We rode through the streets of Madrid. I had a whim to eat doughnuts in Lavapiés. In the doughnut bar the smell of the sizzling oil which oozed out from the enormous frying pans calmed me a little. Hungrily we gobbled down a plate of fritters. The place was smoky and stank. The other men looked at Juan mistrustfully. He seemed very elegant with his black hat and navy blue coat. I clung nervously to my silver fox cape. Pimps, fairies, and bums hang out there in addition to the bleary-eyed, bad-tempered females who come early in the morning with baskets to get the doughnuts. We stayed a short while, eating standing up. An old balding gray-skinned bum fell asleep against Juan's broad shoulder. While the early morning light unmercifully revealed the unpleasant faces, we slipped a bill into the old man's pocket.

Later, what was by then the next day, we drove around and around in the car and I asked Juan to kill me. He laughed, and we kissed each other like crazy near the Plaza del Progreso until we finally bumped into a trolley. I cried a little while. Yes, I confess it. Bitter tears rolled down my unmade-up cheeks while Juan kissed me, holding me tight in his strong arms.

When I calmed down a bit he asked me about my interest in the poor and sick and I confessed to him some of my other life, spilling it out with some regrets. This sort of thing one should never tell anyone. Least of all to a man, to a bastard of a man, even though Juan is really less of a bastard than most.

Afterwards, on other occasions, I told him the rest. One can never stop with half. Even though I tried to blame it all on the wine, he could always guess the truth no matter how strange or odd it seemed.

Now he says that if I don't get on with my story it's because I'm afraid to show my weaknesses. He's wrong. I'm a girl with a great deal of pride and I will tell all. What I won't deny is that it bothers me to put it in words. There are things that are difficult to explain, which spoil when examined.

I haven't forgotten though that when I began to write I promised to be truthful and that's what I'll be. I would have preferred leaving this out, but it's already too late, and the best thing would be to get on with it without any more fussing. When the proper time comes, I will tell all about it, even though it disgusts me. But first I have to mention Espichao.

Two

I met him in the Pasapoga. He came in there one night with a group of friends out on the town. They amused themselves during dinner talking about women. I know for a fact that men really have a ball when they can be together and say a lot of nonsense at our expense. That way they feel terrific—with guffaws and slaps on each other's back. But as soon as women enter the picture they become sour and unpleasant. They start to suffer. When men are alone,

64

they are great guys, capable of taking on the whole world; later they become more humble, as the majority are really very timid despite their big front.

This particular night the whole crew swaggered in staring at us women like big shots. They looked for a table and chose the one next to ours. I was sitting with a friend, Charito, a very pretty girl who was keeping me company.

One of the group seemed familiar to me—Lord only knows from where! Anyway, we greeted each other and he asked me to dance. Afterwards he took me over to his table, where there were several other girls already.

I kept changing partners, first dancing with one, then another. Being a little wary from experience, I finally approached the one I knew. I said what I always say—I am an expensive girl and have to earn my living. I couldn't waste my time with them unless it was profitable.

These things put so clearly always irritate men. They would rather deceive themselves, the poor fools, and forget that one goes with them for their money. Of course there are some women who, either because they are broke, or because they like to have fun, even when there's no money in it, join such a crew in search of dubious pleasures that keep them going the whole night and generally evaporate with the last drinks at dawn. But I'm something else. I always have several possibilities in view, and that particular night I saw two or three other men that appeared to be anxiously waiting for the opportunity of my company. That's why I spoke up. That's why I always speak! What's more, I believe that even if I were dying of starvation and saw myself abandoned by all the men in this world excepting one, I'd still speak like that. One must hammer the truth into them, this truth that hurts so much and makes them so furious. They have me because they pay me, and if they don't pay me, they don't have me.

I told him this and he became insulted.

"Look, Lola, go to hell!"

"Right this minute I'm going," I assured him, reaching for my precious fur cape and throwing it over my shoulders.

"But, what's going on, *hombre?* Don't get excited," one of the group intervened.

"*Caray!* What did you do to her?" another one asked, leaving his feminine companion in peace for a moment and trying to placate him.

"Me? Nothing. It's just that Lola is a whore and can't waste her time with us."

"*Hombre,* leave out the insults—" another one said excitedly, a sickly wasted-looking sort. "The girl is right."

"Thank you very much," I replied sweetly, "but this gentleman is right," I continued, staring pointedly at the first. "Certainly I'm a whore, because if I weren't, I wouldn't be here with you," I finished, fixing him but good. Then I left the table, showing off more than ever my queenly airs. The girls who were with them could thank me, even though it made me furious to realize that now they'd have less competition.

I went back to sit with Charito and not ten minutes passed before I had made arrangements with someone else. I slowly became aware that the fellow who had come to my defense was desperately devouring me with his eyes. I was curious, and I left my night's companion with Charito, a girl one could trust, and went toward the ladies' room. He immediately stopped me in my path.

"I would like to be with you," he stammered, and he nervously repeated "with you" again, this time switching from the formal to the intimate form of address in Spanish.

"I'm taken already."

"You can get out of it. Invent something, anything. I beg you," he implored, agitated.

"I don't like to stand up anyone. I'm an expensive girl but very straight," I warned him, meanwhile seducing him with my eyes.

"You are the most beautiful woman I've ever seen. And my friends acted like pigs with you. Forgive me my part in the insult," he asked, his voice filled with emotion.

"There's nothing to forgive. It's true I'm a prostitute," I admitted very gravely, but with a certain charm of manner.

"No, no," he protested in desperation. "You couldn't be that even though it appears that way. You are an extraordinary girl, very elegant and sensitive. You are a señorita."

"You think so?" I asked, surprised.

"I'm sure, absolutely sure," he repeated very excitedly.

"Thank you."

"*Anda* . . . let's go. Say whatever you wish to that fellow who's with you. Please."

I examined him carefully. He was a ratty-looking fellow, with nervous little darting eyes set in a monkey's face. He was a mess, poorly dressed, and he probably was just a mediocre clerk somewhere who had a lot of dreams about himself and little else. But one should never judge only by appearances, as there are some women of fashion who look like angels but are . . .

"I don't know . . . I don't think I could do that, please understand," I hesitated, trying to test him.

"Just this once!"

66

"Only—"

"Only what? Tell me," he asked anxiously.

"The truth is that I'm in a spot, and if you could help me out . . ."

"I understand your delicacy, your unhappiness at having to speak of these things," he cut in tenderly. "Because that's not natural to you. Please forgive me if I ask you how much you need . . ."

"A thousand *pesetas*," I demanded. The one who was waiting for me had offered me five hundred, and I wasn't going to stand him up for this sadsack unless I got double.

"A thousand *pesetas!*" He became a little alarmed.

"Yes, I need them right away, to give to my little sister."

"I don't have that much on me," he said sadly.

"I'm sorry." I held out my hand. "Perhaps another time . . ."

"One moment, please . . ." he begged me again, seeing that I was leaving. "Yes, I'll tell you what. I'll get the money. I'll be back in a minute. I have to be with you. Can't you understand that?"

"Don't change your mind on the way," I cautioned, resigning myself to his unfortunate body. "Look, give me whatever you have on you now, and that will make it definite, okay?"

He very sheepishly gave me four hundred *pesetas*. I saw that he really meant to get the rest, so I sent the other one away. He could get as mad as he liked. While my hero was getting the money, Charito and I had a good laugh. We gave him the nickname of Espichao—the man without balls.

To his unhappiness, I called him that for over a year.

Three

I'm aware that all this is coming forth without any apparent rhyme or reason and I'm afraid that as my story goes on, it's going to seem even more disordered. I spoke to Juan about this—after all he's responsible for having gotten me started. I told him that I felt incapable of putting everything down in its proper place but at the same time wanted to be sure that I showed a true picture of what my life had been. In real life things happen in a jumbled mixed-up way, and not at all like in books. We talked a little about the complicated ins and outs of my life and I confessed I didn't know how to continue.

He laughed, amused at seeing me so puzzled by such grave problems and doubts. He told me to write freely whatever came to mind according to my mood of the moment. Life also has no rhyme or reason to it, and even though my story cannot precisely copy life—and no story can—the important thing is to write it as naturally as possible.

Now I'm all enthusiastic again. I want to do a good job, which is the way I feel toward anything I undertake. I think that the best plan is to write first about Espichao, who was the most important man in my life during this period. Naturally, this tender little adventure didn't take up *all* my time—he wasn't the only fish in the sea by any means. I'll tell you about the rest in due course.

The poor fellow only had one name—Rodolfo—and I took it away from him, calling him Espichao, leaving him with nothing. He fell hopelessly in love with me, with a gentleness which he still feels for me. He's flat broke, though, so I don't let him come near me.

Juan always takes his part and defends him. He says he's a good man and I acted the whore I am with him. It's very strange, whenever we talk of the "Espichao affair," Juan gets sad and looks at me with a far-off expression in his eyes that makes me shiver. Juan's the one person in the world I can't get at and who can make me feel oddly queasy.

After Espichao returned with the money that night I took him with me to a tavern in the Calle de Válgame Dios. It was a special sort of place and after a certain hour stayed open only for their regular, well-heeled customers. I ate some hot sausages and bread, washing it down with a clear wine. I was starved—this was the first food I had eaten all evening. Espichao hardly touched his sandwich. He nervously kept tapping the table with his restless hands, and every time he opened his mouth he hemmed and hawed like an idiot. All that motion made me terribly seasick. He drank several glasses of brandy and soda to bolster his courage and to cool off. The combination of the heat and my personality were making him sweat.

He babbled on and on. He was the talkative type, one of those men who try to hide their timidity behind a barricade of words.

"I go for you, precious," he flattered me.

"Really?"

"I've had my eyes on you for a long time."

"Funny, I don't remember ever having seen you."

"That's natural. I'm no Don Juan."

"How you do go on!" I exclaimed. That's my favorite phrase when there is nothing to say.

"I don't often frequent these night spots. I find them absurd with their false gaiety and idiotic animation. But I'm

68

tolerant enough to go when my friends want to. Once, several months ago, I saw you in the Casablanca." He had an oddly old-fashioned way of speaking.

"Several months ago? Impossible. For over a year a very rich handsome Italian count kept me isolated from society. He treated me like a queen," I lied, as usual.

"But I'm sure I've seen you," he insisted.

"Perhaps on one of my free evenings, when he was away on a trip." He seemed very sure, so I relented.

"You made quite an impression on me, precious, and I couldn't forget you. . . . Though it would have been better for a man like myself never to have seen you again," he murmured.

"You still have time. I'm not forcing you to stay," I answered peevishly.

"Forgive me, sweetheart. I'm in a very emotional state, and I don't know what I'm—you can't understand what this means to me—" he replied softly.

"I'm no doubt one of many." I enjoyed provoking him.

"No, no," he protested excitedly, bouncing about in his chair like a fool and waving his stubby arms about with the jerky gestures of a robot. "You are a most extraordinary woman, and if I may be completely frank with you, a woman for whom this sort of life isn't fitting."

"You're entirely right about that," I admitted, hoping to get something more concrete out of him.

"I'm positive that some family trouble, some social injustice forced you into this. Your innocent youth has been defiled by the disgusting immorality of these unhappy times in which we live. One only has to look at you, and contemplate the soft sensitivity of your eyes to know how good you are."

"You are a very clever man and it's impossible to conceal things from you," I flattered him. After all, he had given me one thousand *pesetas*—I could waste a little time talking to him.

"Oh, no!" he protested. "In this case one hardly has to be a genius to realize that the atmosphere you live in doesn't suit you. It isn't good for you at all."

"You're right. Sometimes I feel such a need for some genuine affection. . . ." I sighed.

"Really, darling?" His voice rose, while he devoured me with his restless eyes.

"Oh, I wish I could be as far away from here as possible, buried in some remote corner of the earth," I said softly, my face saddening with an air of romantic disillusion.

"I know just how you feel, darling. I, too, long for that.

Oh, if it were only possible to arrange things some day and go off together in search of such a place," he sighed, "some peaceful, tranquil spot. . . ."

"The whole thing is in making up your mind to do it, *hombre*."

"You're right. One must fight." He became carried away again. "I will fight for you. You're worth fighting for."

"You think so?" I asked coquettishly, taking his hand and leaning toward him, showing off my smooth and pearly breasts. I was getting tired of so much chitchat and wanted to get down to brass tacks.

"Yes, you are. I believe that as I've never believed anything in my entire life," he answered violently. "If your face, if your entire appearance belied the confidence I have in you, it would be the most infamous trick of nature."

"I just love listening to you, honey. You're so different from the rest." Well, that certainly was true enough! "Tell me, who are you?"

"Many things, many things."

"Anda . . . come on, tell me, cutie. What things?"

"At the moment an ugly fellow incapable of winning anyone."

"What do you know about these things? I like ugly men."

"Also I'm . . . what nearly all Spaniards are, a lawyer."

"So that's it!" Now I had the picture. So that's why he talked so funny.

"I've nothing to complain about, no, I can't complain at all," he repeated himself, puffing up a bit. "I have some very important clients. Cases involving some of the big electrical companies. Also I've an in with some government business that's, uh, quite worth while—you, uh, understand? No, no, I can't complain. Still, I've earned it. I suffered a great deal during the war."

"My poor little baby," I indulged him, realizing that this trip was going to pay off.

"If you would only help me . . ." he asked timidly.

"Me? To do what?"

"To fight for you. To help remove you from this life, so that you could be mine, completely mine."

"That's a man's affair," I said disdainfully. "I'm not in the habit of having to help people at anything besides spending their money."

"You're right, entirely right," he admitted humbly. "Only tell me the truth, I beg you, my darling. This is a solemn moment which could change my whole destiny. If some day, if some day I could have you and make you mine alone . . . would you love me a little? Could you accept my love? For God's sake, tell me the truth."

70

"I think I might."

"Thank you."

"I like you, *chico*."

"No woman understands me the way you do," he burst out.

"You've been very sincere with me and I appreciate it. . . . Oh, you men are beasts, you're always after the same thing," I tantalized him with my scorn.

"Not me—not me," he protested vigorously. "I'm interested in something more than . . . than your body," he choked.

"But I have a very nice one, see?"

"I can imagine," he replied, putting his hand around my waist. "But you and I, we can't . . . we can't go now, just . . . like the rest."

"Why?"

"Because I love you. I love you a great deal, my darling."

"Listen . . . I'm also going to be frank with you."

"I thank you with all my heart."

"You've guessed a lot about me. Things that no one knows. I come from a very fine family and the loneliness of my life has made me what I am."

"For me you will be only what you want to be."

"Oh, I can't complain. Men have been crazy about me and they always treated me like something special. I've had all that I want, even though I've thrown money to the winds and done whatever I felt like doing with it. But inside, this gay life bores me. Now nothing interests me. I have a strange intuition that soon I'm going to die," I remarked soulfully.

"Oh, God, no, not that! I'm here to take care of you, to pamper you, to protect you against all of life's misery. Oh, my darling, my angel . . ." Tremblingly he kissed my cheek, brushing against me with his lined, troubled face.

"You are so kind. But I won't be a burden to you for long."

"But . . . what do you have? What's the matter with you?" he cried in distress, fearing the worst.

"Oh, not that. Nothing that needs bismuth or Neosalvarsan. It's my heart. I've strained it a little. I'm not very strong, and I may die any day now. Then once and for all my suffering will be over."

"No, my darling, no. That can't happen," he protested, his eyes wet with tears. "Because I adore you."

"Even now I feel a choking, a weakness that could—"

"Oh, forgive my selfishness! It's very late and I'm tiring you with my nonsense—excuse me!" he apologized. "Come along, let's be on our way. You must sleep, get all the rest you possibly can. We will see each other tomorrow. Yes,

71

right away, tomorrow afternoon. We two have a great deal to talk about . . . a great deal."

We took a taxi to my pension in the Calle de la Reina. He discreetly kissed me good-by in front of the door, and I pretended to take the elevator to my room. As soon as he was gone I went down again, grabbed another taxi, went to Riscal, and found there the guy I had met before in the Pasapoga. We got boiled and I spent the night with him in his bachelor apartment in the Calle de Pardiñas. I didn't come home until two the next afternoon. When I passed through the door I couldn't help laughing, remembering the silly kiss that poor Espichao had given me in the same spot the previous night.

Four

Naturally, he fell into my trap. If I've ever seen a man entangle himself, day after day, in my spider's web—a beautiful web, of fine silk threads—it was this fool.

We started to see each other frequently and he began to suffer. I continued the romantic and sentimental byplay. Why, he was afraid even to touch me!

Nearly every afternoon we went out together. He telephoned me at the pension and we met in the terrace of El Abra or in La Elipa, which was airier and caught the breezes from the Calle de Alcalá and the Gran Vía.

I used to wear a very becoming short-sleeved blouse, a rather gay wide skirt which went well with it, and as many gold bracelets as I could stand in all that heat. I really didn't own much in the way of jewelry—just an Omega watch, a good cocktail ring of rubies and diamonds set in gold, and the marvelous bracelet of gold links. My shiny coppery hair made up for everything. It reached down to the middle of my back, waving like a glittering mysterious waterfall. I let a few lighter wisps curl casually around my temples so that my forehead and oval face would be framed to perfection.

In the evening we went either to the garden of Abascal, the University Club, the Retiro, or the Terraza de Riscal. And, occasionally, when he had the money, we went to the Villa Rosa in Chamartín. It cost a small fortune to go there. Espichao didn't own a car and by the time he paid the taxi plus something else for the driver—it was easily thirty *duros*.

When we went out for the evening I got myself up very carefully, very differently than during the day. In the afternoon at La Elipa, El Abra, or some other outdoor café, I tried to accentuate a fashionable little-girl look and hardly used any make-up. In daylight, my marvelous creamy pink complexion glowed like alabaster. I didn't have one wrinkle, rough spot or blemish on my face. My skin looked as though it had been polished and worked over until perfection had been achieved. I have, though, two little beauty marks—one on my cheekbone, near my eyes, and the other near the corner of my lip. All of this, together with the incredible delicacy of my features and the brilliance of my eyes, is what induced Juan to say that my face is a provocation of nature, who delights in showing us her astonishing powers so that we never resign ourselves to the ugly. She wants to awaken in us a terrible craving for beauty. What a crazy guy!

I've always realized that my sole obligation to men was to bring them the incomparable spectacle of my beauty. Once having given them that, I could demand anything without their having been cheated by the deal. This is also something that Juan told me, and he knows a lot about these things.

In those days I dressed beautifully. I really had several breathtaking outfits. I was perfectly satisfied if I owned a Mastida, a Rodríguez, and one or two Balenciagas. But I remember that particular summer I had a chiffon trimmed with black lace which gave me an air of a filmy mysterious butterfly. My other two favorites were a very flattering pink batiste and a dress of natural cream-colored silk which made me nostalgic for my early youth.

Poor Espichao was almost faint with desire whenever he saw me. Whether it was during the afternoon, with my little-girl air and innocent face, or whether it was during the evening, when I was got up like a prima donna, haughty and imposing, men's eyes followed me everywhere. They stared at me—openly showing their desire. Poor Espichao, aware of the stir I created, suffered miserably.

The only man I've ever known who is perfectly at ease with me is Juan. Several times so much so that he's left me alone too long for his own good. More than once the bastard has amused himself by staring at others much less pretty than me, which drives me mad. But that's the way he is and there is nothing I can do about it.

Espichao was just the opposite—always on pins and needles —afraid that someone would give him a few smacks and carry me off for good. Like all small and ugly men, he was touchy and irritable. I have to admit, though, that he was always ready to fight for me and never complained about the trouble I caused him—he being the one who always lost.

We would dance awhile, but most of all, we talked. Which is to say that he talked—always playing the same record for me. He'd begin by peevishly reproaching me for something,

73

nervously making angry gestures with his tiny hands. After an interim of serious reflections about life and bucolic dreams of our future together, he'd finish by making some declaration of pure, true love which was really stickier than a bowlful of honey.

I got a lot of money out of him, though. Shameful, cowardly money. He sent it to me by a messenger from his office in a carefully sealed envelope on which he had written *"Personal and Urgent,"* as though I were some dirty bureaucrat. He saw to it that he never handed me a bill directly. That would have hurt him too much. I was supposed to be something fragile and sacred, worthy of his respect. Just the opposite of Juan, who isn't the sort of man who is used to paying women, and when he gives me something, which is always very little, takes out his wallet and boldly counts out the bills. He flings them to me and says, "Here, something to amuse yourself with." Until one day, when I was in a bad mood, I took the money and threw it in his face, though I don't know why. He very calmly picked it up and after counting it again, put it in my purse. Grinning, he asked me if perhaps I wasn't feeling well, such indifference wasn't like me.

I put Espichao on a regime of pressure and of rationing. Rationing as regards myself—I rarely allowed him to sample me—and pressure as regards his work, as he wasn't stupid and had made very good connections. I urged him to take advantage of this so that it would pay off. I told him I wasn't well at all. The cost of living was very high and I had to have money so that I could have my own apartment and put an end to the nuisance and discomfort of living in a pension.

The apartment would be our love nest and we would fix it up together, planning and building like two lovers. To give him a taste of our future life together, I let him take me to Salamanca for a few days. He went in pursuit of his "tranquil and peaceful paradise" and turned the trip into one continuous guidebook lesson about the monuments in that boring, stupid city. Not one stone was left unturned. Finally I got indigestion from so much learning and we came back to Madrid, and to the subject of that apartment of mine.

Even though it doesn't belong in this part of the story, I remember now that I visited some cities and saw monuments with Juan. But he never tried to explain them to me, even though he knows much more about it than most. He'd simply say: "That is like you—beautiful. That other one—no. There are many of those failures in the world." Then he'd ignore me, annoyed when I asked questions. I know that at times they seemed stupid, but he should have put up with them more patiently. I like it when Juan tells me things.

Five

My darling,

No doubt you will think it silly that I am writing to you. It's only been three hours we've been apart. But I'm very excited about something, and I must talk with you, even though it is in this rather unusual manner.

I've just left the office and I'm sitting at our table in El Abra. Next to me are an engaged couple, and I confess I'm jealous. There is too much loneliness in my life for me not to be. Here, in this spot which reminds me so of you, I seek comfort and solace in my despondency.

Now, I'd like to explain a plan I have which made my hopes surge this afternoon. Yes, my darling, it's about that which pertains most to us, that which will bring us closer together. Things are going along well and very soon I may be able to offer you what you deserve—a home and children. This is a million times better than any amount of money or any amount of attention from those men who appear to love you, but who are really only interested in showing off with a beautiful woman at their side.

My darling, I must be with you—not here, but in some place where you don't know a soul, a place like Salamanca where we spent those few memorable days last year. A place which would allow you to become again the marvelous woman that you are inside, the woman I alone know. The part of you that is mine, only mine. Isn't this so, my precious? I want you to be María Dolores, my María Dolores. Not Lola—this Lolita who belongs to everyone.

I believe I've discovered the perfect spot where we could spend a few days of genuine happiness together.

Twenty kilometers from Calatayud is the famous Monastery de Piedra. Through a friend of mine, I've learned that it is a dream of a place, a veritable paradise with waterfalls and dense, shady groves of trees. In the old building of the monastery is an inn, which is very comfortable and the bus line runs every day between Calatayud and Alhama.

I have to travel through Aragón and Zaragoza because of some very complicated, important legal business of one of my clients—the Alcarreña Power account—and we could make the monastery the central base of our operations. At the same time you'd have a chance to improve your health. It's *important* that you take better care of yourself. Remember, my darling, that if anything should happen to you, which God wouldn't allow, I won't have anything left in this world. You must realize, my precious, that you are everything to me. Of all the women in this world, you are the only one of any real worth. This is apart from your being somewhat pretty.

I am aware that there are many dull-witted men in this world who think that this white dove shall be for them. They don't know that a person who can't dance, who is ugly and almost bald, and in all respects a rather sad figure of a man, loves you too much to tolerate this. Yes, and I will spend my entire life fighting for you, and for you alone. My darling, my precious, my life!

One year has passed since God willed the two of us to meet, and I want you to know that I am grateful to you with all my soul for the immense happiness I owe to you. Yes, dear one, today is the anniversary of our first meeting. It occurred at exactly eleven-ten this evening.

Though you told me this afternoon it would be impossible for us to spend this solemn hour together, I hope, my darling, that at least you are thinking of me a little. I pray you decide to take this trip with me, which is so important for both of us. Yes, I'm positive that you will. God will help me. He understands the misery and loneliness of my life.

For once you must be good to me and not let me go alone to Zaragoza. I have only you in this world. You must leave this awful concentration camp of Madrid. I need you more than ever, darling, because I'm convinced that you are the only decent, honest thing in my life, and even though I realize that I don't deserve your love, the truth is that I love you terribly much more than you could ever imagine.

You can't realize how I've dreamed of having you by my side, away from Madrid. Yes, perhaps even for twenty days! During this time you'd belong to me, and I wouldn't have to put up with some fool permitting himself the luxury of stopping to chat with you in the middle of the street just as though I weren't with you, pretending I didn't even exist. I'm allowing myself to allude to what happened last Tuesday on the Calle de Alcalá. Even though I realize it wasn't your fault, I wasn't at all amused at having that fellow stop you while you were walking with me. He should have known it was impertinent and rude on his part. But that's done with, so we won't say anything more about it.

I have to stop writing now. I've a load of work and the papers are sky-high on my desk. I've had a long talk today with the director who is very pleased with my work. I have to put up with all his nonsense, though, and when he chooses to speak about his stamp collection . . . there's no end.

I don't intend to go out tonight. Your memory satisfies me more than anything I might find—no matter how attractive it might be. I'm very pleased with the idea of this trip. The thought of going to La Granja had appalled me. I've always found it very unpleasant in summer. I despise the ridiculous crowd that vacations there.

Since I've considered the possibility of your accompanying me, I've been delirious with joy. I'm sure you feel the same way and that's all that counts. As long as you're willing, we've no further problem. You will, won't you? I would be very, very hurt if you didn't join me.

I love you more than ever,
RODOLFO

In this manner Espichao pestered me continually. Office boys and messengers knocked at my door at all hours, bringing me his long, cowardly, complaining letters which I never bothered to read. Paulina and Lirio tossed them aside, without even looking at one word. I recently found the above letter in the bottom of a carved chest from Ronda I keep in the foyer. It was buried beneath a mountain of old bills and papers I had been intending to burn one of these days.

Yes, more than a year had passed, one year to the day, and I had gotten my own apartment. I still live in it now, only it's more fixed up. Paulina, an old woman full of intrigue who had been a madam, came with me. She was the cousin of the owner of the pension I'd lived in at the Calle de la Reina. I brought her with me after I'd made arrangements with Espichao pretending she was my aunt. I also brought Lirio ("the Lily") to live in the apartment so that she could help me with my various schemes. She was one of the girls from the house and she'd been nice to me at the time. She gave me five *duros* daily for the rent. She had a steady boy friend from Alcalá de Henares and was a very reliable girl. She never failed to pay me at the end of the month with the money he gave her.

The apartment and the furnishings came out of Espichao's pocket, and another clever source he had tapped. He was so in love and so completely rattled by me that he put up with all my wild demands.

He worked like a horse. He saved all his money for me and I was never satisfied, always needing something else. I treated him badly because he disgusted me, though I'm not really sure why. Much uglier men have been on top of me without producing such disgust.

That's why I didn't go with him—either on the trip which he begged me about so much in his letter, or on any other. I'd had enough with Salamanca and I managed to see that the occasion didn't present itself again. He was rather unpleasant to me for a few days, but later he came back meek as a lamb, telling me that he wanted to show me the marvels of Granada, the cathedral of León, and the sights of Burgos,

77

using all this sightseeing and knowledge as a pretext to win me. I told the poor fool that there are emotions which one can never overlook, uniting two people better than anything. Though, as he already knew, the only thing which united me to a man was plenty of cash.

Hoping to get to me through someone else, Espichao became chummy with Paulina, my fake aunt. They spent hours chatting away. He busily started to engineer some future plans with the old woman. He was afraid that when his money ran out or a new, more powerful boy friend came on the scene I'd drop him.

Paulina was about fifty, a very shrewd operator. That is, until she had fallen for an old retired constable from Armada, and after having played the world for a sucker all her life, she gave herself to him gratis, for old times' sake.

Though Don Octavio, the constable, lived in a pension in the Calle de la Ballesta, he spent every afternoon in my place, and I enjoyed having him there.

He was very old already—almost seventy—and he knew a great deal. He was just the opposite of Espichao. He knew about life from having lived. I liked listening to him. He was widowed twice and had joined Paulina more than ten years ago. She had to manage for him now. He never paid attention to trivial things or fussed about life.

He was a peaceful, serious man, resigned to life. He was strong and had thick white curly hair and a fine handsome face. During the summer he would sit out on my balcony, smoking his pipe and enjoying the fresh air, while in wintertime he'd warm his feet in front of my living-room heater. His deep blue eyes were a little cloudy from age and many people found him a bit of a nuisance, a little unbalanced.

"How are you, Don Octavio?" I teased him, seeing him settled so comfortably.

"Just as you see, girl."

"Remembering things, eh? You don't fool me, I bet you were something."

"If I were a little younger I'd show you right now," he murmured between his teeth, taking his pipe out of his mouth.

"You can show me whenever you like, Don Octavio. I like you better than a lot of other men."

"You've a lot of nerve, child."

"You think so?" I asked in a tiny voice, amusing myself a little by trying to arouse him.

"An old man is an ugly thing, Lolita," he replied soberly. "And at your side, even worse."

"But you're still a very handsome man."

"I was a good man, child. At least that's what women have said."

78

"Oh, you drive us mad with your 'old times.' "

"They were pleasanter . . . ah, you'll see. I'll bring you a beautiful figurine from a Chinese chess set. A marble horseman painted red—a glory to see."

"Don't trouble yourself, Don Octavio."

"You would be the best owner for it. It's like you, Lolita."

"Like me, how?"

"Oh, yes . . . like you. Fine, light and precious. And also hard and cold, like you, girl."

"Oh, in spite of everything, you love me, Don Octavio," I insisted, sitting next to him, the two of us alone on the balcony, hoping for a breeze in the midst of the lazy suffocating late July afternoon.

"We old folk don't love anyone, girl. We're too dependent on what is failing and breaking down in here to love anyone," he insisted, slapping his skinny chest. "But beauty calms and consoles us a little. We think at least there is still that."

"Aren't I good-looking, Don Octavio?"

"Good-looking?"

"Very pretty then, you know what I mean."

"You are magnificent, child. You remind me of a painting of Lippi's and a Venus of Tintoretto. I also have a mother-of-pearl shell, which I had from El Mercante, the store I had in Grao."

"So I'm pretty?"

"You don't fool me, girl. You know that for old men the young have breasts of crystal."

"Mine is of flesh. And very pretty, Don Octavio. Do you wish to see? For you, I'll show it gratis."

"Thank you, child. It is enough for me to see your face."

"All right . . . you'll see!"

"You are a jewel. But a broken and foul-mouthed jewel."

"What nonsense!"

"It's the truth, child."

"I'm a prostitute, Don Octavio."

"Nothing more?"

"Nothing more."

"All right, have it your way," he said, sucking on his pipe. He always gave in when the conversation arrived at an impasse.

"Why do you have doubts?" I asked suspiciously.

"I don't have any doubts," he evaded.

"Come on, out with it."

"A few days ago a new boarder arrived at my pension, Lolita."

"So what has that to do with me?"

"Oh, nothing, nothing. Don't get so excited, girl. This boarder spoke to me at length about a woman."

"Go on."

"He's an old man like me. But he will die before me because he drinks like a fish to dull the pain of a cancer which is eating away his insides. Several times he's mentioned a woman who . . ."

"Bah, nonsense!"

"Who a year ago cared for him like an angel in the hospital."

"All right . . . so what?"

"She was an unusual woman, my child. Because she never tired of caring for the most miserable old men, for the sickest patients."

"Some idiot, no doubt."

"Perhaps, little one, perhaps. But when he told me about her, I don't know why but I was reminded of you. Of this beautiful, beautiful jewel . . . which is smashed."

"Look here, Don Octavio. Don't tire me with any more of your foolishness. You know I don't like people butting into my affairs."

"Ah, in your affairs, girl?"

"Yes, in my affairs," I said firmly.

"You're a brave girl, little one. What a pity that you sing so many different tunes, just like my mother-of-pearl sea shell," he complained, getting up and silently leaving without another word. He was an unusual and gentle man, incapable of hurting anyone with uncalled-for advice.

He died a few months later. He had a heart attack in my apartment. We put him to bed and I took care of him for several days. When the doctor said he was definitely going to die, Paulina begged to have him removed so that he could die in his pension.

She was very nervous and agitated, obviously afraid of something. I didn't want them to take the old man away, but she took advantage of one of my absences to remove him. During the night she and her cousin Loren put him in a taxi and, according to what they told me later, didn't even have time to get him to his bed. He died while they were walking him up to his room. It was on the second floor of the pension in the Calle de la Ballesta.

Paulina and Loren dumped him there, saying that he had had an attack in the street while walking with them. Later, the same night, they went to hear Lola Flores since they had already paid for the tickets.

Six

My apartment suited me perfectly, and I have it still. It has a front and a back door, and it's always difficult to keep track of two exits—while one man has waited in the hall for me, I've often slipped out by the back, with someone better.

My street is very dark and mysterious, filled with all sorts of odd types—couples clinging to one another, hustlers and operators. As it's high up, and there is a low garage opposite, the sun floods my balcony during the afternoon and I don't have to go out into the miserable street below.

The house, like all the rest on the street, is very old and uncared for. But even though I have neither an elevator nor central heating, I don't mind for I have eight beautiful rooms.

It took a lot of looking for Espichao and me to find it, and he had to pay ten thousand *pesetas* for the key. As soon as I saw it, I realized its advantages. For safekeeping, I immediately arranged for the contract to be put in my name. I didn't plan to stay with Espichao forever.

We fixed up the bedroom first, since it's always the bed that interests men most. We made several visits to the Rastro —the flea market—where we found a fantastic double bed, very elegant and beautiful, and I made a gorgeous moiré bedspread for it. We also bought a huge mirror-plated chest and two night tables, all of American oak, which was the last word.

I ordered two lamps with rose shades, a beautiful bell pull of the same color, and to make the whole effect even more rose-colored, had the walls painted a soft pink.

It's a lovely room, and most men are usually surprised when they come in for the first time to see how gentle and homey it is. Only that bastard Juan complains . . . he turns out the lights so he can escape. He says he finds all that wedding-cake frosting cloying. But who expects taste from such a maniac?

Espichao almost wept with pleasure when the room was finished, and jumped about the bed like a rabbit let loose from a cage. I immediately let him know that it all was mine. He didn't have any right to that bed except when I felt like it, which wasn't going to be often.

I'm very strong willed, so I saw to it that in spite of the little apartment and its bedroom, our life wasn't going to become any closer, or more intimate. I forbade him to see me without calling, and arranged not to have him come for several days at a time. I told him some prudish story about my various pains and sicknesses. He was so idiotically in love with me that he swallowed everything just to keep me.

I did a good job of emptying his wallet, the only thing I was interested in emptying. He had saved up about thirty thousand *duros* which he had carefully kept for the time when he would get married. As soon as I found out what he had, I started to dig it out of him, and I made quite a haul. It wasn't difficult, for the poor fool had already promised, "Everything for you, my love, everything for you." He had to save on his shoes, suits, shirts and underwear, and even on tobacco and amusements so that he could send me more money in those famous envelopes marked *"Personal and Urgent."*

We spent almost another year like this, until the spring of 1944. I was twenty-three, on the outside a vision to behold, even though inside things weren't working too well. Don Jacobo, my doctor, discovered something which gave me quite a fright. But he gave me lots of injections, and once more the danger passed; he cured me of eczema on my finger, which I kept bandaged throughout, because of people's foul minds.

The apartment was furnished, though not as completely as now. I had to supplement what I got out of Espichao with my own private earnings. I was determined to have my own home, a place where no one could stick his nose except when I let him. Where I was a queen and a señora.

I ordered some Spanish furniture to be made for me in Ronda. The workmanship was excellent, there were heads carved of wood like real antiques. I did the living-room chairs in wine satin and had a crystal chandelier for the dining room. One room was used entirely for my doll collection—I had loads of them, my favorites were a Mariquita Pérez and a Gisela dressed in a beautiful tennis outfit.

Around that time, around two years ago, Espichao began to speak of his plans. He realized that his money was evaporating and that each day I was becoming more and more independent. Paulina, who was still playing the role of my aunt, backed him up. Don Octavio had just died and the old woman had plenty of time to scheme against me with him. Lirio never mixed into my affairs, being completely taken up by her friend, the one from Alcarria.

They proceeded slowly so that I wouldn't suspect anything. What happens is that passions are incubated quietly, like chickens in an egg, and people don't notice anything until the shell breaks.

Espichao started his campaign by complaining again, threatening me unpleasantly.

"Look here, Dolores, this can't continue," he said one night, while we were enjoying the fresh air on the terrace of the Gijón, on Recoletos. It was a beautiful evening and the moon showed through the branches of the trees. It smelled of acacias, and I was swept away, dreaming of a man I had not yet met, meanwhile amusing myself by flirting with a group of boys who had followed me from the Gran Vía. They had sat down at the next table to see me better.

"Don't begin again, Dolfo," I said, swallowing a yawn.

"But it's necessary. . . . And I warn you, I won't stop talking until you start to listen," he replied irritably, motioning with those annoying little hands of his. "I really have to talk to you seriously."

"Lead on, I'm all yours," I resigned myself, thinking that maybe it would be worth while to make him jealous later with one of the boys from the group.

"You are more than my life, precious. You mean everything to me," he continued, playing a familiar tune.

"I already know, *hombre,* I already know. You tell me all the time."

"But you don't listen."

"*Anda,* come on, Dolfo, don't be a pain in the neck. Please . . . it's such a nice night."

"My dear, my love, I'm obliged to tell you this. And it's important that you heed me, if not . . ."

"If not, what? You know, Dolfo, you're not forced to give me anything. . . ."

"Oh, it's not that, my darling, it's not that," he said, startled. "I'm just very worried about you."

"You don't have to worry about me, *hombre,* I'm grown up."

"Now, Dolores. I'm not going to speak of myself, nor am I going to tell you again that I love you, even though it is the most important thing in my life. Unfortunately, I believe that nothing to do with me interests you," he continued, guessing the truth but not believing it, which is what generally happens to people.

"What things you say!" I protested politely, throwing a tender look at the group next to us, who were really giving me the eye.

"As I've said, it has nothing to do with me," he repeated magnanimously. "It concerns you, Dolores. After all, you're the most important thing in the world to me. I must talk about you."

"I see that I have no choice. It's incredible, that on such a beautiful evening you aren't more romantic."

"Don't change the subject, Dolores. It won't get you anywhere. Once I've made up my mind . . ."

"Okay . . . go on," I replied amicably, meanwhile choosing one of the group to cheat on him with later that night.

"I've spent a great deal of time observing you, precious, even though you may not believe it."

"I believe it. Why shouldn't I?"

"One hundred and five pounds isn't enough weight for you. Your health rapidly is getting worse. There is an immediate danger of tuberculosis and it could attack you when you least expect it."

"I know I'm very delicate—but don't scold me," I begged, looking at him affectionately for the benefit of my audience at the next table.

"Look, my darling. You're free to do what you want, even to insult me, if that's your wish. But there is one thing which I won't allow you to do—to destroy your life," he insisted gravely. "No one has the right to commit suicide, and that's what you're doing in your own way. That's why I've decided to stop this situation before it's too late, my love."

"What are you thinking of doing?" I asked out of curiosity.

"My affairs are in much better shape than I deserve, but God always helps those who live honorably. That's why I dare to ask you to begin to take care of yourself. I ask you this, because if your life is in danger, it is the same as though my life were in danger. You are the only thing in this world that—"

"Yes, I know."

"I've thought that maybe you could get out of the city for a while, away from the heat. Perhaps to the sierras. Afterwards . . ."

"Yes?"

"I believe I have a plan which would provide you with the peace and tranquillity which you deserve," he continued, becoming even more solemn. "I'm not even demanding your love, though I love you deeply. I only hope to make you happy, and then one day perhaps . . ." He stopped, uncertain.

"Yes? Come on, out with it!"

"Perhaps you would marry me. Oh, my love!" He grasped my hand tightly. "I'd be the happiest man in the world."

"Please, Dolfo. Don't make me laugh."

"I'm entirely serious."

"But what would your family think?"

"My mother, who is a saint, dreams about having one more daughter." He became more and more carried away by the sound of his own words. "Yes, my dear, without even having met you, they already love you."

"You're exaggerating."

"Think about me, my darling. My life is worthless, but with you at my side, all that will be changed."

"You're very good to me, Dolfo," I said, trying to gain time. "But—"

"No, for God's sake! Don't put anything in our way."

"*Hombre*, don't be crazy. Marrying is a serious business. And you know I'm a very ill person."

"I will cure you, my precious."

"I'll need many things."

"You'll have everything, darling."

"I think you're wrong about your family."

"No, no. I've already tested the ground, and as they see I'm so unhappy, so worried . . . I hadn't planned to tell you this, my dear, but I hardly eat, and I can't sleep, thinking about you."

"Oh, Dolfo!"

"I'm sure that they'll be happy to see me married. And when they meet you, my darling, they will love you as you deserve to be loved. You are so good, so very good. Life has treated you badly, and people are very evil, they always see the worst."

"That's true enough."

"You'll see, everything's going to work out. Now a vacation in the sierra, and in the fall a wedding."

"I don't know . . . these things take a lot of thought."

"How beautiful you'll look in your wedding dress! What a sight you'll be!"

"I'd make the prettiest bride in the world, wouldn't I?" I became enthusiastic, thinking about my looks.

"The prettiest in the world, my love, the prettiest . . ."

We went on like this for a while. I was carried away by the vision of myself in a wedding dress. But then I remembered that he'd be the one at my side, and I came back to reality. Another half hour, and the whole subject was left up in the air—a wedding was not in my plans for the immediate future.

We slowly strolled along Recoletos, until we came to Cibeles. Arm in arm we went up along Alcalá, and came through on Barquillo, my short little Rodolfo dreaming of our wedding day.

We said good-by before we got to my door, because I don't like the night watchman to know too much about my business. Finally Espichao left, completely elated thinking of the future.

I went inside the doorway and waited for a few minutes. Then I came out again. One of the boys from the group had followed me and I knew that he was waiting at the corner.

I joined him. He was tall, dark and strong. We took a taxi and went dancing at the Villa Rosa. We drank a lot. Later, we spent the rest of the night together.

I stayed in bed the following day, resting up. Whiling away the time, I read two letters Espichao had sent me. Inside one was two thousand *pesetas* . . . like manna from heaven. I was terribly short on cash.

Well, that's the way it goes.

Seven

MY PRECIOUS:

I'm still in Ateca as my work has turned out to be very complicated, and unfortunately the people here don't know much about anything.

I'm in fine shape and this change of atmosphere has been good for me. In Madrid I was so preoccupied that I became ill from lack of sleep. Happiness is never complete, my darling Dolores, and I must admit that I miss you terribly. But one's duties come before one's love, and I must resign myself to being without you for a few more days.

I also think that a few days alone will do me good. You know how the rush and bustle of Madrid gets on my nerves. Here I don't read the paper, I don't listen to the radio and I have no idea of what is happening in the world—the news is never any good anyway. All my thoughts are on you and what concerns you.

I'm going to tell you very briefly about my work. I want you to know a little more of my life so that you will feel closer to me.

I work for the Alcarreña Power Company during the morning, and visit their affiliates in this area. Later, I take a little siesta and when I get up I go for a long walk in the country. This calms me and makes me feel good. I have dinner, read in bed for a while and then off to sleep as soundly as a baby. But I miss you, my darling, I miss you.

When I return you must give me a complete picture of your life during my absence. I won't forgive your omitting even the most insignificant detail, and I want to know if you've kept your promise of thinking about me for at least five minutes each day, the way I asked you to. Oh, my darling, I love you so much that sometimes I even think that

I could resign myself to seeing you with another man, if that gave you your well-deserved happiness. Naturally, I'm referring to your future husband.

I spend my time thinking of the two of you—of your Aunt Paulina as well as of you. I haven't forgotten that it's only been six months since poor Don Octavio died (may he rest in peace). Take care of your sweet aunt, Dolores. Don't abandon her in her hour of need, try to console her with the warmth of your love. I don't know why I'm reminding you of this, as I know you have a wonderful heart, and will look after her with all your usual generosity.

I don't know why, but today I feel a little sad. My soul is heavy, my darling, because I wish that we were already married. But my consolation is knowing that a girl, a girl whose love is worth fighting for, is deeply in love with me.

I realize that I'm unworthy of your affection, but one day I'll convince you of how much I love you, and will continue to love you for my whole life, come what may. There is only one thing which I ask of you—that you always act, my darling, in a manner that will make me feel proud of my love for you.

Well, my dear, I'm going to miss the mail unless I stop, and I want you to have this letter tomorrow morning.

My regards to your Aunt Paulina, and for you, all my love.

RODOLFO

P.S. I've had a bad day. By accident I lost my fountain pen, the one of gold which was given me last winter. But I love you with all my heart and these trivial details don't trouble me.

Yes, we were now engaged. But a very strange engagement, indeed.

Espichao bribed Paulina with loads of gifts and promised her that if she helped the marriage along, later she could live with us just as though she were my mother. The idea of such an easy future completely sold her.

The two of them had been something to see as they whispered huddled together in odd corners of the apartment. She'd acted the role of a Celestina to perfection—playing the *grande dame* dressed to the teeth in black, while seriously and soberly making long speeches about the wickedness and false vanity in the world. He became very soulful, worshiping me like a saint on a pedestal. The poor fool!

The two of them pestered me so that I finally gave in and said yes. I didn't set any date for the wedding, and insisted that Espichao had to earn more money first. He redoubled his efforts and worked like one possessed of a fury.

In order to make our engagement more binding he cleverly

introduced me to his family. First he presented me to a cousin of his, an orphan who had grown up with his family and who was like a sister to him. Then I met the cousin's fiancé, for she was about to get married. And finally, in a rather roundabout way, I met his family in Aranjuez.

They were quite pleasant and cordial to me, particularly Charito, his cousin. She was very friendly and often confided in me.

She adored Rodolfo and told me that he was a very fine man, even if he seemed a bit confused. He worried his family with his fondness for being alone, his unsociability and manner of being apart from the world.

She felt that the poor fellow needed a woman who both loved and understood him, and who could make his life a little happier. No doubt she was right, but it just so happened that *she* picked for herself a very handsome man—it would be very pleasant to make someone like that happy. She overlooked the fact that since she was a very pretty girl and dressed well, Espichao would have probably been delighted to console himself with her.

One day, tired of all her advice, I told her this. She became very shocked, saying that they had always loved each other like brother and sister. But I would have liked to have seen her if Espichao hadn't been so ugly! I get a kick out of these people who are always telling others what to do, always holier than thou, pretending their own lives are perfect.

Her fiancé was a very serious boy, a doctor; he was terribly in love with her. Once, for the hell of it, I let him see my legs and breasts, staring at him in my own unique way. He choked a little, but gritted his teeth and looked back at me with both admiration and disgust. After that, he avoided me. He advised Espichao to act like a man and forget me. I was just a piece of somewhat soiled goods. And it's true—I am.

His parents were a rather silly middle-aged couple, of the sort who had had a lot of formal education. The old man was a magistrate. He had a huge white mustache, wore a high, stiff white collar and always went about completely dressed in black. The mother was very pale and delicate and decorated her dresses with too much lace. The old man regarded me suspiciously with his deep, wise eyes . . . much more intelligent than the eyes of his son. The mother was very sentimental and emotional, and always seemed on the verge of swooning. She took me aside and told me how much she loved her son, he was her entire life, and she hoped with all her heart that I would make him happy.

88

I wasn't at all pleased—particularly with the mother and her gushing. Nevertheless, this relationship with such a distinguished family flattered me. I thought about it a great deal, and I realized that at least for a little while it would be a good thing to follow along. Being connected with a family like this would elevate me in the eyes of the world and increase my future value. Few prostitutes have had the opportunity for a wedding like this.

Eight

At about that time I met Perico. I liked him immediately. Unless I'm mistaken, it was Espichao himself who introduced us one night while we were drinking in El Fénix.

Perico was a real Madrilenian—very high spirited and Spanish. He was rather ugly even though he was quite young, not even thirty. He had dark curly hair and was of medium height. He was full of hell, and a great joker—amusing, wild and witty.

He was a captain in the army. His work had something to do with the legal end of it, he defended the military. When he wore his uniform his cap was always tilted rakishly, so much so that more than once his superior officers called him to attention in the street. But perhaps it was also their jealousy and envy at seeing someone as pretty as me next to him.

We quickly became friends, behind Espichao's back. He asked me how I could resist him since he was the laziest man in Madrid.

We immediately made up a story for Espichao, and went away for ten days to the Hotel Atlántico in Cádiz. It brought back memories of my adventurous youth. Even though I was only twenty-three, sometimes I already felt old.

It was a marvelous trip, the kind I like. Perico's car, a D.K.W., already had a lot of mileage on it, and we had punctures, blowouts, and a breakdown of some delicate part, which I don't know much about. When it goes, you've had it and have to have the car towed in.

It took us six days to get to Cádiz and four to come back. In the beginning Espichao was furious. He was very suspicious—there are men who can smell it when they are being cheated—and it took me two days to calm him down. I managed this with the help of my family, who assumed all the blame and helped me out by sending telegrams, according to my instructions, from Mojácar, which is where they were living at the time.

Perico and I spent a very short but pleasant honeymoon in the Hotel Atlántico. We caused so much disturbance with our craziness we were nearly thrown out of the place. He was in love with me, but he was very shrewd and suggested that I marry Espichao, and we could continue seeing each other. One must take men as they come and I quickly saw that Perico would always be an opportunist. Still, he conducted himself rather well toward me, and freely spent his money during the trip. He bought me several pairs of expensive nylons and a very pretty lace blouse. He also gave me fifteen hundred *pesetas* without too much complaining.

When we returned, Espichao was in a terrible temper and very upset about our forthcoming wedding. I was in a bad mood myself and did nothing to relieve his gloominess. Quite the contrary. We fought every day and on the pretext of being sick I managed to go out several times with Perico. Rodolfo then wrote me several letters like the following, which I found in the bottom of the chest and which I am going to copy out here, before burning it in the kitchen stove.

MY DARLING:

You can imagine how you worried me last Monday with the sad news of your being in bed ill again, and suffering so.

Last Tuesday, at five in the afternoon, I sent you a letter by messenger boy from Fuyma, and I was very startled when the boy came back and told me that after ringing your bell for a long time, a neighbor came out and said that you had left at noon, that there was no one in the apartment. I suppose that you had a marvelous time in the country with some worthless man. . . . What have you done, for God's sake, Dolores? What have you done?

That night I went to the garden of Abascal and I didn't see you. God only knows where you were.

I am very sad and very worried. I suffer, Dolores, I suffer. We can't continue this way—I'm being driven crazy.

In spite of everything, I love you more than ever, I will love you eternally, my darling.

RODOLFO

P.S. I'm neither hysterical nor crazy. And I can't believe that you are someone unworthy of my affection.

We went on like this during several days. Espichao went on and on about the spirit and the flesh, always waving his nervous, stubby little arms. Reproaches, demands, even threats, all glided off me. I was lazily indifferent to whatever he said. Occasionally, in the midst of all his heavy-handed mouthings, he would hit the nail on the head, and

I was moved to make a sharp reply. But instead of giving me a good slap, or leaving, he took it all, and became as gentle as a lamb. And they say that one should love this kind of man!

Afterwards, and no doubt at his instigation, his cousin Charito wrote me a letter from Santander which I wish to put down here. I'm not sure whether the girl was confused, or whether perhaps she was so clever that she was trying to tease me. It went like this (actually I've already burned that one also, and thrown the ashes in the garbage):

DEAR MARÍA DOLORES:

I am writing to you now, even though it is something I should have done long before. Please forgive me and understand that one of my many defects and vices is laziness. I always planned to write you "tomorrow." Finally, today, I became determined not to let another day pass.

My dear María Dolores, I would like to chat a bit with you and tell you everything that I am doing, or rather, the little that supposedly occupies me at this time of being completely alone. *He* isn't here. By that short phrase you can understand how empty my life is. I would love to be in Madrid again, talking to you, and having you tell me all the many things which you would undoubtedly like to. Is there something new? I'm referring, as you can guess, to your personal love life.

I know that you are still in Madrid, and will be there for a while longer. I hope that you plan to be there on our wedding day, so that you can celebrate with us. I am enclosing an invitation. I hope to see you there in all your finery, though you don't need anything to make you prettier. Arm in arm with your lover, you will see me say and do that which very soon, God willing, you will say and do. Are you happy, María Dolores? I hope that you will answer me in all sincerity and frankness. You understand that all you do interests me greatly? And Rodolfo? How is he? I received a letter from him a few days ago, and I'm hoping that he and his father can come here for a short visit.

Forgive me, María Dolores, for taking Rodolfo away from you for several days. However, it may be better this way. These little separations show us where our happiness truly lies. They say that we only know someone after losing him. And, after all, isn't this absence a kind of a loss?

Thank God I only had to be apart from Jaime for three days—even that long a separation is unbearable, and I don't believe that you will laugh, if I tell you that I suffer greatly having him away. However, soon he'll be back and this time he'll be joined to me forever.

Send me a reply by return mail, I want to know all about

you. You will make me extremely happy if you give me all the news, telling me absolutely everything that you do—how you're amusing yourself, and whether you're happy.

You understand, María Dolores, that I want you to treat me as a good friend and to write to me as such. Is this asking too much?

Hoping to see you soon. All my love.

CHARO

The invitation was like all wedding invitations, with the names of the parents and the couple engraved on it and the announcement of a reception afterward in a good hotel—this time the Palace.

I didn't go to the wedding. All that sentimentality and fuss disgust me. I quarreled with Espichao, giving him something to think about by telling him that I liked Perico and was going with him to the country the day of the wedding. What was I going to do with all those silly, stuck-up young girls and so-called decent people? Although they're really the worst of the lot. But that's the way it is in this stinking world.

I didn't go and became even more revolted than usual by Espichao, who was feeling sorry for himself and complaining about the bad time I was giving him. He put up with me, though, saying that I must be ill and wasn't responsible for my acts. He even brought me the menu of the wedding breakfast—dedicated to me and signed by the young couple.

It was September, and during the summer heat, I'd become very thin. My poor condition threatened to give me trouble again and the doctor told me that it was imperative that I spend a few days in the sierra.

I told Perico, to test him, but he was broke. So because of that and Paulina's pestering me, I made up again with Espichao. He was wild with joy and immediately made a "plan" for my trip with the same disgusting care and seriousness that he applied to all things.

He made me completely dizzy. First, Cercedilla was the healthiest spot in the sierra, then Miraflores seemed better. The sun set too soon in Cercedilla and there was a cold evening wind which would be bad for my chest. In the end, he finally picked the Hoyo de Manzanares—the Escorial was completely out of the question. But at the last minute he found out that some people he didn't like were spending a few days in the Hoyo and wouldn't let me go.

Weary of all this, I gave him two hours to make up his mind. As his nervous vacillation was increasing, I told him that if he didn't invite me to spend two weeks in the Parador

Ducal, near Las Navas del Marqués, I would consider him a pig and wouldn't have him around me any longer.

Startled, he gave in and I began to pack. During all this, on the pretext of finding me a good room, he took the train to Las Navas to see what kind of people stayed at the Parador. He came back delightedly singing its praise, which led me to believe that the only people who stayed there were newlyweds, hysterical old maids and boring old men.

I tried to change our reservations for La Berzosa, which was gayer, but Espichao got the doctor to say that the Parador was much healthier, since it was high up in the pines. That's when I found out that the vapor from resin wax is good for the chest and that what they say about the smell of manure isn't so. One always learns something, if you pay attention, the way I do.

Finally, after four days of fighting, I arrived with Lirio at the Parador Ducal. I had insisted that she come. I had no intention of being alone there. I told Espichao that it looked better that way. One always has to be careful of one's morals, and prevent scandal, which is the worst sin of all.

He was taken aback at the terrible expense. It was going to cost him an arm and a leg, but finally he decided to give in. His business prevented him from being in the Parador continually with me, and what I said about Lirio made sense. He hoped to come nearly every night and on the holidays. Oh, this was the worst! The thought of being with me for several nights thrilled him. But I would manage to prevent that, and meanwhile I used my head, which isn't slow by any means, and left him filled with desire.

Nine

Our arrival at the Parador created a sensation. I wore a beautiful dress from Balenciaga, of pale pink which suited my complexion and my copper-colored hair. Lirio was nicely fixed up—at least in clothes she knew how to get her money's worth. Poor Espichao in the daylight looked homelier and skinnier than ever. As soon as we arrived I arranged to confide privately to the director that my husband was a marquis, and that he should give us his very best service. I implied that if we were satisfied there would be good tips for everyone.

The director was a strange, rather gloomy little man. He was bald, squinty-eyed, had side whiskers and always dressed in mourning. He walked with his head bowed, looking down at people's feet. After I gave him a hundred *pesetas,* supposedly from Espichao, he deigned to look up as high as my knees.

We were going as a married couple, and Lirio was supposed to be my sister. That night I found myself in a bedroom with two beds together with Espichao. It was tiny as a ship's berth and very pretty. As soon as I got in bed he began to get affectionate and I had to complain of the pains I felt in my ovaries. We couldn't find a hot water bottle and he spent two hours putting warm towels over my stomach.

He was very good to me. Seeing how I suffered, he became tender and swore to me that, come what may, he'd love me forever and I could always count on having him at my side, ready to protect my delicate health. The pain fatigued me so, that when it started to subside, at three in the morning, I fell asleep from exhaustion. He kissed me on the forehead, and went to bed without bothering me any more.

It was noon when I opened up the window and looked out at the terrace of the Parador. Espichao had quietly left the room at nine to make the morning train back to Madrid. He left a note for me, saying that he loved me more than ever and that because of his unselfish affection he hadn't wished to awaken me. Once more he begged me to think of him for at least five minutes during the day and informed me of his return, the following day . . . ugh!

I immediately saw that the guests in the Parador were very well dressed and well mannered, and I was delighted that I had had the foresight to bring two valises filled with pretty clothes, among them a beach outfit from Bastida which I had wangled out of Espichao before leaving.

I put on a very stylish white piqué bathing suit, and over it a beige silk blouse and navy blue shorts. They went well with the blue canvas sandals I had bought in the Casa Cimarra. I combed my long wavy hair in a very flattering style and used hardly any make-up. Only lipstick—a soft shade of cyclamen of Max Factor's, which according to what I've heard, is the brand that the movie stars use. I also lightly sprayed on some Tabac Blond of Caron. I went out of my room and had to walk the full length of the hall to get to Lirio's, who was sleeping like a baby, despite its being one o'clock.

I shook her violently and made her get dressed in a hurry. I was there for the fresh air and I wasn't going to waste the good weather because of her laziness. After she got ready, we went down and took a stroll around the place to see what it was like.

I liked the spot. There was a lovely terrace with fountains, umbrellas and tables where everyone had breakfast, tea, and later apéritifs. They spent a lot of time there playing bridge. And for those who wanted even more rest in the midst of all this tranquillity, there was a wooded park with roads and marvelous two-wheeled carriages. The cement pool was very ugly, but at least it was always filled with fresh clear water. You could also go swimming in the lake, which was very deep, or paddle about in a boat. Near there was a lookout where you could see the whole countryside, and huge pine tree groves which smelled of the resin which the doctor said was so beneficial for my lungs.

After our stroll, Lirio and I went over to the pool. She went into a cabana to change, but I stayed put and took off my shorts and blouse in front of the curious looks of perhaps twenty people of both sexes, who stared at me both with envy and admiration.

After swimming a bit, we sat down by the terrace in our wet bathing suits without bothering to change, and ordered a vermouth. Then, startling the guests even more, we went in our suits directly up to our rooms to get dressed.

I fixed up my face a little, but not too much. I wanted everyone to notice my wonderful complexion. I put on a white eyelet dress, and a stole decorated in blue which I had bought at Brígada's which went very well with my outfit. I changed my sandals for blue and white pumps and carried my plastic pocketbook, which a friend had recently brought from America.

We ate well. The cooking was good, even though I acted very finicky about what was served so that everyone could see that I was used to the best. The dining room was very elegant and naturally we chose a conspicuous table. After finishing the lunch, we sat on the terrace and sipped our coffee. Later we went upstairs to my room to take a siesta.

I woke up around seven, and had a time arousing Lirio, who always slept too much, a habit she picked up when she lived in a house in Ceuta. After I slapped her face with a towel soaked in cold water, I got her out of bed and we discussed what would be the best way to dress at this hour. The little fool stubbornly insisted on putting on a real flashy outfit, thinking no doubt that she was in the Rex or at the bar at the Palace. Naturally I was opposed to this, and I myself wore a simple beige silk print dress which was both gay and yet appropriate for the occasion. My shoes were of red patent leather and I carried a matching bag.

Downstairs we tried imitating the other guests so that we wouldn't do anything wrong. As the two of us couldn't play cards alone, we killed time by taking two "complete teas," which really were very incomplete and tasteless.

Later, as evening fell, everyone paired off in little groups, strolling through the pine grove and along the various paths. I had a quarrel about this with Lirio. I wanted to go for a walk and Lirio refused to budge more than a few steps. I won out, as usual, and we strolled about for half an hour, until she wouldn't go any further and we had to return to the Parador.

We went straight up to our rooms, but I decided to leave on the same clothes. After all we were in the middle of the country and it would look ridiculous to go to dinner dressed as though we were going to the Ritz. So, after fixing up my face a bit for the artificial light—darkening my eyebrows and eyelashes and powdering myself with *rachel*—we went downstairs, and pretended to busy ourselves with the newspapers. Actually, we were observing everything.

The living room was decorated in a rustic style and had a beautiful stone chimney. As the room was empty, we sat down in the best spot and I looked through *Ya*, while Lirio dedicated herself to *ABC*. She liked that newspaper because her boy friend was a very rich monarchist and had won her to his way of thinking—until she met him she had always been very leftist.

We were alone there for what seemed like ages wondering where the devil everyone was, when finally they started to come down, dressed in the most beautiful evening clothes I had ever seen.

Terribly ashamed of appearing ridiculous in my little print dress, I scooted upstairs again with Lirio for another change of clothes.

I put on a black satin gown with a deep, square decolleté, trimmed with some beautifully worked tulle, and stuck on a gold necklace, earrings and all the bracelets and rings I could find.

I combed my hair more carefully, doused myself with Lanvin's Arpège, and slipped into a pair of suède sandals. On seeing my glorious reflection in the mirror, I actually was moved.

But, as usual, Lirio, the little donkey, gave me trouble. She hadn't brought her black velvet, thinking that she wouldn't need it here, and stubbornly refused to go downstairs, saying that none of those fat sows were going to have the chance to laugh at her. She used a few other choice expressions—despite her refined appearance, she had a vile tongue.

96

We fought again and told each other off, until finally with the aid of a maid we arranged Lirio in one of my dresses, a dark chiffon, which could pass without calling too much attention. Because of Lirio's stubbornness, when we went downstairs the guests had already left the dining room.

Ten

By the time Espichao returned the following night, I had thoroughly studied the lay of the land, and knew what was what with the guests staying at the Parador. I immediately became palsy-walsy with a talkative young boy, in order to get information about one man there who interested me. He obviously was taken with me and couldn't take his eyes off me. The young boy rather bitterly informed me that he was a man of many affairs, who had made a fortune selling underwear to the soldiers in one of the army regiments during the war. He was a shrewd operator, and after that deal ran out, he made a pile bringing donkeys from Portugal, passing them across the frontier by night. He owned a knock-out of a Packard—large as a ship and painted a magnificent cherry. His wife was glued to him and didn't leave him for a minute. She knew what was up and kept giving me dirty looks.

The rest of the guests weren't worth while. There were dull, faded aristocrats, fickle and difficult diplomats vacationing with their wives, black marketeers interested only in their money, honeymooners, a stuck-up Viennese blonde who was being kept by a fat and sweaty shopkeeper, and two or three adolescent boys of a bad age—always melancholy and probably suffering with weak lungs—as well as several ordinary families—papas, mamas, children, and grandparents—who didn't count at all.

But the Señor Pastor did count. And a lot. As Espichao said on one of those occasions when his asperity produced some wit, that pastor has turned his calling to good account —in fact thousands of good accounts. I laughed when he told me that during our dinner, while at the same time I flirted discreetly with the man in question. I was worried, though, that Espichao hardly looked very impressive and this might hurt my chances with Pastor. That little fat man was really big game and I was out to get him.

As life is very complex, I was particularly affectionate to Espichao that night. I had taken a fancy to a beautiful outfit I had seen in one of the shops in the village. The pants were deep blue, made out of "California" material and the short-sleeved jacket had a tailored neckline, trimmed with white piqué. A very pretty girl, the daughter of one of the presidents of Cuba, wore one like it during the morning, and I was determined that Espichao should buy it for me. Naturally he gave in. Though it cost me a lot—for every day he revolted me more—I made myself very available that night. When he put his hand on my body, I felt all prickly, as though ants were running over me. And some people say that whores have it easy!

Espichao left the next morning and I went to work on Señor Pastor. I was so successful that in two days he sent me a typed message. It was in the usual style of those damned married men and went more or less like this:

Señorita: Please forgive my boldness, but your friendliness has given me courage. You are a jewel, a most fantastic young woman. I imagine that you've heard this many times before, but I intend repeating it. If you would be willing to go down alone to the lake tomorrow at eight-thirty, I will arrange to meet you there. In anticipation that you will come, I remain your most devoted admirer. . . .

Signed with false initials, as usual.

I knew immediately he was a common type. No educated man would write a strange woman about "her friendliness."

Lirio told me not to get involved, his wife might raise a stink. There is always an element of jealousy in her advice and, anyway, I like being involved. The peaceful life bores me and I decided to keep the appointment on the following day.

Before leaving I took a leisurely bath perfumed with English salts, which are supposed to be very good. I put on a green silk blouse, gray corduroy slacks, a red silk belt, and my green canvas sandals. I arranged my hair carefully, letting a few wispy curls fall casually about my face and made my face up a little, as dusk was coming and the pine grove would be dark.

I gave myself the finishing touches in front of the narrow closet mirror, feeling very satisfied. I saw myself exactly as I wished to appear in the eyes of Señor Pastor. Young and pretty, with a mixture of innocence and audacity. My face and figure were of a perfect romantic beauty, but at the same time what could be guessed at beneath my blouse was capable of arousing the coldest, most jaded of men.

It was already eight-thirty, the hour Señor Pastor had fixed for our rendezvous. I dawdled awhile, chatting with Lirio, who was in a very talkative mood. One must always make a man wait, this arouses his interest. It was almost nine when I finally went down the winding path through the pine grove which after many twists and turns leads to the lake.

The road was more traveled with various groups of guests and excursionists from Las Navas than was convenient for our plans. Still, instead of becoming scared as Lirio would have been, I continued down it, going deeper and deeper into the woods until I came to a small shaded crossing. I stopped there a moment, not knowing which path to follow and thinking that maybe it would be smarter to turn back. But at that moment some branches separated and in between the evergreens appeared the bald, sunburned head of Señor Pastor who, with more agility than one would have expected, leaped out toward me, panting heavily.

"Shhh! Quiet, child, please! They can still hear us," he whispered. "Over here, over here," he kept repeating nervously, taking my hand and leading me along one of the roads which went down below.

I followed him for a minute, but then I told him that I was tired and didn't want to go any further down. I'd just have to climb back up the mountain later.

"Bah! That's nothing," he said scornfully, filled with youthful ardor. "I'll carry you up in my arms if it's necessary."

"You'd get tired," I said coquettishly, "I weigh a hundred and fifteen pounds." I wanted him to know my exact weight.

"No matter what you weighed, my darling, I'd be delighted to carry you," he replied gallantly.

"That's very kind of you, but this will do. . . . Now you have me here, just as you wanted," I said then, coming abruptly to the point.

"Ah, yes, I'm delighted. How about sitting down a moment on this rock? So that we can talk a little."

"There? Ugh! It's full of insects," I fussed.

"Insects?" He laughed. "Don't worry, I'll kill every one of them," he boasted heroically.

Grumblingly I relented and sat down.

It was almost dark, but I felt completely at ease and peaceful. I only regretted that Señor Pastor couldn't see me more clearly, but then I decided that the dusky light was very flattering. In order to excite him I opened another button on my blouse, and leaning close, asked for a match. The effect on him was instantaneous. Señor Pastor's hand trembled with desire while he tried to light my Chesterfield.

I took a good look at him. He was a bald, fat, ugly man of fifty, with big popping eyes and a very unpleasant drooling mouth. Sun bathing hadn't improved him any. Instead of browning evenly the way young people do, his skin had reddened and become blotchy in huge patches, particularly on his bald, dirty head.

"I don't wish to keep you here long," he said, though what he was really afraid of keeping a long time was himself. He was terrified of his wife. "I just want you to know that I'd like us to become friends . . . good friends," he murmured, clumsily stupid.

"You are too impatient," I replied, stalling for time. I wasn't the one in a hurry.

"I think it's natural being next to you to feel . . . shall we say, rather impatient?" His stomach shook with laughter.

"Are you Catalán?"

"Catalán? Yes, why?" he asked, bewildered.

"Oh, nothing. I happen to like Cataláns," I lied. My love is reserved exclusively for Catalán pocketbooks.

"Well, I'm from Tarrasa, *vaya!*" he exclaimed enthusiastically, revealing his accent which up until now he had nervously hidden. "One doesn't have to ask where you're from."

"Where do you think?"

"From the land of our Sainted Maria . . ."

"No, I'm from Ceuta," I added lie upon lie.

"Really?"

"Oh, and how!"

"It's all the same," he broke in impatiently. "Wherever you come from, I'm crazy about you."

"*Hombre,* you don't have to exaggerate so."

"I'm not exaggerating, and you know it."

"So you like me a little?"

"A little?" he protested heatedly. "Since I first saw you I haven't had a moment's rest. And, at my age, that can be very dangerous."

"You talk like an Andalucian. You haven't any southern blood in you, by any chance?"

"Oh, no. You do this to me. You are delicious, you are the woman I've always dreamed about." He tentatively put his arm around my waist.

"Please, keep calm," I warned him, slowly removing his arm. "Unfortunately we both belong to others. And, what's more, you have a very pretty wife."

"Bah! What has that to do with it?" Like all husbands, he knew when to forget he had a family.

"And as for me . . ."

"That man . . . is he your husband?"

"My husband? No, no he isn't my husband. But he's going to be. Very soon, within two months."

"Ah," he breathed more freely. "I think we're going to get along. Unless you are the type who falls in love."

100

"Me . . . in love? Don't make me laugh, *hombre*."

"I'm delighted."

"Indeed you can be, my friend. So far the mother hasn't been born whose son could make me fall in love."

"That's the way I like it, honey," he replied enthusiastically, putting his arm around me again and squeezing me tightly.

"Oh, I can't please you that much . . ." I let him feel the heat of my body close to him for a moment.

"I'm crazy about you," he moaned.

"I can see . . . but, what are you going to tell your wife?"

"Bah, don't worry about that," he bragged as all husbands brag. "But now . . . it's, uh, getting quite late . . ." Worried, he noticed the time. "Maybe we should begin to climb back up? If anyone comes by, I'll hide. You can imagine the fuss if we're seen together."

"As you like," I answered, revolted. All married men are cowards, and even worse ones if they're Cataláns.

We slowly went back up the mountain, and several times I leaned against him, letting his curious hands explore me. But I didn't let him kiss or touch me with his clammy fish face.

Before we got to the top, we heard voices, and he threw himself behind the bushes, frozen with fright. I continued home by myself. We had already agreed that the following day I'd take the morning train to Avila and wait for him in the station. We'd meet there and spend the whole day together.

Lirio was very against the idea. Naturally, she'd have to come with me to keep people from buzzing. She said that his wife would guess everything and would make a terrible scandal, that she seemed like a strong-willed, resolute female. But I persisted and succeeded in convincing her before Espichao arrived on the eleven o'clock train.

Eleven

We missed the ten o'clock train to Avila and it was past one-thirty when we arrived. Señor Pastor was nervously pacing up and down the platform.

He calmed down after seeing how pretty I looked, but wasn't at all pleased to have Lirio along. When they like you a little, how anxious men suddenly become for peace and solitude! All they want to do is to find a secluded spot so that they can make love. They could contain themselves a little more. They know what's coming and they needn't be so heavy-handed about the preambles. "Should we go

101

here, should we go there, what a beautiful night, what a lovely fox cape, what a beautiful moon!"—"How much I love you"—"You're the only woman in my life"—"I'm a very experienced man"—"I've traveled a great deal"—"I'm used to having women fall in love with me"—"No one can fool me, I've been around"—"When I was in Sevilla there was a brunette . . ."—"When I was in Paris there was a blonde . . ."—"I'm crazy about you"—"You must love me, just a little"—"I understand you better than anyone else"—"You're a very intelligent woman and you can see that I'm no ordinary man"—"Come on, honey, be good!"—"Don't be so cold, woman"—"I know I'm not a boy, but because of my experience I know how to enjoy life more"—"Recently, my business affairs haven't gone badly . . ." Et cetera, et cetera ad infinitum, to use one of Espichao's phrases. And always for the same horrible end. Love-making that is as impersonal and dried as a field of cut hay.

"What did you tell your wife?" I asked him maliciously, while we sipped our coffee in the restaurant.

"Tell my wife?" gulped Señor Pastor.

"So that if she guesses, we're prepared," said Lirio. She had no idea how to be discreet.

"Oh, there's nothing to worry about."

"Well, what did you tell her?" I repeated obstinately.

"Nothing. What should I tell her?" he asked arrogantly. "Look, my dear, I live my life. Without giving explanations, do you understand?"

I saw immediately that he was a man dominated by his wife.

She was very pretty and much younger than he. She dressed well and was very proud of herself. She had a rather languid, distant air, slightly weary, which suited her. Her large eyes had a sad, tender look and she seemed to be a rather harmless woman, but Lirio had got it into her head that she was one to be watched.

"What scoundrels you men are!" I said, letting my voice rise.

"Scoundrels? Why?" he asked curiously.

"No reason, *hombre*, no reason."

Señor Pastor had two little girls. I don't know whether he was the real father or not, but anyway the fact remained that he liked to spend the day with them. They were very small and pretty and he was extremely proud of them. Everyone at the Parador fussed over them, exclaiming over each gesture the girls made. So much that it finally got on my nerves.

"They're yours, the two girls, aren't they?" I asked sharply.

"*Caray!* As far as I know." He laughed heartily.

"I didn't mean that. They could be your nieces or . . ."

"Or my granddaughters, is that what you mean? I'm not that old, my darling."

"*Hombre,* no one would take you for forty," I assured him, realizing that my bad humor might rock the boat.

"Forty!" He was agreeably surprised. "Fifty, my love, fifty."

"No, no," I protested heatedly. "It's not possible."

"Well, it's true, I don't show my age," he puffed up. "I try to live well—as well as my many and varied business affairs permit me."

We continued for a while this way. He understood what I was by now. With Lirio along it was impossible to fool anyone. He tried to arrange for the two of us to spend the rest of the afternoon alone together, but I wanted to make good and sure that I had awakened in him a desire for my body—that was the only thing he would want from me—and I spent the whole afternoon dangling him on a string.

We drove in his cherry-colored Packard to Gredos for tea. We stopped to play in the beautiful fields that were around there, near Tormes. I had a good time letting my feet get wet and eating thistles and leeks which grew alongside of the water. I felt very happy, reminded of my carefree gypsy days. So happy, that I felt even a little sorry for the man at my side who no doubt hoped my presence would give him shelter and warmth, making him forget the coldness of his disillusionment and failure in life.

I was quite friendly the rest of the afternoon. And when we returned to Avila, I told Lirio to pretend to be asleep in the car. I went in front with Señor Pastor, and let him become tender with me.

He was tender, and also something plus, but I was in such a generous mood that I even put my head against his shoulder, something I rarely do. Evening fell and I saw the sierras beneath an orange and lemon sky light up in a thousand colors of twilight. I felt again the goodness of the earth. I heard her deep maternal voice, and I felt that maybe someday I'd be leaning against someone else's shoulder—someone still without face or name, someone born out of the hard, honest truth of the earth.

I daydreamed this way during the whole trip, smoking cigarette after cigarette, not even feeling his curious hands on my body. But after he parked the Packard next to the station at Avila and said good-by to me, I came back to my senses and suddenly realized that my life was like a train moving between two false stations. At my side there was

103

Señor Pastor with his silly laugh and his huge, monstrous hands, which suddenly revolted me. And, at the other end was Espichao. I couldn't stand his insufferable love either, or his accursed tenderness and unpleasant capacity for putting up with everything. Everything. Even the terrible bitterness which I felt growing in me. A bitterness born of memory of old hopes—hopes now crushed by the ambitious plans of my life.

Twelve

My affair with Señor Pastor followed the usual pattern—there are few variations in these things. First there was a fierce competition between the two of us to show the other how much we were worth. I boasted of my successes, my beauty and the men I had scorned and who had been driven crazy with longing for me. I also mentioned the great fortune which Espichao, my future husband, possessed. Señor Pastor had a few doubts concerning my forthcoming marriage, but I showed him letters of proof, finally convincing him and winning the first round.

He was proud of his intelligence, his business acumen, his success with women and his physical prowess. He said that he swam, hiked and always lived intensely.

I don't believe one can live intensely. To me all the days seem the same, even though the date and man change. Only with Juan I've felt that marvelous excitement of not knowing what will happen, what the next quarter of an hour will bring. But Juan's an unusual man who often does wild things, completely out of the ordinary, though other times nothing happens. I'm never bored with him and am always tense with anticipation. Fearfully anxious, I feel that at any moment he might strip me, leaving my heart exposed. But he's very thickheaded and I don't think that he has any inkling of this, even though beneath my make-up the color fades from my cheeks and my hands turn cold.

Lirio says that this shameful anxiety which gnaws at me is what all women feel when they surrender themselves to a man. If my heart feels naked, it's because I've stripped my body so many times—that kind of nakedness is no longer nakedness for me, but like a worn-out dress. Bah! Just Lirio's silly nonsense.

Continuing the story of Señor Pastor, I must say that there was no novelty except for the end of the adventure—and that was quite a shock.

I spent some time with him every day, promising a lot,

giving hardly anything but taking plenty—though not as much as I'd hoped. The old bastard was stingy like all rich men.

We went out for lunch at the Escorial, had tea at an inn and even saw the bulls at Salamanca. His huge Packard ate up the roads. He was completely shaken by desire. An unsatisfied desire, being constantly wounded by my disdain. Enough that at his age he could have a woman like me at his side!

I looked marvelous, my skin baked a clear caramel color by the warm sun. This was the envy of the other women who in spite of their best efforts turned either a dull brown or red as a crab. My tan is quite unique. Juan remarked of it that the tones of my skin were mixed and shaded like the works of the great painters. Beneath the light transparent covering of mahogany, as though behind a veil, one could guess at the pinkish mother-of-pearl cast. I didn't understand what he was talking about. I only knew that I was beautiful.

While I was busy seducing Señor Pastor, our simultaneous absences were beginning to be noticed, and particularly his strange detachment with his two little girls. He spent the whole day with his eyes glued on me, following my movements, and became very absent-minded in his affection toward them.

His wife haughtily decided to ignore me completely, even though she had to swallow plenty. People being catty and envious, more than one was delighted to see such a pretty and vain woman as she made constantly ridiculous.

At night I exchanged the nonsense of my middle-aged lover for the cloying tenderness of my young lover, who hadn't yet caught on to anything. I wanted to burn my candle at both ends, but I felt that Espichao was surer game in the long run.

When he stayed on to spend Sunday, I flirted with Señor Pastor only from afar, and appeared to be very tender with my future husband in public—but only in public. I knew he was probably broke from trying to satisfy all my demands.

We spent fifteen days like this. It was fine for me, I gained six pounds and my health improved considerably. Unfortunately Espichao started to complain about the expenses. So much so that I had to make a scene, reminding him that he had always offered me the "peace and tranquillity" necessary for my health. I threw in his face that now, finally, when for the first time in my life I had this and was with him, he had begun to be unpleasant—as if money was of any importance when measured against the true tenderness and happiness which he ought to feel at seeing me so much better!

Because of his nature, he gave in and I continued to stay at the Parador. Later I found out that he sold a stupendous Leica in order to be able to pay the hotel bill, depriving himself of his hobby of taking pictures, which anyway had been a bit of a bore.

With all my little maneuvers, and as the holidays coincided with the weekend, the old man became impatient at always seeing me glued to Espichao during the whole day. He had a disagreement with him about the government. Like all rich men he complained about how things were going, but as Espichao had suffered plenty in Barcelona during the war, everything seemed fine now to him, and he said he hoped that there'd never be anything again like that.

They ended by quarreling. They raised their voices, but went no further, which is what always happens with men of that class. After that, whenever they met they gave each other fierce looks. Men can always smell being cuckolded, and even though my future husband held his peace until his brief vacation was over, he was suspicious.

When Espichao finally left to attend to his client's affairs, the situation eased. I wanted to make Señor Pastor good and hungry for me because I wanted to get a ring out of him that cost ten thousand *pesetas*. I locked myself in my room for a whole day, stretched out on my bed, and read a novel written by a young girl. Espichao had brought it to me and said that it was the talk of all Madrid. I was curious to find out what it was about.

The old man was completely crazy about me and sent me three urgent notes—all typed on the machine and without a signature—until finally I made an appointment with him for the following afternoon at a place deep in the woods, near the lake.

Thirteen

That afternoon I decided to go for a swim in the lake. It was a very hot day, and not even a drop of air moved through the pines.

I wore a blouse of blue pastel silk and dark shorts, and took with me in my straw bag a bathing suit of green satin which cost Espichao seven hundred *pesetas* and gave me a heavenly figure.

The old man was down below, impatiently sucking on an acacia leaf. As soon as he saw me he acted like a wild animal, and told me that he couldn't continue this way and was ready to do anything for me.

"Anything?" I repeated, doubtfully.

"Yes, anything, absolutely anything, my darling."

"Look, my love," I said clearly, "I'm both an expensive and unusual woman. And I'm not willing to share my man with anyone. Do you understand?"

"Yes."

"Would you leave everything for me?"

"Everything, wife, everything," he accepted desperately.

"Even your little girls?" I pressured, trying to test my power.

"Ah . . . no, not that!"

"I see. I guess I don't merit your love, you take me for just anyone. And me, me who's capable of leaving my husband to join you forever, wherever you like."

"I love you, sweetheart, I swear it," he replied, kissing me and pressing me against his bay window. "And I know how to show my affection."

"Then, you'll leave everything to be with me? I'll give up my whole life for you."

"Yes, I'll leave everything," he lied very stupidly. "But don't let me suffer any more, my darling. If you only knew how much I've fallen in love with you in these few days, my angel. . . . I am completely crazy about you, yes, crazy—"

"Be quiet, *hombre*, someone could see us here."

"Let them see," he cried out. "I no longer resist."

"You no longer resist, do you? You think only of yourself. Let's see if you remembered to bring me the thing."

"What thing?"

"You see? You've already forgotten."

"Ah, yes . . . the ring."

"That's it, the ring," I sulked, frowning. "It's a whim, a little desire of mine to have a souvenir from you, of the happy times I've spent at your side. Nothing more. And if you think it's anything else, I'll never mention it again to you," I replied, moving his arm away, feigning annoyance.

"How silly you are. Let's see . . . how much does the ring cost?"

"Oh, hardly anything! It's a steal. Doña Amparo, the owner, is offering me a real bargain. She's had some difficulty . . . you know what I mean? I already gave you her address so that you could see her."

"You know very well that I haven't gone to Madrid during the last few days."

"You could have gone, instead of being so fresh, and staring at me all the time."

"On top of everything . . ." he said peevishly. "You've no idea how I've suffered, my dear."

"You're selfish, you think only of yourself."

"No, no I'm not. I'll prove it. How much does the jewelry cost?"

"I've told you already, sweetheart."

"I really don't remember. Eight, wasn't it?"

"Eight?" I was shocked. "Out of the question. Ten, *hombre*, ten. Even though it's worth more than fifteen. If it weren't that good, I wouldn't even put it on my finger."

"That seems terribly high," he protested. "But I'm not going to spend the day arguing over such nonsense with you. . . ."

"It's not nonsense. . . ."

"I'll give you the money now. Here, take it. I don't like you thinking that I'm stingy." He took out his wallet.

"Do you always carry so much money on you?" I was surprised.

"No, my pretty one." He burst into laughter. "I carry a blank check."

"A check? I prefer hard cash."

"All right then. If you don't want it, nothing."

"That's enough, hand it over. But, if you're fooling me, you'll pay for it," I threatened him. "You wait and see."

"I'm not afraid. I'm not in the habit of playing jokes on people I'm fond of," he replied, becoming very serious as he signed the check.

"I know, love, I know. One only has to look at you to know immediately that you are a gentleman."

"Here it is, take it."

"Thank you, you're an angel."

He threw me the check brusquely. I took it and while I was putting it in my purse I saw that it was from the Banco Hispano Americano, and seemed in order. Then I raised my eyes and looked at Señor Pastor, who was waiting impatiently. And even now, while I am writing, I seem to see him in front of me, with his expensive light gabardine suit and silk shirt, tieless and with his collar unbuttoned. A pigskin belt held up his pants, which were tight on him due to the curve of the stomach below. He wore on his large, flat feet a pair of white buckskins with thick crepe soles, very American, which he had bought in Portugal. He suddenly removed his marvelous smoky sunglasses so that he could see me better.

When he smiled at me and took my hand he looked like

a stupid, grotesque turtle. The motions of his neck looked like the fleshy sack those animals carry beneath their shell. I smiled back, knowing what was coming. It wouldn't be fair to avoid it any longer. I saw by the expression in his round, bulging eyes that he was so impatient he was ready to get his money's worth right then and there.

"Come on . . . let's go for a swim," I said, getting up.

"Swim now? Are you crazy?"

"Why? It's a magnificent day."

"My lunch hasn't been digested yet."

"Naturally, but if you didn't eat so much . . ."

"Come here, next to me, sweetheart."

"First I'm taking a dip. I feel like going in the water. And you shouldn't be so selfish to your little darling," I remarked sweetly.

"We always have to do what you want."

"How about taking a turn in the boat? You'll see how pleased you'll be with me in my new bathing suit."

"You always please me."

"If there's no one about, I'll change in the boat," I promised. "But don't get fresh, eh?"

"That's fine, come on, let's go," he replied, working up more enthusiasm for the program.

We went to the dock. The platform had almost rotted away from the dampness. We untied a small boat, put the oars in, and started to row swiftly away. We both became tired very quickly and I returned to my idea of a swim.

"Hey, hold on to the oars, I'm going to put on my bathing suit."

"I don't know if this is a good spot to bathe. I've heard something about there being very dangerous undergrowth," he warned me, worried.

"Undergrowth—here? What are you talking about?"

"The water looks awfully black, darling."

"No, it's marvelous." I leaned over the edge of the boat and stuck my finger in. *"Anda, hombre,* don't be silly. Come with me."

"I didn't bring my suit."

"That was stupid. Leave on your undershorts, they'll do."

"A fine sight I'd make."

"But the way you swim . . . I can't believe that you'd be so cowardly."

"I assure you I'd jump in, even with my clothes on."

"Really?"

I put on my bathing suit, and while I was changing, he fooled around with me, nearly capsizing the boat. As he was becoming troublesome, I suddenly jumped in the water. After swimming for a while, I called out to him in a tender little voice.

"*Anda,* come on in."

"One always has to do what you want," he repeated.

"My darling, come to your love, so that we can swim together for a while."

"You're impossible! All right . . . I'm coming. But don't watch me undress."

"Scoundrel. You looked at me."

"You are something beautiful, and I'm something ugly."

"All right, I won't look," I promised, taking a short swim away from the boat, not realizing how close I was to never seeing him again in my life.

He must have undressed very quickly, because I suddenly heard a large splash, followed by a great deal of agitation beneath the water. I swam toward him, but couldn't see anything. Finally a desperate hand appeared above the whirling water, and I swam with all my strength. But he didn't come up, he didn't come up!

The dark, turbulent waters continued to swirl about at the spot where he had jumped in, as though a terrible battle were taking place beneath there, a battle of life and death. I swam and swam, finally coming close. And suddenly I understood. I understood and I became frightened. I was scared and stopped swimming any closer. Avoiding the spot where he had gotten caught, I went around and reached the boat from the other side, completely out of breath, my heart pounding away.

After resting in the boat a moment, I rowed nearer. The waters were beginning to quiet down again. I looked down and desperately searched with the oar. Somewhere, in that dark, rippling, gloomy water, I thought I saw a white light imprisoned by the hungry weeds. Poor Señor Pastor's white buckskins.

I was stunned, not knowing what to do. Later, I understood exactly what had happened, and all that could happen. I rowed like a crazy woman toward the dock, sweating from every pore in my anguish.

Back on shore I relaxed and was able to think a little. I returned to the boat to see if I had left anything which could give me away. The kerchief I had worn over my head had fallen into a corner.

I grabbed it, and put everything into my straw bag. Then I pushed the boat out toward the place where Señor Pastor had disappeared. I looked about to see if I had left anything of mine along the bank where we had amused ourselves before going to the dock. I found two cigarette stubs stained

110

with my lipstick and dumped them into my straw bag.

Thinking rapidly, I walked to another part of the shore, far enough away from the spot where it had happened. I sat down and lit a cigarette. I put my things on the ground and started to yell.

Some crows flapped about nervously, and two wild doves flew out, quickly taking shelter in the trees, but no one answered.

I started to scream again. Nothing. Only the birds paid attention.

I quickly but carefully got dressed. The blouse, shorts and sandals. My hair was hardly damp and I put the kerchief back on my head. I kept my bathing suit in the straw bag, made sure that I had the check in my wallet, powdered my nose and put on lipstick. I looked at myself in my mirror. I was the same as usual, maybe my cheeks just a trifle redder and my eyes a little brighter.

I left a handkerchief on the ground, and also threw down a cigarette butt and the pack of Chesterfields. Then I started back up through the pine woods to the Parador, every once in a while letting out a scream.

Finally they heard me. Two boys, probably white-collar workers from Madrid, out with two girls from Las Navas. They were coming down to bathe.

Appearing very flustered, I told them that just as I was going for a swim, I heard a man crying for help from the other side of the lake. There was a boat nearby, but I didn't see anything else, and I was frightened and came up to look for someone to come with me.

We ran down to the dock, and the boys jumped into the water, diving down under at the spot I pointed out. One of the girls remarked that it wouldn't be the first man to drown there, held down by the undergrowth. Two years ago another vacationer had disappeared forever in the lake.

Finally one of the boys, with the help of an oar, found Señor Pastor. But he couldn't move him. Taking on the solemn and protective air that men assume on these grave occasions, they decided to bring us women back up. It wasn't a sight for us to see. Then, with more people, they went down again to bring up the body quickly in case anything could be done.

We climbed up rapidly, and halfway up, I said that I felt very dizzy, no doubt from so much shock and agitation. The boys carried me back to the Parador half-unconscious, delighted to hold me in their arms. When we arrived I fainted, and they brought me to my room. At least I escaped the first round of the fuss that was taking place below.

I locked myself in my room, and found out through Lirio, who went back and forth to spy, that the wife of Señor Pastor hadn't let them take her to the lake. She was lying down in her bedroom, but hadn't shed a single tear yet. Everyone was very excited and waited for me to pull myself together a little, to smother me with questions.

After a while, when it was almost nighttime, through a crack in my window, I saw them bring up Señor Pastor on a stretcher. I shuddered. A few minutes later Lirio came in and said that according to the doctor, Señor Pastor was stone-cold dead.

Lirio and I talked about it for a while, but I didn't tell her anything about the check. You can't trust anyone in this business. She wanted to pack our valises and get out of there immediately. But I decided to wait for Espichao's arrival, which wouldn't be long. When all was said and done, at least he was a man and could help me.

When he came in, I threw myself into his arms and told him that I felt so ill I was afraid that he was going to lose me forever. He was very upset and tenderly asked me to tell him calmly what had happened. He would defend me to the end.

I told him that it was so hot I felt like swimming during the afternoon and had gone down to the water. Lirio, stubbornly refusing to join me, had stayed up, very absorbed in a boudoir novel. Then I repeated in great detail the same story I had told the others about hearing a man cry and rushing back for help.

After I finished Espichao looked at me very seriously.

"Please, sweetheart, tell me the truth," he finally said.

"I swear by the memory of my mother, Dolfo, that everything I've told you is the truth," I lied, feeling on the spot and not willing to trust him either. "I can't imagine that you don't believe your little girl," I said, starting to cry.

"I believe you, I believe you, my darling," he assured me, contrite. He sat on my bed, devouring me with kisses. "But please try to remember everything, I beg you, for your own sake."

"It's the whole truth."

"But, didn't you see him for even a second?"

"No, Dolfo, no."

"And you didn't run into him going down?"

"No, no."

"Then you didn't see Señor Pastor during the whole afternoon, from the time that you left the Parador to go bathing?"

"No," I repeated firmly.

"Well then, don't worry, my darling, I'll take care of

everything. No one will trouble you with any nonsense," he replied, delighted with his role of being the protective male.

He went down to the living room and spent a long time talking to the guests. He was very good at this sort of thing, being a lawyer. But the wife of Señor Pastor insisted that she wanted to speak with me alone.

Frankly, I was scared when I heard what she wanted. But then I thought about it and realized I'd have to leave the Parador the following morning if I wanted to deposit the check in Madrid the next day. It would be better to clear up the situation with her now once and for all so that there wouldn't be any delay. After a lot of backing and filling about the interview, neither of us wanting to go to the other's bedroom, we finally decided to go down to the living room and meet there.

I dressed carefully for our meeting, and went downstairs holding on to Espichao's arm, sighing heavily. I looked very elegant in my black satin dressing gown, which made me appear taller than I was and contrasted nicely with my reddish hair. I leaned delicately back against the sofa, letting my pink silk nightgown show a little.

Señor Pastor's wife came into the living room immediately after me. She came alone, dressed for the afternoon, and without showing any signs of having wept, even though her face looked somewhat distraught. She greeted Espichao and he very politely kissed her hand. She asked him to leave us alone for a minute.

I began to complain about my heart, gripping Espichao's hand nervously. She looked at me with disdain, sat down, and waited without saying a word. I finally understood that she was ready to wait the whole night, next day, and the day after that. She'd wait a lifetime, if necessary, to be able to tell me what she had to tell me. I wanted to be done with it, and I told Espichao that my dizziness had passed away, he didn't have to stay any longer.

"I suppose that you would like me to tell you what happened," I began, making a gesture of fatigue.

"You're entirely wrong," she replied in a deep voice, filled with hate.

"Well then, Señora, I don't understand . . ."

"I have several things to tell *you*."

"If you only knew how terrible I feel."

"You loved him very much, didn't you?" she attacked, laughing unpleasantly.

"I don't understand you."

"Naturally . . . my poor dear . . . you feel so terrible about this!"

"Oh, yes . . . death upsets me very much," I hastily agreed with her.

"Bitch!" she insulted me without raising her voice.

"You are very excited, Señora," I remarked sorrowfully and with great dignity, firmly determined to avoid a fight.

"Very well, we needn't discuss that further," she cut in with a brusque gesture of repugnance.

"Then, what should we discuss?"

"First, you needn't think that you've fooled me. You went out with him, and you were swimming with him this afternoon when . . ."

"Señora, for God's sake, don't talk such foolishness."

"No. . . . No, I don't believe that we will discuss it."

"Then?"

"What I want to know is how much the check is for."

"What? What check?" I stuttered, shocked.

"The blank check which my husband had in his wallet this afternoon when he left the Parador and which you now have carefully hidden away in your room."

"Señora, I can't . . . I can't tolerate—"

"Go on, go on," she repeated disdainfully.

"You are upset by your misfortune and—"

"And you are going to tell me how much it was right this minute," she replied with a sureness which gave me the shivers. "Because it is the price I am going to pay you in order not to call the police."

"The police? I don't understand."

"I don't wish to prolong this conversation unnecessarily. I find you quite revolting, do you understand?"

"I believe you're mistaken, Señora."

"No, I'm not mistaken. We had intended using that check this afternoon, before he left here, and I know that he had it in his wallet. . . . Now, if you want me to advise the bank and call in the police. . . ."

This was getting ugly. My ten thousand *pesetas,* those ten thousand *pesetas* I had worked so hard for, now threatened to evaporate. The bank, the police . . . what a mess!

"If you decide on doing this, Señora . . ." I tested guardedly.

"I am completely decided . . . and . . . I'm in a hurry. I must go back up . . . to be with *him,* you understand?"

"And what guarantee would I have—?"

"That I wouldn't miss the money, which for you must be the principal thing."

"Very well . . . whatever you say, Señora."

114

"How much?"

"Ten."

"Ten thousand? I can't believe it!" She seemed surprised.

"Well, you can believe it, Señora, you can believe it," I replied, highly offended. "And I really don't think it is so much . . . have you taken a good look at me?"

"So much?" She laughed again maliciously. "But it's a pittance. Generally one doesn't make gifts like that for less than fifty thousand. Bah!" she said scornfully, getting up. "He obviously considered you to be of the lowest category. You can keep that bit of charity, with my compliments. After all, it hasn't cost me much—the price of his murder."

She left, stiffly erect, not giving me another look. I hadn't even time to answer her the way she deserved. But later I was glad I hadn't started a fight. We were able to leave the Parador the next morning and I immediately cashed the check at the bank. The miserable business never gave me any further trouble.

Ah, if Señor Pastor hadn't drowned so inopportunely, I would have said plenty to that wife of his, plenty . . . !

Fourteen

After my stay at the Parador, which finally benefited both my health and my pocketbook, even though at the end I had quite a scare, my life became very complicated.

My stepsister, Magdalena, became sick in Mojácar, and, according to my mother, was about to die at any moment. She had had T.B. for quite a while, there was no hope.

Since I had come to Madrid, every month I had sent her about a thousand *pesetas*, depending on how well I was doing. I did this mostly for my mother, the caretaker, who always had been fond of me and treated me well. With this money, plus the work she did for some of the rich people in the town and her income from a herd of goats (which I augmented little by little with my savings), she had been able to take care of herself and her children. That is, until Malena, who had always been even weaker than I, became ill. According to what I was told she was spitting up blood very frequently.

I became very excited when I heard about this and immediately spoke to Perico. I wanted him to drive me in his car to Mojácar to see my family. I didn't want Espichao to come with me. He didn't own a car, and although he was capable of renting a limousine just to be with me, I didn't want him to use up all his money. With this situation coming on, I might need his money for the future. Perico had a car, and the trip wouldn't cost him much.

I talked about this at great length in my apartment, with Lirio and Paulina. Lirio said that my only reason for taking Perico was that I liked him. Paulina was very annoyed, and said that I was going to lose my chance to marry Espichao. Everything they told me rolled like water off a duck's back. I realized that they both were right. But, as poor Señor Pastor (may he rest in peace) said—I always did what I liked.

Perico and I drove off to Mojácar, happy as two larks—we both liked car trips. We stayed at the Hotel Simón in Almería, taking separate rooms with a connecting door. I didn't want to get a bad reputation in my home territory.

My mother seemed very old and careworn. She had always had a difficult existence—during her whole life the poor woman had worked like a horse. The boy was almost grown up and was able to earn a few *pesetas* here and there. But Malena was in terrible shape.

She was a very delicate, frail brunette with a beautiful virginal face, the kind of looks common in Almería. The poor girl had become so emaciated, though, that she looked like a Mater Dolorosa.

My arrival brought forth quite a welcome. My family had always told people that I was in the theater in Madrid to prevent tongues from wagging. Even the mayor introduced himself and offered his services.

Because of that, Malena's illness was heatedly discussed one afternoon in the local café, Casa Bartolo. The mayor, the doctor, the sergeant of the Civil Guard, and the leader and secretary of the Town Hall were all present. The last did most of the talking. The priest didn't go. Apparently he was suspicious of Perico, whom I palmed off as my fiancé. We were supposed to be working together in a picture at the studios in Madrid.

For several hours they went round and round the same subject. The men really were interested in spending some time with me to relieve the horrible dullness of their lives in Mojácar, a gloomy town that could drive you mad. Finally they made a decision. We would take her to Almería to consult a well-known specialist.

We drove the poor girl there, and on the way she started to spit up blood. So much so that even Perico became frightened. After examining her, the specialist gave us little hope, only a change of climate and a prolonged treatment could cure such an advanced case of T.B.

I spoke frankly to Perico and asked him to take us to

Madrid. He agreed, and the three of us came back here. The trip was terrible. As Perico said, a little put out, it certainly was no honeymoon.

But at least Malena arrived in Madrid alive. After letting her rest a few days in my apartment, I took her to the sanatorium at the Ciudad Lineal, where they could give her good care. With the injections, X-rays, etc., it must have cost me at least thirty *duros* a day.

The expense was more than I had figured on, and I was obliged to give the matter some thought. My finances have always been a primary question, which is why people who study the matter say that everything depends on the economy. What they mean is that it's cash that counts in this world.

Before joining Espichao I earned more, about fifteen thousand *pesetas* a month, but had to pay for my own upkeep. I've already said that I was a girl of the first category and could wait nearly every night until a profitable occasion presented itself. All my acquaintances knew that they had to pay me almost for the air I breathed. And if someone came my way who wasn't prepared to meet my price, either they changed their tune in a hurry or I packed them off.

With the money I earned I paid all my expenses—board, doctor, manicurist, masseuse, dressmaker and hairdresser. I also sent a thousand to my family and nearly every month was able to put four or five into my savings account.

When I took up with Espichao I took a loss in terms of hard cash, and during that period I saved very little. However, on the other hand, I became the owner of a well-furnished apartment which could bring me a good return if at some time I wanted to sell it. Also my personal wardrobe had greatly improved. I always had more than ten outfits in use and at least twenty pairs of shoes. And I didn't forget to look after my jewels. If I remember rightly, I had a pair of good bracelets, a pretty necklace and a Longines watch—all of real gold, which I was so crazy about.

Between Espichao and my adventures during the last few months, though my savings didn't increase any, I had become the owner of a lot of valuable things. And, above all, I didn't have to go out every night stalking game, not a very sporting kind of hunt in any case.

No one realizes what you have to put up with: glasses thrown in your face, holes burned in your dress, fights and yelling one minute, whims another minute—in other words, all sorts of insanity. And to top it all, the worry of the Wassermann at the end of every month, and the terrible fear of Neosalvarsan and bismuth hovering over you after each test.

While I was with that stingy bastard Espichao, at least I was able to live as I pleased and spent very little time with the doctor, in spite of my weakness. At that time my illnesses were more theatrics than anything else. When my family saw me they were very impressed, finding me quite filled out. The fresh air at the Parador and the resin from the pine woods of Las Navas had made me much stronger. In fact, I finally became worried about my figure and started to eat less. I couldn't permit myself the luxury of getting fat like those spoiled, complacent females who spend their lives stuffing their bellies.

The six or seven thousand *pesetas* that I got from Espichao directly in cash, apart from the other things he gave me, plus the two or three thousand that I made behind his back, weren't going to be enough. I needed more than four thousand for my sister, four or five for the running of the house, and also something for the other, an old expense I've had since the time I entered as a pupil in that terrible house. It is the thing that I told Juan about the night I was so excited and angry, when I ended up weeping in the Plaza del Progreso.

I don't like to talk about it. I am both angry and ashamed. There are certain things which should remain private, known to yourself and no one else. It amounted to two or three thousand *pesetas* monthly, depending on the state of things. For the present I'm not going to give any further details.

So I had to take money out of the bank. I couldn't cut down on any of these expenses—not the apartment, nor my sister, nor the other, which has always been sacred for me, more sacred than even being able to eat three meals a day. If someone besides Juan should one day find out, they'd say that I was crazy. Let them! But this expense will continue. I swear by the memory of my true mother, the one I have never known.

Certainly—what was it that Juan said when I told him about it that night? I can't quite remember now—but that's a lie, how can anyone forget such things? I won't say that he didn't say anything, I will only tell you that since then, he loves me a little, a little bit. As much as he's able to.

For many years I've known what a man's kiss signifies. A kiss fools one less than words, and even less than acts. A man can say many things, and even do many things, and still be lying, revealing only his outer intention. But a kiss never lies—at least not when it is received as I usually receive them —by which I mean, with my mind on something else.

Juan is a man of almost forty. I know he loves his wife and children a great deal. And in spite of this there are

118

times when he comes near me and kisses my face, thinking only of me. Why? Why will this man, who seems to need nothing, like me?

He isn't in love. No one can get that guy! I know that other pigs of women care more about him than I do, and he always does just as he pleases. I have never been able to make him suffer for me. Then why does he act as if I were something that belongs to him? Something odd and absurd which he both likes and dislikes at the same time; something which surprises him a little, which attracts and amuses him, no doubt. Does he like to play with fire? Then he'd better watch out. Because I'm going to go after him with everything I've got, and when I get him, I'm going to be hard. I'll lead him along as though he were a lapdog, waiting for me at the end of each corner with his tongue hanging out. Dancing like a gentle lamb, while I laugh right in his face. Yes, I absolutely must get him, and then at last he'll see!

Fifteen

My savings had diminished at an alarming rate after I had paid two months' expenses for my sister. The poor girl was so dispirited that I also had to make sure to bring her something good to eat every day to tempt her appetite. I brought filet mignons, pastry and fruit—all things that she liked. I'm not saying that the food at the sanatorium was bad, only that we each have our likes and dislikes and the sick are even fussier.

It couldn't go on that way. However, I'm stubborner than a mule and I was determined that if it were at all possible I was going to see Malena get better.

I explained my situation to Perico. I'll say for him that he's a big storyteller and slightly crazy, but he has a good heart. And at that time he was in love with me.

Perico promised to help me as much as possible, which wasn't much. His advice was not to abandon Espichao, but keep him on the string until I saw how things shaped up. It was good advice, even though it hurt me to realize that Perico wasn't inclined to look after me.

I saw him frequently, juggling his visits with Espichao's, and behind both their backs finding other productive game which permitted me to look after my interests. I didn't have to take even a penny out of the bank.

My life was divided between these two men, my sister, and the other thing, which took up many of my mornings. All my acquaintances were very curious, considering my behavior scandalous. Paulina and Lirio were afraid that in those odd hours I must be seeing some pimp.

Me with a pimp! How revolting! My "pimps" were poor old sick men, men who had lost all their virility a long time ago, human debris we collected in the hospital. There I was known as Señorita Dolores, the good one, the patient one, who not only was content to pay for four permanent beds, but who came nearly every morning to take care of the sick under the orders of Doctor Villalba, more divine than an angel in my starched uniform, and my hair discreetly hidden beneath my white cap.

I hardly used any powder on my face, wore no lipstick and smelled only of soap and cold water. Every morning I took a shower to rid myself of the heat of the bed I had just abandoned, and the odor of a man who was never anything more to me than a passenger in the night.

Several tried to come with me, others tried to follow. But no one was able to find anything out, anything concrete. My constant secret early morning visits cost me many fights, suspicions, and unpleasantness. All my admirers saw behind the mysterious closed door the idiotic face of another man similar to them. Only Juan was able to . . . All right, soon I'm going to tell everything.

Coming back to my private affairs—what woman creates, man destroys. I had managed, with great finesse, to obtain a favorable equilibrium between Espichao and Perico, but then Espichao ruined it by becoming jealous.

I'm not sure if Paulina whispered something into his ear, but it came to a head when he started to press me about the marriage. He was so persistent that I finally became exasperated and told him quite seriously that I liked Perico.

He turned livid and trembled with rage. He didn't want to believe it, but I'm very obstinate and stuck to what I had said. I remember very clearly that we were sitting in the drawing room in my apartment, next to a marvelous electric heater which he had just given me. It's an old house, without central heating, and this was the second winter I'd spent there.

"Dolores, María Dolores, don't play these games with me," he bellowed at me.

"They're not games, Dolfo, I'm telling the truth," I repeated calmly.

"Then you don't love me, Dolores?" He was startled.

"I love you a great deal. You know that by now, but . . ."

"But like a man, a man," he shouted. "I'm talking about whether you love me as a man."

"Let's drop it, Dolfo. You know that I'm very odd."

"What you are is a . . ."

"Say it. Come on, say it," I taunted.

"No, no. I can't say it. I can't even think it," he replied miserably, hiding his twisted face in his hands.

"As far as I'm concerned, you can think whatever you like," I said coldly. "You know by now that I don't hide my life from anyone."

"But—is it possible, Dolores?" he wondered. "Is it possible that you, my future wife, the woman that I love, say these things to me? Come, darling, tell me that I am dreaming. Tell me that you don't feel well, that you are in a nervous state and don't know what you are saying."

"I'm telling you, Dolfo, that I like Perico."

"Dolores!" he threatened, coming closer to me.

"You heard me," I persisted, confronting him with my deep-seated hatred.

"All right, woman, that's enough," he said with a forced smile on his face, abruptly changing his tactics. "That's enough. You wanted to make me a little angry, get back at me for something. Although I really don't know what it is."

"There's nothing," I answered bitterly.

"Stop it! Forget this nonsense. And let's go out to dinner."

"Can't you admit to yourself that I might be in love with someone else?"

"But I thought that—"

"That I was in love with you, isn't that it?"

"Please, Dolores! All this is very upsetting and very ridiculous."

"Well, I've never told you that I loved you the way one should love a man."

"Yes, that's so. But for God's sake, don't get so angry."

"And I allowed your attentions and even your obsession about getting married only because you begged me. No other reason."

"You're driving me crazy. I feel ill, very ill," he murmured mournfully.

"I think you should go get some rest."

"Naturally, after all this. After having crucified me this way, you expect me to rest. Well, I won't be able to shut my eyes the whole night . . . and with the work I have for to-morrow morning . . . it's an incredible nightmare."

"Do you have anything against Perico?" I egged him on.

"Oh, no, not at all," he denied, like all men hiding his dis-like beneath an attitude of dignified impartiality. "In fact, I think he's a nice guy. But not someone I'd ever advise you to take up with."

"Why?"

"You know how he is. A wild one."

"I like that."

"In that case, Dolores," he said, making a tremendous effort, "I'm going. Yes, it's better that I leave."

"You've been very generous with me."

"Bah! It's not worth talking about . . ."

"Then I won't talk about it. . . ."

"Not about that, but there are other things. It's necessary that we have a long talk, María Dolores. I just can't resign myself to losing you this way, in such a miserable manner. And after having spent such marvelous hours together. . . ."

"If you could see how tired I am of this, Dolfo. Come on, drop it for today, will you?"

"As you like. But I won't say 'good-by,' I'll only say 'until tomorrow.' Or better still—'until forever,'" he corrected, making a grand, final tragic gesture. He tried unsuccessfully to leave the room with a firm, energetic step.

As soon as I was alone I started to fix myself up for dinner with Perico. I imagined the awful letter which would be forthcoming. It arrived two hours later, with a boy from Fuyma. It went as follows:

Friend María Dolores:

I have just left you and I've already taken up my pen so that I could feel near you once more. I can't believe that you mean the terrible things you said and I believe that until God calls you to a better life you must have me next to you, so that I can protect you in these frightful moments when your reason seems to leave you.

You are perhaps ill, my precious? I assure you, though, that you've never suffered the way I'm suffering now.

I feel so dispirited, so alone amidst the hurly-burly of life, that I've resigned myself to my bad luck and don't reproach you for anything. You know very well that I want your happiness, and if you think you'll find it at the side of this man, I must accept your decision.

The man you've chosen can make you happy, and I've nothing to say against him. To the contrary, he seems to be a nice fellow and I believe he has the necessary qualities to bring a woman joy. You deserve this happiness, despite what this evil world might think.

Don't worry about me. My life will be a real hell, but I hope I have sufficient strength to endure it courageously.

I must ask you one thing: you must allow me to see you tomorrow in order to bring you what I have of yours and take leave of you, which is apparently what you desire.

For the last time, permit me to say that I still love you as though it were the first day.

RODOLFO

The following morning, I received another note:

My DARLING:

Don't misunderstand last night's letter. I was beside myself with grief.

No, I can't abandon you. No, no, never . . . Because you are ill, very ill, María Dolores, and you need someone at your side to care for you, someone who loves you. I believe I'm the only one who has this true affection for you, despite your many conquests, and even though you don't seem interested in my love.

The men who surround you only use you as a pleasant, pretty pawn. And your girl friends dislike you, gnawed by jealousy. Only I love you truly and unselfishly, Dolores. Only I can withstand your nervous attacks, your apparent cruelty —because I realize that you've been wounded and are ill. Because I love you.

This is why I believe the first, most important thing is to calm your terrible nervous state. This is why you must permit me to be at your side, like a brother, without any other hopes on my part, or compromise on yours. You must allow me to look after you as you should be looked after. My suggestion is that the two of us go to the sierra, to the Alpine Club, or any other healthy spot where you can regain your strength. I must warn you, Dolores, you are thinner and paler than ever, and I fear that it's come to the point where your health might be tragically ruined forever.

You could stay in comfort at whichever of these places you choose—until you're feeling better. Once you're stronger, away from this inferno of Madrid which has caused you so much harm, all alone and without anyone else's influence, *you can let your heart speak freely to you,* and then with more sureness decide which of the two—he or I—deserves your love.

For my part, I will consider myself still bound to you until you've reached a definite decision. You realize, of course, that my earnings, thanks to the good Lord, are increasing and that I can offer you the life of peace and tranquillity which you well deserve, making you my wife, united forever in the holy bonds of matrimony.

I realize that people will tell you that all of this is nonsense, that the only worth-while thing in life is to have a good time, and not to be bothered with faith or dreams. But I beg you, when you read this letter, to decide for yourself, keeping in mind your spiritual life. And remember, my darling, remember those unforgettable days we spent together in Salamanca that created such a deep bond between us. We've passed many happy hours together. Many hours that I can never forget. Could you forget them?

123

I continue to offer you my unending love, a home, and all the happiness which you deserve.

As always, your adoring

RODOLFO

P.S. I'm sending you a gift for your "little girl." About the coal for the kitchen, I've looked into the matter carefully and I believe that they're sending it over this afternoon.

The present for my doll was two thousand *pesetas*, which couldn't have come at a better time. As for the happiness he was offering me—why do men persist so with the idea that a girl must be happy just because they are?

No, I'll never marry him. Even if he could buy me all the gold jewelry in the world, all the peace in the world, and all the happiness in the world—I'd still turn him down.

Sixteen

After having had a week's good time with Perico, I permitted Espichao to come back to see me, mostly because of the fuss that Paulina was raising. She was his defender, naturally, since he had bribed her with his gifts and attentions. The old woman insisted that he was the finest, most affectionate of all my friends.

And now that the ice was broken, we started to go out together again occasionally, but without any compromise on my part and without his being allowed to say one word about marriage.

At that time Perico would come for me at the end of the afternoon and we spent nearly every night together in my apartment. Actually, we lived together, although he didn't keep me from my regular life, the way Espichao had done. He didn't give me enough money to pay for everything, though, and I had to find it somewhere else. I didn't mention this much, but I didn't conceal it either. He accepted what was necessary, understanding my situation and the large expenses I had to meet.

On account of this, malicious tongues in Madrid buzzed with the news that I had fallen in with a pimp who was taking the money I had earned with so much sweat and revulsion of my body. I, the "Black-Market Queen" of Madrid!

All these were dirty lies to discredit me. Everyone knows that there is nothing a man hates more than the suspicion that his money is going into the pockets of another, a woman's love being the intermediary.

There was a great deal of this sort of gossip about me but fortunately no one with any brains believed it. Because I wasn't in love with Perico, and, anyway, he always gave me what he could, which was plenty, even though it wasn't enough to cover my needs.

Perico isn't a good-looking fellow, but full of personality and charm. We went out dining or dancing together, and on Sundays we'd drive out to the country. He was supposed to be a military lawyer, the defense counsel in cases involving soldiers or something like that, and whenever he had won something, we went off for a few days in his car.

My life was very complicated. I always spent the mornings with my work, except occasionally when I rested lazily in bed. My body seemed to need the rest after so much activity, and the years weren't passing for nothing. I was going to be twenty-four and even though I was prettier than ever, I would get tired the way I never did when I was younger. I generally ate in my apartment. Everyone knows that in Madrid in the morning, there's no business to be had from men. In the afternoon I went to the beauty parlor, the dressmaker, or chatted with Lirio or Paulina. Occasionally I'd bargain with a shopkeeper over a piece of jewelry or an old man in the Rastro over an antique. Almost every day I'd visit Malena. In the evening Perico or Espichao might come over—Espichao only when he was flush, because each day increased the tariff for him. On other nights there was the mayor of Zamarrón, whom I'd known for a long time, or some other well-heeled customer. Then it would start—the same old business until dawn.

This was my daily life and it didn't leave me much time for myself. But I couldn't complain. Aside from an occasional physical weariness which produced a revulsion for my way of life and a cool cynicism toward the world, I was in pretty good shape. Though I wasn't saving any money, at least I wasn't spending more than I should have. Also, Perico was giving me more money. He had picked up a few good fees, and was more and more taken with me.

But nothing stays on an even keel, not even this new-found peaceful tranquillity of mine. It wasn't the kind of "peace and tranquillity" which Espichao had offered me—but something much gayer, wilder and more fun. Naturally this couldn't last, and the end came over something that I could have expected.

I see now that I hadn't really understood Espichao. I had taken him for an idiot, a meek type willingly resigned to accepting everything and incapable of making trouble. But one must never trust a man, and I made a mistake when I assumed that I knew him.

Every day he seemed worse—thinner, paler and more unhappy. Still he never complained. Stoically grim, he kept his unhappiness to himself. As soon as he saw me and was at my side for a few minutes, he humbly was willing to do anything for me. He even went along with me when I went to meet Perico until Perico found out and forbade me to let him suffer that way.

Sometimes, after a batch of complaining letters from him, I would agree to meet him at the hospital during the visiting time with Malena. I arranged it this way because I couldn't stand being alone with him. Often when I knew he was there I purposely came to the hospital very late, or went out with Perico, the mayor, or some other man, and didn't visit Malena at all until the following day.

Espichao would wait for me until visiting hours were over. He'd chat with Malena, who was very fond of him because he comforted her and even dried her tears when the poor girl cried. She suffered a great deal of pain from her illness. According to Malena there were times when he spoke of his love for me and became so upset that he broke down and wept.

One afternoon I completely forgot that I had told him to meet me there and I took the mayor of Zamarrón along with me to visit Malena. He was an old goat who'd been around lots. I'd completely beguiled him and was trying to talk him into making a business arrangement for my benefit.

Before opening Malena's door I heard Espichao's voice. He was speaking softly and tenderly, the way one does to a child. I admit that I could have gone away and come back alone. But I wanted the mayor to see Malena, so that he could be moved by the sight of the poor weak thing, a mere bag of bones in the bed. Then he'd realize how good-hearted I was and how many expenses I had. And since Espichao was always so meek and put up with everything. . . .

When he saw the mayor come in with me he turned whiter than a sheet. He kept his hand in his pocket when I introduced them and didn't offer it to the other man. The mayor was completely taken aback, his hand foolishly suspended in mid-air. Espichao stood still for a minute, absolutely frozen. He stared at me, angry and wild-eyed, his miserable body trembling with some hidden storm. Without saying a word to a soul, he turned and left, almost running.

The mayor was terribly startled. I told him that Espichao was a crazy admirer of mine whom I'd never paid any attention to. My sister became furious, and with the little strength that she had left, forbade me to bring another man to the hospital while Espichao was visiting her. Then she started to weep. She was in a very nervous state and broke out crying over every little thing.

In order to console her, the mayor from Zamarrón gave her fifty *duros* and told her to get something pretty for herself. But the little idiot refused to take it, and I had to keep it for her until she felt in a better mood. Really, Espichao's ridiculous behavior cost me the afternoon.

Still, of all my boy friends it was Perico who upset Espichao the most. Partly because he himself had introduced us and partly because Perico was young, cheerful and easygoing and knew how to flatter and seduce women. But, make no mistake, he never seduced me with any false flattery.

Espichao preferred not to even mention Perico, but when he did speak about him he placed his poisonous remarks with care—in between compliments and calling him "the chosen one of my heart." Everything he did irritated me and I insisted that I preferred Perico, even though this choice was bad for my own interests.

This is the way my life went along for a while—one suffering on account of me, and the other having a good time with me. Until Perico came to me one morning very upset because he'd gotten in trouble. Some money he couldn't account for had been found in an official dispatch on his table, buried beneath some books.

There was a terrible fuss and I don't remember all the details, but this is more or less the gist of it.

Perico, being an officer in the judge advocate's department, couldn't collect fees from the men he had to defend. He had his own affairs on the side, though, and got paid for his legal services. He was a clever, hard-working fellow, incapable of hurting a fly even though he liked a good time just as much as the rest of us. . . .

One afternoon two ladies came to his office, relatives of a man on trial whom Perico was obliged to defend. He met privately with them in his office to explain the situation. I remember it was a Saturday, because right after they left, Perico and I went to the sierra for the weekend. We had a marvelous time, it snowed and I learned how to ski, though I took a lot of spills.

Perico returned to his office on Monday. As soon as he came in the colonel called and told him that after he left on Saturday, after getting a tip from an anonymous source, they had searched his office and found five thousand *pesetas* on the table beneath some books.

Perico panicked, he swore that he didn't know where the money had come from, pointing out that if they had given it to him, he hardly would have left it there since Saturday.

The colonel didn't want to let the matter drop, and immediately ordered an investigation. Meanwhile, the women pri-

127

vately admitted to Perico that they had left the money on the table, not daring to hand it to him face to face, and assuming he'd find it.

Though they told Perico the truth, they didn't dare confess to the colonel. They were frightened that their relative who was under trial might suffer.

What really drove Perico wild was the anonymous letter that had been sent to the colonel accusing Perico of accepting bribes.

Being a clever guy who never let the grass grow under his feet when there was money to be made, he had made a lot of enemies who gladly saw to it that he was suspended from his job. As for the letter, he was positive that it was Espichao's handiwork. The two of them had worked together for a while before Perico had met me and he knew Perico's habits.

This was very bad for me. Since he was suspended from work, his salary wouldn't be paid until the matter was cleared up. I vented all my fury against Espichao, who as far as I was concerned not only had sent the anonymous letter but had purposely arranged it with the two women so that Perico would be caught with the goods.

Several days later Espichao dared to speak to me in the Abra, and I gave him two healthy slaps right in the middle of the bar, winning the undying admiration of several of the local drunks.

Paulina said that I'd done a terrible thing. One day I might need Espichao, especially with Perico out of a job. And as for the letter—I should realize that I had driven poor Espichao to the end of his rope.

Now I see that she was right. She knew more than I, and I immediately began to miss those shy letters of his and what came with them—earned by the hard sweat of his brow.

Seeing how forlorn I was, Paulina must have said something to him. A few days later I received the following letter:

DEAR MARÍA DOLORES:

I am well aware of your present state and how hard it must be for you. I cannot remain indifferent—when you suffer, I suffer.

I realize that perhaps I am somewhat responsible for your unhappiness but I must explain my feelings to you, which you didn't let me do the last time we met.

I'm aware that momentarily you have placed your faith in a man who is really a fraud. In spite of this I want you to know that I consider myself duty-bound to keep on fighting for our happiness together until the time when the good Lord calls you on to a better life.

Since the other day I've become a different man, completely dispirited and saddened. I've the horrible feeling that suddenly someone I've loved has died. The person I loved most of all in this world—you, María Dolores. And I've never been so unhappy in my whole life. In one cruel blow I've aged twenty years.

Why must you be so mean? You treat me as though I were your worst enemy and although I know I perhaps deserve it, I also know that in life one must be generous and forgiving.

I confess I've been following you these last few days. Last Tuesday I saw you in Casablanca. But I couldn't stand seeing you laugh and dance, I couldn't bear watching your face, your special smile, and I left before the orchestra stopped playing.

It wouldn't have made any difference if I had stayed. Twice you've refused to greet me. On Wednesday I saw you at five twenty-five on the Calle de Sevilla, on the corner by Arlabán. On Thursday I saw you on the Calle de Alcalá at six-ten. Both times you saw me and didn't say hello.

I realize that I deserve all this, and perhaps even worse, but I can't hide from you the fact that you've hurt me very, very much.

I've nothing worth-while to tell you now that my life has lost all interest. I speak to almost no one at the end of the day, and sometimes I feel like screaming—like a man gone crazy.

And you? How are you getting along? I must compliment you on the dress which you wore last Tuesday evening. However, I notice you're wearing your hair in a pompadour again, which doesn't suit you at all. Also, you looked thin and somewhat ill.

Do you have some free time today around six-thirty? If you do, and are willing to chat awhile with a poor old friend of yours, let me know where we can meet.

Even if you don't get in touch with me, I want you to know that I'll be waiting for you every day in El Abra and in Fuyma at three-thirty and seven, respectively. Which means in El Abra at three-thirty and in Fuyma at seven. I'll be there every day, absolutely every day, burning with desire to see you. May God grant me the happiness of seeing you soon!

I thank you in anticipation of our meeting. I love you.

RODOLFO

Why, why the devil did this man always have to call on God when he wanted something from me?

Seventeen

I realized that very soon I'd be in a tight spot. Perico was short of cash and under the constant threat of being sent to Guinea. He hadn't been able to completely clear himself. Once one has been accused, something unpleasant always remains. I continued to have very large expenses, and it seemed wise to make up with Espichao. He was the surest bet of all the men I knew, and I intended to get out of him the little money he had left.

We went out together occasionally, but nothing more than that. I continued to see Perico every day, or, more accurately, every night—he generally stayed in my apartment.

This went on for two months and abruptly came to an end around my twenty-fourth birthday, which was a year ago on March 23. Espichao suddenly realized that he didn't have a penny of his savings left, and I couldn't get another cent out of him.

I began to treat him with disdain and, according to Paulina, was completely merciless toward him. One would have thought that he was her child, the way she protected and cared for him. I did terrible things to him, driving him absolutely crazy.

Brazenly mercenary, I told him that he could neither write to me nor see me until some money was forthcoming. He stormed out, furious, and two weeks passed before I heard from him. Finally he sent a note arranging a meeting at Monterrey. Inside the envelope were three thousand *pesetas*. Last year, in '45, three thousand *pesetas* were still worth something.

We went out together and I was reasonably sweet, and so on, with him.

Then several more days passed without our seeing each other, until another letter came arranging another meeting and with four thousand *pesetas* in the envelope. We went out again, and this time I was extremely tender toward him.

This went on three or four times, and though I tried hard, I couldn't find out where the money was coming from. He seemed to be in a terrible state, very jumpy and always giving me deep, stormy looks that were frightening. I was disturbed over his refusal to confide in me and I told Lirio and Paulina that Espichao must be in some difficulty. That mysterious money really smelled bad to me.

And just as bad as I smelled. As though of my own odor! One night while putting my jewelry away in the case I noticed that several things were missing.

Now before I met Juan I always went out decked in all my jewelry, glittering like a Christmas tree. After Juan came along he convinced me that the result was very common, real ladies don't show off like that.

At that time I'd recently been given a pair of diamond earrings and a new ring, and much as I would have liked to, I couldn't wear everything. I put aside several pieces and locked them away in a box in the closet, forgetting about them for several weeks.

I'm always very careful about my possessions. When I go out I never let go of my bag. When I undress, no matter where I am or with whom, I always knot my jewelry in my handkerchief and keep it well within reach. I put it either on the night table, or beneath the mattress, or under the pillow—I never trust anyone. I was even suspicious of Juan. He'd get furious watching my nightly ritual and one time he stole my handkerchief, letting me squirm awhile as punishment for my lack of trust.

Getting back to this business about the jewelry, one afternoon I felt like wearing the diamond earrings and I went to get them out of the case where I kept everything locked up.

The case was in its proper place, but empty. Completely empty. Even some costume jewelry with paste emeralds worth almost nothing was gone.

I was stunned. Finally I pulled myself together and quietly locked the case. I didn't breathe a word to a soul—the thief was obviously someone close to me. The following day I made an appointment with Espichao.

He took me to the Club Avenida. We sat down in a quiet corner and I immediately attacked him.

"You're despicable, you're a thief, Dolfo. One could hardly believe that you come from a good family."

"What are you saying? Have you gone out of your mind?"

"I warn you you're going to pay me back with interest, down to the last penny," I swore at him. "If not, by the sacred memory of my mother, I promise that—"

"I don't know what you're talking about, and I don't like being insulted."

"Insulted? That's nothing, *hombre*. You just wait . . ."

"You are everything to me, María Dolores, I love you more than anything in the world. But this doesn't give you the right to mistreat me."

"With what you've done, eh? Well, I'm going to report you to the police. They can cart you off to prison for all I care."

"Me? Cart me off to prison? You must realize, my darling, that I'm known to be a man of honor. My reputation is not at the mercy of the words of an ordinary—"

131

"An ordinary what? I'll slap your mouth, right here, Dolfo. You're too damned fresh."

"You oblige me to be."

"The only thing I oblige you to do is to return everything that you've robbed from me within the next twenty-four hours. The bracelet, earrings, ruby ring and even the costume jewelry. Absolutely everything, do you understand? And now I'm going—I don't want to see your lousy face any longer." I got up abruptly and left, leaving him huddled in the corner.

The next day he confessed, but didn't return the jewelry. He said it was Paulina's fault. She brought him the jewelry to sell, saying that it belonged to her. But I wasn't fooled. I realized that both of them were in it together. He did it, the rat, so that he could keep me with my own money—she, so that she could have something saved. She realized that her future was uncertain now that I wasn't going to marry her protégé.

After giving her a tongue-lashing, I threw her out in the street. As for Espichao—he had one week in which to bring me fifteen thousand *pesetas* if he couldn't get back the jewelry which had been sold already.

He didn't seem very certain of himself, and knowing that he was broke, I went directly to see his father, a senior magistrate. We had already met in Aranjuez during the time when Rodolfo and I were supposed to be engaged.

He received me in the court chambers. He was quite a big wheel there, and presided over one of the courts. This struck me as odd, I hadn't known that each court has someone in charge. He obviously had a lot of power, the way all the young clerks hovered over him. One of them ushered me into his huge gloomy office. It frightened me with its magnificence.

Don Narciso, Espichao's father, rose from his large leather armchair as soon as he saw me. He greeted me rather arrogantly, with a minimum of polite courtesy, and neither shook my hand nor came toward me. Abruptly he waved his right hand, indicating that I sit down opposite him, his great desk between us.

The light shone in my face. It poured in from a high window in front of me. But the old man's head was obscured in shadow. I could barely make out the white outline of his drooping mustache or the sharp, blue penetrating light of his eyes. He stared at me, filled with both curiosity and disgust.

"You want to talk to me, Señorita?"

"Well, it's like this, Don Narciso," I started nervously. "I want to talk to you about your son, Rodolfo. . . . I'm not sure if you remember me, but—"

"Now, really . . ."

132

"I . . . I was his fiancée when I met you."

"Yes, I remember perfectly. Absolutely perfectly. Now, tell me, what have you been since?"

"Since? I don't understand, Don Narciso."

"What I mean is . . . what relationship have you now with Rodolfo?"

"Uh . . . oh, you know very well that he wants to marry me!" I replied, a little put out.

"I understand exactly. Humph! You're his sweetheart. That's what weak men always call their girl friends. And my son is of the weak variety. But you must know that better than I, right, my girl?" He laughed dryly.

"Oh, say anything you like about me," I replied angrily. "But there are some things that you don't know about your son."

I realized that I had to take care with this old man. Small and thin like his son, he concealed beneath his respectable and learned façade a wicked craftiness and cunning, assuming a pose of scornful haughtiness. In his starched white collar and black tie and suit, he reminded me of a bat. A bat who attacks unsuspecting birds in the night, and sucks out their warm fresh blood.

"Oh, I doubt that, my girl, I doubt that," he replied, toying with a white marble paperweight which was still not as pale as his fingers. "I know Rodolfo very well."

"Do you know that your son has robbed me?" I exploded.

"Now, now . . ."

"You don't believe me, Don Narciso?"

"Young people have such lively imaginations. And you are very young . . . and very pretty. So pretty that you deserve to have something robbed from you," he finished. The sly inclination of his head didn't suit me at all.

"Thank you. But right now I'm not referring to that sort of thing."

"Go ahead . . ."

"Rodolfo stole some jewelry from me . . . in my own home!"

"You must have proof in order to make such a grave accusation. Because if you didn't have, my girl," he continued in his sibilant voice, whistling through his false teeth, "I repeat, if you didn't have proof . . . it would be a serious mistake on your part and could cause irreparable damage to your future peace of mind. . . ."

"Actually, a dishonest old woman who was in my employ stole them from me. But the two of them planned it together."

"Go on . . ." he murmured.

133

"Your son confessed the theft and I—"

"You are ready to do anything, my girl, isn't that it?"

"Well, yes. But very regretfully. . . ."

"You are a very courageous young woman. I didn't believe that the women of today had so much nerve." He looked at me with a cold smile that scared the wits out of me.

"I don't know what you mean, Don Narciso."

"Young lady, I think you should pursue the matter. Make a complaint, initiate proceedings against him," he laughed, mocking me. "Life is so boring for us old people, so monotonous, I find this very amusing, very diverting."

"I hope you do realize that I'm following this through," I replied angrily. "And that your son has asked my pardon."

"Now, now there."

"But I had wanted to avoid the scandal, I had hoped to make an arrangement."

"With me? Humph! I'm a poor old tired man, very used up, and in spite of your appetizing beauty I doubt whether I could—"

"Enough of your jokes, Don Narciso. I wish to inform you that I've asked Rodolfo to give me back the fifteen thousand *pesetas*."

"Lovely sum, young lady, lovely sum."

"Bah! It's hardly anything."

"Maybe for you. But for a poor magistrate like myself it's hardly insignificant."

"If I don't get it soon, then . . . then, I'll denounce him to the police, much as I regret it, Don Narciso, because I don't like scandals."

"But I love them, young lady. I'm wild about them," he went on cynically.

"Very well. I see I'm getting nowhere with you. In view of this, I'll leave you to your own affairs."

"To my own boring affairs," he said sorrowfully. "I'm sorry that you have to leave so soon. But come back, come back whenever you like. I find you very intelligent and pleasant to talk to." He pressed the bell, calling in a clerk. "Roque, accompany this young lady and see that she doesn't go astray. She doesn't know her way through here." A smile broadened his face, making him look like a rabbit. He nodded his head slightly toward me. Our interview was over.

I left in a rage and immediately sent a note to Espichao threatening to cause a scandal if he didn't return the jewels or bring me the money. Lirio warned me that I wasn't going about it the right way, she said that my threats would get me nowhere. His father had the power to bend justice in the direction that suited him, and it would be I who would end up paying for the damages. She said that I should be soft and tender with Espichao. He was a pushover for the sentimental, romantic treatment, and that's the way I'd get the money out of him. As Lirio said, you have to act differently with each man, according to what works best with him.

Eighteen

I'm getting sick and tired of writing about Espichao. I want to finish the whole business in one fell blow, which was the way it really ended for me.

I didn't get the fifteen thousand *pesetas* out of him. After a great deal of patience and a few tender tears, I got ten, much more than the value of the stolen jewels.

He didn't give it to me at one time, but little by little, always accompanied by long, complaining letters that got under my skin. Except the last, which was very short. It was typed, had neither date, place nor signature and went as follows:

MY DEAR FRIEND:
My difficulties in settling my affairs with you continue, despite my fervent desire to terminate this lamentable business. Nevertheless, I'm sending you one thousand eight hundred *pesetas* (1,800 *ptas.*) which together with the eight thousand two hundred *pesetas* (8,200 *ptas.*) make a total of ten thousand *pesetas* (10,000 *ptas.*).

I find myself gravely ill. My nerves are shot, and I'm now in a sanatorium, where a friend of mine has kindly undertaken to write this down for me. I myself no longer have the strength.

If you ever have occasion to think of your poor old friend who is dying, and if your many occupations permit you to leave Madrid, a visit from you would make me very happy.
                                        Fondest regards.

I suppose that the business of the sanatorium was a lie and that he wanted to make himself interesting in my eyes. He had disappeared from Madrid for several months and there were rumors that he had entered a monastery, broken up by my rejection.

This romantic interpretation suited my interests and I always maintained that it was so. The truth is that I never was sure, since I never spoke to him again. Months later, after our separation, I saw him in the distance, hurriedly crossing some street, hanging, like a monkey from a palm tree, on the arm of a female as ugly and deformed as he.

Nineteen

Perico was very worried. The affair of the five thousand *pesetas* hadn't been cleared up and he was still afraid of being sent to Guinea. It's a tropical spot, and I would have been delighted to go along. Unfortunately, I ran into some unpleasantness with Perico first.

What happened hurt me very much. We had practically been living together, he ordered people about in my apartment as though he were the lord and master. Naturally, I'm goodhearted and didn't take from him what I did from the rest. I knew he had nothing.

He made himself completely at home in my place and while he was there I never brought up another man. Lirio, and Basi, a maid I hired after throwing out Paulina, despised Perico. They felt that his presence prevented me from earning all the money which my beauty merited.

One night Lirio came home and told me that Perico went out with other women when he wasn't with me. It seemed absurd, so I paid no attention. But the gossip and rumors continued and I finally became angry. I've never tolerated a man who went out with others while living with me. If he could have at his side the most beautiful woman in Madrid, which is the same as saying in all of Spain, why should he lose both time and reputation with some ugly bitch. If he persists in taking them out, he's going to be minus one Lolita. I've always maintained this position, and always will. Of course, someone like Lirio is more easygoing about these things. She says that the same thing happens between men and women in our field as happens with their legitimate mates. After they've been with us a while they tire, and want novelty, even if it means going out with someone worse. Maybe this is the way Lirio has to live, but I'm a great beauty and don't have to put up with such insults.

Perico burst out laughing at my suspicions. He swore that I was the only woman in his life. Reluctantly he admitted that he occasionally went out on a spree with some others, not as pretty as I. But because of my threats he promised not to do it again.

I trusted him about this. I've always trusted men when it came to other women. Why should they want to go out with some other woman who wasn't even good enough to wipe my feet? Everything was fine until the night Lirio came home all excited, telling me that she had seen Perico in Pasapoga making love to another woman.

I had stayed in bed that day, since I was rather unwell. Perico had gone out in the afternoon, kissing me good-by, full of his usual tender nonsense. Determined to prove once and for all the unfaithfulness which was no doubt amusing all my enemies, I quickly threw on a dress. I ran all the way to Pasapoga, the sparks flying. I was going to catch him red-handed, with his hands on some ugly lump of female flesh.

"*Vaya, vaya*, Lolita! You seem to be spitting fire tonight," Juanito, the doorman, remarked, amused at my hurry. In my impatience I got twisted in the damned curtain which divided the stairway. More than one drunk's broken his head that way.

"Someone's going to sure as hell leave here tonight spitting blood," I answered, putting back on my shoe which had fallen off when I tripped.

"Don't get so excited," Juanito laughed.

I went up to the first floor where several couples were secretly dancing. Perico wasn't there. I continued up to the salon, and couldn't find him there, either. It was difficult to see. They were playing "Brasil" and had dimmed the lights.

I was in a hurry and knew that I had to catch him quickly. Lirio had followed me, and being scared, had told the head-waiter and doorman that I was out for blood. I gave a quick look at the bar, and came back to the salon, pushing my way through the couples on the floor. I saw my reflection in a mirror and was very pleased. My face was freshly washed and my hair was loosely tied back with a ribbon. I looked beautiful.

Finally I found Perico. He was hidden behind a column, buried in a sofa making love to a fat, shameless brunette who was all breasts.

I went toward them. As soon as he saw me, Perico stood up, frightened.

"Take it easy now, Lola, for Christ's sake," he begged, knowing my nature.

But all hell broke loose. I gave her a swift kick and left my mark on Perico's face with a kitchen knife I'd brought along in my purse. The two of them knocked me down to the floor, and even though his face was dripping with blood Perico didn't lay a hand on me. He just left me lying there while he marched off with his girl friend.

She was an enormous greasy female who only attracted men because of her breasts. Which goes to show there's no justice in this world.

Twenty

That's when Perico went off to Bilbao, leaving me alone in Madrid. Alone, that is, in a manner of speaking—I've never lacked for a man. Anyway, the solitude gave me time to think about things.

I took Lirio's and Basi's advice—after all, they had my interests at heart—and decided to take advantage of my freedom and not get stuck again with another man, unless he was very rich.

I went back to my old routine of going out at night, which, believe me, isn't easy. During the morning I attended to my private business with the sick. Afternoons I went to see Malena, who was very ill and spitting blood, and the evenings, well, the usual hunt. It was on one of these nights— maybe April or May last year—when I met Juan. I've gone into that before, and it seems to me that Juan already occupies more space than he's worth in this book. Recently, just as I promised myself, I've done everything I could to draw him to me, hold him, completely captivate him, and make him suffer—yes, suffer—like so many others. But it's no use. The man does what he likes and goes where he pleases, and I can't change him.

But what does he do? What does he want? What does he seek in me? I don't understand him and I'm afraid I never will. I nicknamed him the "Mysterious One" when I first met him. Later I also called him "The Hebrew," as he has large, beautiful, melancholy eyes. Now I call him Juan even though I'm not sure that's his real name. I've never discovered his last name. According to him, the car he drives is in someone else's name. We don't go out often together, and when we do we've never met anyone who knows him. Or at least, if he does bump into a friend he pretends he doesn't know him.

Since our first meeting in the Casablanca, when we argued so over our financial arrangements, I've only seen him there two or three times, generally alone. One night I went to Villa Rosa with my Asturian black marketeer, and to my chagrin he was sitting at the next table, with a beautiful foreigner, a very elegant woman whom no one knew. I know he spent the entire evening staring at me, with my breasts right under his nose, even though he pretended not to pay any attention. I went to the ladies' room, hoping he'd follow, but he didn't budge. Furious, I went back and started to dance with my Asturian friend, stopping almost directly in front of his table. He ignored me and kept right on smiling at his companion.

It was a miserable evening. I was enraged at seeing him

138

with a lovely creature and me with the ugliest monkey that Asturias had ever produced. But what can you do in this lousy life?

Sometimes I even become bored with my writing. If he doesn't love me the way I tried to make him do, why am I wasting my time on this nonsense? It's not as if the whole point of the thing is to please him!

The other day I threatened to stop writing and he said, okay, stop; but so much the worse for me. Because one day my life would be over, and there I'd be, stiff as a board, and no one would remember who I was. But if, instead, I put down everything here, later he'd see to it that it was published. My life would be preserved for the admiration of the centuries. Recently he's been pestering me about a number of things, particularly the subject of my mornings, which is another reason why I've lost my taste for going on with this.

Whenever he mentions this, I jump. He's very stubborn about wanting me to write about the good part of my life, which, God knows, I hate doing. There are *some* things which should be personal. Also, it makes me blush when I have to mention what I do in the hospital. I feel as though I'm doing something wrong in writing it down. That's why I'm so secretive about it, because I'm ashamed. Lola—the well-paid Lola—Lola interested only in herself suddenly interested in miserable sick old men. Ridiculous! Also, there's Doctor Villalba, Father Pablo and the patients—what would they say if they knew the truth about their Lola?

I really don't understand why the devil Juan wants me to write about my hobby. People are never interested in good, only evil is entertaining. And if I've indulged myself and pay for the beds and tend to the sick old men, it's only because I've had this mania since I was a child, and now I've the money to satisfy my desire.

When I was in the orphanage at Almería the Mother Superior always took me with her on the hospital rounds. I like the sick and I like the old. And when they are both ill and old at once, I like them even better.

When I look after them I feel good, a kind of happiness warms my insides. I like putting my hand on their wrinkled foreheads, shriveled from life's difficult journey. I like grasping their trembling hands, which shake like frightened birds unable to fly. I tell them stories I make up on the spur of the moment, silly things I've never told anyone else. Cheerful stories with happy endings about people in love.

One morning Juan came with me. It was shortly after that silly night which ended with me weeping in the Plaza del Progreso. He started to pester me and I finally promised to bring him with me. I said that he was my brother. I didn't want to hear the word "boy friend," or anything like it, mentioned in the hospital.

The hospital is in the outskirts of Madrid (exactly where, it doesn't matter). The building is small, with a pretty little garden around it, very well cared for. Actually, it's a rather special place, and was formed by several rather unusual people who contribute to its upkeep. It doesn't look like a hospital, but more like a rest home for convalescents. There are lots of those in the neighborhood. Everyone in Madrid is always convalescing from something.

My room has four beds and is used exclusively for sick old men. (Never sick old women!) I see to it that it's always kept clean as a whistle. Even though there are several nurses in the hospital besides the two doctors and the chaplain, I spend my mornings caring for the patients. I've always had good hands for giving injections, catheterizing the bladder, washing out the stomach, and cleansing all sorts of infections.

Juan swore by his children never to breathe a word of this to anyone as long as I live—afterwards I don't care what happens. He also promised not to cause me any complications with his infernal curiosity.

Up until now, I must admit, he's kept his word. On that particular morning he walked behind me very seriously and quietly, solemnly nodding at the patients and not murmuring a word while I went about my daily routine. It must have been most appetizing, as Don Paquito, an old wreck of eighty, was in his final throes and in his agony kept vomiting on the sheet.

It bothered me that Juan saw me this way. I felt that he'd lose the illusions he had about my beauty. He was a man who never liked seeing me in daylight or without make-up, and there were many times when he even made me remain still, not allowing me to open my mouth, so that he could contemplate me better. That's when I used to feel like smashing his face. I'm not one of those paintings he admires so much, but a woman of flesh and blood, and, what's more, very alive and kicking.

I watched him angrily while I took care of Pildorillas, another patient, who always had his fingers in his nose, and who had had one arm recently amputated. The wound was frightening to see. It was an enormous open gash, the living flesh a fiery and angry red. I realized that Juan was forcing himself to bear up, so that he wouldn't appear weaker than I. His face was greener than an olive and he sweated like a pig until it was over.

I gloated a little over his discomfort because he often drives me wild with his obsession about beauty. I let him watch all that filth until he couldn't take it any longer and had to go out in the garden to wait for me. "So as not to create a disturbance during your kind ministrations," he said with his customary sharp tongue. When I saw him leave, filling the doorway with his tall, gangling body, I was afraid I'd lost him. He'd never forget the shameful sight.

No, he never has. But he has continued to see me, even though occasionally he stares at me in a very odd way. He seems to be remembering something, searching for something. His eyes go right through me. No one has ever done this to me, and I don't like it at all. Many times I have absolutely disintegrated—me, the girl whom no man has ever made blush.

Then the mood passes and he treats me in his usual manner. Which is to say, making me feel breathless with anticipation, as though something fantastic and earth-shaking were about to happen any moment. Something thrilling which will change the course of my life, the sort of thing which happens in movies and novels. Naturally, nothing ever does happen. He very nicely says good-by to me, and once more goes his own way for a long time. I see very little of him, and I realize that if he had me around more he'd tire of me.

Until now I've known how to hold all kinds of men. Some are drawn to me by their vanity, the contented pride they feel at going out with a beautiful woman. Others are moved by desire, their lust to possess me for a few minutes. And occasionally there is the world-weary type who's made a mess of his life and likes to sit with a whisky and have something that makes him forget his worries. But I don't know why Juan is drawn to me. He has a wife, children, his illusions, his work, he isn't perverted, he can amuse himself without spending money, he is very intelligent, and . . . no beautiful woman would ever refuse him.

No, I really don't know. And this ignorance gnaws at me, making me desperate.

Twenty-one

Soon after I met Juan I ran into some serious trouble. During the summer days, or, more accurately, summer nights, some friends organized a little group which met in the apartment of two girls I knew. There were four men, and I became friendly with one of them, a rich procurer.

I didn't like him at all, but I kept him in reserve the way

I often did for the dry days one inevitably runs into. He was middle-aged, balding and fat. He was also boastful and pompous.

I really think, though, that to describe the way people look is pointless. There are so many men and women in this world who look alike that these descriptions never give an idea of how people really are, inside. That's why I generally pay little attention to people's looks, and only notice the impression that remains after they've left. What I feel when I bring them up to my mind. "Recalling," Juan says. He lacks my charm of speech.

Whenever I recall the procurer, I think of something unpleasantly sticky and sweet, like the aftertaste of candy, or cheap perfume. Something excessively sugary and minus seasoning.

I like to daydream about seeing that fat lump of flesh slowly falling apart in a bath of some sharp acid. How I hate him with his languid fish-eyes and know-it-all air! He is so puffed up with phony self-importance, imagining his stupid boring monologues to be filled with all sorts of weighty significance.

But he makes a lot of money, and though Juan insists that underneath his fancy exterior he's just another poor slob, his friendship is useful to me. But it gives me gooseflesh to have to sleep with him.

The procurer—whose name I won't mention as he's well known among Madrilenians for starting lawsuits—was rather insistent that I go with him to a private party in an apartment. I myself am not fond of those little sprees—they're never very profitable and they bore me to tears. He even called for me at my apartment, which made me very suspicious of what was involved. I'd never seen him so polite and courteous.

In view of that, I emphatically refused to go, telling him I was after a millionaire, and it might hurt my interests if I went. He promised that not a soul would know what went on there and offered me two thousand *pesetas* if I'd come. Finally we settled for three.

He told me to wear my prettiest dress and fix myself up as elegantly as possible. He was going to present me as his fiancée, and not just as someone he had picked up. He warned me to accept graciously the advances of a certain lawyer who had been on my trail ever since he'd seen me dancing one night in Pasapoga.

After I learned the part I was going to play in the evening's program I was ready to ask another thousand, but I resisted the temptation. He deserved being asked, though. One has to have a lot of strength to forego my charms and

142

merely be the intermediary, with me so near and so beautiful.

But as I wasn't having any effect on him, I got there at the agreed hour. Looking like a princess in my low-cut black velvet gown, a new model of Rodriguez's, I was out to place the biggest horns that the procurer's smooth bald head would take. That would show him!

The orgy was taking place in the apartment of the two girls, friends of the men. Two pigs who worked in an insurance agency—an agency that could guarantee everything except the virginity of their employees!

The third woman—we were four all together—caught my attention. Perhaps she was just one of us, but she certainly put on a good front. She was marvelously dressed, with simple elegance, and moved and ate in a charmingly graceful manner. I always notice how people eat. I, myself, am still learning, and sometimes my head gets too close to the plate when I want to scoop up the sauce from the squid. Juan tells me to lean back if I don't want the waiters to realize what I am. At first I got very angry when he criticized me, but now I try to observe how well-bred people eat, so that I can imitate them and have the right manners.

This woman had a casual, delicate way of eating that made me suspicious. The truth is, she looked like real trouble. I saw that the other two weren't up to my level, so I decided not to pay any attention to them. I turned to her and tried to be as charming as possible, but nothing I did made her any less aloof. Though I was furious, I couldn't help noticing that her air of haughty melancholy and embarrassed pride suited her beauty, and I intended to imitate it at the next opportune occasion. She was almost as pretty and interesting as I, which is really saying something.

She was accompanied by a man who immediately attracted me as much as any man ever has. He was about forty and actually seemed worthy of me, really first-rate. What I liked best about him was a peaceful happiness that his presence produced in me. He had a special gift for making one feel that everything was possible in this world. I liked watching and listening to him, and most of all would have liked sleeping with him. I have an idea, though, that he didn't stay with any woman long. In spite of his quiet, serious appearance he was one of those men who are possessed by a terrible restlessness within them, which makes it hard for the women who fall in love with them.

I tried to arouse his interest, and must admit that his companion paid little attention to my maneuvers. The arrogant bitch wasn't bothered by me at all—even though the procurer presented me as *Señorita* de Vélez.

The other two men were ordinary, vulgar examples of

143

the species. All I remember about them is that they talked in the same kind of unbearable sugary gibberish as the procurer. My partner for the night, the lawyer, was one of the two. He wasn't ugly or old, but completely insipid. He had dandruff both on his learned head and also on the no-less learned shoulders of his dark suit, which he wore, no doubt, to impress me.

The eight of us sat in the living room, drinking the cocktails the procurer mixed for us. He was acting as host, though I really don't know why. Naturally, at first, the men were a little overanxious. Not us. Women are always more at ease in these situations. Little by little, thanks to the procurer's martinis of pure gin, the ice was broken and the atmosphere became friendlier.

I began to really enjoy myself. I was brought there by one man, supposed to sleep with a second, and had my eye on a third. I could see that I had a lively night ahead of me, and also that there were quite a few obstacles in the way of what I wanted.

When we sat down to dinner we were all in high spirits, particularly the two girls from the insurance company. For them a good time consisted in bursts of idiotic laughter over every little thing and in wiggling their backsides as much as possible. The procurer watched over the proceedings and I sympathized with his position, because if I got my way, there were going to be two men cuckolded that night. My lawyer friend was dropping dandruff everywhere while the other, the one I liked, had sensed my interest. His girl friend, who put on airs pretending she was his wife, tried to act indifferent to it all. She seemed slightly sour by now, though, about his discreet but insistent attentions toward me.

We were given a cold supper with good wines, iced *sangría* and French champagne. Obviously there was plenty of money floating around. By the time I got to the lobster I realized a few things.

I saw that the fourth man was totally insignificant. He played up to the two stupid chattering females from the insurance company. The procurer was crazy for the good-looking woman, who despised him, but because of some involvement of hers or her companion's, had to be polite to him and tolerate his clumsy manners. Her companion was eager to go to bed with me, even though he seemed very much in love with her. The lawyer was willing to do anything to have me . . . except spend much money. He had all the earmarks of being a selfish bastard, and, to top it off, considered himself young and handsome.

The dinner was very long, and by the time we got to

144

dessert, the fourth man started to make passes at the two girls from the insurance company. He had them all to himself and was delighted with his slice of the pie, seeing a fruitful evening ahead. The other three men had their eyes on the haughty melancholy beauty and me. The lawyer and the man I liked were both after me; the procurer was after the beauty.

Coffee was served in a small parlor. For a little while longer the jokes and giggling continued—the familiar nonsense that always precedes these occasions, serving to mask the hidden desires of some and the boredom of others.

I remained on the sofa between the lawyer and the one I liked while the procurer was being given the cold shoulder by the other woman in another part of the room. The girls took their new friend, now completely stewed, off into another room.

My situation was rather complicated. The procurer still hadn't paid me all of the three thousand *pesetas*. He was a suspicious fellow and had only advanced me half. The lawyer with the dandruff was becoming more aggressive each minute. He pressed against me, examining me with his smart, evasive eyes, and trying his best to please me with his heavy-handed advances. Next to me on the other side I felt the presence of the man I longed for. He was a strange man, and I had hardly spoken to him, but he seemed to me to represent the promise of a golden, fantastic future—something far removed from all the misery of reality.

I leaned toward him, feeling him stir with emotion. I'm one of those women who have a devastating effect on men which goes beyond the physical, reaching the heart as well. I glowed all over, convinced I'd won the admiration of a man who really rated. My looks and personality blossomed under the spell of the mysterious silence, a silence full of promise.

I combed the short, wispy curls which fell around my forehead and were far lighter than the rest of my long coppery hair. In my compact mirror I saw my reflection, slightly flushed and very beautiful. I leaned against him, almost swooning in his arms.

The lawyer abruptly got up from the sofa. The procurer watched, not becoming too angry, being occupied with his new-found companion. I sized up the situation and realized that I could finesse our first bargain. This shift of mine would better his chances of succeeding with that cold, cruel indifferent female—he was so taken with her that he was practically drooling at her feet.

The lawyer suddenly left the room without any explanation. I don't know whether it was to walk off his drinks or take a leak. No doubt, both. I took advantage of his absence to ask the other man for a cigarette, giving him the full benefit of my brilliant smile. While he was giving me a light, we had a short quick conversation, keeping our voices very low. The other woman noticed it, but couldn't get what we were saying as the impassioned procurer was filling the small room with the noise of his monotonous, wandering declarations of love.

"Your telephone number, please," he requested, confidently lighting my cigarette.

"You'll forget it." I didn't beat about the bush.

"No, tell me."

I gave it to him, repeating it two or three times, rather disappointedly. I don't like having my dreams postponed.

"I'll call tomorrow."

"Tomorrow?"

"Yes, after lunch." He was very precise.

"Why not before?"

"Sometimes one hasn't the choice."

"That depends on one's courage." I tried provoking him.

"But I'm a coward," he laughed, completely sure of himself.

"Yes, I can see."

"I don't like offending people."

"You mean her?"

"Yes, her," he admitted frankly.

"But you don't mind offending me." I felt humiliated.

"Bah, little one . . . it's not all that." He laughed again.

"I'm not little, and I don't have to explain things. I'm a very womanly woman, do you understand that?" My voice rose indignantly. I was very angry.

"I've been aware of that quality in you during the whole evening," he smiled. "And tomorrow . . ."

"Let's forget that. Tomorrow is far away, so far away that it may never come. Now or never," I insisted, not knowing how prophetic my instincts were.

He seemed suddenly surprised. He looked over at his companion, who had had her nose in our conversation during the whole time. His gaze was both sad and affectionate. He didn't want to be unfaithful to her, but he realized it was inevitable. He couldn't change his nature.

"All right. Tonight. But it's going to be difficult. And what about your lawyer friend?"

"I'll take care of my business, you take care of yours."

"All right. Then we'll leave now, and I'll come back later, alone."

"Okay." I pressed his hand against mine, hidden from the others by the sofa.

"That's not much," he protested.

"I can't do anything else."

"Coward," he taunted me, leaving me sitting alone.

He called over one of the girls from the insurance company and they went into another room together to talk. I heard the idiot shrieking with laughter, which made me furious. Then he came back to me and sat down on the sofa, smiling lazily and complacently.

The lights suddenly went out in the whole apartment. The stupid females became absolutely giddy, making fools of themselves and giggling like hyenas. He grabbed me roughly in his arms and gave me a hard, short kiss. Then he got up, and wiped off my lipstick with his handkerchief. He murmured something about the fuse box. Snapping open his lighter, he walked down the hall to take a look at it. He was able to fix it in a minute. (I learned later that one of the girls had loosened a fuse.)

When he came back in, his face was washed clean of my lipstick, and the lawyer was with him. My dandruffy friend looked grim. After my companion announced that he was leaving, he soon cheered up. Now it was the procurer's turn to suffer.

Everyone politely said good-by with the usual hypocrisy. The woman was very anxious to go so that she could get him away from me and not be bothered any longer by the procurer. Finally they left. He didn't say that he was coming back, but I knew that he'd keep his word.

I took advantage of his absence to conclude my business with the lawyer. The procurer, disgruntled at being left alone, was in the bathroom meditating on human frailty.

I gave my customer such a good preliminary working over that he ended up by offering me five thousand *pesetas* "in kind." He wasn't used to paying women. The best part was that I managed in half an hour to get him so drunk that when I agreed to accompany him into one of the alcoves he fell on the bed in a stupor and immediately passed out.

I went into the bathroom and put myself together again, for the man had absolutely ruined me with his clumsy jurist's paws, good only for making a speech, taking notes, or handing someone a bill. My only worry was that the procurer might ruin my plans because of his own bitter disappointment.

I looked everywhere for him, until I found him in the kitchen making himself a cup of camomile tea.

He had gotten drunk, sick and tired of the whole business.

It was worth my while to win him over, and I tried to be nice. I quickly finished preparing his tea for him and attempted to cheer him up a little. In spite of my attentions he kept on frowning gloomily. He had guessed what was up.

"*Vaya, vaya* . . . the little dove is in love," he said maliciously. "Take care, girl."

"*Hombre*, don't be ridiculous. Me in love? Don't get things confused."

"He's an imbecile, see?" he exploded suddenly. "One of those jerks who travel around the world not knowing anything about anything. He has no purpose, no roots . . . nothing. Just plenty of luck, like all adventurers."

"And you, you're not an adventurer?" I asked, knowing that I was risking the fifteen hundred *pesetas* that he still owed me.

"Me, an adventurer?" He was furious. "I'm a hard-working man, an expert in my field. Not like some I know. If I wished to talk, my girl, I could ruin many fine reputations. I could take some of those phonies down a peg who think they can snub me."

"You're still an adventurer. Just a rather powerful and successful one," I amended, winking at him flirtatiously.

"Well, I've always known how to adapt myself to what comes along," he said, mellowly changing his tune. "I've what you call—talent for life."

"That's what I'm talking about, *hombre*. When you're away from your important business affairs you're much more fun than most men, including the insipid jerks who are here now. . . . Ah, if only all men were like you!"

"I know how to have a good time, girl. I'm experienced with women, and that's the main thing. As they say, the devil knows more from age than from being the devil. . . ."

"My, you're witty! I see why she is so taken with you."

"What did you say?"

"You heard me. She is crazy about you."

"Christ, it didn't seem that way."

"Oh, you only had to see the way she looked at you!"

"We're good friends, that's all."

"Now, don't lie to me."

"No, really, there's never been anything . . ." he protested, getting all flustered.

"Then it must be because you don't want her. I assure you that if it were up to her . . ."

"I know she's fond of me . . ."

"Fond of you? How stupid can you men get? I said that she was *crazy* about you."

"Why? Explain what makes you think so."

148

"Because women aren't alike. If you want to understand us, you must realize that. She's proud and she would never let on even if she was crazy about a man . . . and especially someone as successful and powerful as you. But there are looks, gestures—a certain something we can't hide when we are in love with a man. Little details that other women immediately understand. You can think whatever you like, but nobody can tell me that she isn't in love with you."

"I don't know what to say . . ."

"You're a Don Juan, and you go from flower to flower. She knows this and is probably afraid. She's . . . uh, his wife, isn't she?" I asked casually, finally getting to what interested me.

"His wife? No, my girl. Those two married! No one's ever tied him down."

"I'd suspected as much . . . quite a situation there."

"She left her husband for him and then—"

"Then what?"

"You're very interested, aren't you?" he asked suspiciously.

"Just curious."

"You're a little more than just curious. You're a very dangerous woman, Lola. I'm beginning to realize that I have to watch out with you."

"Until now you hadn't noticed?" I laughed sharply, worried over his distrust.

"As far as your own affairs go, if you want to be bitten by a snake . . ."

"Snakes don't bite me, *hombre*."

"Maybe. Because they recognize their own kind in you."

"Thanks."

"But this snake is poisonous. Much more dangerous than you. At heart, my girl, you're an innocent baby."

"What things you say!" My classic remark when I can't give an honest reply.

"He's an adventurer, like I said. A man who knows a lot about useless nonsense. Art, music, theater, the movies," he said scornfully. "He used up all his mistress's money for his crazy schemes. Now he's just come back from America with some wild project that's been written up with ridiculous fuss in the newspapers. He'll make it sound good, and as he doesn't lack the gift of gab, he'll get some poor fools to lend him money."

"Then he's broke?"

"Probably. But he'll manage, he always lives well."

". . . and has a pretty woman at his side."

"You women like adventurers, but they're really mediocre types without personality. They're like chameleons, always

149

taking on the color of their environment, feeding on the air of their own fantasies."

"Not me, I like men with money," I broke in, angrily thinking that that kind of man deserved being rich. I had already imagined a long and luxurious affair with him. But in this damned world there's always a hitch, and if the procurer was right, one of the basic elements necessary for my happiness was missing. I was determined to find out for sure, but I would have to be cautious and not be influenced by the procurer's obvious hostility. "Why, the man hasn't been born who could make me live on bread alone, see?"

"I don't doubt that, Lola, not at all."

More than half an hour had passed since they'd left and he hadn't come back yet. He probably wouldn't come and our little tête-à-tête had just been a passing moment in the midst of his busy life. I was beautiful, but men have no taste. No doubt he liked his companion better—even though she couldn't compare to me.

The procurer still owed me fifteen hundred *pesetas,* and I had to get paid. I needed to send five hundred home to Mojácar, pay the week's board at the sanatorium where poor Malena was dying, buy some new spring dresses at Brígida, and pay for the beds at the hospital. I started to get busy with the procurer, putting behind the evening's nonsense. An evening overstimulated by the warmth of a June night plus too much alcohol.

I sat in his lap and stroked his shiny bald head. Suddenly he leaned back against the chair. No doubt he was dreaming bitterly of that other woman. But his gesture of indifference bothered me even more, knowing what he was thinking. I jumped up from my uncomfortable seat as though I'd been stuck with a pin.

"Come on, let's go into the living room. This is ridiculous."

"As you like . . . what difference does it make?"

"I can't believe you've so little interest in me."

"It's not you, Lola. But they've left us here all alone, bored," he wailed unhappily. "One idiot has gone off with the two girls to work off his liquor, and as for the other, your lawyer friend . . ."

"Well?"

"You overplayed your hand with him."

"He's an ass, see? Now if he were like you . . ."

"You don't like him?" he asked, interested.

"Not at all."

"Well, I'm not surprised, even though he's not bad-looking. But you know your role in this . . ."

150

"I haven't forgotten, and don't you forget yours."

"You'll get the money tomorrow, if everything works out right."

"What do you mean, 'works out right'?"

"Don't get so angry. You got to keep his interest up. Put him in a good mood so that I can—well, the rest of it's none of your business."

"My business is the fifteen hundred *pesetas*. Your lawyer friend tried very hard to find out my address and telephone number and wants to see me alone. He obviously intends to bypass you, see?"

"You didn't tell him anything?"

"No, not for the moment."

"You promised me."

"And I've kept my word. However, I'm very short on cash and everything depends on whether—"

"You won't get anything out of him, he's as tight-fisted as they come."

"Maybe not in money. But there are things that one can convert into money. It's called 'payment in kind.' See?"

"Oh, he gave you that line?" He seemed surprised. "That shows he's interested. But don't get your hopes up, Lola, because his 'payment in kind' are recommendations, import licenses, things that would be of no use to you. It's true what he said about that, though. He has a lot of influence and . . . and he pays with that."

"Maybe he'll give me an American convertible, eh?"

"All right, cut the crap. If you're a good girl and soften him up for me I'll send you two thousand *pesetas* tomorrow morning."

"Two thousand five hundred, *hombre*."

"You drive a clever bargain, Lolita!"

"Two thousand five hundred?"

"All right. But no address or telephone number or rendezvous, d'you understand?" he warned me. "Always through me, see?"

"I understood that from the beginning." I knew he was up to some dirty business. "Let's have a drink, to seal the bargain."

"My liver becomes inflamed if I drink too much," he protested. "But, tonight I'll join you. Just one, okay?"

After I'd made a visit to the lawyer who was still stretched out cold on the bed, we sat in the living room, side by side, and started to celebrate, drinking one whisky on top of another. By the time the door bell rang the whisky had made us good friends.

Leaving the procurer stretched out on the sofa, which

151

was too small for his large body, I staggered down the hall. I'd completely forgotten about the other man. When I opened the door, I soon remembered. He stood there, coolly looking me up and down. I was a little ashamed, as though I'd done something wrong during his absence, something he wouldn't like. To hide my embarrassment, I broke out in idiotic drunken laughter.

He smiled, turned around and without a word started back down. I was stunned, and instinctively slammed the door. Sobering up, I opened it again and hurriedly went downstairs, managing the steps as best I could, literally falling into his arms at the bottom.

"Come with me, for what you desire more than anything in this world. Oh, my darling, come upstairs," I muttered drunkenly.

"You seem . . . slightly . . . uh, exhilarated," he remarked, amused. "I think it would be better to leave it for tomorrow, or some other time. . . ."

"No, no, not tomorrow. Not some other time. No, my love."

"Please, my girl. Don't forget that love is a serious matter."

"*Anda*, come with me, please!"

"All right. I'll have to carry you up, though. You don't seem to be able to stand up straight."

He took me in his arms and I know that he liked holding my light, but well-filled-out body. I weigh one hundred and fifteen pounds and am very well proportioned for my build and medium height.

I snuggled up to him like a playful puppy. Then I threw my arms around his neck and kissed him passionately. "Not tomorrow, not tomorrow," I kept repeating with drunken stubbornness.

He walked in the apartment and carried me over to the sofa, dumping me next to the procurer's large, sad body.

The procurer twisted his face into a false smile at seeing him. Then, after murmuring a few polite words, he grossly fell back on the sofa.

I made a beeline for the john, certain that I looked like a complete mess. With a cold towel, I patted my face, neck and eyes. I didn't fuss much with my hair—a kind of wind-blown casualness suits me—but powdered my face, put on lipstick, and perfumed my neck, ears and bosom with Lelong's *Indiscreet*. Slightly more collected, I went back to him.

I sat down next to him and we chatted awhile. He stared at me in admiration, not bothering to listen to what I was saying, which is what intelligent men always do with women in my profession. I wanted to shock him, interest him, some-

152

how arouse him so that it wouldn't end in the familiar one-night stand.

I became very excited. I chattered away, showing how charming and smart I was, my eyes brightly sparkling and my skin flushed like transparent mother-of-pearl.

"You're a very clever girl," he told me, smiling. "But it isn't necessary to prove it. For me, your beauty is sufficient."

"I'm very pretty, aren't I?"

"You are a vision," he assured me, quietly taking hold of my hand.

"I like you too."

"I think I've noticed your . . . uh, affection," he grinned impudently. "But it's really not to your interest to show your enthusiasm for men so openly."

"Oh, usually I'm quite different. I put on quite an act."

"I'm flattered."

"You should be."

The procurer suddenly stood up, snorted, gulped down a shot of whisky and left, muttering angrily as he went down the hall.

"There, now he's mad."

"So what," I said scornfully.

"I thought he was a pal of yours."

"I know a lot of people," I answered vaguely.

"You're lucky you don't need him," he said, helping himself to a cognac. "But I don't think I'll be forgiven."

"Can this cause you trouble?"

"Yes . . . a lot," he laughed.

"Are you sorry?" My heart started to beat faster.

"You're worth it, aren't you?"

"Yes, I think I'm worth a lot of trouble."

"So to the procurer's health." He drank up.

"He told me that you're famous."

"Bah, don't believe it. These rumors are started by money, by a few people who have an interest at stake," he replied scornfully. "Naturally, next to those shitty jerks I seem . . . a less foul piece of shit." He burst out laughing.

"I don't know why, but I think I'd like knowing you."

"Not me—the familiar always cools the heart," he contradicted me. "This business of removing veil after veil, of peeling the onion layer by layer to get to the heart . . . bah! There's nothing of any interest inside. All your trouble, and what have you got? Just a few tears in your eyes!"

"You're a cynic."

"No, my girl, I'm not," he denied, becoming very serious. "I believe in a lot of things. In God, the Devil, in life . . . and at this moment in you, for example."

"You seem very adventurous."

"I'm not sure what I want, you know? And I'm in a hurry to find out, while there's still time."

"And now, at this moment . . . you are not sure what you want?" I asked, suggestively.

"No, in this case I know what I'm looking for," he kissed me, "but for me this isn't enough—no matter how pretty the young lady may be." He smiled gallantly.

I was about to tell him that I felt the same way, when the procurer, the lawyer, and one of the girls came back in. The procurer, who was furious with me and wanted to ruin my evening's plans, woke up the lawyer, shaking him and pouring lots of cold water over his face.

The room filled up once more with people. Unhappily I realized that with the exception of my friend we were all very, very drunk. Particularly the procurer, who had turned ugly. His face a bilious green, he staggered over to the radio and turned on some dance music. Then he went to get the other man who was somewhere in another room with the second girl. He pushed them in their semiconscious state into the living room.

After a few drinks we all started to dance. The procurer ordered us to, and no one dared disobey him. The lawyer grabbed me, and the two girls danced with his fat friend and the procurer. They rudely ignored my friend, who sat alone by himself like an uninvited guest.

This made me angry. I was very excited from drinking so much, and that lousy lawyer had taken advantage of me in a way that disgusted me. Hardly realizing what I was doing, I gave him a push, and he toppled over. Ignoring him, I sat down next to my friend, who was smoking a cigarette, amused by it all.

This immediately started a brawl. The two big shots, the lawyer and the procurer, jumped him, while the two girls squealed idiotically. The little fat guy, staggering and reeling over the furniture, escaped to another room.

Insulted, my friend stood up, and I tried to help him. I may look fragile and delicate, but I wasn't afraid of battling those yellow bastards.

The three of them fought. Being wide-awake and agile, he had the upper hand. But the procurer was out for blood. He purposely smashed the lights in the room, continuing to fight in darkness.

There was a sound of shattered crystal and broken bottles. The men struggled on the floor, panting and moaning, kicking and punching, while the two girls went screaming down the corridor looking for matches.

Somebody hit me with a chair, leaving me with a bad limp for several days. Like a wild beast, I scratched, bit and kicked them back, marking my two enemies, but good.

Suddenly there was a strange quiet in the stuffy, airless room. It stank from the smell of liquor and sweat, and a deadly kind of violence permeated the room. But nobody fought. There were sounds of weary sighs, and I could make out the painful, slow movements of two badly beaten men. But two, only two!

Sensing something in the blackness, I let out a terrible anguished scream. By the time the startled girls got candles lit in the room, I was next to him, having found his broken, motionless body in the darkness in my fright.

The procurer, seeing him stretched out on the floor, horribly pale and immobile, pushed me savagely away. With the lawyer's help he lifted him up to the sofa. Without saying a single word, he went to get the fat man, who had fallen asleep on the bed in one of the alcoves, calmly waiting for the end of the battle. I moved the two curious girls out of the way. Then I cradled his bloody head in my arms and futilely tried to dry with my handkerchief the brilliant little red river which trickled down his temple.

Twenty-two

The fat man ambled in grumbling, took one look at him and suddenly turned his face away. I realized then that it was all over. He was dead.

Apparently the fat man was a doctor and had understood instantly. He immediately assumed charge and ordered us women out, saying that he had to perform an emergency cure that wasn't a sight for our eyes. I shouted back that they needn't try to fool me, I knew he was dead. He said that I was mistaken but that he'd need an atmosphere of quiet in order to cure him. The procurer took us in another room, where he insisted on locking up the three of us. He gave me a sharp warning and left.

I realize that what happened next may seem incredible and ridiculous. But life is full of unexplainable and strange occurrences which are revealed sometime after the fact, in just this way. Things which people often keep hidden for a long time out of collective interest or collective fear.

From our room we could hear them talking in low voices. There were abrupt, nervous interruptions, voices suddenly raised in violence and then subdued again.

155

Unable to stand the tension and apprehension another minute, and exasperated by the two girls' idiotic remarks, I started to shout and bang on the door. The doctor came in and told us that everything was fine. He was resting peacefully and they were going to fetch a car to take him home. The blow had been nothing at all.

I wanted to look after him while they went out, but he firmly insisted that we should stay here. It wasn't our affair, and, anyway, the best thing for him was rest. I took the doctor aside and whispered that he wasn't fooling me—I knew he was dead.

He assured me that I was wrong, and promised that I could go with them when they drove him home. Meanwhile, I was to remain with the girls in the room. If I didn't, it would be so much the worse for me. A scandal would be created which would complicate everything.

The doctor looked rather pale, but not especially perturbed. He kept wiping the sweat off the back of his neck, and seemed to have the situation well under control.

I decided to keep quiet, though I had a terrible feeling in the pit of my stomach that I hadn't been wrong. Still, a scandal wouldn't suit me at all and it wasn't going to resurrect him for me if he was dead. As for his murderers, I'd take care of them later. I've always been a woman capable of handing out justice by myself when necessary.

I lay down on the bed and spent two or three unbearably miserable hours, numb with anxiety. My head ached from listening to the loathsome whining and complaining of my two frightened companions. Finally the doctor came back, and said that the three of them wanted to speak to me alone.

"Where is he?" I cried, not seeing his broken body on the sofa.

"Calm down, young lady, calm down," demanded the doctor gravely. "These two gentlemen and I wish to talk to you. Something very serious happened here during the night."

"These two murderers killed a man," I accused, not mincing any words.

"Please, control yourself. You're entirely mistaken," he insisted.

"Have it your way," I gave in scornfully, "but you better tell me where he is or I'll raise some hell when I get out of here."

"That's what we're getting at, young lady. You're very intelligent. We want to speak frankly with you and immediately put an end to this lamentable and unfortunate accident."

"Accident, eh? Which of the two was it?"

The procurer and the lawyer, who hadn't opened their traps, stared at each other in fright, feebly starting to protest. I realized that they were frozen with fear, paralyzed by the tragic outcome of their drunken brawl. But—which of the two had dealt him the fatal blow on the head? I wanted the truth, the truth at any cost.

"Was it you?" I asked the procurer.

"Stop the foolishness, Lola, and listen to the doctor."

"Or you?" I turned to the lawyer.

"Your questions may prove rather costly to you, Señorita, unless we can avoid complicating even further this terrible accident," the big-shot lawyer threatened me, forgetting his former admiration and becoming suddenly formal in his address. "I suggest you cooperate."

"Last night the two of you had reason to hate him, didn't you?" I continued my accusations. "You were both jealous, weren't you? He had two first-class women, women you had wanted. Well, he may be dead—but you'll never get either of us." I dropped tiredly into a chair. After all, I was a woman, a poor weak woman, and I was beginning to feel weary, horribly, horribly weary. The lawyer and the procurer were completely aghast at my attitude.

"Rest a little while, my dear," the fat one said sympathetically, once more acting the doctor. "I'd like to explain to you everything that happened concerning the night's unfortunate occurrence. You realize, of course, that I myself wasn't even in the room during the, uh, argument. These tragic things happen so often when men are intoxicated."

"All right, say whatever you want."

I'm not writing down his exact words. There were many and I don't remember all of them. He went on at great length, the other two cowards providing the chorus. Outside, the darkness was lifting and dawn was breaking.

According to their version, there had been a minor argument and the man received a tiny knock on the head. The doctor immediately took care of him, and saw no signs of any serious damage. They left him comfortably stretched out on the sofa and went to look for a car (being real hypocrites they hadn't dared use their own to come to this kind of a party). When they returned, the wounded man was no longer here. No, he certainly wasn't! I was a very intelligent woman, extraordinarily intelligent, and would understand—

"Where is he?" I broke in, my heart starting to pound again.

"Calm yourself, please," the doctor begged me again.

"I want to know where he is," I insisted, rising from my chair with an ugly look on my face.

157

"Downstairs . . . in the patio," he murmured. "During our absence he . . . uh, he threw himself out of the window."

"You dirty rats! So now he's dead, eh?"

"The poor boy was terribly unlucky," the lawyer said sadly.

I wanted to go down to the patio to see him, but they held me and even though I bit, scratched and kicked them, I couldn't get away, and finally started to weep like Mary Magdalene at the Cross—terrible sobs coming from the depths of my soul.

The three men waited—the doctor had signaled them to let me cry in peace. Both the procurer and the lawyer were very impatient, it was difficult for them to keep from stopping me.

Though the tears were running down my cheeks, I was able to collect myself and think more clearly. My grief was subsiding and I felt a little better.

They'd killed him during the fight with one blow, just as I'd suspected. And now nothing and nobody could bring him back. Maybe that's why I'd felt such overwhelming urgency last night to give myself to him. Perhaps I had an inkling that his time was coming to an end. He was dead, stone-cold dead. I knew it in the dark when I heard the panting of his two enemies, while he lay there, the breathing of his virile chest already stopped. Nothing, nothing could bring him back any more.

But, who killed him? The procurer or the lawyer? Who broke his head? Who, who? I was positive now that they didn't know. Being drunk, they flailed the air, threw bottles, and crashed into chairs and walls. Who, who? No—they didn't know themselves and that was what bothered them most. They'd remember that crime for the rest of their lives.

I felt weak and asked the doctor, who was most solicitous, for a glass of cognac.

Why had he gotten mixed with it? It wasn't fright—he hadn't been in the room when it happened. Friendship? I don't believe that would have influenced him in something this serious. Money? That was it: money, money, money!

And that would be my revenge—money, money, money. . . .

I felt very ill, exhausted by unhappiness. Nothing and nobody could bring him back to me now. It was already morning, the "next day" he'd been so happy and confident of. In the end he had to forfeit it to death. But these men had to pay, and they would. They'd pay plenty.

"I don't think anyone will believe your story," I remarked coolly.

"The truth always triumphs," the procurer replied in his usual hypocritical fashion.

"Anyway, Señorita, this has nothing to do with you," the lawyer warned me.

"I didn't realize that you were so in need of the money," I turned to the doctor, "but I suppose your price was rather high?"

"You're out of your mind, young lady, absolutely out of your mind. The excitement's been too much for you and you don't know what you're saying."

"Bah, I'm telling you this merely because I'm a very expensive woman," I said scornfully. "Frankly, I only see two solutions."

"Tell us," the lawyer urged anxiously.

"Pay me . . . or . . . throw me out of the window as well." I smiled dryly.

They paid. They paid a lot. We started to bargain fiercely, but I maintained my position, realizing that whatever they paid me, they'd have to give to the doctor as well. He'd sold himself very cheaply, which I could tell by the way his voice went up when he heard my price. A price of six solid digits, which I won't mention here out of delicacy.

Twenty-three

I got the money the following day, before I made any official statement. No stupid notary was going to make a fool out of me. It was in huge bundles of thousand *peseta* notes. I kept them hidden in my apartment for a while, not daring to bring them to the bank.

This business turned out to be really costly for the procurer and the lawyer. Even though they managed to explain things satisfactorily to the law—helped by the doctor, and by my silence, and by the ignorance of the girls, who backed them up all the way (*pesetas*, lots of *pesetas!*)—there was a terrific scandal.

The "accident" didn't appear in the newspapers but everybody knew and was talking about it. For a long time an unpleasant aura of suspicion hung over the two rats. It died down eventually the way those things always do. All of us have some skeletons in the closet. . . .

I kept my word, I didn't tell a soul, not even Juan. I had my vengeance, though. Those two shysters were trapped by their own fears, gnawed at by their own doubts. I want to write here what really happened, to show up and shame those two miserable cowards. Any man with guts would have admitted the truth, and would have been better off.

They were so in the habit of lying, always using the law to cover up their dirty work, that all they knew how to do was to scheme their way out of trouble. They even turned on each other, each blaming the other one to save his own reputation.

They were frozen with fear, the fear of seeing themselves in the place where they'd sent so many others. In court they brazenly tried to pass off the incredible lie of it having been an accident, and to help themselves, even stooped to insulting the women who had been at the apartment. They called themselves "respectable married men," and said that they had nothing to do with us.

I gave my version to the court in few words. I said that, feeling very dizzy, I had left the living room after the party and lay down on a bed. Then I heard the terrible soft thud of a body falling on the floor of the patio. Nothing more. Later I also told the procurer that if I ever heard that he was going after the dead man's mistress I'd tell the whole truth even if it meant my spending some time in the clink. He assured me that he hoped to forget the whole troublesome business. His health and position had suffered greatly, and he had no desire to see anyone who had been there that night, not wanting to bring back unpleasant memories. That's what he might want, but they'll soon find out, both of them, the procurer and the lawyer, what happens when one of us who kept quiet needs more money. The fear of those imbeciles can be a gold mine. . . .

For the moment, I'd completely resolved my financial situation. But the pile of bills that I kept hidden beneath a table in the apartment disturbed my peace of mind. I hated to leave the house, afraid that Lirio or Basi would smell out the hiding place and steal the money from me. Still, if I stayed home I became furious at not being able to enjoy the money. I didn't dare try to change even one of the bills. I've often read in detective stories how they can trace them by the numbers on them. Also, since that night, I figured that those two murderers were plotting to get rid of me—I knew how afraid of me they were.

After a few months had passed and when I already had begun to trust Juan, I made up a very complicated story about the money so that he could help me invest it. He seemed rather surprised at all I had, even though I reduced it to half. Later, he told me that he hadn't believed my stupid story and had immediately detected a bad smell about

160

the money. As it wasn't his business, he introduced me to a friend of his on the stock market so that I could get some good securities at a fair price. So with my first blackmail money I became a shareholder in a respectable real estate venture!

I was well aware that in confiding to Juan I'd weakened my chances of getting money out of him, and for that reason waited awhile before telling him. I couldn't go on hiding the money though, and, anyway, Juan wasn't a man to be led by women. He never gave me more money than suited him. Occasionally, when I'd put on an act about not knowing where the next meal was coming from, something I did out of habit, absent-mindedly, he would merely smile ironically but he never reminded me point-blank of my money.

During the summer months Juan was the principal man in my life. Perico had returned from Bilbao but we saw each other infrequently. He came back in a bad mood. The business of the five thousand *pesetas* had never been properly cleared up, and he was being sent to Guinea. He wrote me some very nice letters while he was stationed there.

I devoted myself mostly to Juan and the mayor Zamarrón, whom I talked into setting me up in business by buying me an interest in a dry-goods store on the Calle de Fuencarral. I worked him over so well that in two months everything was set. I even had another buyer ready, as I intended to sell out my share. Naturally, I'd lose something in the transaction, which is what always happens when one sells in a hurry. The investment was going to cost the mayor thirty-five thousand and I was only going to get twenty-five thousand. But I had no intention of going into the dry-goods business, and anyway I'd still be left with a nice sum—twenty-five thousand free and clear.

Unfortunately, a mean bitch ruined it for me. She had known the mayor from before—he'd often come to Madrid. She told him a lot of nasty things about me, making him so suspicious that he canceled the project, though he continued to give me a little monthly allowance the way he'd always done.

At about that time, my mother, the caretaker, died from a blood clot. I went by train to Mojácar but arrived too late. The poor woman was already dead.

I felt badly for two reasons. First, because I'd always been fond of my mother and second, because she took with her to her death the secret of my birth. She had always refused to tell me, saying that it was better I didn't know. On the way back I stopped in Almería, hoping to see the Mother Superior of the orphanage, but she also had died. I spent two or three days there trying to find out something about my real parents, and why they'd sent me to the orphanage, but I couldn't unearth a thing. The mystery of my birth has to remain a secret forever. This doesn't bother me much, for I can pretend that my parents were marvelous people, which they can't really have been.

At least I was able to settle my affairs, so the trip wasn't wasted. I'd brought Malena to Mojácar with me so the neighbors could see her amazing improvement, and after my mother's funeral, I arranged it so that she and the boy who looked after the goats would split the income that the flock produced. This provided for them very nicely. Then, on the way back, I met a fellow in the Hotel Simón in Almería who was going through to Cartagena and I persuaded him to change his plans and come back to Madrid with me. I promised him that for ten thousand *pesetas* I could arrange a matter in Madrid involving the purchase of a truck which had been left pending in the Department of Commerce. I arranged things so well that I kept the ten thousand and the fellow wasn't able to say a word. When a man's been an idiot the only thing to do is to keep his trap shut and profit from his experience for the future.

All this helped improve my financial situation considerably. I was a stockholder in an important real estate holding, mistress of a large, well-furnished apartment, owner of a very nice savings account, plus a flock of over five hundred sheep in Mojácar. Though I didn't get any money from the last, at least I no longer had to support my stepbrothers, or take care of Malena.

But I didn't get swelled-headed. I know that money never stays in one spot, and goes as quickly as it comes. I also wasn't forgetting that even if I took good care of myself, I still only had four or five years left of my beauty until I reached thirty. I wanted to hurry up and get as much as I could out of all the men I met in the little time that was left me. I was going to need lots and lots of money for my old age. I intend becoming a business woman and traveling around the world, using my intelligence to hunt something more interesting than just suckers.

When Juan hears me speak of this—and he's the only one I confide in—he looks at me in his special fashion, half-mocking and half-admiring. Even though he laughs at me, I know that he believes I'm capable of being a success in whatever I set out to do. And I will succeed, there's no doubt of that! First with a beauty parlor, then a whole salon like Elizabeth Arden's, then a dress shop. . . . But all that must wait—for the moment I'm still my most profitable source of business. I am biding my time, calmly and unhurriedly, and in the meantime studying and learning all I can for the future.

For the past year I've been having lessons with a professor whom Juan found for me, who charges seven hundred *pesetas* each month just to come here three afternoons a week. My reading and writing have greatly improved. I was very poor in that. And I've also picked up all sorts of odds and ends. I'm even beginning to learn English from a very ugly Englishman. Soon I'll show the world what I'm capable of!

Part III

❧❧❧❧❧❧❧❧❧❧❧❧❧❧❧❧❧

One

I've already written how and when I met Juan. I've also told more about him than anyone else. I'm not sure whether it's because he was the one who started me writing, or whether it's because he's on my mind too much.

Anyway, even though it must seem rather odd, I can't treat him here the way I've written about all the other men who've stumbled across my life. Juan always escapes me. Even when I try to put him down on paper I'm left with something which isn't really him. That's why, so far, I've put him in little by little, but once and for all I'm going to really devote myself to him, damn him! I'm afraid, though, that he'll slip through my fingers again. I won't deny that all my efforts at getting him and making him fall in love with me have failed miserably. Considering his attitude, I really don't know why he continues to go out with me.

In the beginning, I didn't find him very *simpático*. First, because, as I've said before, I don't like tall, thin types—they always make life unpleasant and complicated. Second, because I soon realized that he went his own way entirely. But when it finally dawned on me that I hadn't the slightest idea of what his own way consisted of, I became frantic with curiosity.

"Do you want to go out tonight with me?" he asked me on the telephone soon after we'd met.

"Tonight . . . I'm not sure," I stalled, trying to make him a little angry.

"Forget it. Excuse me for having disturbed you," a hurt voice answered at the other end of the wire. "So long."

"But, listen, *hombre!* Don't hang up like that," I shouted, not wanting to lose him. "You're getting angry over nothing."

"I'm not angry, *chica*. I just don't like bothering people," he said, suddenly becoming quiet.

"Hey?"

"What?"

"I thought you'd hung up."

164

"No, not yet."

"Where do you want to go tonight?"

"We could go for a spin, after dinner."

"Oh, you don't intend taking me to dinner?"

"No, I can't."

"You're afraid of being seen with me, eh?"

"Maybe. . . ."

"Aren't you the mysterious one," I said scornfully. "Listen, you know that I can't waste my time. I've my living to earn."

"You won't waste your time."

"All right. What time are you coming for me?"

"At eleven, downstairs by the corner."

"Okay."

"And make yourself very pretty, girl. That's what I like."

"You don't have to tell me that. I look beautiful already."

"See you then."

"Okay . . . until tonight."

We went to La Capitana. It was very dull there that night, but we danced and chatted awhile. We drove back to Madrid while it was still early, talking nonsense all the way. He stopped by the railing of the Retiro at the end of Alfonso XII. I was just thinking, here comes the same old business, because I like to get down to brass tacks and skip the nonsense, when suddenly he asked me to be quiet for a while so that we could hear the trilling of a nightingale in love.

I stared back at him in amazement. Then I decided that it was rather nice, at least it wasn't the familiar routine. As I remember, it was a wonderful May evening; the air was pleasantly warm and there was a bit of a moon. The large dark trees of the Retiro gave off a pleasant fragrance while the tiny bird sang, cocky and courageous, guarding his mate who was warming their nest.

I liked that. Cozily I curled up next to the man by my side. Filled with emotion, he looked at me for a moment in the misty light cast by a street lamp in the distance. Then he seemed to shake himself out of it. Brusquely he took out his wallet, handed me a small gift, started the car, and, without having uttered another word, deposited me on my street corner. When I opened the door the bank clock struck one-thirty. It had been a long time since I'd come home that early.

Since then we've gone out only occasionally, despite all my efforts to tie him to me more securely. He always cut short my little maneuvers and one night he told me very seriously that if I didn't stop my lying and professionally phony advances he wasn't going to see me any more. We were sitting at some spot along the Castellana, cooling our-selves in the hot night with iced *horchata* shakes.

"We should see each other more often, my love," I re-marked, leaning against his shoulder.

"What for, little one?" he asked, pushing my head back where it belonged.

"How unpleasant you are, *hombre*. For the natural reason. Aren't you in love with me?"

"Yes, a little. But not in the way you think," he laughed.

"There's only one way of being in love it seems to me."

"We don't look at things the same way, girl."

"All right, let's see—you explain your kind of love. Per-sonally I think you're nuts."

"Uff! It's too long, complicated and difficult . . . it's such a beautiful evening, don't you think it's better to leave it for some other time?"

"No, I'm very curious and impatient. Come on, tell me. Do I please you, darling?"

"Please me? No . . . You really don't please me at all."

"Then why the devil do you go out with me?" I asked, getting angry.

"Because I'm in love with your beauty, your incredible beauty," he said, completely seriously.

"Are you kidding?"

"Not at all."

"Then I'll give you my picture, so that you don't have to be bothered with my presence, sweetie-pie. Naturally, you'll have to pay me for it."

"A picture's of no use to me."

"Oh, you're impossible to understand!"

"In that, you're absolutely correct."

I kept quiet for a while, offended by his rudeness. Sulkily, I sipped my *horchata*. He kept staring at me, smiling quietly. Until finally his silly grin made me blow my top.

"You can go straight to hell, see? You men are all bastards!"

"You've no reason to get angry, little one."

"No? Well, if you think—"

"It's been a long, long time since I've seen a woman as beautiful, as amazingly beautiful, as you."

"If you pay me enough I'm capable of sending you my head so that you can stuff it. That's what you really like about me, isn't it?"

"You're very clever, *chica*," he laughed. "I'm happy that you finally understand."

"But I have a beautiful body, haven't you noticed?"

"I've noticed, girl. But, truthfully, it can't compare with your face."

"Now, you wouldn't happen to be an artist by any chance?"

"Perhaps. . . ."

"Are you a painter, or what?"

"Maybe."

"*Hombre*, I'd love a good painter to do my portrait."

"We can talk about that later," he said reluctantly. "But you'd make a difficult model."

"Why?"

"Your coloring, your expression, the sparkle in your eyes. . . . I don't see how all that could be captured on a piece of canvas. I've told you before the beauty of your face is really fantastic."

"Thank you, my love," I replied, mellowing at the sincerity of his words. "But don't you love just a little bit your pussycat who loves you so much?" I tried to kiss him.

"I don't know you well enough yet." He kissed me unenthusiastically. "Also, our first encounter wasn't something to make me go wild about you. Nobody, nobody, has ever treated me that way." His voice suddenly became harsh.

"I don't know what you're talking about," I assured him, even though I clearly recalled my haggling that night in the Casablanca.

"It's better forgotten."

"Your trouble is that you're very suspicious." I hoped to get him on another subject. "But I've more admirers than I know what to do with, and if I didn't really like you much more than you think, there'd be no reason for me to go out with you."

I said it out of habit, but immediately realized that there was a little—just a little—truth in it. Even if I hadn't had the money from the procurer and the lawyer, there were always plenty of generous men ready to take me out. And Juan was certainly among the least generous. He was obviously unaccustomed to paying women and he gave me a gift of thirty *duros* with the same grand gesture as another man offering me a fur coat. Even though I didn't like his being tight, I was curious about his strange ways and also I wanted people to see us together. He was obviously first-rate.

"I don't believe that you're fond of any man, little one," he contradicted me. "You're sick and tired of all of us, you're only in love with yourself."

"What things you say!" I laughed, trying to cover up with my usual remark the truth of his discovery. Why should

I pretend? I've never met anyone who could compare with me.

"You know perfectly well I'm telling the truth. And I understand how you feel. We men are stupid, ugly beasts in your opinion. Even though you're a rather spoiled little animal yourself, still it's thrilling to watch you."

"You—you think you know everything."

"That's one of my defects. I see things too clearly. And that makes my life hard, very hard, my girl," he said sadly. "It makes it difficult for people to fool you, and even more difficult to fool yourself, which is the necessary ingredient for happiness."

"You shouldn't be so mistrustful."

"I'm not as suspicious of people as you think. I've lived a lot and I've had some experience with women. You probably think I'm lying, but I've usually had luck with them."

"I believe you. According to what they say, you're very good-looking," I said, thinking that I sounded flirtatious.

"According to what 'they' say?" He burst out laughing. "But not for you, eh?"

"I don't get carried away over anyone," I confessed. "But I don't dislike you, and that's quite a compliment. You seem intelligent and I won't try to fool you with my usual nonsense."

"That's precisely what I wanted to ask of you. And as long as we've started this rather serious and almost inappropriate conversation, I want you to know that I would like to see you from time to time, but on one condition."

"Speak up."

"That you stop your boring play-acting with me."

"As you like," I replied. He was a difficult fellow and the best thing would be to humor him.

"And I'll never be taken in, not even if I'm dazzled by your beauty, when it comes to the farce which your . . . uh, your work demands of you." He had to hesitate a moment over his choice of words. "It bothers the hell out of me that you think you can treat me like an imbecile."

"Maybe I'll fall in love with you," I said to be contrary. I was irritated by his cool reasoning.

"No, beautiful," he protested violently. "If there's one woman who could never fall in love with me, it's you."

"You might be wrong." His certainty made me furious.

"I'm sure I'm not."

"I seem like such a silly idiot?"

"Thank you . . . but it's not that."

"Then . . . what is it?"

"Because you're shriveled up inside, your soul's all twisted."

"That's true," I laughed.

"And even if it weren't for that, I'm not the man you'd fall in love with."

"How do you know?"

"One can always tell, unless one's vanity gets in the way."

"You're a conceited ass, do you understand?" I yelled. "You think you're cleverer than anyone else and that everything you say is right. You can be wrong, too, just like the rest of us."

"In that case it would be a very pleasant mistake," he said gallantly. "Because once I'd like to hear you truthfully tell someone that you loved him. *Caray!* Just thinking about that drives me wild."

"Well, who knows? Maybe it will happen after all," I said prettily.

"No, cut it out, Lola. I want to be a good friend to you, all right?"

"As you like," I replied, thinking that it was worthwhile getting to know such an unusual sort of guy. I was curious to discover his Achilles' heel. In the end, I'd find it. I hadn't the slightest doubt of that.

Two

I must confess that if he has an Achilles' heel I haven't found it yet. Even though I know Juan very well when it comes to the way he acts with me, I'm completely in the dark about his other life. All the information I've unearthed has been contradictory. There are some people who think he's very smart and others who think he's a nitwit. Some find him *simpático,* others very unpleasant. The only unanimity has been among the pretty women who've known him. They are all very proud of having been acquainted with him. This is rather strange. After all, he's not all that.

Very soon after our conversation I gave him a spiel about my life which naturally didn't have a single word of truth in it. I made myself into a very interesting woman, ruined by all sorts of misfortune.

We were eating a marvelous country ham in the gardens of the Bolonia, hidden beneath the leafy outdoor arbor. He seemed to be swallowing the whole story, listening to me very intently. But after I finished, lowering my eyes demurely like one who has suffered at the hands of fate, he burst out laughing. He congratulated me for having such an entertaining imagination and said that he hoped some day to merit my confidence so that he could hear the real story of my life. He was sure it was far more interesting. The truth always is.

What he said is idiotic. The truth is always stupid, and what's worse, boring. But I kept my thoughts to myself. Nevertheless, I must admit that from the way he spoke and the things he told me that night I realized that he knew more about me than anyone else. He wasn't in love with me but when he spoke of my beauty a kind of music seemed to fill his words. Somehow he was always ahead of my thoughts, going carefully, step by step, leading me along until I was left absolutely without a shred of anything to hide behind. Angrily, I decided not to go out with him any more.

There were many reasons for my decision. The most important was the business of money. The little he gave he did in the manner of a small, obligatory politeness and never as my just payment. Also, I hadn't been able to make him change his habits and take me out with him in public, which would have been useful to me. Unfortunately, he wasn't propelled by that productive vanity which makes most men want to have pretty women along, and was content to go with me secretly.

Still, there was some bond between us. Generally, husbands make the best victims, but this one wasn't, as is always the case with those who get along with their wives. It's easier to catch fish who are swimming in more troubled waters. Give me any time a man who's failed in something, especially in marriage. They're the best game. I, myself, have never liked dealing with those types who after a short quick fling go back safely to the tender, loving arms of their wives.

The "Mysterious One," as I called him at that time, was both serious and crazy, a fatal combination. He calmly made the wildest statements, with an astounding self-confidence that prevented him from appearing a fool.

"You're a good girl," he suddenly said the other night while we were jammed in the Villa Rosa.

"Me—a good girl?" I protested. For me that's the worst insult.

"Yes, little one, most definitely. Maybe a little disoriented, but fundamentally good. You don't fool me. . . ."

"Well, you're wrong. I'm a very dangerous woman."

He burst out laughing and I had to contain myself from slapping his impertinent face.

"Forgive me, Lola, but really you're very amusing."

"Then go buy yourself a monkey, see?"

"I couldn't find one as pretty and *simpática* as you."

"*Simpática?* That's not what other people call me. Women hate me from jealousy, and men hate me because of my price. I'm the most expensive woman in Madrid. Everyone's heard about me, I'm called 'The Black-Market Queen.' Didn't you know?"

"No, I didn't. But my wallet's gotten the idea."

"Your wallet . . . what nerve!"

He suddenly became serious, an almost childlike look of sorrow wiping out his usual worldly expression.

"I'm sorry, Lola. I didn't mean to annoy you," he apologized sadly. "Even though you might not believe it I've not had much experience in these . . . these things. These feminine financial matters. Sometimes, I forget that when you go out with a man it's to earn your . . . your wages."

"I have to live."

"There are many ways of living."

"But this is mine."

"I'll try not to forget it again."

"You better not," I replied curtly. "Listen, why don't you buy me a very pretty little ring? A real bargain, my sweet."

"Because I can't."

"Then how about a beautiful dress that I saw yesterday in Rodriguez? It's just a whim, see?"

"How much is it?" he asked doubtfully.

"Two thousand five hundred, because it's for me."

"Impossible."

"I can have it put aside, and you pay when you can." I tried somehow to trap him. "You'll see how pretty I'll look in it."

"I'm sorry, but I can't."

I gave him a dirty look. I was put out because I knew that if I persisted I might lose him. I controlled my anger, swearing to myself that one day I'd get his entire wallet away from him and he'd have to buy me not just one, but lots of dresses, if he wanted to keep me around.

In the meantime I'd put up with it. I was getting to know him and was carefully spinning my web to trap him. Even strong fortresses eventually give way and surrender.

After that conversation, the "Mysterious One" disappeared for several weeks. I'd given him up for lost when he suddenly telephoned me for a date.

"Listen, Lola," he said to me as soon as he saw me. "Do you want to stop all the nonsense?"

"What nonsense?" I asked, surprised. Truthfully, I don't remember all the things that men tell me.

"The discussions that we always get into."

"Ah, I see! You're referring to our economic question, aren't you? That's not nonsense, *hombre*."

"I understand, but it takes away all my illusions about you," he admitted frankly. "Let's clear the air once and for all."

"Unfortunately, it's too clear already, don't you think?"

"No, it isn't." He went on very seriously, not a man for half-measures, "I'm not a very good bargain for you because I've made a niche for myself now in life. My marriage has been happy and I love my family. I don't feel bitter or a failure. I've nearly always done as I like. I haven't had to fight too hard for money even though I work a lot at various things. I live well enough, but day-by-day, without saving anything. And rest assured, I won't deprive my family of even a penny that they might need. Which means that I can give you very little, much less than you deserve, but much more, I can assure you, than I'm accustomed to. But . . . perhaps it might prove a good investment for you." He smiled ironically.

"A good investment?"

"I'm excited by your beauty. You please me, I find you amusing, Lola. And I think that one day I could pay you for all this."

"Ah, now I understand. You're like one of those securities that start low and later climb."

"Exactly, Lola. I find your business acumen enchanting."

"I've very important friends and I like to listen to what they're saying, see? I know from a very good source that *Los Dragados* are going up. Why don't you buy it?" I generously offered him my advice.

"Thanks, but I don't like the value," he snapped back angrily. "I intend to buy *Navales*."

"But they're so low . . ."

"Like me," he burst out laughing. "But like me they're also going to climb," he remarked, very amused.

"If you say so. . . ."

"Listen, do you want to buy *Navales*, or not? You understand what I mean."

"Okay."

"I'll give you the little that I can, and you won't complain any more. Agreed?"

"All right."

"You're not going to breathe a word about our . . . our friendship and you'll resign yourself to our going out secretly."

"You're the boss."

"And if you see me with someone else, your pride won't be wounded, eh?"

"That you can be sure of."

"Perhaps."

"Is there anything else?"

172

"Yes, little one," he went on calmly, "I want to see you always as well dressed and as pretty as a queen. With make-up, perfume, and always by night."

"Worse for you. In the daytime I'm a vision to behold," I snapped, getting angry.

"I'll have to renounce that."

"Very well. Anything else?" I was controlling myself, curious to see where this was going to end.

"Look, Lola," he said, becoming serious again, "I need your beauty. I'm in love with it, can you understand that?"

"*Hombre*, you're an imbecile. And crazier than a goat."

"I don't like goats because they have horns."

"Ah, because I might put them on you!" I laughed, as it was becoming funny.

"You never could," he replied easily. "Because I'm not in love with you, and I've no need of you. Just of your beauty. Your incredible beauty. However, if you don't want to give it to me occasionally . . ."

"Okay, okay, let's dance. You're becoming a pain in the neck," I said curtly. After dancing awhile, I'd tell him to scram.

But he wouldn't budge from the table. He told me that some friends of his family were sitting next to the dance floor and he didn't want them to see me with him. That was the last straw. I told him to take me home. We drove back by Chamartín in silence. Then finally he parked the car near the new ministries and started to talk, not about me, but about what my beauty signified for him.

His words were rather odd, but they comforted me. I felt fresh, as though inside me a river of clear water was running through the dry desert of my soul. The man was crazy, crazy and nervy, no doubt of that. But he was a special kind of man, he had more spirit than most. He cleansed me, and made me feel young again and I remembered the innocent, free happy life of my childhood. That's why I went with him again to hear the nightingale of the Retiro, and that's why I kissed him so idiotically while the bird sent the arrows of his sharp trills flying through the clear and starlit night.

Three

We went out together frequently during that summer. I realized that I was being very impractical in seeing so much of him, which enraged me. But he never got angry at my sharp, bad-tempered thrusts, only at my fake sugary tenderness, which little by little I dropped when I was with

173

him. Where we went depended on the state of his wallet. Sometimes we drove to the Villa Rosa or the University Club. Other times we walked along the Retiro, stopping for a cool drink along the Castellana. We talked endlessly, of all sorts of odd things, and often fought. Still, it was a good summer for both of us. But we always stayed at the same point, and when I tried to make headway I found I was knocking my head against a stone wall.

When I'd wake up alone in my large double bed or when I found the man next to me unbearable, I'd think about Juan—off God knows where, and my blood would boil with rage. I even lost my appetite. Frantically, I whipped up fancy new hair styles, exotic ways of making up, and wheedled some fantastically beautiful new dress out of some poor idiot who had had the bad luck to cross my furious path.

But it was useless. Even though all other men melted like wax near a hot flame when they were with me, Juan was like solid granite, despite his being the most enthusiastic of all concerning my beauty. Maybe it was precisely because of that.

I'm no fool and I'm very capable of understanding things. I realized that he was an odd character and I'd never weaken his will. His reasons for going with me were very different from the rest, though when it came to performance, he was better than any of them. I didn't understand his reasons then, and I don't see it very clearly now—though I've spent over a year trying to. I've finally resigned myself to merely guessing at what goes on behind the iron curtain he draws. But earlier, during those crazy, idyllic summer nights, I couldn't accept his rebuffs, and each defeat inflamed me more and more until I hated him more than I had ever hated anyone in my eventful life.

"Do you know what I call you?" I asked him one day, trying to get a rise out of him.

"You tell me."

"'The Mysterious One,' *hombre*."

"Why?"

"Because in my whole life I've never seen a man as mysterious and odd as you."

"As I?" He was shocked.

"You don't deny it, eh?"

"I certainly do, Lola," he smiled. "Because I don't find any part of myself mysterious, no matter how hard I look."

"Come off it, *hombre*."

"If you're referring to the fact that I don't like to be seen in public with you, please remember that I've a happy marriage and don't want trouble."

174

"That isn't it."

"Then what is it, little one?"

"Tell me your name. Come on."

"What for, girl?"

"So I can call you by it. A woman wants to be able to call her . . . her . . . well, her fiancé, her—well, whatever he is—by his name. You understand?"

"Yes, I see." He smiled. "But I'm not your fiancé, or your . . ."

"So, what are you?" I asked him, very hurt. "Come on, *hombre*, say it. Once and for all."

"Don't get so excited, beautiful. Even though you're very pretty when you get mad."

"I'll do as I please. Now, once and for all, out with it."

"All right, girl, all right." He laughed again. "The truth is that I'm nothing to you. Nothing."

"Nothing?"

"Nothing."

"Go to hell, *hombre*," I growled. "You're a first-class idiot."

"Probably," he admitted coolly.

"So you're nothing to me?" I lowered my voice the way I do when I'm upset. "So I'm putting up with you while you're nothing to me, and meanwhile losing marvelous opportunities to get money out of some sucker? I don't deserve that at all," I finished, holding back my tears. I didn't want him of all people to see me cry.

"Don't be silly, Lola." He took my hand, becoming serious. "Even though I'm nothing to you, I love you very much. That's the truth," he insisted vehemently.

"That's white of you. . . . Really, there's no point in discussing it." I became calmer. "No doubt you're wondering if because of what you said I'm going to try and get more money out of you."

"Yes, I was," he admitted frankly. "But I'm surprised you realize it." He laughed. "To you, getting money out of a man is an organic function, something as natural as breathing."

"Bastard!"

"Sometimes you're concerned with money for money's sake, other times it's something else. In this case, it's the something else."

"Ah, so maybe you think I've more than I need, eh?"

"You? Never. I didn't mean that."

"What did you mean?"

"Getting money out of me signifies something very important for you."

"Go on. . . ."

"It's as though you're conquering me. Cutting me in pieces and chewing me up with your pretty little voracious teeth."

"What nonsense!"

"It's not nonsense, it's the truth."

"You're a miserable coward, and your trouble is that you're afraid of me. Afraid, afraid, see?" I suddenly felt I'd made a discovery.

"Not of you, Lola. Maybe of your beauty."

"What crap is this about me and my beauty? I'm only a woman, a beautiful woman. Me, Lola. I'm sick and tired of your fantasies."

"That's natural."

"And if you're nothing to me, and I'm nothing to you, well, then . . .?"

"You mean a great, great deal to me."

"What are you trying to say?"

"—I would hate losing you."

"I don't think you're going to have long to wait."

"That's what I'm afraid of."

"You're afraid of that? And what else?"

"Nothing else."

"Coward, coward, coward . . ." I spat at him. He merely smiled and lit a cigarette.

Later that night I managed, for once, to get a rise out of him. After having apéritifs in a spot at the end of the Castellana he took me to the Villa Rosa and we sat down at a table near the dance floor. Generally Juan chose a table more in the back where there were less people, but I was so angry I didn't notice his gesture.

As usual, I created a sensation. I looked fabulous in my garnet silk dress, a Balenciaga that I'd gotten out of the old Asturian recently.

"You see how they look at me?" I pointed out to him. "At this moment they all despise you."

"But not me them, beautiful."

Whether or not he hated them, he started to stare nastily at an ugly creature seated next to us. With her was a man who didn't take his eyes off me from the moment we sat down.

"Would you mind your manners, please, and stop looking at that pig," I warned him.

"At what?"

"At that ugly bitch next to us."

"Ah, yes. Why? Don't you think I find her attractive?"

"Who the devil knows!"

"I find people's faces very interesting. Even the ugly ones."

"If you keep looking at hers, you better watch out."

And he kept looking.

To retaliate, I started to flirt with the fellow with her, much to his surprise. He was young, but very ugly—had a face like a plate of mush. Aware of my scrutiny, he nervously started to arrange the knot in his tie and his voice became louder. He put on a special performance for my benefit. His thin mouth, hidden beneath his mustache and nose, curled in a malicious smile. He gave Juan a smug, condescending grin. Precisely the effect I'd hoped for.

"I think that's enough now, Lola," he suddenly warned me, after having pretended for a while not to have noticed.

"What did you say?"

"That's enough, don't you think?"

"Forgive me, but I don't understand."

"If you keep looking at that guy, I'll walk right out of here," he threatened, his voice breaking a little.

"Oh, don't tell me! You're not jealous, are you, my love?"

"Listen, cut it out. Jealous or no, if you don't stop your little game you'll find yourself alone."

"I never lack for company, you can be sure of that."

"I'm quite sure. And I'd just as soon leave you to someone else if you go on this way."

"*Hombre,* how demanding!"

"I seem to be in the way, and, I warn you, I don't like being a fifth wheel."

I didn't answer, but continued to stare at the other man. I was more discreet, but I kept it up to annoy Juan. He seemed to be oblivious, apparently having such a good time —we even danced once or twice—that when he got up and left me, I thought he'd only gone to the john—certainly he'd forgotten his threat. At least that's what I thought until one of the car attendants brought me a note from him wishing me a pleasant evening and advising me that in the case that I lacked company, there was a paid taxi waiting for me by the garden door.

But I didn't lack company. There were plenty of men and I had a fight with one of them. It was quite a night. I got boiled and didn't come back to my apartment for two days.

Four

Later that week the "Mysterious One" called me on the phone, and calmly, as though nothing had happened, suggested that we go out. We had a few words, or, more accurately, I had them, and plenty of them, and I angrily turned him down. But when he called back several days later I changed my tune and agreed to see him. The truth is that I missed his craziness. We never mentioned again the business at the Villa Rosa, and I never dared look at another man while I was with him, except swiftly, out of the corner of my eye—always afraid that he might walk out on me.

Actually, I had a good time when I was with him, and I decided not to get mad any more about his idiosyncrasies. I either had to take him as he was, or leave him once and for all. I was well aware, though, that he took what he wanted from me without ever having to commit himself in return.

I'm very talkative and love to chatter away. But when I'm with men I become the mysterious sphinx, aloof and quiet. That's the way to arouse their interest. Also, a loose tongue always brings fatal contradictions, which end in trouble. I don't know what the devil happened to me when I was with Juan. I couldn't keep myself from chattering, and very soon he knew everything about me. The real, unvarnished truth, without any other fantasies except the dreams natural to a girl of my imagination.

He was very adept at getting it out of me. He never got excited over the things I did, and always knew how to laugh at the right time. He was particularly interested in my past experiences, and listened to those intently. So intently that I talked on and on, forgetting that he was a man, and my deadly enemy. When at some pause I remembered it, it was already too late. He already knew too much about me, and insisted that I go on.

Beyond this, his curiosity flattered me. He never was bored by me and my stories amused him. This was a new triumph for me. I had always conquered men by very different means. Cynical, desperate means, born of bitterness. I attacked my victims with the cruelty of a master bending his slave to his will. And they, when they no longer needed me, tossed me aside contemptuously, hardly aware that I still existed. Until they were beaten by life, and had to come back to me again, debasing themselves to make love to me, hoping my closeness would brighten their filthy lives.

With the "Mysterious One"—Juan—this never happened. He was crazy, full of nerve, but he was as interested in me when he met me for a friendly supper as he was when he spent the night making love. And even though his interest was clearly limited and sometimes rather superficial, he didn't modify it according to the heat of his passions, but always remained the same.

This surprised me very much. It was completely new to me. At first I thought it was a clever tactic of getting a bargain and avoiding giving me money, something I'm still very suspicious of. I don't trust any man. But suspicious or not, I still had to keep on living and at that time he was undoubtedly a big part of my life.

One day I learned that he needed me as well. He'd often told me that, but I'd always assumed he was lying. Until one night, while I was nibbling away at a marinated partridge in a small, gloomy tavern, I suddenly realized that I also meant something to him. Something very vague and confused, that I'd probably never be able to understand, but nevertheless —something.

I'd gone out with another man earlier that night because I needed the money and because Juan hadn't telephoned me. When he came looking for me in the Casablanca I was dancing a samba with my friend, who was young and good-looking. I waved to Juan, who was standing alone, looking terribly lonely. After the dance was over, I sent him a note with the flower vendor saying that I was busy now, but that he should call me the next day so that we could go out together.

Being a woman, I was very pleased at first to put him off. Especially as he could see I was in such good company. But when he rushed from the room as if he were angry, I realized suddenly what I'd done. I didn't want to lose him and I was afraid he'd never forgive me. This fear ruined my mood for the rest of the evening.

The Bank of Spain sounded three when I came home with my companion for the night. We walked down the empty street and our steps resounded with that special emotional sound that one hears in good films when the dramatic moment is coming. Neither my friend nor I spoke, even though we were arm in arm, like two lovers. God knows what he was thinking, but I was in a foul mood, furiously thinking what a stupid jerk this rich young fool was.

Beneath the flickering street light I saw Juan's parked car at the end of the corner—a gray convertible Lancia, very pretty. My surprise made me hesitate, and my companion firmly grabbed my arm, thinking I had tripped. I was afraid of walking past the car with him. The street was deserted and I didn't trust Juan.

I stalled, trying to send the guy away on some pretext. Unfortunately he was a young man of the sort capable of any perversion but never rudeness. He insisted on bringing me to my door. We argued awhile until I realized I had no choice. I dropped his arm, putting a cool distance between us. I looked bedraggled, unmade-up, faded and lackluster, a piece of soiled goods. When I reached the Lancia, my cheeks flamed and I felt like what I was. I didn't dare raise my face, fearing to look at those two steel-like eyes glittering with anger and humiliated pride.

But I was all wrong. The Mysterious One waited calmly for me until he saw my friend leave. Nervously, I went over to his car. Perfectly pleasant, he said that he felt like seeing me. I hadn't eaten anything so he took me to a local tavern which was open late. We drank a bottle of red wine and I had marinated partridge, along with a salad of lettuce, olives, tomatoes and onions.

We sat in silence because it was difficult for either of us to say anything. He kept staring at me so intently while I ate that I began to feel worthless again, filthy from use.

What was he looking for in me? Why did he want to humiliate me? Then, while I was nibbling away, I realized that he needed me for something. Something dark and nameless. If he hadn't some need of me and what I was—a thing corrupted, dirty and used—he wouldn't have come for me, he wouldn't have brought me to this miserable, awful tavern, filled with the shrieking laughter of drunken couples.

Excited by my discovery, I drank a great deal, and unburdened myself, ending by weeping in his car at dawn. He didn't say one word of reproach, but aloofly rejected my embraces. Finally, he brought me back home and instructed the watchman to help me to my apartment. I couldn't make it alone.

The following day I became serious, something which rarely happens. I don't like becoming too involved in things.

"Listen, why'd you come looking for me last night?"

"Because I wanted to see you."

"I'd told you I was busy."

"Yes."

"And you could figure out that I wasn't coming back home alone, couldn't you?"

"Yes, I'd thought of that."

"You upset me a great deal, see?"

"You—upset? Come on, Lola, don't exaggerate."

"But—what did you take me for? Come on, say it."

"I took you for what you are. A very pretty girl, very *simpática*, and very amusing," he evaded me, laughing wickedly.

"Okay, Mysterious One, either you tell me why you came last night and waited there for me, or you won't see me ever again," I snapped, tired of his nonsense.

"I told you, silly. To see you."

"To see me with someone else, eh? To see me disheveled by another man, despoiled by another man, dirtied by another man. To see me sold to another man," I continued, completely losing my control. "And to rub my face in it, right?"

His eyes shone with a strange light at hearing my words.

We were seated in a spot along Rosales, trying to relieve the suffocating evening heat with some cold *horchata* shakes. The street lamp cast a light across the bottom of his face, while an acacia branch, quivering in the warm breeze, shadowed his forehead, his eyes and half of his nose. His smile was both cynical and tender, and his large eyes, hidden in the shadow, glittered with pleasure.

"Ah, you like doing that to me, annoying me. Isn't that so, you bastard? Well, I'm getting tired of your little mysteries, see?"

"But there is no mystery, Lola," he protested, smiling. "Only in your mind, woman."

"Tell me why and with what intention you came by last night and maybe I'll believe you."

"My reasons had nothing to do with hurting or humiliating you, I swear," he replied very seriously. "I wanted to see you, that's the truth, and—"

"Men don't come to see someone that way, just after she's . . . I suppose I looked horrible."

"Not horrible—but not too good either."

"How'd you expect me to look, you idiot?" I shouted at him. "On top of everything else—now you tell me that I'm not pretty. I'm *always* pretty, *see?*"

"Not last night."

"Ah, now I'm beginning to understand you, Señor. You wanted to see me bedraggled, used, soiled. Well, for your information I'm beautiful without make-up, with my face only washed with soap and water."

"Maybe with your face washed, but last night it wasn't," he commented dryly.

"He didn't even kiss me. I don't let just any man kiss me, see?"

"It has nothing to do with that," he broke in, irritated. "*Anda*, Lola, let's forget about it."

"No, no, I won't. I won't forget about it because you and I have to have a serious talk. And right now," I insisted excitedly.

"In all this heat. . . ."

Suddenly what I had said reminded me of Espichao. I remembered how he always had to speak very seriously about something with me. Tirelessly involving me in complications, in problems that had to be cleared up immediately but that never could be because they only existed in his imagination. And I remembered how I never shared his impatience, and how I always begged him to forget about it, to stop being ridiculous.

The memory embarrassed and shamed me. I didn't want to act or sound like that poor fool, and even though it was hard for me to hold my tongue I decided to keep quiet about all but one thing. I had to ask the Mysterious One a question, and I had to do it right away.

"All right," I gave in. "Let's forget about it. But I want you to answer me about one thing truthfully—truthfully, d'you hear?"

"The truth . . ." he groaned, "can be awfully tough, girl."

"Promise?"

"All right, for once."

"Listen, *Misterio*—Damn it, I won't call you that any more, see? Either you tell me your name or I'm leaving right this minute."

"Then . . . then call me Juan."

"But that's not your name, is it?"

"No, but it could be."

"Well, for me, you're going to be Juan for the rest of your life."

"As you like."

"Look, Juanillo, tell me the truth. Why do you go out with me?"

"Because I like you."

"You promised to tell me the truth."

"But was that what you meant?" He burst out laughing. "*Caray!* I imagined something more serious."

"Well, now you know . . . Juan. I want you to answer me right this minute. Why do you go out with me?"

"I can't really answer you. I'm not sure myself."

"You know everything. Anyway, I can refresh your memory so don't worry."

"Is this a confessional?"

"You promised me."

"All right, girl, have it your way," he replied, resigned.

"People are always attracted by something. Why do you follow me?"

"Oh, but I . . . Christ, you're right! I do follow you." He seemed genuinely surprised.

"Look, stop acting like an idiot and answer me once and for all."

"I'm very fond of you, Lola. I've already told you that," he answered impatiently.

"You like my face, isn't that so?"

"It's fantastic."

"And I please you?"

182

"A great deal."

"Also I amuse you . . . you find me *simpática*."

"Yes."

"And as a woman, I'm not exactly a bag of bones, eh?"

"Definitely not."

"But, well . . . as for being in love with me, the way they mean when they say a man loves a woman, you don't feel that, do you?"

"You ask too much," he grumbled.

"I know that you don't love me, Juan."

"You're mistaken, silly," he protested. "I suppose the only thing to do is to get things straight. You're very mixed up about us, girl."

With a kind of casual determination, he pushed himself forward in his chair, and fiddled with the knot of his tie and stared at me a moment. In the dim light of the street lamp I could see a slow smile spreading across his face. You couldn't deny he was handsome, but he was crazy—crazier than a goat.

"There are some things which are very difficult to explain, Lola. And anyway, I don't believe in explanations. You can never say what you mean to say and people never understand you the way you want to be understood. Words rarely help us explain things. They only complicate matters."

"Forget the trimmings, *hombre*. Just call a spade a spade."

"Okay, then I love you. And let's not talk about it any further." He stretched himself out in the chair.

"No, go on. I like to hear all your crazy ideas."

"You won't understand."

"Please."

"It's very clear, beautiful. Your trouble is that you're looking for a double meaning where there is none."

"You're nuts."

"I don't see why."

"You don't see why, eh? Can't you understand anything? Okay, then tell me what's so clear and simple to you."

"Do you remember how we met?"

"Perfectly."

"And I haven't forgotten, either. Neither the haggling nor the payment in advance."

"So what you want is revenge, eh?"

"How silly can you women get?"

"Personally, I think it's bad taste to bring that up."

"If I do, it's so that you know that from the first moment I found you interesting—a very unusual sort of girl."

"Don't tease, *hombre*."

"I'm too grateful to womankind to ever tease any one of

183

them. Listen to me a minute, Lola," he said impatiently, pushing his chair next to mine. "You've always interested me, since the very beginning."

"It generally doesn't seem that way."

"First, because your beauty is miraculous."

"We've already been through that," I grumbled. "You're making me tired of hearing it."

"Your beauty makes me happy because I'm one of those unfortunate men who only feel good when they are near something lovely. Your face, your liveliness, remind me of all the good moments of my life. When you're with me I forget the bad parts of my past." His voice filled with emotion. "You are so beautiful, so refreshingly beautiful. Like a murmuring spring, a never-ending stream of fresh water— water which purifies and calms my soul."

"Some storyteller you are," I said, for the sake of saying something. Actually I liked his crazy thoughts.

"That's why I hesitate, that's why I don't dare . . ."

"Dare what, *hombre?*" I asked, dying of curiosity.

"Dare possess this flowing water which races on and on, and can never be held still even for a moment because of its fluidity."

"Oh, so you're afraid of me! Frankly, isn't that it? I think, if you wanted me to, I could get along very well with you, Juan," I said, trying to encourage him.

"Maybe . . ." He seemed preoccupied.

"I love you very, very much, silly . . . and . . . and I even think I love you enough not to cheat on you with anyone."

"But what are you referring to?" He seemed surprised. "I wasn't thinking of that sort of thing." He burst out laughing. "Thanks anyway for your proffered faithfulness. Even though I don't believe it, girl."

"You should be ashamed of yourself."

"I want to capture your beauty. To make it into something immortal, something that will last forever," he tried to explain—as if his words ever really explained anything! "But I'm afraid, because running water stagnates when it's imprisoned and held back from its natural course. One day, though, I'll have to try. Nothing will come of it—but I'll try. So that you won't end up just another woman finally conquered by the years."

"Listen, you. I'm only twenty-four!"

"I know, Lola, but one day you'll be forty. And then—"

"Bah, don't worry! I don't plan to reach old age."

"Why?"

"Because I'm rather ill."

"Ill?" He seemed startled. "With what?"

"With a weakness . . . of the heart and chest." I immediately guessed what nasty thought was on his mind. "I've everything except the thing you're worrying about."

"Are you sure?" he asked, alarmed.

"Sure," I replied, bitterly disappointed in his selfishness. He was just like all the rest. They don't care if you're ill, or whether it's the heart, the chest, the liver, the kidney, the head, the nose or even the whole body—as long as it's not the other thing. So that they can remain clean. One could rot, scream with pain, choke, and die like a dog if necessary. As long as they, the dirty pigs, remain strong and healthy.

"Poor baby," he comforted me in a softer voice. "All beautiful things are delicate and fragile. Though, despite your delicacy, you give a rather healthy appearance and I'm sure you're exaggerating. But we'll see. Just what is your trouble?"

"I've told you already, *hombre*. I have a weakness."

"That's meaningless," he replied impatiently. "What happens to you when you feel ill?"

"Are you a doctor?"

"No, I can't say I am."

"So what business is it of yours? The only thing that should concern you is that I'm fine as far as that other thing goes," I remarked sarcastically.

"I'm glad of that, I won't deny it. But I'm also concerned about the rest," he said soberly.

"Really?" Now it was my turn to be surprised.

"Really, Lola."

"Well, I think it's the heart, see? I get fainting spells and I feel very weak."

"Have you seen the doctor?"

"Yes, lots of times."

"And what does he say?"

"Just that, *hombre,* don't be so thick-headed. That I've a weakness up on top, and also in my heart below. And I have to take care of myself."

"But you don't."

"No, what for?" More to the point to have asked—for whom?

"Your health is important," he replied after a short silence. He must have guessed my thoughts. "You're a girl who could make a man very happy and it's wrong for you not to take care of yourself. I'm going to take you to a good doctor so we can see what's what."

"Doctors cost a lot of money."

"It doesn't matter."

"But you said that you didn't have much money?"

"I can find it for this," he said with a firmness that filled me with warmth.

"You're an angel, my love." I cuddled next to him, for once with the truth on my lips.

"I'm a mere man, that's all," he replied, obviously not believing my affection.

"And also a louse who doesn't believe one word of what I say," I added. "I happen to love you, I love you, you crazy fool, whether you believe it or not."

"I've had a lot of luck with women," he admitted, completely unabashed. "But I don't foresee it with you, baby."

"What makes you so sure?"

"I'm thirty-six, Lola. I've had too many flight hours, do you understand? By now I know a little about life."

"And me, I don't, eh?"

"Yes, you too. But in another way. Down deep you're really very innocent."

"What nonsense!"

"You're marvelous. You've no idea of how you really are."

"So tell me, *hombre*. I always like hearing about myself."

"You're capable of doing anything to get ahead. Duties and limits don't exist. You go straight for what you want, blindly determined. Any faltering of spirit or weakness of will spells retreat. You find it humiliating. To fall in love for you would be like falling into hell."

"You're painting some picture of me," I laughed.

"You're well capable of robbing—assuming you haven't already done so. . . ."

"Now, wait a minute," I protested feebly, for the sake of protesting.

"And in the perfect circumstance, the absolutely perfect circumstance, I believe you're capable of killing, if it's worth your while."

"No, that I wouldn't do!" This time I meant it.

"But in spite of everything," he continued, not listening to me, "you're a wonderful creature. Alive, beautiful and cruel. Like some free, indomitable force of nature. So alive, so beautiful and so cruel that . . . that I fear you have no soul," he finished abruptly.

"Each day you get crazier." I laughed.

"That's why I see you, Lola, do you understand?" He spoke rapidly, the words suddenly pouring forth. "Your beauty alone is of no use to me—any more than the beauty of marble or of a painting. But I need your freedom, your happy, cruel freedom and simple blind strength. My soul is able to breathe, I'm purged of my apathy, my moods. You're like the rain, like the wind, like the snow, like the flowers—

186

and like a graceful, beautiful bird. You remind me of a tender warm place in the sun, a frozen winter night, a hot summer noon and sometimes a beautiful storm that's just clearing. To tell you the truth, I think you're capable of being everything—with one exception."

"What's that?"

"A woman."

He suddenly stopped talking. He sucked on the straw of his *horchata* shake and leaned back again against his chair. He obviously was nuts and there was no point in daydreaming about getting him. He was clearly no good either for screwing or for being a companion to a woman. Even if she loved him and didn't try to get much money out of him.

I stared at him awhile without saying anything, distracted by the shadow of the flickering acacia leaf against his dark face. Was he teasing me? Did he love me a little in his own crazy fashion? All I was sure of was that he would tell those things to any number of women and he'd upset them with his crazy talk. I knew he wasn't in love with me, and, although he liked me a lot, he really didn't need me for anything else but to listen to his nonsense. What an idiot I had been! For a moment I'd actually thought that he couldn't live without me.

But this thin, lively crazy fellow was incapable of ever sacrificing himself for a woman. This didn't suit me at all, not at all, and I didn't intend to go out with him any more. *Hombre,* what nerve. To tell me—me—that I wasn't a woman!

Five

He phoned me two or three times but I'd given orders to both Lirio and Basi to say that I wasn't at home. And, just as I'd suspected, he didn't bother himself again with me.

If I remember rightly, most of the summer passed before I heard from him again. Even though I didn't forget him entirely, the mess I had with the procurer and his friends during those weeks took first place in my mind. At first I was furious at that murder, and afterwards was busy wondering what to do with the money I had hidden in the apartment.

Then finally I saw him one night in the Villa Rosa, hidden behind the pool with a very well-dressed woman. The two of them were acting very lovey-dovey and romantic. They were dancing alone on the small floor, acting like idiots in the moonlight.

I was with my Asturian friend. The money hadn't gone

to my head and I was working on a very interesting black-market deal with him, but I felt very badly that Juan should see me out again with such an ugly guy. Nevertheless, I wanted to get a good look at them and I maneuvered my guy closer to the pool, so that we, too, could make love in the moonlight. Juan ignored me. Irritated, I went to the hat-check room and sent a note with a busboy calling him to the phone. I wanted to have a few words in private with him.

The Mysterious One, Juan, or whatever the hell his name was, didn't come. He understood immediately what was up and told the boy that he'd telephone me another day. And that's precisely what he did do—very calmly—two or three days later.

I really had intended to tell him to go to hell, but instead I went out with him the very same night he called. I wanted to find out who the bitch with him was—I had been dying of curiosity.

We went out for dinner to the Samba. At that hour there weren't very many people there. By the end of the dinner his rigid look and manner began to make me very nervous. I realized that I'd acted very badly, for there are some things one shouldn't do to a man; but recently I'd been through a lot and I was in a very jumpy state. What's more, I couldn't find out who the magnificently dressed creature with him had been.

People tell me that when I get vicious there's no one worse. I always know where to plunge the knife. That night I must have surpassed myself, wild with rage. At the end of the meal, a little under the influence of the wine, I made a terrible scene.

We had been talking for a while about all sorts of trivial things. He didn't reveal a thing, so while we were eating the crayfish I took matters into my own hands.

"Well? Don't you have anything to tell me?"

"Yes. Every day you get prettier and prettier."

"I wouldn't have thought that beauty mattered to you, *hombre*," I laughed maliciously. "You haven't paid any attention to me and you go out with an old bitch who should make you hide your head in shame."

"I don't like to bother people who don't come to the phone. As for the señora who was with me the other night . . . well, she's not so bad." He smiled his eternal smile.

"Ah, she calls herself a *señora,* eh? The nervy pig!"

"Let's drop it, please?"

"Anyway, I've seen her around before. She goes with a friend of mine, an old geezer with lots of money," I invented wildly.

"I think you're mistaken."

"She's a foreigner, isn't she?"

"I don't believe so."

"I think, I believe," I mimicked him. "For Christ sake, don't you even know her?"

"Look, Lola, I never know anything about one woman when I'm with another, do you understand?"

"Oh, I couldn't care less about that bitch. You didn't suppose I would, did you, *hombre?* With me it's only cash that counts, see?"

"I've always known that."

"I only wanted to see you today to ask you for some money—I'm broke."

"You're coming to a fine source, girl."

"Listen, Juan, or whatever your name is, and which I don't give a damn about, let's drop the nonsense. I'm a prostitute and if I go out with men it's for money and only for money."

"I know that already, Lola."

"And as I've always acted fair with you, you have to get me out of this hole—that is, if you ever want to see me again."

"I'm very fond of you, but I don't have any money."

"And the other night?"

"With her, money has nothing to do with it."

"The filthy bitch! Her kind takes a man for all he's got."

"Without a doubt."

"You're a conceited ass, an insufferable smart aleck and a miser."

"Thank you."

"You have a car, you can do as you please," I went on, getting angrier and angrier, "but you don't have even two thousand *pesetas* to give to a woman who has always been generous with you, and who is having a bad time and needs it."

"I just don't have it. Though even if I did I wouldn't give it to you," he said soberly.

"Just what I thought!"

"But I'm glad to offer what I have on me if it's of any use, or any other help that I can give you."

"Thanks."

"Are you sick by any chance? Because if that's the case—" he murmured.

"No, I'm fine," I interrupted curtly. All he was worried about was V.D.! "I'm better than ever, healthier than ever, prettier than ever. But I need money, lots of money, see? Money for jewels, money for dresses, money for perfume, money for drugs, and money for my pimps, if I feel like having them."

"I think you've had too much to drink," Juan warned me. "Though, indeed, you do look prettier than ever. But go on."

"I want two thousand *pesetas* from you, two thousand measly, stinking, filthy *pesetas* so that I can buy myself a ring that I want, and which I only intend to wear once."

"You'll have to be content just wanting it, girl."

"You have the money, yes or no?"

"I told you, no."

"I'm the most beautiful and expensive woman in Madrid, don't you realize that?"

"It's quite possible."

"If you don't give me the money you'll never see me again. Then you won't be able to admire my beauty which you've praised so much, or enjoy 'this clear flowing spring which refreshes you so,' " I threatened him. "But naturally, since I'm not a woman, what difference does it make. I'm the rain, the wind, the day, the night and . . . the devil only knows what all else—naturally I don't deserve anything. All of that you can get gratis, just by going outdoors."

"Oh, come on, don't be silly. Now stop, eh?"

"I don't feel like it."

"If you don't stop, I'll leave."

"So scram."

That time he didn't go, but called the waiter and asked for the check. The two of us were silent while he put it on the plate, carefully folded, to hide the astronomical figure. I felt my blood rising with an anger I couldn't control, and I abruptly opened my purse and threw down a thousand *peseta* bill before Juan could stop me.

"Take it out of this, please," I commanded. "The gentleman is a little short tonight," I explained, looking sorrowfully at Juan. "And divide the change among yourselves and the boys in the orchestra—so they can drink to my health, okay?"

"Thank you, thank you, Señorita," the waiter murmured, grabbing the money and running before Juan could say a word.

Actually, he didn't even try to stop him. He was silent for a moment. Then he burst out laughing. I didn't like the forced sound of it at all.

"Thanks, Lola. It's quite a thrill to be taken out to dinner by a woman like you! And so generously, too!"

Later, we went dancing at the Villa Rosa. We were very polite with each other during the rest of the evening, the kind of frigid politeness you use to cover anger. When it came time to pay, I picked up the check again, provoking his nasty laugh a second time.

We drove back through Chamartín in strained silence. After a while I noticed that instead of entering Madrid by the ministries we were speeding along toward Cuatro Caminos and Tetuán.

We were already at Fuencarral when I asked where we were going.

"For a drive."

"At this hour? You're crazy."

I didn't dare say too much because I didn't want him to think I was afraid. Even if he was going to cut my throat or tear me to pieces, I wasn't going to show my fear. Instead, I quietly gazed out at the beautiful evening. It was the end of summer and the large August moon lit up the night.

We passed through Fuencarral and got on the road to Miraflores in the direction of El Mesón. I thought he was going to stop there, but he put his foot on the gas and raced through Colmenar Viejo like a madman, obviously trying to frighten me.

"How fast are we going?"

"Ninety-five kilos."

"How fast can the car go?"

"One hundred and ten."

"What a shame! I'd like to go a hundred and thirty. The other day I was in an American car, a brand-new Buick, and the speed was fantastic. I adore going fast."

I glanced sideways at him. The moonlight cast a beam of light, like translucent water, against his sun-tanned face. He kept on smiling with that little smile of his that can be sad, or happy, or tender, or ironic and cruel, but always remains a smile.

He slowed down slightly, just to be contrary. After passing some miserable ramshackle houses, he crossed over to another road which bordered the Santillana lake. Suddenly, he stopped the car right alongside of the water.

"What are you doing?"

"Come on, let's get out."

"*Hombre,* you're out of your mind. At this hour what reason have I to start exploring?"

"You seem frightened, my dear," he joked.

"Me frightened—of you?" I immediately jumped out of the car. "Really, *hombre,* all I am is tired and bored."

"They say it's very healthy to go for a stroll before going to bed. Doctors recommend it highly, particularly to calm the nerves."

He took me firmly by the arm and propelled me toward the edge of the lake. Suddenly I remembered Señor Pastor and the man who'd just been killed and I thought that maybe my hour had come too. Perhaps Juan was really crazy, criminally insane. Perhaps he planned to weight me down with rocks, tie me up, and throw me in the water. Perhaps this was his moment of revenge, for Lord only knows what mysterious hurts he had buried within himself through the years.

Everything is possible, and though in real life these things happen only occasionally, in films we see this all the time. What did I know about this man who held my arm so tightly as he steered me toward the cold, lonely water streaked with silver? He probably wasn't even really named Juan. True, we had had several conversations together, we had dined at the same spot several times, had gone dancing in various night clubs and had had some good times out—the usual sort of thing for men and women to do. But I'd also heard the nightingale singing in the Retiro, and I'd revealed the dark truth about myself to him, bringing burning tears to my eyes and a distant smile to his lips.

The first part I'd done with all the men, more or less—the second had only happened with him. That's why I was struck by this strange man, who gave the impression that beneath his smile he was hiding a terrible inner restlessness. Once this wild force was freed, there'd be no limits to his violence. Maybe he was crazy. I let him lead me toward the water, pretending to be merely bad-tempered and annoyed. Actually I was petrified.

With that terrible lucidity that comes to one in moments of stress, I felt that my final hour had come. I felt a terrible rage swelling in me against that stupid man who had never understood me. That miserable beast who could have made me happy if he had ever taken the trouble to recognize the way I was feeling, to realize what he had stirred up inside me with his foolishness. But then I decided that maybe it would be better to end it this way, without his knowing anything. I didn't feel capable of telling him, of explaining the agitation in my heart—I didn't understand it myself. I became strangely calm, filled with an odd bittersweet melancholy, longing for him to finish what I feared he had begun. I wanted him to be the one, that man who was at the same time both so distant and so close to me. I wanted him to finish my stupid life. This paltry idiotic life that he had no love for, that was of no use to him. And as for me—beneath my beauty, my astonishing, fantastic beauty—something had awakened. Juan had made me for the first time in my life feel like a woman. Ah, but after what he'd told me that terrible night, he would never, never know it, the idiot!

While I was thinking all those things we came to the edge of the lake. The moon was shining across the water, and a fresh breeze from the sierra ruffled the enormous sheet of gold. I looked over at the solid mass of mountains and shivered. The Pedriza was livid, as though red wine had been spilled over it.

Juan just stood there. He dropped my arm, stooped down, scooped up a stone and threw it, breaking the bright silver water with black wounds which dissolved slowly, leaving the surface calm and smooth again. Then he sat down on a large rock, and suddenly pulled me down on his lap, kissing me savagely. I didn't care. I wasn't going to resist. He could do what he liked.

Without a word he brusquely took his mouth from mine, seized me by the waist, and turned me face downward across his knees. Pinning me down with one arm, he lifted my skirt with the other. He pulled down my pants and spanked me until, in a fury, I was able to grab one of his legs and bite him.

Later, everything seemed to happen very fast. When I got loose, I cursed at him with all the vile language I'd learned in my time as a prostitute. He smiled at me calmly, as though I were giving him compliments. Worn out, I suddenly started to weep. Why, oh why did that man always make me cry? Finally, in between my sobs, I was able to speak. It burst forth like a torrent—I was in such a hurry to unburden myself that I tripped over the words.

I don't remember most of what I said or what Juan answered. But even if I could, I wouldn't put it down here. There are certain things which are meant for oneself and should never be told to anyone—particularly when you've led a life which has already obliged you to show more than you should.

I lost my head that crazy night and it's all very hazy, like a confused, happy dream. I only remember that our love-making ended at dawn and that the price I paid—a heavy chest cold—seemed well worth while. It was the one time in my life that I suffered illness happily. But not once did he come to see me during the four days that I ran a fever, all alone in my pretty and solitary bed.

Six

I know that for a few days I went a little crazy. We went out a lot together and I told him the whole truth about my life. In the beginning I mixed the truth with all shorts of lies but little by little I became so involved that it was impossible for me to leave out or change anything, even the awful bits that made me sound bad. As soon as something occurred to me, I couldn't rest until I'd spilled it all out to that accursed Juan. But I never understood his reactions. Whenever I thought he'd get angry, he laughed, very amused, and whenever I thought he'd be amused he'd become grimmer than a judge with ulcers.

What I poured out during those nights were things to be heard rather than to be put down here. Once the truth had been unlocked I couldn't stop. I told him all that I've already written up to now about my life, maybe embellishing it a little, but not hiding anything. And when we'd left each other, I'd feel feverish and stay wide awake all night. I was afraid that he might leave me, and I wouldn't have anyone to talk to. I realize now that since I'd been a child I hadn't revealed myself to anyone, keeping everything buried in a gnawing silence.

My excited state didn't prevent me from noticing Juan's mood. I was so aware of him that I often stopped talking, being afraid of tiring him with my words. But since he always smiled back sympathetically, I kept on going. Until finally one night it occurred to me that while he knew everything about me, all my secrets, I still didn't even know his real name. I remember that I stopped short then like a suspicious mule who stubbornly refuses to go on.

"What's the matter, little one?" he asked immediately. Nothing escapes him.

"I don't know why I'm telling you all this."

"You're telling me because you can't stand it any longer, because you've reached the bursting point," he replied, smiling.

"And . . . you think that's the only reason?"

"Yes."

"Listen, I just don't understand you, Juan," I said angrily. "You're unbearably conceited, and a big idiot who can't see the nose in front of your face."

"*Anda*, Lola. Forget about that and keep on talking. I find your past very interesting," he said, conveniently going off on another tangent.

"Interesting!" I grumbled. "All that interest of yours annoys me."

In a flash I became aware of something, something that wounded me in a sensitive spot. I realized that in his great interest, his patience in listening to me, his insatiable curiosity to learn everything, appearing to be making notes in his memory . . . he was studying and observing me as though . . . as though I were a *thing!* I was enraged. That wasn't what I had wanted—not at all.

"Okay, it's all over, see?" I yelled. "I'm not some queer insect."

"Stop talking nonsense, Lola."

"I'm not, Juan. While I've been pouring out my whole life, completely confiding in you, you've kept on being mysterious and haven't revealed a thing. Why, I don't even know your name!"

"A name doesn't mean anything. But I can't be anything more than me myself—you see?"

"Why haven't you ever given me your telephone number, so that I could call sometime if I needed you? Come on, tell me. Once and for all."

"But—but I thought that it was very obvious, girl," he said, smiling. "Because I don't want you to phone me."

"You've got your nerve. But anyway, at least you're frank. That's something."

"Sometimes I am . . . sometimes I'm not, Lola. With the others, the other women I mean."

"Okay, okay. I already know that you go out with others, you needn't remind me. I know very well that I'm nothing to you. That you don't love me. That's it, you don't love me at all, not even a little bit, Juan."

"I'm very fond of you, Lola."

"Thanks. I'm the most expensive woman in Madrid, and I don't need your charity."

"Naturally."

"Look, Juan, why don't we put the cards on the table?"

"Those games generally end rather badly. But if you insist . . ."

"Certainly I insist," I said firmly. "Even if it ends badly, still it will end—understand?"

"I understand very well that you no longer have any need of me."

"I never did, *hombre*. What did you imagine?"

"Suit yourself."

"Now come to the point."

"The point is often something very ugly, and you are something very beautiful."

"Leave the joking for another time. This little bee isn't in the mood for honey. Listen to me, Juan. I'm asking you as a favor, and I never ask favors from anyone," I cajoled him.

"You never ask favors from anyone? Come on, Lola, you don't have to exaggerate."

"You don't have to make yourself into a bigger idiot than you are." I became angry again. "All right, obviously I ask, and I ask plenty—but this isn't asking, it's only collecting what's due me, see?"

"Forgive me," he murmured. "You're right. Only I hate having such serious conversations when you're with me."

"Listen, Juan, I have to know why you go out with me."

"Are we starting that again?"

"Truthfully—are you married?"

"*Caray, chica!* Yes, truthfully," he laughed.

"And you love your wife, don't you? I'm sure, completely sure, of that, and don't try and deny it," I warned him, becoming very excited.

"I didn't intend to deny it, just the contrary. I love her very much," he said, completely unabashed.

"I bet she doesn't understand you at all."

"As a matter of fact, we understand each other extremely well. And we've a very happy marriage. One of the few left in this world," he added, very satisfied with himself.

"Maybe. I won't argue about it with you. But as for understanding you—and by that I mean a complete understanding—that's almost impossible. One would have had to have been through all life's shit, and yet at the same time have remained more innocent than a baby at the breast to make sense out of you. Yes. Juan. One would have to be both angelic and evil, simple and clever, pretty and ugly—all of that at the same time, to really know what you're about. That's why neither she, I, or anybody—even you—can understand yourself."

"Christ, what a character I must be!" he laughed uncomfortably. "But—where did you learn all this?"

"Flight hours, *hombre*, flight hours."

"When you speak seriously, you're always right," he admitted. "It's one of the few things I dislike about you."

"Don't change the subject, please. I want to know what you think you're doing with me."

"You're like a record that's gotten stuck."

"Because you haven't explained, see? It makes no sense. You're not one of those failures who want a woman like me so that they can forget things. You have nothing to forget with me."

"But maybe I have something to learn from you," he replied gravely.

"Yes, I know that. I've known that for a while. . . . I don't enjoy knowing it, I assure you."

"But it's worth your while, Lola. And now I'm telling you the truth."

"I'm not interested in that kind of 'worth,' see?"

"Okay, okay . . ." he purposely pretended to misunderstand. "For you the only thing that counts is—"

"That's right. Money . . . or . . ."

"Or what?"

"Oh, there are so many things that can interest a woman. Didn't you know?"

"Jewels, dresses, comforts, luxuries . . . money, always money, isn't that it, Lola?"

"You're pretty sharp, Juan," I snapped.

"Are the cards on the table now?"

"Hardly. They're more concealed than ever."

"Then let's deal them, once and for all."

"Juan, what do you plan to do with me?" I asked, after a short pause during which I decided to be completely reckless.

"What?" He jumped. "I don't intend to *do* anything with you. God save me from that!"

"Look, Juan," I asked, persisting. "You have to answer me. I beg you, I ask you for the sake of . . . for . . . well, I don't know . . . For something that you're very fond of."

"Then, for Lola," he replied gallantly. "For what Lola means to me—something for which I've extraordinary respect."

"Respect? That word hardly seems to suit me."

"Respect, Lola," he repeated firmly. "Because you are beautifully alive and filled with a savage strength, like a dramatic phenomenon of nature. . . . I'll answer anything you like, I promise."

"Are you rich?"

"*Caray!* You sure come quickly to the point, girl," he laughed. "You really want to know, eh?"

"Yes, I do. I'm always interested in knowing whether a man has money or not. And in this case it's of more than usual interest to me."

"Much more?"

"Much more, Juan."

"And for what reason?"

"Oh—it's very difficult to explain, and probably you wouldn't be able to understand," I said elusively. "Because there are some things that you don't understand, either. In spite of being so smart."

"I'm sure of that, Lola," he replied, slightly put out. "But coming back to your question, girl. I'm not rich."

"You swear to it?"

"I don't swear lightly, beautiful. I give you my word of honor and that's enough."

"All right, *hombre*, don't get angry. But what do you call not rich?"

"I call not being rich having to spend my days scrounging around after work like a dog, accepting each lousy thing that comes my way—even when it's badly paid and loathsome. I have to keep my mouth shut and I never say what I really think. I'm not able to do the things that give me a sense of strength, of well-being and inner honesty. I do all of that to earn enough money to be able to exist—provided I live very carefully and deprive myself of many satisfactions. That's what I call not being rich. When you don't lack for anything essential, but are not really free."

"And you live that way?"

"Yes, Lola. I live that way."

"Please, swear that it's the truth."

"I don't want to. I've already given you my word."

I scrutinized him carefully. No, he couldn't be lying. Not with such an open and straightforward expression. But how many times in my own life had I looked like an angel when . . . Naturally, I'm a prostitute and live off my ability to lie, but he . . . no, no, he couldn't be lying, I was positive of it.

Once again we were sitting in the gardens of Bolonia, hidden in the courtyard, listening to the music of the orchestra, muted by the trees and the distance. They were playing "Caravan" and I felt both sad and happy, knowing that Juan didn't have money. Sad because if he had had some I could have been very happy with him, with him alone. I was weary, terribly weary of my life. Only with him I was never bored. I was happy because the reason he had treated me this way, not giving me what the others did, and always less than I deserved, was because he didn't have much money —not because he thought I wasn't worth more. And even if I wasn't exactly rich myself, since the death of that poor friend of the procurer's, I had enough to see me through my own funeral and I could allow myself the pleasure of wasting several evenings with Juan, and accepting some miserably small bill from his hands.

"Don't you believe me?" he asked brusquely, breaking into my thoughts.

"Well . . . yes, I do. Because even though you're smart enough to fool me, you wouldn't."

"Then continue with your questions."

"You don't love me?"

"I've told you, I'm very fond of you."

"But . . . not, not in love, right?"

"*Caray!*" He laughed again. "I haven't lost my head over you, but . . ."

"Look, Juan. . . . You men go out with women for two things. I mean, with women like me. Either because you're in love with them, despite yourself, or because they give you

198

a good time when you feel like having a good time, see? And with me I don't think it's either. So what is it?"

"I don't consider you a . . . a woman 'like that,' Lola." I'd never seen him look so serious before.

"Oh, I know," I laughed sharply. "You don't consider me a woman at all."

"My God, how murky it's all becoming! And on such a beautiful evening," he sighed regretfully. "Come on—let's go listen to the nightingale for a while."

"They don't sing in September."

"They sing during the whole year, if you're able to hear them."

"If you haven't lost your head over me, if I haven't driven you crazy, like the rest, and if I'm not even a woman to you—why do you go out with me? What are you looking for?" I continued, getting very excited.

"Christ, leave me in peace!" he protested with irritation.

"You have to tell me," I insisted.

"But if I don't know, Lola—if I don't know?" he cried desperately.

"Then—" I thought, and suddenly I felt terribly happy. "But I'm sure you know. Think a little, and you'll see that you know," I insisted, rejecting my own thoughts firmly.

"Maybe," he admitted pensively. "But it would take a long time to explain and I don't like making speeches to people."

"Try to say it in just a few words—the way the truth should always be said."

"Look, Lola . . . haven't you seen those films where the hero or heroine has a sort of double personality and leads two distinct lives?"

"I rarely go to the movies, but I know what you mean."

"Well, without being anything as extreme as that, something a little similar has happened to me," he confessed.

"Hombre!" I laughed incredulously. "Don't tell me you go around killing people when the mood strikes you."

"Oh, I'm not talking about that," he replied impatiently. "I just used that as an example so that you could understand what has happened to me."

"Go on."

"I think I'm realistic. I take care of my obligations, and, what's more, I enjoy the pleasant, orderly, convenient life of family and work in my own familiar world. In fact, I like it too much ever to give it up."

"In other words, you love your wife, children, and job. You like a pleasant life without complications or adventures," I replied, disappointed.

"That's right."

"You take the easy way out."

"Yes, up to a point—I won't argue that."

"Good! But—what do you really *do?*"

"Oh, lots of things."

"But what are you, *hombre?* Doctor, engineer, lawyer, black marketeer or what?"

"None of those things, Lola." He laughed loudly. "I'm in business, respectable business," he admitted, almost ashamed. "Which gives me plenty to do. And, in addition. . . ."

"In addition, what?"

"In addition I'm also someone completely different," he continued with more pride in his voice.

"But what, what?" I yelled. "A thief, a criminal—what the hell are you? I'm losing my patience!"

"I'm . . . I'm also a poet."

"A poet?" I was startled. "You're bats."

"Perhaps it's the same thing."

"So you write verses, eh? . . . then you can make a pretty one about me."

"No, I couldn't. I never write verses."

"Really now . . . it's impossible to understand you."

He laughed. "Oh, you're wrong. You see, that's just why I go with you—because you *do* understand me."

"Don't try and softsoap me. I'm not in the mood, see?"

"What I mean is that in addition to being a decent, hard-working, serious man, and a good father and husband, I'm also a troubled, curious, wild adventurer. I live in an imaginary world which is as necessary and real to me as the humdrum daily grind."

"Then I'm . . ."

"I need you. I need your astonishing beauty and spontaneous charm, your cruel and lively strength, your marvelous lack of sentimental complications, scruples and worries. I need you because you are the prettiest, loveliest, purest little animal that I've ever encountered in my life—in my poet's life."

"Ah . . . so I'm the nightingale," I said, finally understanding.

"Yes, Lola. You're the nightingale who sings, and the gazelle who runs and the newborn duckling who cries and the sea gull who plays with the wind."

"And the clouds and the snow and the running spring and the storm. I'm all of those things, every one, right, Juan?"

"Right, Lola."

"Everything except a woman, isn't that it?"

"No, you're also a woman—and a marvelous woman. No one could improve upon you," he conceded laughing.

"But only on the outside. Inside, I'm not, right?"

"It's difficult to have everything," he admitted. "Anyway, it's not your fault."

"Sometimes you act like the world's biggest fool."

"A poet, Lola."

"A dope." Wouldn't he ever see? "And you can go find someone else for your . . . for your poetry."

"It won't be easy."

"You go out with other women . . . don't you?"

"Well . . . well, yes. Once in a while."

"See what a bastard you are? See how little you love me?"

"Let's drop the subject now. Shall we dance awhile? I don't think there's anyone that I know here."

"No, I don't want to dance, see? I want to drink, I feel like drinking."

I drank plenty that night. And at dawn I started to cry again—those hot, acid tears which were always brought on by that accursed man so that he could later tenderly wipe them away with his kisses.

Seven

I don't want this to seem like a boudoir novel about the upset Juan caused in what he always called my "mechanized" life. Our relationship wasn't at all sweetly sentimental, just the opposite. I just want to put down here a brief reminder of the way we were together—or, more accurately, of our insoluble problem, which is really best forgotten.

I remember very clearly that after that drunken night, I decided not to go out so often with him, but to continue to treat him as a good friend in whom I could confide. Only one thing I kept hidden. Something which was happening to me for the first time in my life, and worried me a lot, despite there being long periods when I forgot about it.

I very quickly told him about the procurer and his friends, about the money I had hidden in my apartment, and about my sick old men. I never neglected that part of my life, even though I liked less and less to speak of it.

As I've already said somewhere else, the money didn't go to my head. I was well aware that it wasn't enough for me to keep on living in high style, spending freely and buying whatever I liked. It was just a little help, that's all.

Juan was very good about all of that. He said that he didn't want to interfere in my affairs or give advice, since it never did any good. But he couldn't resist telling me one thing. He warned me to select my friends more carefully since I was determined to keep on living off them. And suddenly, unexpectedly, he volunteered to find and pay for a good teacher who could improve my meager education.

He did this rather reluctantly, out of a sense of duty, almost hoping that I'd refuse. I realized that he was afraid that once I was educated he wouldn't like me as much. But I accepted his offer, and during the last year I've studied with a very serious old gentleman Juan sent to me. Recently, I've also added an Englishman, whom I pay myself. I want to impress people with my cleverness and, too, I'm practical. As everyone knows, those who speak this language are going to be managing the world for some time to come.

I must admit that I like learning things. I've always had a curious nature and I find it very absorbing to learn about what happened in the past, and what is going on now. That's why I like histories and biographies more than novels. To Juan's great astonishment, I became interested in mathematics and grammar. He says I'm a woman full of surprises. But no matter how much I try, I can't satisfy him when it comes to understanding all the ins and outs of art and literature. For me they're pretty pictures and fairy tales that men make up to avoid the sourness of real life. (Me, I like things clear, be it in the past or present.) Sometimes Juan gets carried away and goes on and on about all sorts of things, until suddenly he stops, almost startled to find it's me he's talking to and not one of his literary friends. I think he's even beginning to be sorry that he started the lessons. Just a little while ago he told me that he was afraid that he had made a mistake. All this knowledge wasn't going to make my life any happier. Indeed, it might make things worse. Of course he's wrong. I just adore the lessons—but not for the reasons he thinks. Now I have a chance to bowl people over with something besides my looks, and I'm delighted. Of course, I've no intention of letting my smartness make me get all worked up like Juan. It's strange, the more he knows, the nuttier he gets.

This past year has swept by almost without my realizing it. I guess when one isn't so active outside, and instead of dashing about, calms down and concentrates on something in the mind, the days seem to fly without leaving the slightest trace. One lives apart from time, in a sort of limbo.

On the surface I spent those months the same as in the past, often busying myself with my hospital beds. Underneath, I confess I was wild with rage at not being able to capture that crazy Tenorio.* Oh, he's fond of me and needs

* Don Juan Tenorio. (Translator's note.)

me much more than he thinks, and even much more than I think when I'm in one of my black moods, but that's not enough!

I'm running into trouble with my writing. I've lost some of my illusions about literary things and I'm no longer so easily impressed. Since I've become so educated it all seems trivial. I know now that there have been other lives just as stormy as mine, even though I'm sure that the protagonists weren't so pretty. According to Juan that's one of the results of culture. One loses one's certainty. Be that as it may, I intend finishing. I'm a very stubborn girl and always see things through. Anyway, I still enjoy it when I'm writing about myself.

Now, looking at it squarely: What prostitute has had my success? How many of them have received as many proposals to get married for real, in church? And, indeed, who is as pretty and beautiful as I and who looks the way I do in the morning with my face freshly scrubbed, without even a drop of powder? No one, I'm absolutely positive of this. Juan may be a dumb fool who doesn't realize what a prize I am, or maybe he's incapable of falling in love, but that's no reason for me to feel so angry and miserable.

And I do feel that way. Miserable—good and miserable. Gnawed away inside by something which won't let me live in peace. Only now I don't feel as angry as I did. I know that there is nothing to be done.

Eight

I met Ricardo Cienfuegos that summer in San Sebastian —his name may mean "much fire" but Cienvinos, "much wine," would have fitted him better. He was always loaded. In August, guessing that Juan would be there with his family, I decided to abandon the heat of Madrid for the cool air by the sea. With great difficulty I managed to see Juan once or twice, until the rat took matters into his own hands and went to Biarritz, protected by the frontier, a barrier I couldn't conquer. And after he said that he was so poor!

In San Sebastian, like everywhere else, I created a sensation. The young things from Ondarreta and the Bar Vasco were miserable because I stole all their boy friends. You should have seen me in my American bathing suit, a divine blue outfit which cost me over a thousand *pesetas*. I also had a beachcoat from Rango and two Balenciaga dresses. Indeed, I was spending a lot of money on clothes and was getting quite a reputation for being well dressed.

I was always surrounded with the most eligible men in San Sebastian, which is like saying in all of Spain, since everyone who counts goes there for the summer vacation. I had decided that month to spend some money on myself, and it's really amazing what money can do for you when you're young and pretty. But I must admit that I wasn't as happy with my success as I should have been. Whenever I thought about that man who always slipped through my fingers, I became enraged and snapped at whoever happened to be with me, or else I suddenly seemed more stunned than a hen in a strange coop, until after a few minutes the bad feeling passed and I came back to my senses again.

During my vacation I met Ricardo at the tennis courts one evening, and he immediately fell for me. He's a dumpy little guy, but very rich and from an excellent family. Ordinarily, I'd feel flattered by my conquest, particularly as he had quite a reputation with women.

That night, trying to forget about Juan and soothe my anger, I got dressed up to go on the town. I wore a pretty little headband and the Balenciaga, a hand-printed dress with yellow and green flowers. The skirt outlined my well-shaped hips, clinging snugly to my thighs, and the low-cut neckline showed off my breasts provocatively.

My evening's companions were Don Alfonso Tapia, someone very important in the movie industry, Luis Arrigorrechabala, a Basque shipowner, wealthy and very *simpático,* and José Antonio Cortés, a mature type, around fifty, who had plenty of money and prided himself on having reached the age where he didn't have to toss it away on women—in other words, a guy who's only good for taking up space and filling a pair of pants.

The Maître received us very obsequiously, leading us to a first-rate table with a good view of the tennis grounds. Arrigorrechabala obviously had a lot of pull at the club. Immediately all the other men at the club started to stare at me intently, while my three escorts, feeling very satisfied with themselves, started to act foolishly considering their age—although justifiably considering their millions.

José Antonio Cortés was the most playful, gaily waving to all his friends, dancing continually and in general behaving like a giggling adolescent. He made such a spectacle of himself that Señor Tapia, who had the most brains, sharply called him to order.

I admit that I let myself be fondled by him, being quite tipsy. I danced with him, glad to get away from the table. The dinner was frankly inferior and I didn't enjoy it, having learned to be fussy about what I put in my mouth.

Later that evening that idiotic Cortés started to boast that he could get into France. He had a pass, something very difficult to obtain then, the frontier being closed. This reminder of Juan made me very despondent. I asked him where along the coast Biarritz was. Pointing to a distant light across the dark sea, he showed me the lighthouse of the French port. I became melancholy, and sadly listened to the soft sound of the waves beneath the noise of Kurt Dogan's orchestra, quietly wondering whether in Biarritz nightingales also sang.

To cheer myself up I asked for another bottle of French champagne. After it had taken effect, and I was acting gayer, Ricardo Cienfuegos came over to our table, all spruced up and full of smiles. Though presumably he came to greet the men, he immediately asked me to dance.

He held me tight while they played *"Tres Palabras,"* and finding him rather charming, I started to enjoy myself with him. We arranged to meet later, after the others left me at my hotel, which by some lousy coincidence was called the Biarritz.

I found it quite difficult to get rid of them. Cortés was one of those tiresome jerks who stick to you like glue, and who think that you have to put up with their insipidness, their boredom and their grossness just because they have several millions, plus a chalet, pool, and black American limousine. He took me home and then suggested that we go for a drive in it on the Paseo Nuevo, along the coast. We went. He showed me the Biarritz lighthouse again and made such an aggressive pass that I pretended to have a dizzy spell, so that he'd take me back to the hotel. He's one of those men who's only used to going out with some poor greasy pig and has no idea of how to treat a high-class, expensive woman like me.

Finally I was alone, although only for a moment. Ricardo Cienfuegos came for me right away. We went out on the town, drinking in all the taverns and bars that were still open, for it was almost dawn. Later we swam at Zarauz—a treacherous beach where I almost came to the end of my days while peacefully another day was breaking.

Nine

I felt rather sympathetic toward Ricardo. He was one of those men who never are a nuisance. Naturally, before I devoted myself to him I found out about him, through his friends. They immediately told me all the things that could have prejudiced me against him. I learned that he was separated from his wife, that he was a complete alcoholic, conceited, a fool, and had two grown sons. Apparently he had run through a great deal of his fortune, but from what I could see he still had enough left to spend plenty on women. I was soon to learn from my own experience that he was an expert at getting rid of the green stuff.

The best thing about him was his drunkenness. When he was stewed he became peaceful and quiet, and was content to have a pretty woman at his side, and even sometimes an ugly one. Alcohol makes everything beautiful for some men.

Ricardo only spent a few sober hours each day. From morning until after lunch. He was a military man and had to report to his post for a while. Then he started to drink English gin. From after the siesta until dawn the following day Ricardo drank steadily, peacefully falling into a happy stupor. Nothing escaped him and he never made a disagreeable spectacle of himself. Even though he oozed liquor from every pore of his body, he never lost his beautiful composure or his equilibrium. He merely kept still, buried in a soft velvety dream, removed from this world, for better or for worse.

Naturally he wasn't one of those hectic drunks who want to be in a million places at once, nor did he become cloying or personal. My affair with him all boiled down to an occasional dance and going along with a pal of his whom he called The Bird. He was an odd character who always said *"Palagalaga"* whenever Ricardo said *"Chaguagua."* This meaningless gibberish was his favorite verbal means of communication.

For these two men everything, absolutely everything, could be expressed by those two nonsense words: *Chaguagua, Palagalaga.* Admiration, surprise, scorn, fear, desire, envy, bitterness, good humor, the most cruel sarcasm, affection, and even greed. Everything was meant by *Chaguagua* and its constant reply—*Palagalaga.* The Bird never said *Chaguagua* or Ricardo *Palagalaga.* The two drunks in their quietly inebriated state never permitted any change in the order of the linguistic ritual which was as unchanging as the rain which always comes down and never goes up, or the sun which never confuses twilight with dawn. When I told Juan about it he said that it was something more than nonsense words; it was the symbol of the survival of the intellect. I don't understand this pedantic lingo—maybe I'm stupid but I don't see why things can't be said clearly, the way I do. But Juan is very strange in many ways, and among his oddities he's a philosopher, or something like that.

Coming back to my story, I should say that I immediately realized that Ricardo was something more than just the usual

sucker. In his drunken, lovesick fascination for me I saw
something that could be of help to me when my life was no
longer so glittering. He might give me security, maybe even
a little affection. These gentle drunks often become very
attached to one, if they're astutely handled, and allowed to
go their own way. Why, The Bird has managed to live off
Ricardo for ten years by always knowing when to say
Palagalaga!

I let Cienfuegos see me all he wanted to. He was crazy
about me and there were certain advantages. He made my
reputation in San Sebastian for the entire summer, always
treating me like a queen. The young Basque girls as well as
several married women were delighted at how deftly Ricardo
managed to chase away the crowd of idle loafers who constantly clung to me because of my beauty. Still, I didn't tie
myself down to him and I preserved my freedom. I wanted
to proceed step by step and make my decision after I went
back to Madrid.

But that was much, much more involved than I had
imagined. As soon as I abandoned the Basque countryside for
Madrid, guessing that Juan must have returned from his
escapade, Ricardo canceled the rest of his vacation and came
running. Actually, I had left him in San Sebastian during a
brief fit of bad temper.

As soon as I arrived home I tried to catch up with Juan.
In twenty-four hours I spent more than fifty *duros* on taxi
fare looking in all the places where I figured he might be, for
him or his car. But the earth had swallowed up both. Disgusted, I threw myself into the waiting arms of Ricardo, and
made do as best I could. Finally, after I'd given Juan up for
lost, we ran into the crazy Tenorio one night in the gardens
of the Villa Rosa.

It was a beautiful moonlit September night, heavy as liquid
gold, and so still that you could almost feel the air with your
hand. The cloying night left a sweet perfumed taste in my
mouth, and I remembered that September is one of the worst
months—a month filled with anguish, and approaching death.

I looked marvelous. My black Rodríguez was very décol-
leté and flattered my figure. Over my shoulders I draped an
ice-blue fox stole, a present from Ricardo, which made me
look like a queen. I sat between him and The Bird and didn't
deign to look at anyone. But down deep I felt very weary, as
though an evil spell had been cast on me, a spell extinguish-
ing one by one the lamps of my happiness.

"What's happening to my girl this evening?" inquired
Ricardo. "What does my little princess want?" Even though
he's Castilian, he has a lot of the sugary Andalucian ways.

"I think I've caught a chill, I don't feel very well," I replied fussily.

"Poor little baby. Tomorrow we'll bring her something that will make her happy," he consoled me. "Right, Carlos?"

"Oh, without fail!" The Bird said, making a great effort to keep himself awake.

"Maybe a pair of diamond earrings?" I asked hopefully, becoming more cheerful.

"Perhaps, perhaps. . . ." Ricardo murmured.

"Oh, my darling . . . how much I love you!" I exclaimed, snuggling next to him like a contented pussycat.

"Chaguagua," he said, smiling peacefully.

"Palagalaga," answered The Bird, hiding himself behind his plumage. He was like a soft plump drowsy bird, whose feathers had become stiff from an inner cold—a cold no drink could ever warm.

We danced two sambas. Then, when I sat down again, I saw Juan. Taken aback, I dropped my purse and, what's worse, broke the mirror of the compact inside. Luckily, I was flanked by the two men, and was able to hide behind them, concealing in time the unhappy expression on my face.

The bastard naturally had someone in tow. Some conceited bitch, who put on grand airs pretending to be a lady just because she had on an expensively elegant dress and hat, which was the only ladylike thing about her. But I had magnificent hair and didn't need a hat—hair she'd have given her eyeteeth for. Preoccupied with themselves, they talked on at great length and sat down at the next table without even noticing me. This made me even more furious. Finally, Juan turned his face in my direction, and his eyes suddenly met mine, smoldering in fury.

Now I ask you: Wouldn't another man, with less brass than he, have gotten up on some pretext and left? The very least he could have done was to have changed tables. Out of common courtesy he could have shown some delicacy for my feelings.

But that bastard did just the opposite. When he first saw me he seemed rather startled, but then he smiled back amiably and admiringly, as if to indicate by his expression that he found me good to look at. Jokingly, he waved to me. Yes, jokingly—I swear by the memory of my mother, the one I never knew—and that's what made me lose control.

Redder than a poppy, burning with all the wine I'd drunk, I went over to him in a fury. Not giving him time to think, I wiped that amiable smirk off his face with the best, most resounding slap of my entire filthy career.

Ten

After that mess I spent several days hardly ever leaving my apartment, at odds with all mankind. Disgusted, I wasn't in a mood to put up with any of them. After I calmed down a bit, I decided to have a strong talk with Juan. It was time a few things were cleared up.

I found him, and we agreed to go out the following night. He didn't seem angry about either the slap or its consequences. It had caused a terrible fight and scandal, but these things amused him.

I must confess that I spent the entire day dressing and perfuming myself, anxious to have a powerful effect on him. I don't know whether it was my nerves or so much putting on and off of make-up, but when the time came I was much less pretty than usual, and in a lousy mood.

"What's the matter, Lola?" he asked, after we sat down at an isolated table at the Granja Florida in the Retiro.

"Nothing, absolutely nothing, *hombre*. Why?"

"Oh, I don't know. . . . You don't look too well."

"So I'm ugly, eh? For your information the traffic stops when I walk out in the street."

"Now, after all. . . . You don't have to exaggerate that much," he laughed.

We kept on pussyfooting about this and that, until, after gulping down three brandies, I came to the point.

"Listen, Juan, we have to have a serious talk, see?"

"How horrible! Just as soon as you get me in your clutches you decide that we have to have a serious talk, as if we had some terrible problem!"

"If my wanting to talk bothers you so, I'll keep quiet. And if you don't like my company, I'll scram. I've more boy friends than I know what to do with."

"I saw that the other night, thank you, baby."

"As for you, you've lost every ounce of shame. Going out with such a creature . . ."

"You know her?"

"No, nor do I want to. I know her kind. She'll take a man for everything he's got."

"Really?" He looked amused. "Why, she has more money than the Bank of Spain."

"She'll get something out of you, I warn you." I found his smugness infuriating. "And, anyway, you don't have to be so insulting."

"Insulting? To whom?" he asked, surprised.

"Just because I have to earn my living in a bad profession you don't have to throw it in my face."

"Now, Lola—take it easy."

"I'm sure that bitch didn't have to sweat for her money. Some man of the family earned it. It must be very pleasant to be rich like that, *chico*," I muttered angrily.

"Maybe you're right. Now, let's forget this foolishness."

"Okay. Let's forget lots of things."

"All right."

We sat quietly awhile, and he took advantage of the opportunity to stare at some female. That man, he couldn't keep his eyes still. Why, he'd even be interested in a stick of wood if it was dressed up in a skirt.

"Please, Juan, listen to me for a moment," I implored softly, realizing that I wouldn't get anywhere fighting with him.

"Anything you like, precious."

"I don't see how we can continue this way. At least I can't, that's for sure."

"Continue what way? What are you talking about?"

"You're making my life miserable with your craziness."

"Me? Making your life miserable? But you live better than all of us," he said, surprised. "A dab of powder on your face, a dash of lipstick, a few flirty smiles and caresses and presto! You've hooked your fish."

"You think it's that easy?"

"Naturally. All the dramatic nonsense about the miseries of the life of sin is only literature—literature for adolescents. The ones who really have a tough life are our honorable mothers, our respected heads of the family. So don't come to me with your nonsense."

"I have to think about myself."

"Think about yourself—for Christ's sake, that's all you do twenty-four hours of the day. Even when you sleep."

"I see that I can't talk to you. I might as well not try."

"Now look here, Lola, I know what you want to tell me. You've hooked this Ricardo Cienfuegos and you no longer need me as client—in fact I'm in your way, isn't that it?"

"No, Juan. What you say is true in one way, but you've gotten the meaning all wrong."

"Who the devil can understand you?"

It was strange—his asking the question I had so often thrown at him.

"I think you don't want to understand me. You're all wrong about that night. I swear, by the memory of—"

"Leave your mother in peace, eh?"

"I love you, Juan, I'd give up everything for you if you wanted me to." There—now, it was out!

"Lola—don't tell me I've won the lottery!" He looked at me in astonishment.

In a desperate fury I told him everything. What I said has no place here. I remember that I wept, scratched, and lost all my pride. I begged that bastard for what one should never beg of a man. At first he listened with a sort of suspicious curiosity, but finally he, too, was swept away by passion. By passion, mind you! We spent a wild night together. The best, most beautiful night of my whole life.

Nothing really changed, though. The following day he was very tender with me, but carefully advised me not to lose my friendship with Ricardo. This made me so ill that I had to stay in bed several days. I became very upset and my health suffered so that Lirio had to call the doctor. He gave me something to calm my nerves—they were really shot.

Eleven

In view of this, after taking stock of my affairs, I decided to establish a definite relationship with Ricardo, but without breaking off with Juan. Actually, he's the only man who really understands me, the only one I can be myself with. I don't have to humor him with all that boring nonsense I'm so weary of.

If I'm in a bad mood I can show it to him, if I feel like smoking a small cigar I smoke it, if I feel like unburdening myself and telling all the awful things I've done, I do it. I never have to be afraid with him—in fact, he's the only one who really looks out for my interests and gives me good advice. He's even convinced me that the worst thing I could do would be to abandon my present life for him—even if I had enough money to assure me a comfortable future. He says that the reason we understand each other so well is because we never try to fool each other, or become too demanding. Since it's impossible for us to live together, we should be good friends and each lead our own lives. I don't really think that it's so impossible—when a man loves a woman he manages to find the money somewhere and gives up everything for her. This guy is so bats, though, that probably in his own fashion he does love me. Anyway, I find it a consoling thought and he assures me I'm right. He insists he loves me far more than I realize.

For quite some time now I've known who he is, and he no longer attempts to conceal his identity from me. I don't want to cause him trouble, so I can't reveal his name here. He has a good job, generally is quite responsible and hardworking. But like so many men I've run into in Madrid, he has a kind of double personality. The poetic, rebellious side of his nature occasionally forces him to flee from life. Disgusted, he escapes into a world of fantasy, and becomes involved in all sorts of adventures with women. He has some silly notion about prostitutes and how he needs women like us to find some kind of inner freedom. Really! As if my kind were good for anything besides going to bed with a man or spending his money!

Being outspoken (and also because I wanted to discourage him from seeing other females), I've told him many times not to act foolishly. We women are what we seem and nothing better. But he laughs and tells me not to throw stones at my own house. He says that he needs us women as sort of a drug. A drug that opens the dangerous threshold of the imagination. Which is why the louse says that he can't live without some woman constantly at his side.

What with all these long discussions, plus other things which I won't mention, I calmed down somewhat and started to look after my own interests. They were a little shaky due to the fuss a while back. But I didn't give up my idea of catching Juan one day by dint of my patience and my beauty—and even by smothering him if necessary. Now it's become a matter of pride and I'm capable of doing anything to get him.

Meanwhile, I handled Ricardo very well. I swore by my mother that I wouldn't see Juan again—he had smelled something fishy there, something that put horns on him—and he was perfectly content.

Until that point I'd managed to keep my independence, but then he decided to set me up in a little villa in Chamartín. It was very pretty but rather isolated for my tastes. He rented it in my name and also signed my name on the bills for the furniture, just to be on the safe side. I didn't give up my apartment, but kept both places. I had my plans. Once again in my life I was embarked on another honeymoon with someone new, and I meant it to pay off.

At least this time it wasn't too inconvenient. I slept the entire morning, as this is *de rigueur*, then had drinks either at Loto, or the taverns of Correos or Aguila in the Calle Serrano. We had lunch in the neighborhood, and in the hot weather a drive and a siesta. Not bad at all. With what was left of the afternoon I amused myself dressing for dinner. We usually went dancing afterwards and I tried to amuse myself as best I could during the *Chaguaguas* and the *Palagalagas* of Ricardo and The Bird. After a tour of Riscal or Samba we returned home to sleep. At nine in the morning I'd hear Ricardo get up and shower. He's a man of fantastic stamina and never needed much rest. He'd leave, looking more serious than a judge, off to Army headquarters with a bottle of

212

whisky or gin hidden on his squat body. When there was something doing at headquarters or when some relatives were visiting, I'd see Juan. First I did it very discreetly, then each day more and more openly. He was going mad with boredom and I gladly risked anything to see him.

During the fall, my sister, who was back in Madrid, got much worse again. She guessed that she was going to die and she begged me to bring her back to Mojácar. She didn't wish to end her days in a strange place, away from home.

Hoping to kill two birds with one stone, I tried to convince Juan to drive us down in his car. I wanted to make her happy and, also, I looked forward to the return trip with him. But the guy's stubborn as a mule and he refused. Finally, I had to resign myself to using Ricardo's car, accompanied by The Bird, who was sent along as defender of my chastity. Ricardo was quite right in having complete confidence in him. The Bird's only interest in life was alcohol. As soon as he heard some bad gossip about anyone, he ran to tell his master. His kind I could never get around.

Another month passed. Malena died and we buried her in Mojácar. This relieved me of quite a drain, believe me. I had spent a fortune on her.

By the time winter rolled around, I was so snugly entrenched in my easy, idle life that I'd begun to fill out, and even had the start of a double chin. Juan made fun of me and said that I was becoming very bourgeoise. With the help of dieting and massage I got my figure back and by Christmas looked marvelous, down to one hundred and twenty pounds. Of course, Juan insists I still look huge—but he's crazy. He's been acting impossible lately. He's taken a dislike to Ricardo, though he refuses to tell me to leave Ricardo for him. That would be too much responsibility! In this ridiculous state, the year 1946, in which I am writing still, is about to end. I am almost twenty-six and I have to be very careful. This is the danger point when the wrinkles start appearing—though so far I haven't even one.

As far as money goes, I can't complain. Ricardo has a healthy little pile, and I am trying my best to leave him nakeder than the gizzard of a skinny consumptive chicken, one who had long since forgotten what it is to lay an egg.

Part IV

ॐ—ॐ—ॐ—ॐ—ॐ—ॐ—ॐ—ॐ—ॐ—ॐ—ॐ—ॐ—ॐ—ॐ—ॐ—ॐ

One

If it hadn't been for a new success which recently brightened my life, I wouldn't have taken up my pen again to continue my scribbling. That crazy Juan has always had the eye of a prophet and he was right in predicting I would become famous, remembered by posterity for something more than my beauty—a beauty so many men had paid so much just to possess for a brief while.

It didn't happen quickly, the way it does in novels, just little by little, step by step. It started with a contest—"The Calico Dress"—organized by a popular Madrid newspaper. I won second prize. Some dirty rat ruined my chances for the first by telling the jury stories about my sinful life.

But before going into that, I should mention that nearly another year has passed, and now we're in the fall of '47—a dreary time that will go down in history, according to Juan's sarcasm, as the year when Madrid went wild over a new slow, sickeningly sweet flowering of the tango. I remember it as the year when I couldn't manage either to shake off Juan or to get him to love me, which is what I wanted.

During the past year, up until the contest nothing interesting happened, except that Ricardo was nearly ruined. The poor guy even had to sell his classy limousine, my demands were so high. With the money I got out of one man, I was going to set myself up fine with another. But don't think that Juan became my pimp. I wasn't born to have one, nor he to be one. What I mean is that Juan only gives me what he can—very little considering the kind of woman I am—and no one worries.

This period was spent more or less the way it started—that is, with the *Chaguaguas* of Ricardo, the *Palagalagas* of The Bird, and horns on all of them. I must admit that when something good comes my way, I know how to take advantage of it. It relieved my bad mood to take his money from him, hoarding all the gold like the thieving magpie that I am.

Living a life of ease made me much stronger, but my

214

former happy-go-lucky high spirits vanished—perhaps even forever. Juan says that these feelings never return. Instead of idiotically bemoaning the past, the thing to do is to find substitutes, and the world is full of them. Obviously for him it's easy. He always has the name of some woman, and is constantly substituting one for another!

Lately, though, he seems very downhearted. What's more, he says it's my fault. I've made him lose his respect for many things he used to do, and he has realized that for the few days we have on earth it's better to live the way we want, and without hypocrisy. At first I was happy at seeing him this way, thinking that this would bring him to me, but later I realized that he couldn't live with only one woman, that he had to change them, the way the days and the seasons constantly have to renew themselves. He's a difficult sort of man and I think that I understand him less and less as time goes on. If he really loved me the way he says, why doesn't he join me once and for all?

I also kept on with my classes, learning many new things, though sometimes people smiled at my cultured remarks. Until suddenly, not long ago, Juan forbade me to continue with anything except literature, English, and spelling. I've never understood what caused this whim of his, and whenever it comes up he becomes rather sad. He says that knowledge brings a great deal of bitterness and unhappiness and that my best quality is my savage animal nature. At first I was very annoyed, taking what he said as an insult, but now his remarks slide off me like water off a duck's back—we all have our manias and his is to say that I'm a pretty little animal. Though you may not believe it, he made me drop many things that had really begun to interest me. He was very insistent, saying that if I continued to be so bougeoise I wouldn't see hide nor hair of him again.

But going back a few months . . . Ricardo became more and more attentive to me. He must have realized that once his money was gone I was going to slip through his fingers like an eel. He gave me a fabulous summer. We drove through the whole of the north and Galicia, and even went to Portugal where we spent several days in Estoril—a stupid place where men's money is sucked away from them in a ridiculous game which seems to me neither clever nor amusing.

In October I returned to Madrid looking like a fashionable foreigner and prettier than ever. I couldn't find Juan anywhere, which threw me into a fury. Every summer, without even saying good-by, he evaporates for several months. He says he doesn't like scenes. One fine night he says, "Well, I'll be seeing you," and that's that.

215

I found out that even though his family had already re-turned to Madrid, he was still away. (I've said before, I'm very *au courant* about his affairs.) Jealously, I wondered whether he'd gone off in his car with some pig heaven knows where. He's always telling me fantastic tales about how he can't stay in one place, and is only happy when he's burning up the roads.

Finally, my maid, Basi, seeing me so nervous, brought me a faith healer. He knows how to deal with these things, and how to cure fits and strange obsessions.

We had several sessions in my own apartment—I didn't want Ricardo to find out about it.

Uncle Rufo, which was what he called himself, was a middle-aged man, dark and wizened, like an old prune. A weird expression filled his half-closed gray eyes, which were almost hidden in his ratty face. Everything came together on top of his nose. His shaggy dark eyebrows formed a thick line directly above his eyes and his eyes pierced your heart like a steel blade.

Uncle Rufo listened seriously to my troubled story. I showed him Juan's picture, which I had cut out of the news-papers, and he screwed up his face, gravely warning me that this would be a most difficult case. I asked him why and he made me a short speech about the significance of a face like Juan's. This disturbed me. I knew there was something odd about Juan's expression—something that had always eluded and bothered me, troubling me to the very depths of my soul.

Nevertheless, Uncle Rufo assured me that we could accom-plish a great deal if I had confidence in him. And for over ten days we busied ourselves with preparations, until Ricardo began to be suspicious, realizing that I was disappearing for a while each day.

First we darkened my living room, then he circled around me, making wild motions over my head and body, flinging himself about like a man gone berserk. I had to laugh de-spite his warnings that if I took it as a joke we'd both lose— me money, and he time.

Later there was some mumbo jumbo with Juan's picture and he gave me a potion to drink so that I'd forget my ob-session. I must confess, I didn't take it, even though I man-aged to fool Basi and Lirio, who had continued to live in my apartment. I had absolutely no intention of letting them think that I might not want to forget Juan. I dumped the medicine, and told the faith healer that it didn't have any effect on me, so instead of circling me he better produce some magic to make Juan fall in love.

Uncle Rufo did some more odd things with his picture and

216

with a silk handkerchief I had taken from Juan on a certain occasion in the past, and had such success that two days later the crazy Tenorio phoned me.

In view of that, I decided to give him a potion to make him really fall in love with me, but—would you believe it?—no matter how many times I tried to give it to him, each time he slipped through my fingers, suspecting something. After getting plenty of money out of me, Uncle Rufo informed me that Juan was a man of diabolic moods and there was only one way of striking back—by having a baby. I burst out laughing and said it was out of the question. But I must admit that I gave it a great deal of thought and one day, before seeing Juan, arranged for Uncle Rufo to take care of it.

He stretched me out on the bed and made three crosses over my chest, thighs and stomach, accompanied by lots of swinging motions, bows, et cetera. I wasn't quite sure whether I wanted him to be successful. I'd be happy to have Juan's seed in me, but I'd have to be out of my mind to try to become pregnant by him. It would be no small deal to convince him that it was his doing, while I'm living with another—who isn't exactly one-armed either.

Two

By then I had made up with Paulina, who was always hovering around. These procuresses always cling close to first-rate women, like flies to honey. She is a woman of great experience and an excellent front, even though her fingers have a way of sticking to things like my jewelry box. The cost of living was going up, Ricardo's money was running out, and Juan was being his usual vague self. All in all, it was time for me to think of my financial security and start the hunt afresh.

Paulina got busy and found me some good opportunities. She told the men that I was the daughter of an important family (which isn't exactly a lie since I've always suspected that my real parents were from the nobility, even though they had gotten into some trouble), a family that had suffered after the war because of political sympathies. She said that I was very well educated, cultured and serious, and that I had a millionaire friend who was crazy about me, one whom I wouldn't risk losing unless it was for a lot of money.

After she gave the men her spiel there was a formal interview in the apartment of Angustias, a friend of Paulina. I received there as though I were a royal princess—looking beautiful, aloof, and murmuring phrases that showed off my knowledge whenever the occasion presented itself. Some of the men laughed, but most of them swallowed Paulina's story. Men are really children and the best way of taking them in is to excite their imagination with foolish, ridiculous tales.

My demands were high, and none of them were able to meet my price, so it all came to nothing. I didn't care. I prefer losing several men of little value and aiming for one who's worth while, even if it means a long wait. Whoever I hook will be strewing gifts, gold and good thousand-peseta bills before he gets anything from me.

Around then, several weeks ago, I was at the point of concluding a negotiation which didn't jell because of what happened in the "Calico Dress" contest. I wanted to buy a marvelous pension which occupied a whole floor in the Calle del Barquillo. Paulina was very eager for me to get it, anxious to run it herself. They asked me more than three hundred thousand *pesetas* and I couldn't come to a decision, since Juan wasn't very sure about it either.

I remember that I was very downhearted about him then. I couldn't stand *Chaguaguas* and *Palagalagas* any more and my body was becoming weary of going from man to man, even though they paid me well. In low spirits, I went to Uncle Rufo so that he could give me the cure again, hoping that he could dream up something better.

Uncle Rufo listened to me as calmly and seriously as always—he is a very solemn man. I opened up and poured out my heart to him. So much so, that after giving it a great deal of thought, he informed me that he was going to try a new ceremony which was very important—and if it succeeded it would bring Juan to my feet for the rest of his days.

I was delighted. I gave him one hundred *duros* and we started to organize the thing. It was rather difficult, as it involved bringing Juan to the faith healer's house, where, with his magic, he'd make Juan surrender to me.

Knowing the weaknesses of my man, I saw to it that one day while we were all in my apartment Lirio innocently let drop that she knew an old man who had a fantastic painting in his house. A painting which I bought ahead of time from an antique dealer in the Plaza del Angel for eighty *duros*. At that price it should have been good since it was very small. It showed a couple holding hands in a room while, unknown to them, a curious ugly fellow merrily peeped through the window. The antique dealer, a sharp little rat, insisted that it was Flemish. Anyway, to me it seemed very cute. I brought it to Uncle Rufo's place and he put it in a convenient spot in the dining room where it would be easy for him to work on Juan when he came to see the picture.

We went—naturally we went. As soon as I acted unenthusiastic Juan insisted that we go see it, lecturing me in the bargain about how selfish I was, and what little interest I had in his hobbies.

Uncle Rufo lived in Las Ventas near the market of Canillas. We arranged to go in the morning. According to Uncle Rufo this was the best hour for the operation. In order not to spoil things, I made sure to lead with my right foot when I left my house in Chamartín. Then I spit three times over my left shoulder toward the east, which is where all things are born.

The outskirts of the market were jammed; everyone knows that meat is much cheaper there than in Madrid, and even society ladies go there with their maids, accompanying them to see that they don't get rooked. Everyone steals these days. The hurly-burly, and the sharpies and the tricksters of the quarter warmed my soul.

We wandered through the market and bought tickets in a raffle for a white rabbit from a woman with enormous tits. It was a fat little animal and I would have liked eating it with rice, but we didn't win. Naturally, these raffles are always fixed beforehand. I walked along behind a little kid who was selling fish in a basket and I became so excited, recalling my good gypsy days on the road, that I stole a lemon from him that was a joy to behold. Juan, crazy as usual, amused himself awhile with a blind old geezer who spent his life there calling out—"Give to Grandpa, give to Grandpa . . ." with a hoarse shriek that sticks in your ears for the rest of the day.

In the middle of all the commotion I tried to filch a string of Jabugo sausages but some bitch in the store saw me and there was a terrible scene which I cut short by throwing a hundred-peseta bill on the counter, so that they could see I didn't lack cash. At first Juan laughed, but then he became annoyed and asked me if I had taken him there to demonstrate my pickpocket talents or show him the picture. I was rather sad as I realized that the agility of my fingers wasn't what it used to be—everything changes in time.

We finally arrived at Uncle Rufo's place and we waited for him in the dining room while, hidden behind a curtain, he spied on Juan. He had warned me ahead of time that before coming out he had to observe him carefully. Juan twisted about impatiently, and he finally appeared. I examined his face, looking for some sign of the impression Juan had made. His eyes pierced Juan like a sharp needle, but his dark, shriveled face showed nothing.

Juan didn't care for the painting and wanted to leave. But

Uncle Rufo managed to detain him by mentioning another one owned by a friend of his which he could show Juan whenever he wanted.

While he was talking, he went closer to Juan, gesturing and jumping around him like a wild man, taking Juan completely by surprise. Irritated by the weird goings on, he grabbed my hand and led me through a dark sloping passageway toward the door of the faith healer's hut, which I must admit looked like a bandit's haunt.

In the middle of the passageway there was a kind of matting which served as a curtain. Juan pushed it aside and suddenly there was a terrible noise and an iron bar fell on top of him, sending up clouds of dust and debris. He was stunned momentarily, slightly bruised. Then he came to and jumped on Uncle Rufo, messing him up a bit, while the faith healer screamed that next time he wouldn't do anything for clients if they were going to end by beating him up.

At first I was frightened by the noise—the iron bar had somehow missed me—but then I noticed that Uncle Rufo was taking advantage of the confusion to make some strange signs over Juan's head and chest, not to mention other less apparent places, and I realized that he had cleverly prepared this. I don't know whether or not it was a coincidence but for the next few days Juan was marvelous to me, telling me that I was the most absurd, charming woman he had ever known. Happy as a lark, I gave five hundred *pesetas* to Uncle Rufo.

It still didn't go any further than talk and compliments —we didn't arrive at anything definite. That's the way this man's love is: tiny in action, big in talk, and his head always remaining squarely on his shoulders.

Three

After all of that was over, I realized that things weren't going the way I'd hoped and I became very melancholy, imagining that something terrible was going to happen to me. Juan laughed and said that the fat I was putting on was what was making my heart sad. Looking at myself in the privacy of my dressing room I noticed that the base of my neck had thickened a little, my small breasts were filling out, also my belt was a wee bit tight. I put myself again in the hands of a masseuse and spent several unpleasant weeks hungry and bad-tempered. I got back my figure the way Juan liked it, even though other men, includ-

220

ing Ricardo, preferred a little more flesh to hold on to.

Sobered by my dieting (there's nothing better to sharpen one's wits than an empty stomach), I found out about the "Calico Dress" contest. The girl in the best-made dress of that fabric would be elected "Miss Madrid." Naturally, she would also be the prettiest and best made herself. After hearing that Lirio, who always had a good opinion of her looks even though she'd been put under a curse by someone, intended to apply, I decided that what she could do, I could do—better. I immediately went to my dressmaker and ordered a dress. It clung to my flesh as tightly as my own skin, revealing my breasts and hips, and the back of the skirt trailed to the floor in a very daring, gypsyish style.

I entered the contest just like any other well-bred young girl from my district. But when I met the journalists from the paper that was sponsoring it I gave them such provocative stares that the newspaper came out full of mistakes that afternoon. Ricardo was rather annoyed, but I held my ground and informed him that this could affect my future. They'd probably give me a movie contract afterwards. But Juan, on the contrary, was delighted with the idea and with his usual cynicism advised me to participate. Exactly the opposite of what I would have liked.

The contest took place outdoors in the gardens of Bolonia, which were jammed as far back as the trees with a happy, tumultuous mob. Juan was there, though he had refused to accompany me. Ricardo, however, had taken to his bed after lunch, and started gulping down gin with The Bird. He got terribly drunk because of the scene I had made with him. He was very much in love with me and his eyes filled with tears whenever I got angry. He didn't dare try to prevent me from going to the contest, fearing that I'd leave him flat. He had hardly any money and the end was near.

The gardens looked lovely beneath the colored lanterns. The floor was packed with jealous females who had come to criticize the looks of the contestants.

Indeed, they had a right to in many of the cases. Everyone had entered the contest—an old hag who could barely move her miserable body, a piggish bitch who for five *duros* was known to lean up against the darkened railings of the mansions along the Castellana during the hot summer nights, and a big fat greasy brunette who lived in the neighborhood. A revolting collection, even though I hate to admit it. They were so awful that when they walked across the floor into the spotlighted area there were catcalls and hissing—it sure took nerve to pass oneself off for good-looking with the mugs most of those pigs had.

When I came out there was dead silence. Then, as I walked into the spotlighted area, accentuating the roll of my hips and the firm curves of my breasts, a deafening sound of masculine admiration burst forth. Truthfully, I was something to see. Even Juan admitted that I was magnificent.

The jury held a worried conference, comparing our charms for over an hour in a private room which was reserved for the purpose. Despite my success they took the first prize—"Miss Madrid"—away from me, though they gave me the one for my district.

Apparently the judges were delighted with me, and I don't doubt it—they are successful men of both intelligence and taste. Only, as I've said, some louse had a grudge against me and talked more than he should have. The judges don't like any scandal so they had to give the prize to another female who obviously couldn't compare with me.

The choice was so obviously phony that it caused an uproar when they announced it. My fans threatened to break up the chairs in the garden and I finally had to come out again to calm them down and thank everyone. I was feeling very sulky myself, I must admit, and to top it off I found Juan in the company of a pretty blonde who hadn't been in the contest. But, anyway, he very nicely soothed my feelings and told me that I looked prettier than ever, staying with me until dawn.

After the contest some very busy days followed—photos, banquets, parades, the newsreel, and finally Don Laurentino Balbin himself appeared on the scene. But that's another story.

Four

Don Laurentino Balbin is a producer. According to what they say in Spain, they're the ones who mess up films so that everyone can make a profit. Don Laurentino is skillful in the art of making money—particularly at the expense of others.

He's an old guy, but very lively and *simpático*. He nearly always has a cigar dangling from his lips, and his owl's face twisted into an astute smile. In spite of his weight and his years he doesn't make a bad appearance and one could go out with him without looking ridiculous.

Don Laurentino saw the newsreel and immediately found out my address through the newspaper. He sent an intermediary, a sort of secretary of his, to find out if I wanted to see him in his office. Naturally I wanted to. The secretary became a little sticky and I realized I had to deal with him first. I delivered him at once his percentage—in kind—and of the best kind, since the currency used was myself. I promised him further payments if he helped me with his boss.

Don Laurentino was more of the same. After several interviews, and some night clubbing with the good Señor, I had to sleep with him in order to make progress with my movie career. As Juan says, most of our movies are made in bed.

I continued to pay my tolls along the way. I slept with the director, the production head, and the conductor, a fellow with no manners who was only interested in patting himself on the back. I even included the manager of Balbin Films—only escaping the cameraman among the upper echelons of that crew. He was a foreigner and didn't care about women.

Rapidly, within a few weeks, I made a film which has just finished a successful run in a theater along the Gran Via. Naturally, I wasn't the lead, but according to what I've been told I acted very well. I myself wasn't very satisfied with my role. It was too small, and I didn't like the costumes I had to wear—it all took place in the olden days—which is what the movie people here like, I haven't the vaguest idea why. But now we're going to begin a terrific spectacle —*The Gypsy Princess*—and I think I'll be a sensation in this one if I get the lead. Tinito, Señor Balbin, has promised it to me.

With all these goings on, my relations with Ricardo are a little up in the air, though I haven't broken with him yet. I've a very clear notion of what a guy will put up with, and I leave the rope a little slack until I'm sure it won't hurt my interests to cut loose. As for Juan, we go along the same as usual, with an occasional fight over his impossible behavior.

Several days ago, for example, a group of us from the studio were dining at Villa Romana, which the fickle public is now jamming to the hilt. I was very cheerful, in high spirits at having two escorts at my side. But during the dinner I saw Juan come in and sit himself down at a front table—not hiding himself the way he does when he's with me. He was accompanied by two women, which surprised me since he isn't fond of parties of three.

The evening was a mess. I managed to get through it, and at dawn, tipsy from drinking, I confronted him once and for all next to the pool.

"I see that you've got plenty of company, Tenorio," I snapped at him.

"How are you, Lola? As pretty as ever, I see."

"As pretty, and as pampered by the men, for your information."

"*Anda,* girl. They're waiting for you and might get angry if they see you with me."

"My congratulations to those two princesses. They're with such a handsome man," I said sarcastically.

"Don't start up again, girl . . ." He pushed me in the direction of my table.

"You don't have enough any more with one, eh *hombre?* You're in bad shape, very bad."

"You've drunk too much, Lola. And I'm telling you to go," he persisted, grabbing my arm and shoving me a little.

The blood suddenly rushed to my head. He was standing next to the pool and his two women friends were waiting behind him. They stared at us, like two idiotic birds, with their silly well-bred little smiles. I couldn't stop myself. With all the strength that alcohol gives when one is soured inside I pushed him into the pool. Everyone burst out laughing. They laughed so hard that I jumped in myself to make them laugh even more—it bothered me to think that he was made to look ridiculous all by himself.

Five

I stopped my scribbling for a while because neither my activities nor my mood permitted me to continue. *The Gypsy Princess* was a very difficult film to work on—not from the technical end, as there was none—but because of the intrigues and jealousy of the cast. I can be very mulish once I start, and despite the competition, I got the part of the protagonist (it's a very difficult word, but it sounds important, doesn't it?). We finished making it very quickly and now the film is doing the rounds in all the local theaters, but with a much more provocative title—*The Beautiful Gypsy*.

There was a great deal of fuss about the title. Some wanted to leave out the "beautiful" part, others wanted to call it *The Queen of the Sacred Mountain* and Laurentino, who is the real expert, was stuck on *Love Magic*. But I was also very persistent. I wanted "beautiful" in it and at the time my whims were law for Señor Balbin, who was crazy about me.

Since a lot of money was thrown about, the film got a good reception in the papers. The public, however, proved more obstinate. We were surprised that the film didn't do well in the local houses, but no doubt that was due to the high cost of living. A day's wages barely pays for oil and beans. Juan, who never holds back his dirty tongue, insisted that the public was getting tired of taking so much abuse just to fill the wallets of a few fat rheumatic gentlemen. No matter what he says, I know that I looked magnificent, and, according to my friends, am not a bad actress at all. True, a nasty critic on a rival paper did say that I was a beautiful specimen of a woman but absolutely nothing more. So? Isn't that enough, mister? Are there so many beauties walking around?

But in spite of my success I'm not what I was once, it's true. Up until last year life was filled with mystery and promise for me. Now I feel as though I know beforehand what's going to happen, and none of it seems very worth while. Juan says that this always occurs when we realize that our lives are mediocre, and then there are only two solutions: either we must courageously throw ourselves into the arena to fight the bulls of our madness, knowing that we'll probably be gored, or we must put up with life's monotony. According to him, I had chosen the second course, in spite of always seeming so gay, while he has picked the bull ring, even though, if you ask me, it will be cows rather than bulls that gore him.

Recently he was involved in an awful scandal with a rather pretty blonde, someone else's wife. And to think that I spend my life lecturing him not to get into trouble. When a man is married the least he can do is to hide his occasional larks so as not to complicate his life. But he acts like a man who wants complications, and I'm afraid that all these entanglements of his are going to end badly.

He responds to my advice by laughing. No doubt he thinks that if I'd been the cause of the scandal I would have been delighted with his recklessness, even if it ended badly for both of us. But though I've always been gay and carefree, now I feel differently. Occasionally I feel a sudden urge to end things—to end something that is traveling along the wrong track. I shudder to think what will happen to me when time starts to destroy my beauty—when this pretty face of mine becomes wrinkled and my eyes no longer sparkle and my figure is ruined. I don't like to dwell on it because, as Juan says—and in this he's right—I live only for my beauty, and for nothing else. But he's the one person who shouldn't reproach me for this, as if he had wanted to . . .

I had earned some money out of the movie, and also out of Señor Balbin's wallet, which is really part of the same.

Commercial or not, my films did well, even though it was strictly because of my looks. On account of this, Don Rómulo Villa, a Mexican producer, wanted me to go back with him to Mexico to shoot a film with Armando Calvo. He says he will make another María Félix out of me. I've a much better figure, and the closest I could be compared to another star—though actually I'm unique—would be a mixture of the best features of Rita Hayworth and Ava Gardner.

I let the matter dangle as I wanted to think it over carefully before deciding to leave.

Often I wake up suddenly at night with a strange sensation. I feel as though some part of me is in my room floating in the air. Floating and thinking weird thoughts which I can't explain, but which cause me a terrible anguish. Then, when I return to normal, I remember my unknown parents, the orphanage in Almería, my stepmother and my adopted sister. Most of all, I remember my thieving gypsy days along the roads of the south. I think now of all the things that can never be, and I realize that when I was a happy, carefree young girl I thought only about all the things that *could* be. But now all those possibilities seem a little foolish. The only things that interest me are money and people's admiration, and I realize that you can get tired of these. I feel flat, like food that needs salt. A nastiness has come over me that never existed before. I used to do mean things when I wanted something—generally money. Now I play with people just for the sake of playing and to avenge some obscure thing that has saddened my heart. That's why men say that I'm very bad and, down deep, they hate me the way a slave hates a tyrannical master. But I'm not bad. No, really I'm not.

Six

My melancholy increased and I told Juan about it. At first he took it as a joke but then he became more concerned, fearing that he was the cause of my troubles. Not because of any sentimental attachment, or passion—he never thinks about that—but because according to him he had started me on the road to knowledge. I've read and learned a great deal these past few years and my personality has completely changed. I used to act blindly, like a wild bird. Now I don't dare utter a word without first reflecting.

After giving it some thought, Juan advised me to see a friend of his, a psychiatrist, one of those doctors who appear in so many American films.

Several years ago I would have slapped a man's face if he gave me that kind of advice. Now I'm aware that those doctors aren't only for lunatics, but are occasionally helpful in brushing away the dust that settles on our souls. So I went there, to see if he could give mine an airing.

Doctor Gándara lived in a rather ordinary apartment in the Calle de Claudio Coello. I had expected that his home would be mysterious, like a faith healer's or fortuneteller's, only more classy. I confess I was disappointed, it was just like anyone else's place. In the waiting room there were two or three other people who didn't seem at all unusual, yawning from boredom, calmly waiting their turn in the line even though it wasn't a Saturday. Juan informed me that nowadays the craziness is very deep inside, and that we're all so crazy that we don't even notice our insanity. The lunatics in asylums are prehistoric remnants of an insanity of long ago, something concrete and clear, like cancer or pneumonia, and completely distinct from our present hectic nervous disorientation.

Juan continued with his speech, embellishing it more and more, until the door of the waiting room opened, the doctor appearing in a white uniform. He was a young man—healthy, blond, and bald. He smiled, sweating slightly beneath his eyeglasses, looking like an amiable traveling salesman peddling cosmetics.

We went into his office, rather poorly done up with furniture of chrome tubing and a couch of the same. He had some books lying about, and some odd gadgets in the windows. He immediately asked me a lot of questions. Juan had had a talk with him ahead of time so they weren't too indiscreet. After writing it all down on a large piece of paper, Doctor Gándara took my pulse and blood pressure. He made me walk across the room in a straight line with my eyes closed, then he had me extend my arms and placed a thin paper on my outstretched palms to see whether my hands trembled. He banged my kneecap with a rubber hammer and pressed down on my eyes. He finally spoke, telling me that if I wished to place myself in his hands I had to treat him as though he were a sort of confessor, a spiritual leader, a lay priest. I should unburden myself as though I were in a confessional.

I must confess that I never went in for that sort of thing. The only person I've ever confided in has been Juan. Maybe it was time that I spoke frankly to someone besides Juan, maybe that way I could get rid of all my fears and unhappiness. My most recent obsession, which is what made me come for a consultation, is that I can't stand looking at myself in the mirror. I become disturbed when I see my reflection, as though a strange being were staring back at me—someone who wishes me no good, and who is lying in wait to do me harm. I start to sweat from fear and have to stop looking at myself. It's incredible that this should happen to me. Why, I've spent my entire life living off my beauty and looking at myself in all the mirrors I could find!

The doctor laughed, and instead of irritating me, it calmed me down. I was sure that if there was something very wrong with me he wouldn't laugh. Indeed, he suggested that we should continue our sessions so that he could psychoanalyze me. In an involved conversation with Juan he explained the necessity of destroying my complexes, removing them from my subconscious and placing them in front of me. Listening to him I began to think that "complexes" were like those stones that they remove from the gall bladder when people turn yellow as a pumpkin and aren't cured by letting water.

According to Doctor Gándara, psychoanalysis is a very complicated process. The only way I can explain it is that it clears out the muck that time leaves in us, which has become so clogged in a murky depth that it destroys our joy in living. It didn't sound bad at all. I'm a very clean girl and have never permitted any filth or nastiness to remain on my body, and I was delighted with the idea of being rid of the foul mess. I told him that I didn't see how this waste was going to get out, since the soul doesn't have holes like the body in order to throw off what it doesn't need.

The doctor replied that, more than a purge, it consisted in repairing and rearranging things in their proper place. He added several more odd phrases. It struck me as very pretentious of him to talk of the troubles of the soul and these repairs as though he were treating a liver or opening a stomach on an operating table. Even though I've been careless with my life, I believe that these things belong to God. At times Doctor Gándara acts like a madman. He bursts out into weird laughter, completely uncalled for. He is very vain and suffers from a nervous habit of constantly putting on and off his glasses and wiping away the sweat which glows on the bridge of his nose. One day I finally asked him if something was wrong. Drawing himself up proudly, he very seriously informed me that he had a terrible phobia. Being curious, I tried to find out what that was, but without any success. I decided that the doctor was amusing himself much more with me than I with him and I cut short the interview. I was very suspicious of this business of having to see him alone, stretched out on that miserable chrome-tubed couch covered in some material with huge revolting red roses. I began to wonder if the man might not be interested in removing something more than the complexes from my body.

Finally, I became so leery of him that I told Juan that I didn't intend to continue. He said that if I didn't have to, it would be the best thing since one should only go to doctors out of desperation, and with the same lack of faith that one plays the lottery. For the next several weeks I forgot about Doctor Gándara; but then I had to go back, "out of desperation," as Juan says. My phobias were getting worse and I hardly slept at all at night.

Seven

I had a fight with Juan over my going back. I wanted him to come with me and he refused. Then I asked if he'd be willing to stay outside in the waiting room while the thing went on, and he didn't want to do that either. He was so unpleasant that I told him that either he wasn't a man, or else he was out of his mind. It was very obvious what his doctor friend had on his mind with all those secret interviews, and though Juan nastily said that he wasn't jealous of my other admirers, he was still a pig to send me in there alone with such a greasy fellow.

He got angry and I didn't hear from him for several days. But when I got worse I called him up and said that I'd go to see Doctor Gándara. I didn't intend being more popish than the Pope.

I went to see the doctor after lunch and he made me wait a long time. Finally he received me, more friendly and unctuous than ever, and asked me to lie down on that miserable couch, putting a clean napkin at the head. He picked up an ordinary notebook, the kind used by store-keepers, covered in stiff black and cream-colored paper, and sat down behind me so that I couldn't see him. He scribbled away, scratching the paper with his pen. The telephone rang and there was a discreet, mysterious knock on the inside door of his office. He picked up the phone and in a solemn voice told whoever was calling that he couldn't be disturbed before five as he had a patient in the office. The patient was me and, realizing that, I began to feel more important.

Already outstretched, I made sure to lower my skirt, which bothered me by continually riding up—I didn't want any trouble with that particular man. Finally the session started.

"Make yourself comfortable, Señorita. Relax all the muscles in your body," he advised me.

"I'm just fine, thank you."

"And if you're wearing a tight girdle or corset, you should loosen it."

"Do you think I need those things?" I snapped.

"Oh . . . I don't think anything, Señorita," he replied prudishly. "I'm merely giving you the usual instructions."

"There's no need to concern yourself about that, Doctor."

"Very well. Now, tell me, what are you thinking of?"

"The truth is that I'm not thinking about anything."

"What do you think about me?"

"About you?"

"In sincerity, Señorita, in all sincerity," he admonished. "If you don't want to waste your time and money."

"But I'm not thinking about anything. . . ."

"One always is thinking of something. Especially about others," he insisted. "Now . . . what are you thinking about me?"

"That you're a very likable man," I answered finally, for the sake of saying something.

"Ah!" He became excited. "With this *likable* and *man*," he repeated, savoring the words. "Now we have something very interesting. . . ." He scribbled something on the paper, scratching furiously with his pen.

"Well . . . yes, that's right."

"Keep on, keep on. In all candor. It's essential for us to know the impression that the doctor makes on his patient before initiating psychoanalytic treatment."

"I have no further thoughts, Doctor."

"Come along, make an effort."

"I'm trying to think."

"I assure you that at this moment I have no personal feelings, Señorita. Treat me as though I'm a recording machine, I beg you, and . . . and, if it is necessary, I order you to, as your doctor," he added in a deep, solemn voice.

"Okay, I think you're bats. Really, I assure you," I confessed, laughing.

"Marvelous!" he exclaimed, writing rapidly. "A case of transferring the obsessive trauma from the patient to the doctor. I had suspected as much, but it was necessary to confirm it. Excellent, excellent," he repeated, satisfied. "Now, I must warn you, Señorita, that your feelings toward me will undergo many changes during the treatment. At the beginning you'll be extremely mistrustful; then when your problems come to the fore you'll be filled with rancor toward me; later you'll avoid the sessions and probably stop the treatment entirely, deciding that it's a waste of time. Not feeling well, you'll come back again. Then finally, feeling extraordinarily alive and possessing a new inner sureness, you'll elevate me to the category of a thaumaturgian and even fall in love with me. . . ."

"What's a thaumaturgian, Doctor?" I broke in curiously.

"Please, don't interrupt me," he admonished, irritated. "All these responses, whether they be complimentary, or hateful and resentful, lack importance. They only signify the normal reaction to the treatment I must apply to your deviated personality. Consider me, Señorita, at the fringe of all that. My only interest is in curing you."

"In other words, you don't think I rate."

"Let's proceed," he announced, clearing his throat slightly. "Relax, free your mind from all thought as much as possible. When I say a word, no matter what it is, tell me the first thing that occurs to you. Spontaneously, without thinking about it, without withholding the reply in any way. Say it as soon as it comes to your lips. Ready?"

"Yes, whenever you like."

"Then we'll start, after a moment of silence."

He became quiet and stopped writing. I suddenly was afraid. Afraid that this strange fellow would cast some spell over me. Hypnotize me so that he could do something horrible when he had me in his power. The silence continued, and I couldn't prevent myself from letting out a scream and sitting up to see what he was up to. But he was only smiling patiently and waiting.

"Now, now . . . take it easy," he advised me paternally. "I'm not surprised by your alarm. It happens frequently. Lie down again and calm yourself."

I stretched out once more and very shortly I noticed an unmistakable unpleasant odor. There wasn't the slightest doubt. The doctor's feet smelled, and the vapors reached my nostrils. It was a rather warm February day and he was sweating.

"Tree," resounded the voice of Doctor Gándara, breaking into my observation.

"Cheese," I replied without thinking.

"What kind of cheese?" he asked with the anxiety of a hunter.

"I can't tell you."

"Concentrate, concentrate. . . ."

"I can't, I can't," I groaned.

"Edam? Camembert? Gruyère? What kind of cheese, please? This could be very important, Señorita," he warned me.

"Cheese of the feet, Doctor."

"Ah!"

He wrote something down in his notebook, but I noticed that he instinctively pulled them back. And after a short while he artfully moved away the chair, separating himself even further from my unfortunate and imprudent sense of smell.

Eight

We went along that way for several more weeks, with nearly daily sessions at the doctor's as well as doses of Bellergal pills. I felt calmer. The sessions distracted me and I felt that if my troubles could be cured with a few silly words, they couldn't be too serious. So I continued my visits, even though I had to shell out a lot of change.

Doctor Gándara had a strange way of collecting his money. After giving me a speech about the need of cementing a good relationship between doctor and patient he informed me that I should deliver him his fee, ten *duros* a visit, every two weeks. I had to keep track of the amount myself and give it to him in a sealed envelope on the day when the payment was due without uttering a word about it. This was so peculiar that I decided the poor man was completely off his rocker. I decided to take advantage of his lunacy and make the cure more economical by subtracting a few sessions each time I had to pay him. And he never said boo.

He advised me to continue my regular life and not to take any medicine except that which he prescribed. I could drink, go dancing, work on my films, if it was necessary, and amuse myself all I wanted. But then, during the three-quarters of an hour that the session lasted, he rinsed away as much of my soul's muck as he could. After the first few times spent throwing out one or two words without any meaning, the doctor had me speak of my beauty and of myself. Since I always enjoy chattering about myself this wasn't hard, though naturally I played my cards close.

One time we'd discuss only one subject, other times we'd move about, depending on what occurred to me.

"Water," he said.

"Road," I replied.

He insisted later that I said that because without realizing it I had nostalgically remembered my vagabond youth when I traveled along the Andalucian roads, and the sweet fresh smell of that countryside after the spring rains.

Sometimes my mind would go blank for a short time,

and a terrible anguish would overcome me, as though I had fallen into a deep hole and, without knowing why, could no longer grasp the thread of my thoughts. Then Doctor Gándara would try to ferret out the cause of my odd silence, so that he could catch some dirty rag of my being and wash it for me thoroughly. Actually, only unimportant nonsense not worth mentioning came out, but the poor fellow wrote it all down in his ugly merchant's notebook of the soul.

I also remember that one day I became very excited. He said the word "old" and I immediately became faint and nauseous. I became so ill that we spent several days circling around the word until he dug out of me the business about the beds of the sick old men that I pay for in the hospital. I regretted telling him. Later he constantly spoke about it, preening himself with his find.

As I soon felt better I considered dropping this silliness but I remembered what he had told me in the beginning and I decided to continue a little while longer. This guy is much smarter than you'd think. He knows how to get a good grip on his patients by telling them in advance that they'll feel like leaving him. Then, just to be contrary, they stay.

Around that time he conducted a very peculiar experiment which consisted in putting large pieces of paper with ink spots in front of me and having me tell him the first thing that came to mind. The idea was to catch by surprise the foolishness which occurs to one.

"What do you think of this, Señorita? What do you see in it?" he pressed me.

"In where?"

"Here, in this spot."

"Well . . ."

"Say it, say it without any embarrassment."

"I'm considering it."

"Please, Señorita, drop all this consideration if you don't want to waste your time."

"I see a man."

"What's he doing?"

"Nothing."

"In what position is he?"

"On his feet. Yes, very stiff and erect."

"And *how* is this man?" he persisted, heavily accentuating the *how*, giving it a quality of mystery.

"I don't understand, Doctor."

"Is he naked perhaps? Tell me everything, Señorita, even though it may be ugly and repugnant. I'm sure you see something ugly . . ."

"Well, you see, Doctor . . . The man is . . . is masked."

"Masked?" he exclaimed, scribbling away rapidly in his notebook. "Masked, you say?"

"Yes, he's wearing a mask over his face."

"Keep going, keep going, please."

"And the mask—"

"It's horrible, isn't it?" he broke in nervously.

"No, not at all. It's a mask that is laughing."

"Ah, so it's laughing, eh? Very good, Señorita. Now we'll continue. And here what do you see?" he asked, showing me another spotted page.

"A crab."

"Nothing more?"

"Nothing more."

"And here?" he asked, rapidly placing another one in front of me.

"Well, another man."

"Go on, go on . . ." He became excited. Whenever there were men in it he practically jumped out of his skin.

"A dead man."

"Dead?" he asked while he was writing. "Dead? Dead from what, please?"

"From old age."

"Ah, fine, fine. And how do you know that he is old and dead?"

"I can see, Doctor. Just because I know."

We went on that way for a while. He insisted that I find ugly things in the ink blots. Things about men or women that are never written of in books, even though in real life people spend plenty of time making jokes about them. But all I saw were strange figures—masked men, old men dead from life's misery, crabs, caterpillars, spiders and finally a broken mirror.

When we finished, Doctor Gándara looked very grave. He had me lie down on the couch, took his usual position behind me, and started to speak.

"Señorita, I don't wish to conceal from you that I just did a . . ." and he said a very peculiar word, something like *Rosas,* a *Rosas.*

"That's all right, Doctor."

"And the Rorschach never lies."

"Is that possible? It's very peculiar never to lie."

"Unless the patient has done it before and is familiar with the technique."

"You mean that patients pick up bad habits like animals, eh?"

"No, not that exactly."

234

"You can relax. As far as I'm concerned, no bad habits are involved in your *Rosas* business. It's the first time in my life I've seen it."

"Therefore, Señorita, unless you tell me the truth—crude, hard, and unpleasant, perhaps, but indispensable—I can't continue my treatment. The scientific discipline which my calling and professional ethics demand of me obliges me to abandon you to your fate."

"But what have I done, Doctor?" I exclaimed, ready to shed a few tears if it was required.

"To me nothing, Señorita. Absolutely nothing. But perhaps you are trying to fool science and that is very serious," he warned in a deep, solemn voice.

"But what for? I don't understand."

"Tell me the truth, I'm asking it for your own good," he inquired in an insinuating voice. "Isn't it true that you have seen lurid images, erotic, libidinous, and pornographic figures in those ink blots?"

"Not one, Doctor. I swear by the memory of my true mother, who is now in her glory," I replied without hesitation, sitting up straight on the couch. I'd only seen nonsense on those sheets of paper. Some deal for me to have to see pigs in ink blots after having had to put up with them all my life!

"Is it possible you're telling me the truth?"

"And how!"

"In the name of science, Señorita—again, I demand the absolute truth."

"Don't act like that, Doctor. I've told you everything I've seen. There isn't any more."

"I don't dare believe it," he said doubtfully. "You would be the first case among thousands and thousands of tests who hasn't suffered from a sudden erotic resurgence. . . . Ah, aha, I think I've hit it. Naturally, that's it. . . ." he continued, scribbling away rapidly. "I should have thought of it before."

"I'm glad you hit the nail on the head, Doctor. . . . Now tell me, is it very bad?"

"Well, a . . . we'll speak of it further on, when I judge the moment to be propitious," he hedged. "But don't worry. I assure you that it's coming along fine, very fine."

"That's something at least."

Several days later he made the diagnosis. It was very complicated and I don't know how to explain it here. Apparently I didn't have "trauma or psychic shock in my infancy, but vague, hysterical and neurotic reactions provoked by the discomforts of my life." In other words, I lacked the proper comforts—something I already knew very clearly. That's more or less the gist of what Doctor Gándara said, only his was a more roundabout and discreet way of saying it. What I finally managed to understand was that he thought that I wasn't satisfied with myself, and that I'm very timid and unsure. Me—timid. What a nut!

He became very curious about the business of the old men, which I had confided to him in a weak moment. He said that I took pleasure in their suffering as a vengeance against the way men had humiliated me during my entire life. That when I saw them—old, sick and rotting away—I experienced a kind of spiteful compensation.

He also insisted that my body had become frigid—even though I told him that it's obviously quite the contrary. I've had relations with so many men, the doctor said, that, though I don't suffer from any organic damage, I've lost all warmth. My feelings have become distorted and my soul embittered. My principal vice is greed. An example of this is the way, thinking he wouldn't notice, I filched part of his fees.

My "syndrome" (I've never understood what that means though he explained it to me several times) is obvious. All my feelings and passions have directed themselves to an all-absorbing slavish love for money, greediness provoked by my fear of the future and insecurity concerning myself. According to him, I only believe in my beauty. As this beauty can't last, I've begun to feel as though worms were eating away at me.

I asked him why I feel so badly and if he had found out what was preventing me from gazing contentedly at my reflection in the mirror.

Doctor Gándara said that my vegetable system (he called it "vegetative") had lost its equilibrium because of the pressures of my psyche, producing "disequilibrium and disturbed feelings." Worried, I asked him if I needed a Wassermann, and he firmly replied that had nothing to do with it.

As for the mirror, this must have originated from my fear of becoming old and ugly. The strange anguish which I suffered when I looked at myself, and the chills which later went through my entire body were nothing more than the "vegetative symbol of my subconscious anxiety."

Naturally, I didn't pay too much attention to this gibberish, but got down to brass tacks—whether or not he could cure me, and how expensive it would be. He assured me that I would respond very well to treatment, as my soul (only he said "psyche" instead of "soul") had responded very well to psychoanalysis. There were still many unknown factors to be cleared up. (There was one thing in particular he hadn't been able to find out. I had drawn a curtain over this part of my life, probably a subconscious defense.) Dying from curiosity, I asked him what it was. He's a very slippery fellow, as crazy as they come, and wouldn't commit himself.

We agreed to continue the treatment, and after a little haggling on my part I talked him into reducing the sessions to forty *pesetas*. I realized that there'd be plenty of them and I wasn't inclined to send myself to the poorhouse paying Doctor Gándara.

Nine

I like less and less continuing my writing. Even though the reason I started this now strikes me as absurd, a rather odd affection for these pages makes me go on.

There's no doubt but that I'm much better now. All the anxieties that I suffered several months ago have left me. But since I've gotten rid of all my shame and have let the air get at the backside of my soul I feel rather sad and depressed. As we like to imagine things being much more beautiful than they really are, we never like knowing the truth. Doctor Gándara's psychotherapy and my reading have made me learn much more than I should know.

Juan tried to console me, telling me that this is inevitable, and that's why he has suspended some of my lessons for a certain time, but that if I continue my learning I can overcome this bad period and will once more be able to enjoy lots of other things.

Only now it will be pleasure in different things. I can no longer return to what I once was—when young and free as a bird I ate thistles and leeks along the roads of the Andalucian coast.

Actually I don't want to mention any more of this to Juan, because I think he's to blame for all of it, although Doctor Gándara says this isn't so, that no one is to blame for anything. It's just life, he says, and it can't be helped. Ridiculous!

I've just returned from a trip with Juan and in a few days will go back to see the doctor who is trying to "reorient me" in his ugly tiresome manner of speaking. That's just what I need. I've got myself in a mess and I don't know how to get out of it.

I was a little nervous about driving down to Valencia in Juan's Lancia. It was falling apart, ready for the junk heap.

237

Juan must be a little hard up. He hasn't bothered to replace what it's lost on the roads or to repair the dents from the streets of Madrid. If it didn't belong to him I wouldn't get in it for anything. I'm really embarrassed to be seen in such a piece of tin. Still, it never stops running and it's the most popular car in Madrid. The paint stains, crumpled fenders, rusty bumpers and constant noise make it unmistakable. People always know what Juan's up to, which makes him furious.

But, jalopy or not, I wanted to be with Juan and decided to go on the trip. My departure was made very difficult by both Ricardo's and Señor Balbín's suspicions. I arranged things cleverly, telephoning my family to send me a telegram from Mojácar requesting my immediate presence on an urgent family matter. I showed it to both men and they both wanted to drive me down, but I let them believe I was postponing the whole thing, and then took them by surprise by suddenly calling them a few minutes before leaving. I'm never very sure of Juan and wanted to make sure we were going, so I waited until the last minute before phoning them from a bar in the Plaza de Manuel Becerra. Tinito, Señor Balbín, took it in a very dignified manner, but Ricardo wanted to send his cousin, The Bird, down with me, and was ready to leave headquarters to see that I got off all right. I told him not to bother about his car, that I already had my ticket on the Jaén-Granada Bus—hastily leafing through the phone directory, I'd picked out the name of some bus line at random—and finally he was satisfied.

After these delays we left Madrid on a rainy April morning in a wildly crazy mood, crossing the sierras of Cuenca.

We started out later than we planned, and stopped to eat in Tarancón. I looked lovely in a clear beige lace dress, happy as a lark to be on the road again. The brisk air made my face sparkle, my cheeks glowing rosy as an apple.

Snow still clogged the ditches along the sides of the road, and a clear gray light colored the earth. We talked excitedly, the Lancia bouncing over the holes at an incredible speed, while we admired the vivid ochres, purples, reds and greens of the sierras. Though I've seen a lot of country, I've never, never contemplated anything so savagely beautiful. A tremendous upheaval surged inside me. I forgot the tawdry world of Madrid, deserting it for a beautiful dream—a dream from long ago, but now even more varied and more beautiful.

Drunk on the earth and fresh air, I was like a bird that is finally liberated and flies free. Filled with happy excitement, we dawdled along the road, not noticing that night was falling.

Neither of us knew the way after Minglanilla, and with the last lights we became lost in the scary crevice at the threshold of Cabriel in Contreras. In the dusk it looked like the mouth of hell. Suddenly, almost beneath the wheels of the car there was a steep drop to the rocky, clifflike panorama below. Looking down at the incredible view, I saw in the distance slopes covered with tiny pine trees. Slowly the car started down the continually winding road.

Beyond, in the open, the last gray misty lights of daylight were falling, but the inside of the pass was as black as a fox's mouth. We drove in deeper, slowing down the car while we rounded the treacherous descending curves. Suddenly, as we neared an inn below, several men of the Civil Guard jumped out in front of us, demanding that we halt.

Juan, very surprised, got out of the car and went into the inn to show his papers. They must have been important. I noticed that the sergeant saluted him very respectfully. He even accompanied us back to the car and apologized for having disturbed us. Juan asked the reason for the fuss and the man became very mysterious, refusing to give any information. Then Juan took him aside and in the glare of the headlights showed him another paper which he took out of his wallet. After examining it, the sergeant told him everything.

It had to do with an attack. At two in the afternoon in the hills of Contreras several strange men had stopped the bus from Valencia to Madrid. They'd wounded the driver and held up one of the passengers, the director of a big Valencian company, who had a lot of money on him. Since three the Civil Guard had been searching the road for the bandits. According to the sergeant they were very well armed.

Juan asked me if I wanted to stay. "Here we'd be well protected by the police."

"*Anda, hombre,* on our way."

"You're not frightened?"

"Yes—but what can we do here during the whole night? Some joke!"

"They could take care of us, Lola."

"So what?"

The sergeant said that the gang probably had taken the road to Cuenca and that the road to Valencia was clear, so we decided to leave. We continued driving until we reached the bottom of the crevice. Suddenly Juan gave me a terrible fright by suddenly stopping the car.

"What's the matter?" I yelled nervously.

"Nothing, honey, nothing," he assured me. "Listen, Lola, you better learn your lesson."

"What lesson? You're crazy."

"Now just pay attention to me," he ordered very seriously. "I'm a movie script writer, also work in radio, and I live off what I earn. You're a model in a fashion house, you live on what you make and you hardly know me. I'm giving you a lift to Valencia where you're going to see your family. Get it?"

"All right, as you like. But repeat it once more. Is some of this true, by the way?"

"Not one word, Lola. And remove that jewelry store window that you're wearing. Unless you want to be left without it, girl."

He was right, and I became panicky. I always like to bedeck myself and had on earrings, a necklace, four bracelets and two rings. Juan always reproached me, saying that it was very vulgar and in bad taste to be so showy, but I've never lost my delight in jewels.

I was really miserable. I think I've already said that whenever I go with a man I first remove my jewelry and carefully hide it in a handkerchief beneath the mattress, never forgetting about it even for a moment. Only with Juan have I relaxed my vigilance a little.

"What should I do with this, Juan?" I asked, knotting my jewels in my handkerchief.

"Hide it."

"Hide it? Where?"

"Underneath the floor—anywhere, Lola."

"No, no," I refused, alarmed. "I could lose it."

"Give it to me, I'll hide it for you."

"No, I don't want to." I pulled back my hand, hiding it in my lap.

"Then whatever happens will serve you right, girl." Angrily, he started up the car again.

"Do you think that they'll capture us?"

"No, but it's best to take precautions. I don't look forward to being held prisoner in some bandit hideout in the mountains here. These parts are filled with them."

"I can imagine."

We continued our descent, crossing over the river, which glittered below like a curved blade of steel. After reaching the other side we laboriously started the slow climb upward.

Scared, I held on tightly to my bundle of jewelry, ready at any moment to throw it in a ditch or hide it somewhere fast.

We climbed up very high, straining the motor more and more. At the entrance to a tiny village several men jumped in front of us.

"Halt!"

"What is it, Juan?" I screamed.

"Nothing—the Civil Guard again."

They surrounded us and once again we had to explain everything. Juan didn't show his papers, and they treated us badly.

"Keep driving," ordered one of the men.

"Whereabouts are the bandits?" Juan asked.

"Keep going and don't ask questions."

"You could be a little more helpful," Juan grumbled. "If they're nearby, we'd rather spend the night peacefully in the village."

"They're over there, in the hills," one of the younger guards informed us, looking at me.

"Way in there? Good God!" I exclaimed, smiling at the young boy, hoping to dig out more. "I'm terribly frightened. Are you sure they're not down below?"

"No, Señora, they're not. They've hidden themselves behind the rocks."

"Keep going and stop worrying about it," the other guard interrupted curtly.

We kept driving but were stopped again on the outskirts of another village.

"This stinks, Lola," Juan swore, using another expression that I won't put down here out of delicacy.

They became much more polite and told us what they knew. We were shocked to find out that the bandits were somewhere on the road. The Civil Guard hadn't been able to capture them.

"Should we stay or go?"

"What do you think?"

"The best thing is to keep going, it's probably just a false alarm."

"Fine with me."

"You there," Juan called to one of the guards. "Is there any risk in continuing?"

"Not if you don't stop."

"What do you mean—don't stop?"

"If someone signals, or if a man or truck is blocking the road, don't pay any attention. Just keep right on going," he advised us.

"A truck?" Juan became alarmed. "How the devil can I keep on going if a truck is blocking the road?"

"Oh, you'll find a way," he answered vaguely.

Juan swore in disgust.

"And don't pay any attention to any women either, even if they're lying stretched out on the road."

"Uh, thanks a lot," Juan interrupted him, starting up the motor. "That information sure is a help," he grumbled, driving away. "The best thing to do is to forget about the whole affair."

We continued on. The road soon started to flatten out toward Valencia and we were able to work up some speed. We were driving over seventy kilometers an hour—a fantastic speed for that car—when we saw a parked truck hidden in the shadows alongside of the road.

"There they are!" I screamed. Juan cursed and, unexpectedly, pulled out a pistol from I don't know where, cocking it rapidly with a sharp, dry little sound.

"Don't pass," I begged.

"There's room."

"They'll capture us!"

"No, they won't."

And they didn't. We went right by them, the Lancia dangerously close to the edge of the road. I shuddered, looking down at the sharp drop below.

A little later we saw a parked touring car in the center of the road. Passing it, we saw a man in shirt sleeves moving his jacket in front of a searchlight.

"Did you see? He's signaling," I observed.

"It's your imagination. Who the devil could he be signaling?"

"The bandits, *hombre*. They're hidden in there and he's calling them, so that they can come down and escape the guards."

"Nonsense, Lola."

"So what's the guy doing with his jacket?"

"Christ only knows."

"Listen, Juan, I'd be happy if they didn't get the poor fellows."

"Poor fellows? They wounded a man," he replied bad-humoredly. "You women are ridiculous!"

"You listen to me—I know you don't want to see them hunted down like dogs either," I hinted.

"That's their tough luck."

"But would you hunt them?"

"Oh, leave me alone with your nonsense! I've got enough trying to drive this piece of tin."

He drove very well, but with one hand on his pistol ready to shoot at anything in our way. I realized that he was a little uneasy, but for him it was a pleasurable emotion. He enjoyed trouble, and at the drop of a hat would be ready to join in a fight.

We drove like lightning through Utiel and Requena, bouncing over the holes in the road, which got worse and worse as we went along. On the outskirts of the second village we ran into a taxi from Valencia, filled with people. Juan stuck close to it—he had been afraid that the bandits would seize our car for a getaway, but with two cars together it would be more difficult, and we were able to relax a little.

Soon after joining the taxi we saw a miserable little light in the distance, almost lost in the dark night, which barely lit up the pump of a small gas station. There was no village, and it had the air of being a solitary roadhouse. The taxi started to slow down near the pump, and we followed suit. We didn't want to be left without company.

Suddenly someone fired shots at both our cars. The people in the taxi as well as Juan started to shoot back, aiming at the flashes which were coming from the shadows beyond the side of the road. A terrible battle started. I took advantage of the commotion to hide my jewelry beneath the car seat.

Everything happened very rapidly and ended in the most unexpected manner. The Civil Guards suddenly appeared from out of nowhere, surrounding both the cars, and making us come out with our hands up, with pistols pointed at our bellies. You guessed it—we had fired on the Civil Guards and the bandits had been in the taxi from Valencia—no less than seven of them!

Despite our futile protests they locked us up in a room of the roadhouse while they took care of the other business —the men resisted, so there were deaths, and all. It took us over two hours to clear up everything, which we managed finally to do thanks to Juan's papers.

When at dawn we actually arrived safe and sound in Valencia with all my jewelry intact, I breathed a sigh of relief. That kind of trouble is no joke. I'd clearly heard the whistle of the gunshot and we could have easily remained in the blackness, dead, like the rest. When they let us out to look for our papers I saw one of the young boys lying face downward in the ditch, bathing his grave with blood. I felt sorry for him because I like men who know how to lose a fight courageously. Juan very gravely told me that one should never be the first to shoot. And they had shot at the poor bus driver. But who knows what really happened?

Ten

After Juan finished his business in Valencia and Barcelona we came back to Madrid by way of Zaragoza as we had planned. The trip took ages as something happened to the clutch plate of the Lancia—I don't quite understand what that is, but it has a nice sound—and Juan had to continually scrape it with sandpaper to keep it working.

The radiator was leaking, and since Juan forgot to fill it with water in Lérida, shortly before reaching Zaragoza the motor exploded in a terrible mess—boiling water over everything, even burning my legs a little. We were finally towed into Zaragoza late at night, weary yet amused by it all, and we got a room in that depressingly dull and chilly hotel that the local citizens are so proud of.

After waiting two days for the damage to be repaired we left Zaragoza for Madrid, delighted to abandon that dusty, windy city. Beforehand we ate in a good tavern and had the best cooked rabbit that I've ever eaten—it still makes my mouth water when I remember it. We washed it down with good red wine, and, gay as larks, started the trip back.

We took the wrong road, and night started to fall while we were near Alhama. Juan looked at some maps, which meant nothing to me—he's always fiddling with them when we take a trip—and decided that we should sleep in the ancient Monastery of Piedra which was somewhere nearby.

That was worth seeing—Espichao was right when he had wanted to shut himself up there with me. Leaving Alhama behind us, the earth ahead shone a flaming red in the dusky light, while beneath the rose sky the road curved along a deserted, unreal countryside until we finally came to an oasis, the trees already darkened by nightfall.

I'll never forget that short trip. The lingering twilight created a sight such as appears in only the wildest dreams.

Late that night, driving along with our headlights shining as brightly as they could, we finally came to the ancient monastery, now an inn. A fresh, springlike breeze was blowing through the air, rustling through the young freshly opened leaves of the ash trees, smelling of newly fallen rain.

All was unbelievably perfect—the fresh breeze, the dark-shadowed towering trees, the soft smells and even the sounds of the Aragonesian voices of the people who took care of our baggage. When the door of the inn opened, and we entered the large white hall of the monastery, I felt happy, so happy that it hurt; shuddering, I leaned against Juan, burying myself against the heat of his warm, strong body, wanting to share my intense and unexpected joy with him.

Our bedroom was lovely, with two high beds on a red waxed tile floor. There was a small living room with a divan, a wonderful bathroom, and two balconies which opened out on an open gallery. When I walked out on it I could hear the murmuring music of a thousand waterfalls.

Juan was delighted and said that there was nothing better than arriving at unknown beautiful places in the darkness of night—since you're not able to use your eyes in exploring, all your other senses become remarkably alive and sensitive. I can't express myself like him, but I remember I felt as though I were floating in a wonderful new world.

We had to cross the long clean white halls to get to the dining room, and after eating something we came back to our room, bringing with us a bottle of Catalan champagne. We spent our time well and were almost lulled to sleep by the heat of an electric stove which purred like a contented cat.

It must have been very late when we opened the door and went out on the balcony to listen in the fresh night to the music of the waterfall. Then we went to sleep, each of us in our own high bed. Juan fooled around in his, peeking out from underneath the white sheets with his dark head and taking out his pistol to defend himself against imaginary bandits who were attacking the monastery. I smoked a cigar which transported me into a state of bliss. And I fell asleep, wonderfully happy.

Eleven

They were two fantastic days, spent amid the constant murmur of the water. What was odd was that even the daylight couldn't destroy our mood.

We went down to see the waterfall, ran through the green woods, climbed up the hills, and peeked through the lookout windows after examining the tombs in the old monastery. Juan said that there was only one superfluous element—people. Some honeymooning couple from Zaragoza, very ordinary people, carried on stupidly, screaming about, in and out of the foliage. Soon it started to rain and we were finally left alone—splendidly alone—in the midst of the great orchestra of the water.

Soft May breezes were blowing, and we huddled together in the gallery, hardly speaking. Juan read while I fixed my nails, mended stockings or combed my hair in front of the mirror. When it cleared we ran across the earth once more, coming upon a school of trout in the deep part of the river.

It was the morning of the last day, several hours before we left for Madrid, when I finally understood it all.

Juan, interested in a book, was reading in the gallery. Tired of roving through the woods and along the waterfalls, I had started to climb back up the hill toward the monastery. I remember I was wearing a gray skirt and a sport shirt of natural silk underneath a sweater of Juan's that was much too big for me, but which tempered the cold morning air.

I started up and could see him from where I stood—peacefully and comfortably reading his book, his face absorbed in concentration. I called out to him and he stood up, leaning against the gallery railing to observe my progress.

While I scrambled toward him all out of breath, while he watched me smiling, I suddenly experienced something very strange. As though he belonged to me and I to him, as though we were bound in a secret marriage, sacred and indissoluble.

I reached the top running like one possessed and threw myself into his arms.

"But what's the matter?"

"How I love you, how I love you!"

"I love you too, little one."

"I want to give up everything for you. Everything, absolutely everything. I want to live only for you and . . ."

"My little baby . . ." he murmured, patting me as though I were a capricious child.

"I'm very serious, Juan. Couldn't you arrange things?"

"It's difficult."

"I don't care if you don't have money. We'll live as best we can."

"Lola!"

"I'm telling you the truth."

"I know . . . but it would be a truth that—that wouldn't last very long," he predicted sadly.

"You think so?"

"I'm sure."

We were quiet for a moment and I moved closer to him, hearing the rapid beating of his strong heart—did it really belong to someone, that sound?

"What's wrong?"

"Nothing. Why?"

"You're not happy, Juan, I can tell."

"I don't pretend to be, either," he informed me, lightly removing his arm.

"But I am—when I'm with you, I am," I exclaimed.

246

"What luck, my girl," he remarked, a touch of rancor in his dark eyes.

"If you loved me more you'd be happy too."

"I love you a great deal, Lola."

"What's the matter with you, my darling? Tell me."

He hesitated a moment, his thoughts causing his face to cloud and darken and his eyes to fill with sorrow. He didn't speak—he couldn't speak—and once more all was buried inside, in the deep recesses of his soul which no one could ever penetrate.

"You have nothing to say, Juan?"

"No, nothing, I admit it, Lola. Before I used to speak constantly. And I don't believe anyone understood me. Not even myself."

"But I love you, Juan. You're the only one in the whole world I love, I swear it," I said desperately. "And you love me too. . . ."

"Yes, yes I know."

"Then let me go with you, to be with you forever—and you can do whatever you want with me."

"No, I can't. I can't let you. I love you too much to . . ."

"That's a lie, a dirty lie," I broke in angrily. "You don't love me too much, you love me too little . . . just a tiny, tiny bit . . . something that occasionally pleases you to be with, which amuses you when you're in the mood. That's the truth of it, Juan," I shouted, starting to cry.

"No, Lola . . . please let me explain. . . ."

I couldn't listen to any more. Again and again he'd begin his long talks, trying to fill the emptiness between us with pleasant, consoling words—that horrible yawning hole which I constantly tried to cover up while at the same time he persistently undermined it. Why did it have to be like that? Why?

Quickly I left him standing in the room and started to run down toward the large waterfall which rushed in a foamy white horse's tail down the cliff. He shouted, trying to overtake me, but couldn't as I wasn't running along the paths but was throwing myself down the mountain. I reached the edge of the precipice with tears sorrowfully streaming down my face. But I didn't throw myself into the swift roaring river below. No—in the end I couldn't jump.

And several hours later, in the afternoon, we returned to Madrid, hardly opening our mouths during the sad trip back.

Epilogue

It was a day like any other, several months ago. The mediocre, monotonous hours were drawing to their usual close. I felt bored —weary of all the ridiculous effort, foreign to our nature, we go to put money in and out of an indifferent wallet. I was tired of meeting people who were constantly making demands—all in the name of the most imaginary rights—of putting up with their stupid sensitivities and even my own foolishness; and of having constantly to tell every woman that she was the most beautiful, the most intelligent, the most wonderful of them all.

I felt as though I were drowning in a terrible gray sea of papers, telephone calls, books, smothered by the petty notions of fashionable critics who try to make us succumb to their phony literary values. Indeed, I was ready to commit the wildest, most explosive act to free myself from the stupid mediocrity of my life.

I remember that just then the telephone on my table rang. I took the receiver off the hook and left it lying on top of a book so that I wouldn't be bothered by it. But suppose it was someone new who was calling? Someone you are sure exists, and is somewhere to be found, but is prevented from meeting you by the confusion of life—someone who may bring you a little mystery and added pain.

Anxiously I grabbed at the receiver. But no one new after all! Just Juan.

"How are you? What do you want?"

"Are you very busy?"

"*Hombre*, you know. The usual nonsense."

"I'd like to see you for a minute."

"Perhaps tomorrow. . . ."

"No, today."

"But it's almost nine, and—"

"And you're in a lousy mood, eh?"

"Something like that."

"It would be better to meet outside because—"

"Because you want to escape from that damned *retreat* you've made in your apartment, from that coffin of books which threatens to mummify you alive."

"What a lot of crap."

"Come right away to the bar of the Palace."

"What for?"

248

"You'll be interested, I guarantee."

"All right, I'll be there."

We sat at a table next to the window. The branches of the acacias on the Carrera de San Jerónimo softly fanned the night, filling the bar with the aroma of spring.

Being early, it was deserted. Those people who come there every evening, growing a little older in front of the same cocktail, hadn't yet come. One still had a little time to talk.

"What the devil's the matter with you, Juan?"

"Nothing."

"Then I don't see the reason for all this urgency, *hombre*. And, as for that," I warned him, pointing to some papers which my friend was carefully carrying in a portfolio, "I'm not in the mood to put up with any manuscript."

"Oh I think you'll put up with this," he laughed. "Because it has to do with women."

"Precisely . . ."

"*Vamos, hombre*—don't prejudge."

"All right—but what do you want me to do?"

"Take it and read it. It will help you to write a novel."

"And why should I write another novel?"

"That's your business, *chico*."

"I assure you I don't intend to write any more novels."

"You're that depressed?"

"Depressed? Not at all. Quite the contrary," I insisted energetically. "I'm just beginning to believe less in literature."

"You?" he asked, somewhat surprised and contemptuous. "I don't believe it. Merely a new literary phase of yours."

"Look, Juan," I interrupted brusquely. "This kind of ironic and superficial conversation bores me a great deal. If you want to have a serious talk, I'm ready. If not, the devil with you and your papers."

"What a terrible temper!" he protested, affectionately slapping me on the back. "Very well, *hombre*, we'll speak seriously. But first tell me whether it's true that you don't believe in literature."

"Perhaps not to that point . . . but I think the time has come to sweep away all the old dust, and, above all, I'm convinced that it is much better to make one's life a work of art than to write masterpieces, assuming that one has the talent to write them."

"Ah, you're coming over to my camp. I'm not surprised . . . you're almost forty and . . ."

"We're the same age, Juan."

"Perhaps in years, but not the rest . . . I feel much younger than you."

"Will you come to the point and tell me why you've brought me this?"

"Tomorrow I'm going away, Darío."

"Where?"

"Quiberon."

"Where's that?"

"You should know your geography better. It's a tiny village in the southeast of Brittany, situated on the edge of a long narrow

249

peninsula that juts out into the sea, according to French guide-books."

"And what are you going to do there?"

"Me? Nothing—nothing at all."

"Ah, some trouble, eh?"

"Much more complicated."

"Ya, ya. I've heard some talk about that. Be careful with literature, Juan. Because in books things are tolerated—but in real life . . ."

"Literature—me?"

"You are the most literary person in the world. In your flesh and bones, you are literature."

"As you like," he replied scornfully. "But let's get to the point."

"The point is those papers, isn't it?"

"Don't be so precipitous, *hombre*. We have to start at the beginning."

"All right, out with it." I resigned myself, fortifying myself with a shot of port which is one of the few wines I've a taste for.

"Listen to me, Darío," Juan began, leaning toward me confidentially. "A few years ago I met a woman . . ."

"How unusual!"

"If you don't immediately change your attitude, I'm leaving and you'll lose something that—" he faltered angrily.

"It's just that I've a horror of people confiding in me," I warned him. "We Spaniards are *anticonfidential* and all our admissions are completely false, merely our rancorous vanity masquerading as confidences. So if it's that sort of thing, you can find someone in France to unburden yourself to."

"Are you finished now?" he demanded brusquely.

"Yes, I've finished."

"You have to learn how to listen, Darío."

"I'm Spanish, Juan."

"And how! But this will interest you and you're going to make an effort."

"What will? This woman?"

"Listen, if I remember right, you've been fooling around with a sort of novel that's completely different from what you've written up to now, isn't that so?"

"Not exactly," I protested. "But something like that. For some time now I've stopped believing in a certain kind of literature. In literary literature—do you understand?"

"I think so."

"I also believe that while men live the novel won't die, even though it wipes out their tormented past. That's why I believe in literature that's alive and not mummified, and why in the midst of my life's stupid activities I've stopped to reflect a little on the possibilities of creating a living, breathing novel with the least possible amount of literary morphine in it."

"And here it is," he replied, solemnly handing me the papers in the portfolio.

"What did you say, *hombre?*"

"That here it is."

"If *it's already written*, I'm not interested Juan."

"It is and it isn't, Darío. Depending on you."

"It's nothing of yours . . . because, well, forgive me . . . but I don't think God has called you along that road."

"Now you know that my interest is in living," he replied contemptuously. "And I don't believe literature serves any use except in hunting women."

"And who is she?" I asked, carelessly leafing through a few filthy pages, written in a childish hand. "Because this handwriting . . ."

"She just recently learned how to write."

"Ah, *caray!*" I was beginning to be interested. "This could be important."

"Everything written there is true," Juan informed me seriously. "And I think you should interest yourself in it."

"Maybe you're right . . . I'll read it and then we'll see," I vaguely gave in. "But I'd like to know something more of this woman."

"I never intended to confide in you, you can believe me, Darío," Juan murmured. "I know that in our country we men don't like to reveal our inner feelings. We're particularly reserved and sensitive."

"We're ill at ease with friendship."

"Because friendship is always soft—charming and feminine."

"And she?"

"It's all there—complete and true—in the pages of her memoirs that I made her write."

"Ah, in other words you— Were you in love with her?"

"In love?" He seemed surprised. "Christ, no!" he laughed.

"Are you also in those papers?"

"Yes, but not very much. Why?"

"Oh, nothing, *hombre*. Vanity has so many masks. . . ."

"I repeat, she was not in love with me," he replied, irritated. "Nor I with her, even though I sought her company."

"Was she pretty?"

"Pretty—what a dull, ordinary word! She was much more," he exclaimed. "Like a . . . no, I don't want to talk about it. You have it all there," he pointed to the pages.

"Evidently she was worth while."

"Yes, very worth while."

"Did she die, Juan?"

"No—not that I know," he answered, troubled.

"But you keep referring to her in the past. 'She was like this, she was like that.'"

"You'll see why. Just a manner of speaking."

"Which means that she's disappeared—died—from your life, doesn't it?"

"Yes, I suppose so."

"I'll read these papers. And if they're of use to me, I'll make a novel from them."

"Try to respect them as much as possible."

"That's my affair."

"You won't spoil them?" he asked, anguish in his voice.

"I'll take good care of them, Juan, I promise you."

He sipped his champagne cocktail in silence. I could see by his face that he was thinking of this woman, unwinding some of the first reels from the film of his memory.

"And you, Juan?"

"Oh, as for me—you know me by now," he confessed sadly.

"How vain you are!"

"You want me to say that I was in love with her?" He became irritated again. "At first I thought she'd be of use to me."

"To you?"

"Don't act like an idiot," he warned. "You, more than anyone, know the disgust reality inspires in me. The awfulness of our filthy, daily existence. And that—" Suddenly he hesitated.

"Go on, go on."

"And that my consuming interest in life is to know everything concerning it, to blow up everything near me with all the explosives I can find."

"You're a terrorist," I remarked in embarrassment, mostly for the sake of saying something, actually I understood Juan rather well.

"We won't be happy," he started to become excited again, "until we end our dirty, hypocritical self-righteous concern with what we call reality. We have to pass on to other considerations."

"That wouldn't help. You'd only end up with another kind of reality."

"Reality is madness—a piggish, convenient madness. I attack it whenever I discover it in front of me."

"With some rather pleasant allies, it seems," I remarked dryly.

"With anyone who wishes to join me in my battle."

"But actually, Juan, women are great realists."

"That depends. One has to know how to exploit their cruelty, audacity, imprudence, and, above all, their insatiable curiosity."

"I believe they suffer from a rather limited imagination."

"There's a masculine imagination and a feminine imagination, and one bears no resemblance to the other."

"Perhaps you're right."

"Their imagination is completely selfish, totally unromantic. But it's always hungry, always thirsty. You have to throw it a lot of meat to chew on and a lot of blood to drink," he announced, being ridiculously dramatic.

"How theatrical you are, Juan!"

"I'm not theatrical, Darío. I'm theater. We're all theater, except that most of us have drawn the curtain."

"You're tremendous tonight," I told him, feeling myself swept away by his violence.

"Do you want me to tell you what a woman's most important quality is?"

"Go ahead."

252

"Adherence."

"Perhaps."

"Let them stick to you and they'll surrender everything to you —or almost everything. . . . But enough of this nonsense," he burst out laughing.

"And this one . . . did she stick to you?" I asked, already searching for concrete information.

"I didn't let her, and that's why . . . well, she left."

"*Vaya, vaya* . . . this little girl is beginning to please me."

"I don't think you'll like her at all once you've read those papers."

"Why?"

"Do you remember those words of Jehovah in the prophet Hosea? No, I'm sure you don't," he anticipated rapidly without giving me time to reply. "I'll refresh your memory: *I strip her naked and set her as on the day she was born, and make her as a wilderness and set her like a dry land, and slay her with thirst. . . . I will hedge her way with thorns and make a wall, that she shall not find thy paths.* That's how she was—a desert, a dry land, because she was surrounded by a terrible hedge of thorns and couldn't find her way in life."

"Then the poor girl had a bad time of it," I sympathized, without wishing to stop the flow of his words, on the lookout for something that was beginning to excite me.

"Yes, but there was more than that to her—much, much more, Darío."

"I can imagine."

"She was a dark mirror. The dark mirror that Saint Paul speaks of. You remember that, don't you?"

"Yes, in the first epistle of the Corinthians," I replied, pleased. *"Now we see ourselves in a dark and clouded mirror; more truly, we see ourselves face to face."*

"That's it, that's the way she was—a dark mirror. But behind, in the shadows, was God. Because God is always behind all clouded and dark things, behind all unreal things."

"That's a very interesting thought. I confess, though, that I didn't imagine you so well versed in biblical culture," I remarked, quite surprised.

"The Bible is the most passionate, the most rebellious, truthful book ever written," he replied enthusiastically. "And Christ is truth's leader in the battle against hypocrisy, rhetoric and utilitarian reality."

We were quiet for a while. There was little to say. The bar had filled up with people. Each of them had the same face, the same body, the same drink as always. Seeing them, I felt like screaming in terror.

"What's the matter?"

"Do you see Guillermo in the bar? It's been twenty years that he's combed his hair that way. See Tontolín come in now? For the past forty he hesitates when he enters a place. See the duke who's staring at us? For years he's been staring at people like that.

253

See Almenit smiling? He's trying to smile the way he smiled fifteen years ago. They're corpses who are dragging along their own cadavers."

"You're not well."

"No, one can't be well here. There are too many dead in the city. Their stench fills our nostrils."

"Why don't you come with me to Quiberon? I'm going by car."

"And your office, Juan? And the farm, the radio, your family and all the rest?"

"There are times one has to spend alone and naked, one's skin exposed to the air."

"I don't have any money."

"I do. I always have a little money," Juan smiled. "Enough for us to go."

"What kind of a car do you have?"

"A small Renault—the kind you see around now."

"What a coincidence! I bought one too."

"Down deep we have a lot in common, don't you think so, Darío? We're cast from the same mold."

"Perhaps. . . . But tell me—do you plan to drive to your Quiberon in such a small car?"

"Naturally."

"What insanity! I haven't dared to go beyond the outskirts of Madrid in mine."

"I've traveled from Madrid, to Le Havre, from Le Havre to Toulon, from there to Valencia and from Valencia to La Rochelle and Saint Malo and back again. You'll see. . . ."

"Maybe I could arrange things," I said doubtfully.

"If you arrange them, you won't come. Come without arranging them. And there you can write this novel, perhaps the best novel of your entire life. Naturally you'll change the names of its characters. Because of course she wasn't called Lola," he laughed.

"Perhaps I could title it *Lola?* Without any literary fanfare. *The Dark Mirror* wouldn't be bad either, with the quotation from Saint Paul in the beginning. I'm not sure. . . . Maybe *Lola* would be better as I want to forget all the dazzling literary tricks. . . . *The Dark Mirror* could add a lyric quality without sounding like literature. It needs thinking about, Juan."

Now I know that tomorrow we will leave together and in three or four days we will get to the long curving peninsula of Quiberon swept by ocean breezes, traveling from sea to sea. Daily, the Breton sailors spread out their nets along the huge stones of this rocky, healthy paradise, where under the clear skies the villages are clustered beneath the church like tiny chicks beneath a mothering hen. Late at night, one hears the grave song of a vigilant foghorn, while during the day one is warmed by the sun along the immense sandy stretches. There one is stripped of everything and comes face to face with oneself, overpowered by the fantastic miragelike beaches.

"I'll come, Juan. But, what about the passport? And the exit permit? And the Spanish Institute for Foreign Currency? And the

254

Security Police? And the French Visa? All that means papers, red tape, and days and days of looking after details. What misery to live in such a complicated world!"

"That way, I would never go anywhere. Fortunately, Darío, when one has courage there are no guards or frontiers. We'll go without a single paper."

And we went, the two of us—he and I—though I was almost entirely obscured by him.

Quiberon, 15 of August, 1949

Other SIGNET Books You'll Enjoy

MAN OF MONTMARTE   by Stephen and Ethel Longstreet

A novel about the tormented genius, Maurice Utrillo, and his strange life in Paris during the great period of modern painting.   (#D1617—50¢)

ROMAN TALES   **by Alberto Moravia**

Stories of the exuberant life in the back streets and slums of Rome, by Italy's greatest living writer. (#S1612—35¢)

AND QUIET FLOWS THE DON   by Mikhail Sholokhov

An undisputed masterpiece about the vigorous, violent lives of the Don Cossacks of the early 1900's.
(#T1661—75¢)

THE ROMAN SPRING OF MRS. STONE
by Tennessee Williams

A daring novel of a frustrated woman who turns to younger men for love, by the author of *Cat on a Hot Tin Roof*.   (#S1664—35¢)

THE TIME OF THE DRAGONS   by Alice Ekert-Rotholz

An epic novel of the Orient and of three sisters who seek emotional fulfillment in their turbulent world.
(#T1668—75¢)

THE WOUNDS OF HUNGER   **by Luis Spota**

The shockingly brutal story of an impoverished boy's struggle to become a top matador.   (#S1684—35¢)

MANUELA   **by William Woods**

A desperate girl offers love to get freighter passage and unleashes a violent chain of events. (#1704—25¢)